CAPTIVE LOVE

Gently grasping Alexandria's quivering chin, Joshua raised her head. "Look at me," he commanded tenderly.

She anxiously obeyed, slowly pulling her hesitant gaze from his smiling lips. Their eyes met and fused, liquid green with molten blue. "Relax," he coaxed softly. "I'm not some ogre come to devour you. I ask but a kiss to sate my starving soul."

His head slowly came down toward her. Disarmed, she permitted his mouth to explore hers in a long and deliberate kiss. He plundered her mouth with a skill to match his piracy at sea. Several kisses later, her arms went up and around his neck. As his masterful lips branded her mouth, face, and throat with his fiery touch, she was quickly lost to all reality; she had returned to that wonderful dreamland—from whi there would be no escape. . . .

EXCITING BESTSELLERS FROM ZEBRA

STORM TIDE   (1230, $3.75)
by Patricia Rae
In a time when it was unladylike to desire one man, defiant, flame-
haired Elizabeth desired two! And while she longed to be held in the
strong arms of a handsome sea captain, she yearned for the status
and wealth that only the genteel doctor could provide—leaving her
hopelessly torn amidst passion's raging STORM TIDE . . . .

PASSION'S REIGN   (1177, $3.95)
by Karen Harper
Golden-haired Mary Bullen was wealthy, lovely and refined—and
lusty King Henry VIII's prize gem! But her passion for the handsome Lord William Stafford put her at odds with the Royal Court.
Mary and Stafford lived by a lovers' vow: one day they would be
ruled by only the crown of PASSION'S REIGN.

HEIRLOOM   (1200, $3.95)
by Eleanora Brownleigh
The surge of desire Thea felt for Charles was powerful enough to
convince her that, even though they were strangers and their marriage was a fake, fate was playing a most subtle trick on them both:
Were they on a mission for President Teddy Roosevelt—or on a
crusade to realize their own passionate desire?

LOVESTONE   (1202, $3.50)
by Deanna James
After just one night of torrid passion and tender need, the dark-
haired, rugged lord could not deny that Moira, with her precious
beauty, was born to be a princess. But how could he grant her
freedom when he himself was a prisoner of her love?

*Available wherever paperbacks are sold, or order direct from the
Publisher. Send cover price plus 50¢ per copy for mailing and
handling to Zebra Books, 475 Park Avenue South, New York, N.Y.
10016. DO NOT SEND CASH.*

LOVE ME WITH FURY

JANELLE TAYLOR

ZEBRA BOOKS
KENSINGTON PUBLISHING CORP.

ZEBRA BOOKS

are published by

KENSINGTON PUBLISHING CORP.
475 Park Avenue South
New York, N.Y. 10016

Third printing: July 1984

Printed in the United States of America

For

Joe and Betty Taylor,
who already know the many, many reasons why . . .
But, mainly for their son
Michael
who embodies each of my heroes . . .

A MYTH

In times long past when the face of the mighty Atlantic Ocean was dotted with the wooden ships of Good and Evil, a beautiful goddess watched over her watery world and gave her aid to those deserving ships and captains who found favor in her eyes and who were in grave danger of destruction by the forces of greed.

When a certain ship and her captain proved worthy of survival and success in her eyes, she protected them with a veil of misty darkness. For when such a noble ship was set upon by those who would plunder and dishonor her, this benevolent goddess removed the silvery pins from her midnight tresses and trailed them over the chosen ship, concealing it from the eyes of her enemy.

To those eyes of evil, her stygian hair appeared as a mysterious and deadly black mist. No sailor knew from where it came, nor to where it vanished. But once the black mist lifted, one ship sailed on in safety while the other lay forever lost within some encompassing realm of magical nothingness. The goddess then replaced her shimmering pins and once more the sky was clear, filled with silvery, twinkling lights to guide the chosen ship to a safe port.

As the War of 1812 became imminent, once again the

forces of greed and evil drifted upon the serene face of her watery domain, endangering the ships and proud men of a newly born nation. That promising land mutely cried out for help. The Goddess of the Black Mist heard and witnessed their plight, taking special note of a certain brave ship which bore the name of her legend . . .

I

"A pair of star-crossed lovers"
—*Romeo and Juliet*, William Shakespeare

Late April, 1812
Liverpool, England

"But, Papa, you don't understand!" Alex shrieked, anxiety and dismay flooding her youthful body with dread. "How can I wed a total stranger, some strutting peacock who must ask his dolting father which way is up! I can't!" she heatedly vowed for what seemed the hundredth time in the past seven months, her emerald eyes flashing rebellion and obstinance. Why did he insist upon ruining her life? she wondered sadly.

Lord Charles Hampton wearily shook his graying head and sighed loudly in exasperation, vexed by this now familiar battle against his only child: the beautiful, but willful Lady Alexandria. "You must control that tempestuous nature, my little spitfire. You will hear me out this time," he stated firmly, half pleading and half demanding. He dreaded the inevitable day when he would be forced to bend her stubborn, defiant will to his own.

She jerked her tawny head upwards to meet his steady gaze, curly tresses falling enticingly around her

9

slender shoulders. She pouted impishly, jutting out her dainty chin to expose her irritation. Yet, her green eyes softened to the hue of newborn leaves as they lovingly caressed the striking face of her cherished father, her only parent since childhood. Hoping to halt this talk before it could continue, she quietly declared, "But there is nothing new to discuss, Papa; it has all been aired many times before. Surely we both grow weary of this same tiresome speech. I shan't marry some boring piece of frippery. I won't, Papa; I simply won't!" she insisted, her silvery voice sounding a bit strained. Her father bristled immediately.

Seeing the ill effect of her rash declaration, she tempered her tremulous tone with a hint of sadness and urgency, "If you truly love me, Papa, you will never afflict such a dreadful fate upon me. I could never endure such a stifling, pretentious union . . . even without love. You must not press this issue if you do not wish to break my heart and chain me to some fop who will simply view me as another piece of his property. Can't I wait for real love like you and Mama shared?" she entreated, frowning slightly when his noble features remained stern and insensitive.

"You're nineteen years old, Alex. You have been wooed, chased, and courted by the richest and most notable lads in all of Great Britain. Yet, you've stubbornly and vainly refused each of them!"

She hastily injected, "That isn't fair, Papa! What have pride and tenacity to do with a coerced marriage? Why should a woman meekly and cowardly submit to such an unjust fate?"

"We each have our destinies to fulfill, Alex. Since you were born a female, you must accept your responsibilities as one. You are not a man, and you cannot live and think as one! You have conjured up a Sir Lancelot which has blurred your vision to all else. Your choices are countless, my child. Surely there is at least one deserving man among your many suitors!" he shouted angrily.

Annoyed by his display of tension and impatience, he snapped, "You cannot continue to scorn every man and send him away! I will not allow my only daughter to become labeled a heartless haughty femme fatale who arrogantly treats titled Englishmen as beneath her! You will not become a source of gossip or ridicule!" he shouted angrily at the misty-eyed girl poised gracefully before him.

He fumed silently. Why was his bright, vivacious, normally respectful and obedient daughter behaving in this defiant, insolent manner? Such alliances were arranged every day! What had clouded her mind with these dreamy notions of love and romance? Foolish ideas which he must cruelly strike down before they became too destructive and too tempting . . .

Alex also fretted silently. How could she explain her innermost fears, dreams, and emotions to her aging father? How could he comprehend the desires and drives of a woman? He could never understand what it was to be a female. He had chosen his own love; why couldn't she do the same? She was no less intelligent than a man. To Alex, his primary concern appeared to be seeing her "properly wed." She would readily confess to being proud and steadfast; such traits were not evil or wrong. She would also admit to her disillusionment and disappointment with the numerous men who constantly sniffed around her fashionable skirts. Fools! Dreamers! she contemptuously sneered to herself.

She had eventually grown to despise the inane banter, the subtle flirting, the false gaiety, the snobbish milksops who refused to leave her alone. Society's rules and expectations nettled her. There had to be more to life and happiness than becoming a docile wife and selfless mother! What about her own needs and dreams? Such intense yearnings for adventure and freedom coursed through her veins! Sometimes she desperately wanted to run away in search of that forbidden, enticing destiny which called out to her in her dreams. Yet, women were wrongfully chained to compulsory roles which society placed upon them. No matter how much she craved such a life, it would be stupid and perilous to chase after it. How could she survive in a male-oriented world? How she wished she had truly been born an Alex. Then, she, too, could select her own love and destiny. Alas, it was impossible to change who and what she was: a helpless, obliging daughter . . . a mere female in a masculine world.

Choices, her father had claimed. She had met no man who could flutter her heart and steal her breath away, who had made her happy to be a woman. She was not a blind fool; she knew what most of those persistent suitors wanted: servile behavior, an exquisite face and lusty body to enjoy and to flaunt; her huge wealth; and her elite status. She had yet to meet the man who was deserving of them!

She bitterly vowed that she would become no man's lovely possession, his meek and dutiful wife, his brood mare, his legal prisoner! She knew of her compelling position as an excellent and valuable catch. Her bloodline was nearly matchless; her fortune, hefty and envious. Yet, she desired a valiant man who wanted her for herself, a man who was both strong and tender. Was that so much to expect, to demand? Was it too idealistic, too romantic?

She studied her father closely in the brooding silence. Warily she weighed the depth of his determination. How far could she push him? What wily logic could forestall her threatened fate? He seemed so adamant and the situation so hopeless. Would he honestly coerce her into a loveless marriage to some fawning duke or middle-aged lord? Naturally he would never choose some irresponsible, faint-hearted wastrel to take possession of his only child and the Hampton Estates. Yet, she could imagine none of her present suitors as an appropriate man for her husband. Still, her prominent father knew countless men and their circumstances.

A lifetime without love and fulfillment . . . How could he? Of all men alive, he should know the heights and rarity of love, real love between a man and a woman such as he had shared with her mother. That love had been so strong and special that he had been unable to find another woman to take her place.

13

Following her mother's untimely death, he had focused his love and attention upon his only child. Their resulting relationship had been close, unselfish, and warming; now, he was about to carelessly destroy it by sending her away from him and her home, by thrusting her into a loveless marriage.

"Please, Papa," she softly implored. "Just another year? Is that so much to ask? You're speaking of my entire life, my daily existence until death. The social season will be opening soon in London; perhaps I'll meet a proper young man there," she wheedled in her velvety, persuasive tone as she had done so often in the past with her adoring, frequently too lenient, father.

Astutely reading her wily scheme to attain more time, he instantly shook his head once again. "The matter is settled, Alex. I'll brook no more insolence or disobedience. It is past time for you to settle upon a worthy mate. Since you have failed to do so, I must accept this task myself. I hope and pray I can cull a suitable man who will meet your discriminating taste and willing approval. There are certainly plenty of prospects to winnow through. I would not find this course of action necessary if you did not persistently discourage every man who comes to call," he chided her.

"But, Papa, a woman shouldn't marry just any man simply to be wed before twenty! Name one of my beaux who would be compatible with me! Tell me which of my many admirers qualifies to inherit me and the Hampton holdings!" she objected.

Taken aback, he tersely snapped, "Fiddlesticks! There are hundreds of available men whom you haven't met before. Do not allow your impetuous, fanciful nature to hinder any hope of love and happiness by denying him and your impending marriage your very best efforts," he warned the wide-eyed girl.

"You cannot be serious, Papa! I beg you to reconsider; at least wait until this season's over. I swear to search very thoroughly for the right man," she promised, hoping to sway his decision to have this revolting matter over quickly.

"Right man!" he shouted impatiently. He, too, wanted this dire problem solved before it drove a wedge between them.

They had always been very close, sharing nearly every facet of their lives. But the time had come when childhood must be left behind, when her future must be settled. The numberless days which had been spent fishing, riding, hunting, and with other typically boyish activities must be put away forever. It was past time for Alex to realize she was a female—one perhaps too beautiful, too ingenuous, and too spirited for her own good. It had been foolish and wrong of him to allow her so much freedom and to constantly permit her at his side until now. For one who sounded so ensnared by love and romance, why wasn't she out pursuing some knight and enjoying her femininity?

In all honesty, she was not wholly to blame for her unusual feelings and personality, for he had unwisely encouraged many of them. She was such a bright, enjoyable, artless vixen. Unknowingly he had treated her as a son; now he had to force her to become a daughter.

Calling upon all of his inner strength, he declared to her, "Not all of the men you've met could be classed as dolting fools, vain peacocks, silly popinjays, or stupid and spineless rapscallions as you've proclaimed them. At least three of the bachelors and one of the widowers are notable choices. Too, there's that French count who purchased the Wilford Estate to be seriously considered."

"Andre DuBois? He's a sadistic rogue! Ask your friends about him and his sexual preferences. He simply wants some high-born wife to protect his notorious image. As for James Hartley, he drove his first wife to an early grave with his harsh demands upon her. Besides, he can always marry his mistress. Who needs a husband who must spend part of his time with other women? And what about those refined bachelors . . . did you know I have to fight them off every time I find myself alone with any of them? They paw over me like I'm some cheap doxy. I despise them all," she promptly and truthfully maligned each man mentioned.

"Malicious gossip cannot be taken at face value, Alex. As for your eager swains, can you fault them for being enchanted with you, perhaps overly zealous for your attention and hand? You're just spoiled and fanciful, my dear Alexandria. I can partly blame myself for these childish, unfeminine traits. I've been too indulgent and generous with you. I shouldn't have let you traipse around the countryside dressed like a boy and acting like one. I've given you free rein much too long. You're not a child or a boy; you're a ravishing beauty with grace, charm, wit, and refinement. It's time to leave your girlish dreams behind and to face real life," he advised.

"But, Papa—" she began, but was interrupted.

"No more talk. In time you'll grow to honor and love your new husband. Don't spoil your chance for happiness with these romantic illusions and foolish notions of yours."

"Foolish notions, Papa? Become a docile, mealymouthed wife just because I had the misfortune to be born a daughter instead of a son? Am I to have no say in my own destiny? If Mama were here now, she would never permit this outrage, this cruel injustice," she protested miserably.

A glimmer of sadness and lingering pain filled his blue eyes. She was instantly sorry for her insensitive words. In a hoarse tone he murmured, "But she is not here with us, Alex. If she had lived, we would not be standing here discussing your forthcoming betrothal and hurling stinging insults and cruelties at each other. I have been sorely remiss in teaching you to become a woman; for that, I am truly sorry."

"I do not mean to hurt you or to disobey you, Papa. Must it be this way?" A teardrop eased down her flushed cheek, its presence revealing her inner turmoil.

"You have your responsibilities to yourself, to me, and to your heritage. In time you will agree this

17

decision is for the best," he stated with finality. "Soon, it will be done."

There would be no changing his mind now; she was trapped like a butterfly in a spider's web. Did he already have some frightful creature in mind? Surely not one of those he had previously mentioned! Defeated and distressed, her sadness was unavoidably replaced by anger and resentment. She bitterly scoffed, "Best for whom, Papa? Why are you suddenly so desperate to be rid of me? How much longer can I enjoy my unladylike freedom? Have you already selected some mollycoddle to take me off your hands?" Hurt by his seeming callousness, she childishly struck out at him, trying to pass some of that suffering along to him.

He noticeably flinched as if she had delivered a physical blow. "I will not tolerate your disrespect and impudence, Alexandria Hampton! You possess manners, breeding, and intelligence. Use them wisely and promptly," he warned, annoyed at having to throw his weight around with his obviously unsettled daughter. "You are far too headstrong and wild for a young lady of your standing. It's time you realized you're a grown woman, not some mischievous tomboy."

"As you wish, Papa," she replied in a frigid tone, her lovely green eyes sparkling with glacial defiance.

"It won't be as terrible as you make it sound, child. You have but to use your beauty and wiles to have your new husband entwined around your finger," he tenderly encouraged her, praying to soothe a few of those fears and doubts. "It isn't uncommon for a young lady to dread such changes in her life. Your panic and apprehensions are not rare. Face them and subdue them."

Alex walked over to the bay area of his library and gazed out the window into the tranquil garden. Poised before the clear panes with the warm sunlight falling upon her silky head and taut body, she appeared an innocent girl who had been magically transformed into an exquisite statuette of priceless value. Her whole world was being torn apart, and there was nothing she could do or say to prevent it. "When is this happy event to take place? With whom, may I be so rude and bold as to inquire?" she pertly asked without turning around, choosing not to view his tender expression and ignoring his softened tone.

"Please, Alex, don't make this matter any harder on either of us," he pleaded, coming to stand beside her. He gently caught her arm and pulled her around to face him. He suddenly looked old and tired. "Don't spitefully destroy our closeness."

Her destroy their special relationship? she pondered. That statement would be absurdly funny if it wasn't so sad and false. "How can it be difficult for you, Papa? You won't be the one who is forced to sleep with some foppish knave. You won't be the one to smile demurely and to bow meekly to a crude stranger. You won't have to perform any repulsive wifely duties or to bear his whiny children. I'll become little more than a slave to this nameless beast. I will be the one to live with your decision, not you. I shall surely stick a dagger into his heart the first time he dares to touch me!" she boldly vowed.

"Cease this foolish prattle, daughter! You will not speak in this vulgar manner. It is a wife's duty to obey her husband and to bear his heirs. Besides, a husband does not ravish his own wife," he reasoned, highly vexed by her crude insinuations.

Tears began to roll down her flushed cheeks. Her pride and strength were taking a terrible beating as she pleaded and reasoned with him, knowing it was futile. "I will surely die if you commit me to such a slavish, humiliating existence," she stated dramatically.

"No, Alexandria, you will not. You are a Hampton. Your pride and breeding will not permit you to dishonor either of us. Once the banns are posted, you will see where your duty lies, and you will bravely follow it. You need not fear your husband or the marriage bed, for I would never wed you to a brutish swain. If it stings your vanity to have your father find you a worthy husband, then perform this necessary task yourself."

She brushed away her tears and sniffed, trying to control this lucid display of anguish and weakness. "If I knew of any distinguished man among my escorts, I would marry him tomorrow just to please you and to halt this vicious battle between us. I only want a man like you, Papa, one who is strong and smart, one who is also tender and special. I want a man who desires me for myself, as I truly am, not for my name and wealth. I want him to be handsome and virile, a man I can love and desire. He should be honest and valiant, a man to be respected and treasured. I want a man who works with his holdings, not one who wastes his time and money on gambling and lazy living. All I want, Papa, is a real man. I could not endure a man who was weak in body, spirit, or character. When I look at him, I want my heart to flutter and my breath to catch in my throat. I have not met any such man, not one who even comes near to being a real man. Surely there are men out there with traits such as you have," she reasoned.

He smiled, then chuckled mirthfully. "Should he have blue, green, or brown eyes; should his hair be black, brown, or the color of yours?" he teased his dreamy-eyed daughter as he caressed her cheek. "I wonder where I can find the man you just described . . ."

She frowned at him. "You're making fun of me, Papa, and that isn't like you. The color of his eyes and hair makes no difference to me. I simply want a striking, compelling, and stalwart husband. Surely you are not one of a kind, Papa," she returned his playful jibe. "You contradicted yourself earlier. First you said I would not be allowed any more time to find my own husband, then you said I could perform the task myself. Which is correct?" she questioned, clinging to this one ray of hope.

His eyes glistened with intrigue and suspense. "There is some other news you should hear before I answer," he hinted, his tone changing perceptibly.

"Other news?" she echoed. "What could be as important as discussing my destiny?" she jested saucily.

21

"In spite of how you feel at this moment, Alex, I am not heartless. I only want what is best for you. It isn't wrong to have such high expectations, but I fear you're blinding yourself to any man who does not fulfill all of them. You see me as perfect, child, but I am far from it. I am weak and foolish, for I let you forget you are a woman. There are countless things which you do not know about me and how I conduct myself away from you. It required many years and numerous experiences for me to become the man you view before your prejudiced eyes. The young men who come to call on you lack these years of training and refining. If we carefully select one with great promise, then he will not disappoint you.

"Just as you asked and deserve, you will have a little more time to seek out this dream man of yours. In about two weeks, I'm sending you to visit your Uncle Henry in America. You will remain there for a month or so. Who knows, you just might discover a Sir Galahad living there. Men who face such dangers and who bravely conquer new worlds and challenges are surely exciting, fearless, and unique. No such adventurer could be called lazy or weak in spirit and character," he jested playfully. His eyes twinkled devilishly as he tried to ease the tension between them.

It was vital that he get her to America as quickly as possible and without any suspicion. Surely the threat of marriage would entice her to readily agree to his cunning plans. He was uncertain as to how much longer he could conceal the reason for his anxiety, restlessness, and moodiness. Worst of all, if discovered, both of their lives would be in grave danger. He could not place his cherished daughter in peril of her life. Lord Hampton had to use any measure needed to get her to Henry's, no matter the price. In time, she would understand and forgive him.

She stared at her father in disbelief. "America? But America is a raw, uncivilized, dangerous wilderness! She is a traitor to the Crown. What about the Orders in Council, Papa? It is forbidden to trade or to travel to America. There's been conflict with the Colonies since before I was born. There hasn't been peace since the war of 1776. What British ship would dare to sail into an American port against the King's orders? The Americans despise us; they would probably blast our ship out of the ocean. The Americans are wicked, ungrateful, treacherous bumpkins! What honorable, intelligent man would turn against his own motherland?"

"Your Uncle Henry and many of our friends have become Americans. Is that how you view them now?" he challenged.

"That's different; they're Englishmen," she argued.

"All Americans came from other lands, my naive girl. When you arrive there, you will see just how mistaken you are."

"Even so, Papa, how could I possibly find a proper mate in that savage land!" she suspiciously inquired. "You would never consent to Alexandria Hampton's wedding an oafish clod, some uncouth rogue, not when so many men of noble lineage have asked for my hand. What is the meaning of this new plan?" she softly demanded, eying him for any hint to this perplexing enigma.

He laughed heartily to dispel his tension and to disarm her. "I do not consider a holiday in America as a threat or punishment, daughter. This might well be your last visit with Henry before you settle down. You wanted excitement and adventure; was it only idle talk? If you happened to meet some lion-hearted man who is well-born or of noble heritage, I see no harm in marrying him. Many sons of the best families have gone there. I hear talk of strong, proud, courageous men who have carved a new empire from a vast wilderness. Perhaps your dashing knight resides across the ocean. It seems obvious you cannot find him here." His eyes glimmered with amusement and mischief. He laughed as he witnessed her look of astonishment.

"You're actually saying if I meet some valiant man that I love, I will be permitted to marry him?" she asked incredulously, shocked and bewildered by this implausible news. "Even an American? But what of the troubles between our countries?" she asked. "Our loyalties would be to different lands. We would be enemies! How can I marry an avowed foe, a traitor?"

"America is no longer a wilderness, Alex. She has her own culture; she has great promise. From what Henry writes, she is little different from Great Britain. You forget one critical fact: America is not the aggressor in the hostilities we now face. As much as I hate saying this, we are responsible for the continual

24

animosities. America is not the one who is crippling world commerce and my own business; France and Great Britain are. We cross the ocean in mighty frigates to attack her; she does not send her ships here to battle us."

Astounded by his comments, Alex did not grasp his implications. He softened his tone as he announced, "The arrangements have already been made. I planned it as a surprise. You are to leave within a fortnight. I have spoken with Captain Burns of the *Moon Maiden*. I've dealt with him many times in the past. He is dependable and honest. Feigning to be an American privateer, he can hoist their flag and sail safely into her ports. This has been done many times. He frequently exchanges letters between me and Henry. We had a very profitable business going before King George stirred up this new hornet's nest. Henry and I are trying to find some way to survive until this new conflict is settled. These are facts best left secret, Alex, considering the strained relations between here and there. It wouldn't do for anyone to discover that we are trading business secrets which often hurts other firms and merchants. If it wasn't safe, Alex, I would not send you to America."

He smiled tenderly and advised, "Enjoy this brief reprieve, look for your dream man, if one exists. When you return home, you will be affianced within the year, be it a man of your choice or mine. I might as well confess; I am presently considering several young men. While you are away, I will carefully examine each of them. When you come home, I will introduce you to my selections. If you still refuse to accept one of them, then I will take it upon myself to do so. Is that clearly understood, Lady Hampton?" Their eyes met and clashed.

His unintentional harshness made her prior irritation return. "Yes, Papa, I understand perfectly," she replied. Mentally she added, no, Dear Heart; I will never be forcefully coupled to a crude rake. Banns . . . betrothals . . . consummation of vows . . . unquestionably and finally, imprisonment and suffocation . . .

"Excellent, my child. The affair is settled for now. I must see to some pressing business matters. At dinner tonight, we will discuss your impending trip to America."

With that dismissal, Alexandria gracefully swept from the stuffy library. She mindlessly rushed to her room to change clothes. She did not put on one of her costly velvet riding habits; instead, she rashly pulled on a multi-colored cotton skirt and a white peasant blouse. Barefoot, she stealthily made her way from the huge stone mansion to the stables. Without saddling her snow-white stallion, she leaped upon his broad back and quietly walked him from her ancestral home.

A safe distance from the hedge-enclosed yard, she gently prodded Ivory into a swift pace. They raced across the meadows as if spiritually and physically joined as one wild and carefree being. The wind whipped through her tresses of golden wheat hair and fanned them out behind her. The warm air nearly snatched the breath from her throat; yet, she refused to slow her urgent speed. It was rare moments like this when she truly felt alive, free, and venturesome.

She instinctively headed for her secret haven, her refuge. She lovingly pulled upon Ivory's mane and softly spoke to him, bringing him to a gradual halt. She agilely slipped from his back and affectionately nuzzled his nose for a few moments of solace. He would remain where she left him, for he was intensely loyal and well-trained. As she skipped off through the grass and wildflowers, he began to nibble at the luscious covering beneath his hooves.

Alex approached a thick line of trees and underbrush. She ducked and weaved her way along the well-known, but concealed, path into her own private world. Whenever she was troubled or desired total privacy, it was to this hidden sanctuary she fled. Within moments, she emerged from the dense circle of tangled trees and thickets to enter into a sunny, serene clearing.

She halted briefly to allow her pleased gaze to scan her utopian surroundings. The small pond snuggled into the land like a clear blue lagoon upon a deserted tropical island. The water was always lucid and warm. The trees and thickets allowed no eye to discover her or this spot of total harmony. She had always felt happy and safe here; a warmth and serenity filled her each time she came.

She aimlessly paced the small area between the tree line and the water's edge. The conversation with her father and its dire consequences whirled round and round within her head.

Admittedly she could grasp her father's point of view, but what did that understanding profit her? How could she willingly submit herself to a man she did not love or desire, a dreadful stranger? Love and desire . . . what did she really know of such wild and wonderful emotions? In fact, love was as much a mystery to her as carnal sex was. What she did know was that no man had ever made her feel warm and tingly inside. She had never lost herself in the smoldering depths of any manly eyes or experienced the overwhelming desire to boldly fondle a virile chest or to caress a handsome face. Was that so utterly unthinkable, so unrealistic, so foolishly romantic? Surely real love was something unique and all consuming . . .

Irritable and distraught, she yearned to surrender her cares and tensions to the encompassing and soothing arms of the inviting water. She chided herself for not bringing along something in which to swim. Even though this area was completely private, she had never gone swimming in the nude. Her strict, moral upbringing and inbred modesty had never allowed her to think such a wanton idea.

But today, she was pervaded with restlessness and anger; she was infused with defiance and daring. The mid-day sun warmed her body and silky head, increasing her desire for release. She glanced around, noting her solitude.

Did she dare to wickedly strip off her clothes and go for a swim? What harm could it do? No one could see her. Impulsively she cast aside all modesty. She yanked off her garments and carelessly tossed them upon the grass, then dove into the pond. The water was cooler than she had imagined; yet, she relished the feel of it against her smooth skin.

She could do little swimming due to the smallness of the lakelet; yet, she could float and dip with gay abandonment. The water was like a cool and silky caress, vanquishing her tensions and cares. A wonderful sense of reckless adventure flooded her. She laughed to herself, weighing this wanton streak which had just emerged, seductively savoring it.

Growing weary of floating, Alex climbed upon the grassy bank to lie in the warm sunlight. She fanned out her long hair like a silvery gold halo. She lay upon her back and closed her tired lids, allowing the sun to dry her from head to toe. Her fatigued mind and relaxed body were gradually lost to peaceful slumber.

Not far away, another young defiant person had just faced a similar stormy confrontation with a loved one who did not comprehend the inner forces which drove him. The younger lord of Farrington Manor had recently returned home for a genial visit with his aging, revered grandfather, only to have his joyful arrival spark a war of wills.

Spencer Farrington headed his chestnut roan to that one spot of solitude and refuge which he had accidentally discovered as a lad, a secluded area which bordered the next landowner's property.

His thoughts were as swift and as urgent as his breakneck pace. His mind raged at the helplessness which he was experiencing, an annoying emotion which only his grandfather could inspire. A man unaccustomed to failure, uncertainty, and weakness, he fumed at these undesirable emotions and the bitter cause for them.

How could he tell his cherished grandfather that he had not only come home to visit with him, but to secretly spy for the American government? The patriotic old cuss would never comprehend his many reasons for wanting a hasty and lasting peace between the two countries which he loved and honored. Yet, his own loyalties lay with his adopted homeland across that wide and wonderful expanse of blue which he had so recently conquered. How could he explain the importance of a mission which would appear treasonous to Grandfather Will? How could he possibly convince that old fox that only by outsmarting and outmaneuvering the Crown could real peace be won? America was not the one who had instigated the rapidly growing troubles between them; Great Britain was the aggressor. Great Britain, along with Napoleon, was gradually crippling American commerce with the Orders in Council and the Continental System.

He couldn't tell Grandfather Will these things for several other reasons. His furtive missions and his disguise had to be guarded well. He would place the old man in grave danger and great distress by confessing the truth. For at the crux of these covert matters was his deadliest secret of all. How could he possibly confide that he—Spencer Farrington—was the notorious Captain Joshua Steele of the privateer ship Black Mist, scourge of the British navy? A spy . . .

a privateer . . .

He shook his full mane of raven black hair which fell loosely over his temple. Devilish lights of rebellion and stubbornness sparkled within his grayish blue eyes, eyes which could take on the brittle coldness and stony hardness of deadly steel. His strong jawline and chin appeared to be of finely chiseled granite which revealed a fearless contempt and total disregard for danger and authority. His towering frame of over six feet rippled with muscles of smooth, firm iron. His slightly weathered, tawny skin spoke of an existence among the raw elements of nature.

Perhaps it had appeared insensitive and even cowardly to brashly swagger from Farrington Manor right in the middle of their heated dispute. Yet, it was clearly evident their verbal battle was taking a toll upon the enfeebled, elderly Will who continued to rule Farrington Manor with an iron hand and unbending nature. Things hadn't changed; Will persisted in viewing him as an unruly, selfish, irresponsible youth. Will blindly refused to recognize the obvious changes within his grandson, who would eventually inherit his powerful position and large wealth.

The quarrel had centered upon the same three topics: home, marriage, and a respectable Farrington image. Spencer could understand Will's desire for his permanent return to Farrington Manor. But, Will could not accept the fact that his only heir was now firmly and happily entrenched in a new life in America. Will had scorned the carefree, bachelor life which Spencer was reputed to enjoy with numerous women and under very dangerous conditions. Will had stormed about the "wild oats" which he mistakenly presumed Spencer was indiscriminately sowing and rapaciously reaping in that crude frontier called America.

But marriage had been the main concern of his dear grandfather, a man who had been like a stern and loving father to him from the age of fifteen when his father and mother had both died of an unknown disease.

Marriage? Stephen Spencer "Joshua Steele" Farrington? The independent, enterprising, adventurous bachelor who guarded his freedom and pleasures as closely and fiercely as his life! No way! Besides, he had yet to meet any female who had more to offer him than a lovely face and a compliant body. Women were to be enjoyed, not wed and then chained by his side day and night for the rest of his life. Marriage was a stifling trap which he fully intended to avoid like the plague!

Sir William Farrington wanted nothing less than for Spencer to instantly select some highborn lady from his endless list of eligibles and to marry her within the next month or so. Will had shouted and even threatened Spencer with disinheritance if he refused to settle down within the next year, present the proper image for a Farrington, and have children who would be the future heirs of the Farrington prestige and fortune.

What was the big rush? he fumed. After all, he was only thirty-two years old. There was plenty of time to snare some mildly acceptable female whom he might learn to tolerate at his side for at least part of the time. At present, his life was too complicated, too perilous, too blissfully full to settle down. And, a vicious war was brewing . . .

From his own observations, husbandly duties slowly drained a man of his prowess, his sense of adventure, his contentment. It gradually choked and entrapped him until he was nothing more than a rotund lord sitting before a cheerless fire, smoking a smelly pipe, waiting for several noisy brats to be put to bed, dreading his marital duties with some witless and plump wife, sneaking off to join his expensive mistress, taking care of mundane business affairs, growing old and weak and useless, missing out on the very best years of his life, wishing his boots were firmly planted upon the rolling deck of his ship with the ocean breeze caressing his serene face . . .

What angered Spencer the most was Will's audacity in actually approaching another lord about an arranged marriage to his no doubt dumpy, spinster daughter! What female of any value, would permit a repulsive union with a total stranger? What lady of any quality couldn't find her own mate? How dare Will take it upon himself to imperiously choose him a wife, a proper mother for his future sons, a woman to share the most personal and valuable parts of his life!

Spencer could almost hear Will's amused, mocking laughter and none-too-gentle scolding. What if she was wealthy, refined, vivacious, charming, and beautiful! Oh yes, Will had also mentioned a noble lineage and rebellious air to match his own! There were plenty of available women with those same traits. What made Will think this particular female was so rare, so deserving of becoming Lady Farrington? Why would Will force such a spoiled, haughty lass upon his grandson? Spencer had no time for taming a pampered she-cat. If this female was truly so matchless, why was she still unattached at nineteen? Didn't her constant refusals to countless suitors betray her vanity and undesirable traits? She surely had Will fooled!

Men could be selective in marital matters; women could not, Spencer speculated. What gave this vain, willful female the right to scorn so many men whose genteel births and family fortunes made them valuable conquests? What kind of man could she be waiting for, if she even desired wedlock?

Baffled and annoyed, he wondered why these men discarded their pride to grovel at the feet of an ice maiden. He was sorely tempted to meet her just to satisfy his curiosity. But time prevented such a spiteful pleasure. Will would not take kindly to his deflowering and disgracing of Lord Charles Hampton's daughter. No doubt he would retaliate with an enforced marriage to the little tempestuous Circe! Lady Alexandria Hampton was a dreadful disease to be wisely avoided . . .

A low, humorous chuckle came forth. He hadn't even asked any questions about her. He had overheard enough colorful gossip to size her up accurately. His debate with Will had ended with his adamant refusal to meet or to further discuss Lady Hampton. No matter, he would never marry any woman under such despicable circumstances. He growled to himself in his black mood, "If and when Spencer Farrington weds, it will be to the most fascinating, unique woman in the world. And I certainly won't be the one to melt that hard, cold statuette of ice!"

A man of his reputation and prowess didn't require any assistance in that particular field. If there was one thing Spencer could too easily accomplish, it was to have any woman he desired. He considered women as weak, frivolous, sexually ravenous, and dull-witted creatures. He had grown weary and bored with their clingy, possessive, irritating ways. He despised the flagrant flauntings, the crocodile tears, the rash threats, the foolish and annoying pleas, the voracious appetites, and the irritating farewells: the whole, sticky process of never being satisfied with the only parts of himself which he was willing to share: his sensual body and his lusty appetite. Never would he share his heart, his mind, his freedom, his soul!

His turbulent thoughts whirled madly within his handsome head. His impending mission entered his already crowded brain. This trip would not be a tranquil one. There was great peril in his daring plans to steal the maps and documents from Lord Grantley's safe and to spirit them back to President James Madison. Still, he had willingly taken on this dangerous mission; he was probably the only one who could pull it off with any measure of safety and success. Then, he was to head to Spain to confer with Joseph Bonaparte, that ineffective Frenchman to whom Napoleon had given the Spanish Crown.

Napoleon wasn't fooling anyone; it was no secret that he was holding King Ferdinand VII prisoner in Bayonne. It was also no secret that the Spanish had held elections in Cadiz, proclaiming a liberal constitution and suppressing the infamous Inquisition, futile and heroic as it was.

But Spain controlled Florida, that area too close for comfort if lost to hostile British hands. Since France ruled Spain, Spain owned Florida, and France was presently battling Great Britain, the natural thing for them to do was offer the capable Americans a stronghold in Florida to protect her and America from British invasion. Now, all Spencer had to do was convince Joseph Bonaparte to agree to their location in San Augustin as mutual protection for both sides. It seemed a logical and reasonable proposition. Trouble was, the Bonapartes were not known for their wisdom, tolerance, or kindness.

Spencer was intrigued by his unknown British contact who had demanded that an American representative hurry to London and steal a package of maps and papers which he claimed could affect America's survival and defense. Why wouldn't Madison divulge that man's identity to Spencer, his trusted friend and employee? Madison should know by now that nothing could extort anything from Joshua Steele! In this case, Spencer felt Madison was being too secretive and protective. Still, Madison frequently jested, "A man can't let slip what he doesn't know, Spencer. Besides, I gave my word of honor that his name would never depart my lips. One day you'll meet him; that I promise you."

Since his present visit had reopened old wounds, the only course left open to Spencer was to pick up the package in England, complete his mission to Spain, return to America with the dispatches and report from Bonaparte, and later return to Farrington Manor to bravely face the odious marriage that Grandfather Will wanted so desperately before he passed on. However repulsive, Spencer would eventually grant him his wishes.

Spencer reined in his horse, curiously studying the white Arabian stallion lazily grazing without a tether or saddle. He wondered why anyone would be so careless as to allow such an exquisite beast to roam freely. No matter, he had enough problems of his own without giving time and energy to some stranger's foolish dilemma. He tied his reins to a nearby bramble bush.

He strolled over to the thick line of trees, avidly searching until he found the path into his secret hideaway. It had been many years since he had ventured here. He hoped the small pond was still there, as harmonious and entrancing as ever. It would be a miracle if the enclosed area was not completely overrun with tall grasses and tangly vines.

Pushing aside the last hanging branch, he stepped into the sunlit clearing. He halted and closed his blue eyes, slowly taking in the fragrant, fresh air. He gradually released it once he had savored its heady, pleasing essence. His intent gaze began to lazily pass over the azure pond and the small gray boulders at the far end of this unique haven.

His inquisitive orbes of steel blue stopped abruptly in stunned disbelief as they settled upon the magnificent creature who was sleeping so peacefully in his private domain. He rubbed his eyes in astonishment, then shook his head to clear it of this breathtaking illusion. He crossed the short distance which separated them in three easy strides, his black boots whisking silently over the lush grass. He wistfully gazed down at the enchanting goddess who lay slumbering at his feet.

Was she real? Who was she? How had she come to be here in this paradise? The steady rise and fall of her bare bosom told him she was indeed alive and much too real.

He bent down beside her, just at her tiny waist. His smoldering gaze began at her tawny head and leisurely moved all the way to her neatly trimmed toenails. Spencer's respiration grew strained and labored. His senses ignited and flamed with acute desire; his groin tightened and pleaded for release, and his lips curled up in an appreciative curve.

She possessed the exquisite face of an angel, the seductive body of a goddess, and the magnetism and mystery of a sea siren. Since she was boldly trespassing upon his private property and was wantonly lying naked in broad daylight—did that give him the unquestionable right to take advantage of this delightful situation?

His torrid gaze drifted over to her garments which

had been so impulsively and immodestly tossed aside to frolic *au naturel*. He grinned in satisfaction, for they were definitely the vestments of a commoner. What menial with a face and body like hers could still remain a virgin? No doubt her skills were tremendous and her experiences numerous, Spencer surmised.

No female had ever denied him anything he wished. The idea that this sensual girl might resist or refuse him was totally absurd, impossible! A pleased smile claimed his sensual mouth; everyone knew that a ravishing serving girl belonged to any nobleman who could seduce her . . . He glanced around at their secluded, dreamy setting; no one would disturb their play. A devilish gleam flickered in his eyes and settled upon his striking face. He selfishly concluded that she was his for the taking. Anyway, if she were not a passionate woman at heart and a spirited adventuress, she would not be lying naked and inviting in his Elysium . . .

Perhaps this beguiling vixen was actually waiting for him, plotting his own seduction, he mused. He should generously and chivalrously comply with her needs and wishes. This diversion was just what he needed to ease his tensions and to take his mind off of his troubles. It had been weeks since he had found a woman he wanted to bed. He stood up and non-chalantly stripped off his own clothes, dropping them beside hers in a neat pile.

Observing her and his swollen manhood, he made his irrevocable decision . . .

II

"These violent delights
have violent ends."
"A word and a blow."
—*Romeo and Juliet,* William Shakespeare

Towering over Alex, Spencer stared down at her, his eyes fusing to an igneous cobalt shade. Her hair surrounded her head like a halo of intermingled gold and silver. It was long and wavy with impishly wispy curls dancing upon her oval face. Her complexion was flawless and silky smooth; the lines of her lovely face were exquisite and sensually appealing. Her lips were soft and pink; a defiant pout claimed them even in deep sleep. A dainty chin hinted at that same willful, stubborn air. Spencer knew she couldn't be less than seventeen or more than twenty.

Although her breasts were firm and ample, they seemed to be still blossoming. Her waist was the smallest he had ever seen; her hips were nicely rounded and slim. Her shapely legs were supple and slender; her dainty ankles were small and strong. She had surely broken the hearts of countless swains. Yet, her obvious power over men irrationally vexed him.

In past experiences, Spencer had discovered that extremely beautiful women were usually impetuous,

41

haughty, and spoiled. They used their beauty and sensual appeal as weapons to force men to grovel at their feet, just like Cassandra!

Cassandra . . . that spiteful, little witch had actually pulled the two lowest tricks in the book to try and subjugate him after his casual dismissal of her. After attempting every ploy and using every wile and charm she possessed, she had vindictively allowed him to catch her in bed with another man—his own bed at that! When that disgusting idea failed miserably, she had taken a bejeweled dirk and maliciously tried to castrate him, to deny him possession of any other female. No doubt her broken arm had smarted for quite a long time afterwards! Spencer grinned satanically as he sneered; no scheming female would ever get the best of him.

He wondered why that little witch had come to mind after all these months. Gazing down at the nymph at his feet, he knew. Cassandra had boasted of nearly this same color hair and this same defiant expression. Yet, Cassandra's beauty could not hold a candle to this ravishing creature's. He absently wondered if Cass had finally married President Madison's assistant. If she had cunningly managed to become Mrs. John Lindsdale, it was only to remain within arm's length of the man she truly craved: himself!

With that thought, he instantly eyed the third finger of Alex's left hand which lay negligently over her flat stomach. He astutely noticed there was no wedding band there and sighed in relief; however, he carelessly failed to take note of the softness of those graceful hands which clearly proved they had never known menial labor.

He gingerly positioned himself beside her, propping his head upon his hand. He cautiously snuggled his stalwart, nude frame against her golden flesh, resting his throbbing manhood at her hip. The coolness of her flesh felt good next to the fiery texture of his torrid extension. He stretched out an anxious hand to gently fondle the satiny flesh upon her stunning face, slender neck, and inviting shoulder. He ever-so-lightly traced his forefinger over her neck, down the hollow between her breasts, over her abdomen, and down her leg for as far as he could reach without moving at her side. She shifted and sighed. His touch was as light and warm as a summer breeze at mid-afternoon.

He lowered his head to allow his mouth to confiscate hers in a pervasive, delicious kiss. He then trailed feathery kisses over her closed lids with their thick lashes and across her velvety cheeks, savoring their smoothness against his lips. He nibbled at her earlobes and parted lips. His hands deftly and boldly encroached upon her enticing body, very provocatively, so as to titillate her rather than to startle her. His assault was deliberate and sensuous.

When he drew moist circles around her erect nipples with a warm tongue, a drowsy moan of rising passion escaped her lips. Alexandria sighed contentedly in blissful relaxation. Her lids fluttered, then opened to reveal eyes the shade of precious emeralds. They slowly roved the handsome face and virile chest which loomed above them. A natural, innocent smile greeted him, bewitching him beyond reason. She sleepily gazed up into eyes of molten steel upon the face of Apollo.

He sent her a beguiling smile in return, enrapturing her heart and enflaming her dream-blurred senses. His skillful fingers wandered into her amber curls, feeling the vitality and glossiness of them. He tenderly caressed her cheek with the back of his strong hand, admiring the soft perfection of her golden flesh. In her half-wakeful state, Alex snuggled her cheek against the hand which had halted its pleasing action.

His head leaned forward; his mouth covered hers once more in a thorough and engulfing kiss. A tingling glow suffused her. She was instantly adrift upon a turbulent ocean whose powerful waves feverishly washed over her body, gradually pulling her into a dangerous whirlpool of heady desire. As he kissed the tip of her nose, liquid green eyes were captured by potent blue ones, expertly drawing her deeper and deeper into their seemingly bottomless depths, imprisoning her senses in an all-consuming abyss.

Captivated by this stimulating dream, her arms went up to encircle his neck. Dreamily entrapped, she greedily held his mouth against hers for several more devastating kisses. Her senses reeled freely and wildly, filling her with the same carefree abandonment she experienced when racing the wind upon Ivory's back. For the first time in her dreams, her elusive perfect man was at her side. He was kissing her, touching her, and holding her as no real man ever had.

Her body soon felt the same overpowering heat and

hunger which his did. Her skin prickled and flamed. A gnawing ache which she did not recognize made her hunger for a nameless satisfaction. Her breasts were taut, pleading for a new onslaught by his lips and hands. She instinctively and voraciously responded to the bronze-skinned, sable-haired, blue-eyed knight above her who mutely demanded her helpless submission.

Alexandria's unbridled response to him heightened Spencer's own desire and encouraged his assault upon her. Her growing ardor and urgent need for him grew greater and greater. He ignored the artless way in which she kissed him and reacted to him. He adamantly refused to comprehend she was totally innocent in mind and body.

Passion's flames engulfed them in a fiery glow which only total fulfillment could douse. His hands freely roamed her luscious figure, bringing her uncontrollable tremors of molten desire. He gently forced her lips to part and accept his assault. His tongue probed the warm and tasty recess of her mouth, and he savored the sweetness he discovered there.

Even the weight of his virile body failed to release her dazed senses from their perilous enthrallment. He gently ravished her entreating mouth and tantalized her body until she was mindless of all reality except the godlike, magnetic creature who was driving her into a bittersweet frenzy. The thick mat of black hair upon his brawny chest aroused her to an even higher level of excitement as it rubbed against her sensitive breasts. She uttered feverish moans as he nibbled at her ear, his warm and erratic breathing sending tremors over her pliant body.

Her hands anxiously stroked the rippling muscles in his firm back and upon his powerful shoulders, finally burying themselves in his full stygian hair as she inaudibly pleaded for some resolution to this torment of intermingled pleasure and anguish.

Alexandria was totally oblivious to his gentle parting of her thighs and to his determined probings at her resistant maidenhead. Her mind was incapable of understanding this ravishment, and her own arousal aided his success. Suddenly, a searing, burning pain shattered her Eden as Spencer feverishly drove his manhood into that guarded place where no interloper had ever trespassed before. Even amidst the pain and shock, her body greedily accepted the invasion. But suddenly her Galahad became a malevolent demon who was fiendishly invading her innocent body and brutally trampling upon her purity.

A piercing scream of sheer agony was torn from her lips as the unexpectedness of the pain ripped into her rosy world. She shuddered and attempted to escape this horror, but was pinned beneath the phantom's unmovable body. Tears of pain and fear filled her eyes and eased into her tousled hair as her dream became a nightmare.

Startled by her cry, Spencer leaned away from her and stared down in utter disbelief at the panicked girl who was fearfully gaping up at him. A look of confusion and anguish flooded those lucid pools of green. They darted over his astonished features, then glanced around them as if trying to decide where she was and what was happening to her. Strange, she appeared totally befuddled! He was shocked.

She inhaled sharply. Her lovely face went stark white. She glared at him. This was not a fantasy! He was no fanciful Galahad! Aware of the bleak reality and stunning implication of the situation, she began to beat upon his chest with ineffectual blows. She screamed at him; she threatened him. She sobbed in anger, pain, and humiliation. She fought him like a tigress, trying to claw herself free from this degrading position beneath his naked body.

"Get off of me this instant, you vile beast! My father will kill you for this! How dare you sneak in here and brutally ravish me! How dare you touch me at all! Get off of me!" she screamed again at the bemused Spencer whose ears were still ringing from her first shrill cry. Her hair was dishevelled; her respiration was erratic. Daggers shot from her narrowed eyes. But unknowingly she provoked him even more.

Spencer knew he should feel some pangs of guilt and alarm, but he was too intoxicated by her to do so. "Ravish you?" he taunted devilishly, his wits quickly returning. A mischievous leer flickered upon his mocking face. His eyes twinkled with renewed intrigue and daring. "My little naiad, you are the one who nearly ravished me. I merely complied with your pleas when I but stole one kiss from those sweet lips," he teased her, trailing his finger over her lips.

Shocked by his nonchalant mood and infuriating

explanation of his vile deed, she fused a deep crimson as she shamefully and gradually recalled what she had mistakenly believed to be a dream. She inhaled sharply in rising distress as these memories flooded her terrified brain. "I was sound asleep! I was dreaming. I never meant to encourage you! I mean . . ." she wildly stammered in alarm and panic as she realized her own guilt.

My God, she thought, I did respond to him! How could she behave like that with a total stranger? She mumbled weakly, "I thought I was only dreaming. I didn't know you were real or that we were actually . . . You took advantage of me! You're a devil! How dare you try to blame this outrage upon me! I've never . . ."

Blushing and shaking with unleashed fury, she halted. How did one handle such an embarrassing situation? How had he gotten into her private world? Why had he calmly and arrogantly violated her body while she slept?

She paled as he genially smiled down at her and seductively whispered, "You have now, my carefree nymph. Tell me, my lovely angel, how have you managed to remain untouched for so long? A woman of your matchless beauty and sensuality is impossible to ignore." His appreciative and burning gaze boldly swept over her frozen features. He chuckled in amusement.

Astounded and enraged by his indifference to his vile deed, she drew back her hand and attempted to slap his smug, mocking face. He easily blocked her hand, gently and firmly imprisoning it within his strong grasp. "You filthy animal!" she retorted. "Not all men are rutting beasts who prey upon sleeping, defenseless maidens! Even so, I would slay the first one who dared to lay his disgusting hand upon me!" she stormed at him, her eyes freezing into chips of green ice.

She began to struggle with renewed strength and determination. She savagely clawed at his shoulders, and angrily bit him bringing pain and more blood. Yet, Spencer never even winced or cried out.

He seized her other flaying hand and pinned her wrists to the ground near her head. She wiggled and thrashed about, trying her best to free herself from his grip of iron. She shrieked unladylike insults at him; she cried in fury and frustration: all to no avail. He would not release her or move from atop her.

His eyes had narrowed and hardened when she had rashly bitten and scratched him. He casually glanced over at his bleeding shoulder with its lacerated nail and teeth marks. His fathomless gaze shifted to the helpless, struggling girl beneath him. His satanic glare slowly and deliberately eased over every inch of her body which was visible to his insolent gaze. She uncontrollably trembled under its glacial intensity.

When he finally spoke, his voice was deceptively calm, "Now that you have painfully branded me with your mark of affection, where shall I place mine upon your lovely body?" he asked, instantly vanquishing the smug smile which had flickered briefly upon her radiant face at the mention of the pain she had inflicted upon him. "Perhaps upon one of these delectable breasts? Or here, where everyone can see who has taken you first?" he snarled, stroking her upper chest and trailing a finger over her collarbone.

Alex shuddered and paled. Unbidden tears stung her entreating eyes as she softly whispered, "Please don't. I'm . . . sorry . . ." From the way she had spoken that last word, it sounded to him as if this was the very first time she had ever uttered an apology!

A heady sense of power and unruly desire entered him as he gazed down at the girl-woman who lay imprisoned in his embrace. "Apology accepted with no further need for reprisal," he insouciantly announced to the stunned girl. "Besides, you're much too exquisite to mar and definitely too wild to be corralled by any one man," he hoarsely murmured, running his finger over her parted lips.

As Alex nervously awaited his next move, her gaze helplessly travelled each line of his compelling face. He was the most striking man she had ever seen. She had never even imagined a male could be so devastatingly attractive, and she knew she was at his mercy. An inexplicable and magnetic force irresistibly drew her to him like the moth to the flame. What magic did he possess? How had he come by such staggering prowess and enormous charms?

Spencer curiously observed the ever-changing lights flashing in her eyes, and felt a novel tug of tenderness and passion suffuse his taut body. He instantly quelled such foolish and dangerous feelings.

His manhood throbbed its reminder of need. He

leaned his head forward, assuming she would no longer reject him. He was wrong.

Noting his intention, Alex turned her face away from his approaching lips. Heart-stopping fear gnawed at her senses; she stiffened and trembled. "Please don't," she softly pleaded just above a whisper. "If you let me go now, I promise not to tell anyone what you did," she said demurely.

"Nor what you did, my seductive naiad?" he merrily quipped, a soft chuckle escaping his full mouth. "It's a bit too late to stop now or to return what I've already taken. Show me that fire and eagerness once more," he huskily entreated.

She made a careless mistake when she jerked her head around to glare up at him and to indignantly shriek, "But I . . ."

Before she could complete her denial of guilt, his lips possessively and hungrily came down upon her mouth. His lips again burned those sweet, forbidden messages across her unsteady senses and hazy brain. Her pulse raced madly. His kisses and caresses were insistent, demanding, and persuasive. Alarmed by this odd warmth and novel hunger which sent her logic spinning away, she briefly enjoyed his new assault.

His strained voice murmured into her ear as he nibbled at her lobe and sent shivers over her nude frame with his warm breath, "Yield to me, my siren, and ride the waves of ecstasy and magic . . ."

Panicked by the heat and temptation of his husky words, another struggle ensued, alas, to no avail. But when Spencer began to move gently within her, the former pain had somehow lessened to a dull soreness. Alex realized he was determined to have her, to complete his enforced seduction, to sate his carnal lust.

In spite of her terror and resistance, Spencer used all of his skills to rekindle her heated response to him which had nearly driven him wild with passion. He could detect her rampant desire for him, her almost urgent need to put out the flames which he had fanned within her luscious body. Yet, he eventually noticed that she retained just enough strength of will to deny him any success this first time. Consumed by a roaring inferno within his own body, he reached the point of unrelenting need which erupted like a potent volcano.

When his spasms of sheer delight had subsided and calmed, he sighed in satisfaction and contentment. He propped upon his left elbow and stared down at her. What was it about this particular female who had given his body an intense hunger and overwhelming ecstasy which far exceeded any other sexual experience of his entire life? She was totally unskilled, unresponsive, hostile, and innocent! Who was she? Why had she been lying here in the sunlight, naked and alone? Why had she shifted from fire to ice?

He lifted a finger to wipe away the teardrops which were slipping from her tightly closed eyes. Where had all that eagerness gone? Why had she suddenly resisted him so fearfully and so fiercely? Had she merely panicked at the last minute?

Virgins were reputed to fear the unknown, that final parting with innocence and purity. Since he had never taken one before, he could not venture an accurate guess as to her feelings. Perhaps he had hurt her . . . he had not been particularly gentle, but neither had he been rough. How was he to know this would be her first time! In the beginning, she had been a lusty ball of fire. She had practically demanded that he ravish her!

Twinges of guilt and remorse nibbled annoyingly at him. He tenderly inquired, "Are you all right, love? Did I hurt you?"

At those softly spoken words, more tears eased out from under her lids. She shuddered as she drew in a ragged breath of air, but did not answer him. He began to fret. Had she truly believed him and this situation to be a dream as she had alleged earlier? Could she have been that drowsy, romantic, and innocent? Surely not . . .

He persistently tried another approach, "What's your name, love? I can't keep calling you 'my little naiad.' Where do you live?"

Alex tensed, dreading his beguiling manner. In a tremulous voice she asked, "If you're quite finished with me, may I go now? Release me, please. I want to go home," she stated wretchedly, her lips quivering. Her attempt to sound forceful and brave failed miserably.

He immediately knew he would never see her again if he complied. For some reason, that mattered greatly to him. "Not until you tell me where home is and who you are," he replied, concealing his abundant concern and growing affection for her, hoping to stall things until . . . Until what? he mused curiously.

She opened her misty eyes and glared up at him. "No," she declared coldly.

So much for thinking her charmed and intimidated by him! Who was this girlish woman who could rebuff and withstand him? Had he lost his magic, his devastating prowess, his magnetic allure? According to her expression and behavior, he most assuredly had! Unknowingly she challenged his masculine ego . . .

"Why not?" he casually questioned.

Her sea-water eyes chilled into pools of stormy green. She couldn't believe her ears. This ruthless scoundrel had just ravished her, and now he conceitedly wanted to know where to locate her in case he wished to seek her out again! Of all the unmitigated gall! She would never confess her name and residence to this criminal. He would never be granted the chance to pursue her and to soil her name and reputation as he had just done to her body. "Never!" she stormed in outrage, gritting her teeth.

"Never is a mighty long time to lie here making love," he taunted her, caressing her cheek. "Until you answer me . . ." He dramatically left that imposing threat hanging in the air.

Her jaw dropped; her eyes widened. "Making love!" she retorted incredulously. "You call that repulsive, bestial attack making love! If such is true, then I shall die an old maid!" she vehemently swore.

He laughed heartily. "It is always uncomfortable, perhaps even painful, for a woman on her first encounter. Or so I'm told. Having no prior experience with beautiful virgins, I really don't know for certain," he felt strangely compelled to impress her. "I promise you'll experience just as much pleasure as I will the next time," he boastfully vowed.

"Next time . . ." she hesitantly repeated. "Surely you don't intend to repeat that crude act again! You have no right to touch me in any manner! It is not only painful, it is also disgusting and humiliating. If you try to . . ." She halted when she realized the futility of her threat. "If you release me this instant, I'll keep this encounter a secret between us," she promised bitterly, clenching her teeth in resentment and frustration.

He threw back his head and laughed. "Tell anyone you please, love. I fear no man," he boldly declared with arrogant confidence.

"My father will kill you for this! He will have you arrested and hanged from the nearest tree!" she exclaimed, her eyes sparkling with false bravado.

"First, he will have to find me," he mocked her. "Second, he must prove you did not willingly submit to me. What will dear father say when I earnestly vow that you not only gave in, but you were lying here waiting for me, naked and hot-blooded? What will you say to your many friends and admirers when they come to court each day to hear the spicy, intimate details of how you wantonly provoked me beyond my resistance? Naturally I shall plead not guilty by reason of powerful temptation and willful provocation upon your part. Far worse, my love, how will you fend off all of those lustful swains whom you've obviously denied until now? Will those 'rutting beasts' be content to accept a haughty refusal after I am forced to reveal that fiery and passionate nature of yours? I'll weave the most sensual, colorful, exciting tale ever told in public. Besides, with the fame of my great prowess, would anyone believe I had to force you to lie with me?" he devilishly quizzed the distraught and shocked girl, her lovely face losing more color with each added threat.

"You couldn't possibly proclaim such filthy and damaging lies! Why should I permit you to violate my honor and then go free as if nothing happened between us? Damn you! I was asleep. I thought no one knew of this secret place. I've never gone swimming like this before. I was upset and I needed to relax. I never imagined anyone would come here. I didn't lead you on. You cannot destroy my reputation as well as my honor and purity! You cannot be allowed to go around attacking innocent girls!" she heatedly argued. "I was asleep! I didn't know you were real," she stressed her point emphatically.

"You could tell the court I was the incarnation of your dreams," he playfully mocked her denials, baiting her for any additional information which she might spill forth during her rantings.

"You, my dream man? Never! I despise you! You defiler of innocent, defenseless girls!" she screamed at him, pained by his taunting words about her foolish notions of a dream lover. Papa was right, she sadly conceded to herself. I am nothing more than a rosy-eyed, naive child.

"Girl? You? If you're a mere girl, love, then I'm the devil himself," he merrily parried, eying her with appreciation and admiration.

"That's the first honest statement you've made so far!" she snapped.

He agreed, "You are absolutely accurate, love. As I made my daily rounds of earth, I saw a vulnerable and beautiful angel all alone and waiting patiently for some lucky devil to come along and to claim her body and soul. Can you blame me for being susceptible to your charms?"

"You're making fun of me. Stop it this minute! Please let your jokes and punishment be over," she entreated him with a wounded glance. "Let me go home now. Please . . ." she added softly, hoping to touch any faint chord of conscience within him.

"But I wasn't making fun of you, love. You are in truth the most beautiful and desirable woman I have ever seen. Have you never looked closely in the mirror? Doesn't your father have to continuously beat the eager swains from your doorway? Alas, what was I to think and feel when I saw you lying upon the grass so . . ."

She hastily placed her small hand over his grinning mouth to prevent any more intimate words from coming forth. She blushed and flustered, "You shouldn't say such risqué things, sir!" For an instant, she forgot their intimate contact and her precarious situation.

He roguishly delivered an enticing kiss onto her palm, allowing his warm tongue to sensually moisten its smooth surface. She quickly jerked her hand away. Confused, she gaped at him, wondering at the tremors such a silly kiss had sent charging through her body. "Why did you do that?" she naively snapped, vexed by her physical response.

Seeing her instinctive reaction, he laughed, nettling her further. "You, my little angel, are too rare and exquisite to be real," he murmured tenderly, allowing his gaze to charm her. He beseeched her, "You must confess; are you a goddess or a real naiad? Perhaps some bewitching mermaid who has magically lost her tail? Will you vanish from my arms and life before I can learn your name and fate?" Their faces and bodies were much too close to think clearly.

Snatched off guard by his disarming tone and mellow mood, she smiled shyly. The pleasant expression upon his strikingly handsome face compelled her into spontaneously replying, "Neither, sir; I fear I am only a mortal woman. Can you vow the same?"

"May I see you again if I promise to behave the perfect gentleman?" he asked, carelessly bringing her back to full alert.

"Certainly not! You, Sir Demon, are a cad and a despicable rake! We shall never meet again," she retorted.

Their gazes fused and clashed. "Then I shall never let you leave my side. It would be an unforgivable crime to lose such a valuable treasure," he stated.

"You cannot keep me here forever!" she protested.

"I could surely try," he replied. "If not, I might

take you with me and hold you captive until you relent."

Apprehension set in anew. She had to get away from this disturbing and mysterious stranger. But how? she speculated. He was too strong to physically overcome. If he carried out his threat to take her with him, the truth would be out like wildfire. If anyone saw her dressed in her peasant garb or if she were forced to seek help from some passerby, she would be humiliated and disgraced, stained for life! If he dared to imprison her secretly within his home, she would find escape impossible. Distressed, she decided, if he conceitedly thinks for one instant that I will succumb to his charms, he is vastly mistaken and exceedingly vain! No man treats Lady Alexandria Hampton in such a manner!

Succumb . . . Her cunning mind was quickly at work upon this problem. If she could trick this egotistical man into thinking she might willingly accept him and his touch, perhaps she could escape him. A weapon was what she needed to even the odds between them. A desperate plan came to mind. Without meeting his steady gaze, she meekly asked, "May I wash off in the pond? I feel soiled."

Why not? he generously deliberated. Perhaps a short swim would release some of her tension. It might be wise to relent slightly where this fragile girl was concerned. She was as skittish as a newborn mare. After all, she couldn't escape him, he smugly concluded.

"First, a few kisses to earn my patience and kindness. Then, I will free you to bathe," he promised, an engaging grin curling up the corners of his sensual mouth.

She stared at him, weighing those strange and powerful emotions which he had borne within her, deciding she must bravely comply with his demand if she hoped to flee him and this place. At her look of uncertainty and anxiety, he murmured, "You are not sullied, my radiant sun goddess; you have simply become a woman. Your downfall was inevitable; you are far too beautiful and tempting to ignore. It would be a grave sin to be so lovely and to remain so incomplete. I cannot return what I have taken from you; it is mine to treasure and remember forever." He kissed the tip of her nose and smiled into her wary eyes.

Such unknown and stirring excuses . . . Such crazy thoughts and frustrating feelings . . . Perhaps he was in truth some resistless demigod from another time and place. Why did he make her feel and think such strange things? Still . . . "You had no right to forcefully take what was mine alone to give to the man I love and choose," she scolded him.

He sighed heavily, then smiled: that same way which set her senses to reeling madly and her mind to dreaming. "Need I refresh your memory, love? You came to me willingly and eagerly in the beginning. In spite of my normal control, I was past turning back when you changed your mind. Once the raging fires of passion have been ignited and fanned to such a torrid state, there is but one way to extinguish them. It would be prudent of you to remember that fact in your future . . . contacts with bedazzled, hot-blooded young suitors," he advised in an almost fatherly tone, his sober expression serious and tender.

As she silently deliberated upon those curious words, he added, "Had I known of your innocence and dreamy state of mind, I would not have persisted when you panicked and withdrew from me," he declared candidly, bringing a look of utter surprise to her face. "When you smiled up at me and hungrily responded to my kisses and caresses, I was bewitched beyond reason. When you tried to reject me, I merely judged you a coy tease who had panicked at the last minute or a cunning doxy who wished to levy a hefty price before continuing along your chosen course. Since the damage had been done, there was no need to halt our final union," he reasoned aloud, also trying to assuage his own disturbing feelings of guilt. "Remember that old adage about the danger of playing with fire and burning one's fingers? There is no flame more potent or perilous than the unbridled fire of passion. We are both at fault here."

Alexandria's brow knit in deep thought. Could he possibly be telling the truth? Had she unknowingly incited him beyond logic and control? He had positively done that exact thing to her. But he was a man of experience and knowledge in these intimate matters. Was he craftily seeking some excuse for his bestial conduct? There was none!

To defend herself and her own wayward actions, she

vowed in irritation, "But I didn't know what I was doing; you did! I honestly thought you were only an illusion. What real man could possibly look like you or kiss like that?" she foolishly spouted, then moaned in annoyance at her unwitting slip.

A broad, pleased grin flickered enchantingly across his face as he chuckled. "It isn't funny!" she cried, tears filling her eyes.

"No, love, it isn't," he easily agreed. His left hand was playing in her honey tresses while his right index finger was drawing tiny circles upon her left cheek. His touch and expression were disquieting, yet wonderfully exciting. Even though his actions were tantalizing, she wanted him to halt them and leave her alone, fearing another loss of her self-control.

"I promise I won't hurt you again. This time, you'll know only pleasure and contentment. You are far too special and fragile to abuse. Come, love; let me prove my claims . . ."

Next time! the words raced through her mind with lightning speed. Glimmers of alarm sparked terror within her wide emerald eyes. Her body tensed and trembled. "You cannot do that wicked thing again! Please . . ."

"Such feelings and reactions are natural and normal, love. You're experiencing emotions which are new and confusing, even frightening. Why is it wicked to feed a hunger which is as old as time itself? Your strict upbringing has taught you to fear and to reject such innate responses. Can you truthfully deny you enjoyed my kisses and caresses? Can you disclaim the fires which swept through your mind and body? Admit it, love; you desired me as much as I desired you. You're just too stubborn and afraid to tell me, perhaps even admit to yourself," he boldly challenged her, the ghost of a triumphant and knowing smile teasing at his sensual lips and mocking eyes.

Another annoying blush colored her face. She silently cursed that weakness which revealed her innermost feelings and thoughts to a stranger! How she wished she could prevent that vexing habit forever. She softly parried, "A kiss is one thing, sir, but seducing an unsuspecting girl is quite another matter. If you cannot judge the vast difference between the two, then you are indeed some crude ruffian! I demand you let me leave here this instant!" she exclaimed, her velvety voice lacking real conviction and courage.

He laughed with genuine amusement. "Not until you reward me with several kisses and tell me your name," he merrily retorted.

"Reward you!" she shouted in disbelief. "Pray tell, for what? Indeed, I should slit your miserable throat!"

"For chivalrously lying here exchanging banter just to relax you rather than making passionate love to you over and over . . . which is exactly what I yearn to do?"

She inhaled sharply. Her stomach knotted. She swallowed the lump in her throat with great difficulty. She paled visibly beneath her golden glow. "You, Sir Demon, vastly overestimate your kindness and manners!" she sarcastically sneered, abruptly becoming aware of the aristocratic bearing and noble breeding he exuded. His cultured, educated speech could not be denied. This was no country bumpkin or lawborn rogue! But why would such a man stoop to ravishing young ladies of his own class? Had he mistaken her for some vulnerable peasant girl with whom he could while away his leisure hours? Even so, it would not excuse his conduct!

Totally unexpectedly, she questioned him, "Who are you? How did you find this secret place? Where did you come from? Since I was a small child, no one has ever discovered or entered my haven." But Spencer paid no mind to her last comment.

So, she wanted to know his name and identity. Why? Did she wish to turn him over to the British soldiers for imprisonment? Was she so intrigued or spiteful that she would attempt to procure an enforced marriage?

Such ideas brought a bitter taste to his mouth. Marriage was irritating enough as some distant threat over his head, but to be forced to wed a mere commoner was utterly preposterous! Not that she wasn't the most beautiful, desirable woman he had ever known, but to marry her to save her honor? Frankly, she did reveal a charm, wit, and intelligence which he found refreshing and stimulating. But the unwritten laws of marriage within one's own station were ingrained within him. In spite of his rebellious and masterful air, that was one area of his life which he had never questioned or resisted. When that revolting moment for marriage arrived, his sense of pride and duty would wed him to a proper lady of matching bloodline and social rank. At such a time, it would be a tasty paramour such as this peasant girl who would make a stifling marriage tolerable. Still, she could make trouble for him with accusations of rape, trouble which he could not afford at this time. In fact, the limelight could spell disaster and death for him . . .

No, my exquisite sun-goddess, you shall not trick me with those bewitching eyes and that innocent air, Spencer thought. I will not permit you or anyone to endanger my mission or family name. He smiled engagingly and lied most convincingly, "For five kisses you can have your answer." Having no intention of revealing either of his identities to her, he decided a false one might tempt her to spend time with him while he was here. Charmed or ignorant, she couldn't cause any entanglements with the British forces here. If he managed to win her over and if she were still around and available in a few years, she might be persuaded to become his mistress.

Years? Available? Twinges of jealousy and anger nipped at him as visions of her lying beneath other men flickered before his mind's eye. Now that she was no longer pure in body—thanks to him—she might see no reason to remain pure in mind and heart either! She might recognize her value as some nobleman's mistress. Or she could become some highly paid harlot with her looks and charms. He had shown her passion; he had taken away her virginity. She could never return to innocence. With that picture before him, Spencer vowed to sate his desire for her before leaving

Great Britain; for as she had said earlier, they would never meet again . . .

"Put your arms around my neck," he tenderly commanded, his voice calm and reassuring. "Tell me your name and then give me five kisses. In return, I will give you mine; then I will release you . . . if you still wish to leave me."

Alex's emerald eyes brightened with a ray of naive hope. Her trusting nature foolishly accepted his devious promise. Anyway, what was the use of fighting him? She was powerless to prevent his intentions, but she might forestall a painful assault. Her only hope for freedom lay in outwitting him, if she could.

An undeniable aura of tightly leashed power and restrained violence could be felt around him. If he so wished, he could easily do what he pleased with her. Yet, a genuine streak of gentleness and intoxicating charm flowed from him when he allowed it to surface. It was obvious to even her naive mind that he did desire her; his body told her that much, as did his blue eyes.

She was completely within his power and control; yet he was attempting to gently seduce her rather than to savagely rape her. Why? Did he prefer her willing and eager beneath him? Or, was it that she was no doubt the first and only female to ever reject his ardent advances?

He was unlike any man she had ever met or known. He was power, passion, and masculinity all rolled neatly and perfectly into one tight mold. He was a complex puzzle which she could not decipher to form an understandable picture. His moods were like quicksilver. Clearly he wanted and demanded his own way, but disliked having to forcefully extract it or to subtly plead for it. She frowned in dismay.

"Well?" he impatiently growled. "Do we have a bargain?"

"Your word of honor you'll release me afterwards?" she implored.

"My word of honor, love. Afterwards, I will let you go," he stated clearly, closing his trap around her as she failed to note his sultry inflection upon the key word "afterwards."

She sighed in artless satisfaction and trusting relief. A dazzling smile came to her suddenly relaxed features. Yet, even gullibly accepting his false word, she sweetly gave him a false name, "I'm called Angelique." A perfect choice since he had previously called her an angel! She smiled, not at him, but at her guile. He was insane if he thought she would reveal her real name! She would make certain he could never locate her or abuse her tender soul and traitorous body again. He was much too clever and skilled to risk seeing again. Yet, he was most tempting and compelling . . .

"Angelique," the name rolled upon his tongue like a lover's caress. "Your father named you wisely and accurately," he remarked favorably, completely taken in by her lie and mood.

"I've always liked it. It's difficult to say in an angry or harsh tone," she murmured softly to make sure he did not doubt her honesty, which he didn't. She smiled

67

timidly and asked, "And yours, Sir Demon?"

"Stephen. My close friends call me Ste; you may do so if you wish," he smoothly misled her with the same ruse she had used upon him. His confident expression and disarming tone never altered as he deceived her.

He studied the luminous eyes which demurely slipped to his manly chest. She was frightened of him and unsure of herself. She wasn't familiar with this kind of situation, denying her the right thing to say or do. She was a rare gem, ready to be cut into a valuable and precious stone by the right craftsman. He mentally sharpened and honed his skills, savoring this heady task which lay before him.

She flushed a deep rose as she felt his discerning blue eyes watching her. She refused to meet that intense gaze which alarmed her senses and curiously appealed to her rampant emotions.

He pushed a stray lock of silvery gold silk aside. She nervously flinched at his searing touch. "Don't be afraid, love. Look at me, Angelique," he tenderly commanded in a deep and rich tone. He gently grasped her quivering chin and raised her head, bringing her eyes up to his lips. "Look at me," he said again.

She anxiously obeyed, slowly pulling her hesitant gaze from his smiling lips. Their eyes met and fused, liquid green with molten blue. "Relax," he coaxed softly. "I'm not some ogre come to devour you. I ask but a kiss to sate my starving soul," he teased.

His head slowly came down toward her. Disarmed, she permitted his mouth to explore hers in a long and deliberate kiss. He plundered her mouth with a skill to

match his piracy at sea. Several kisses later, her arms
went up and around his neck. As his masterful lips
branded her mouth, face, and throat with his fiery
touch, she was quickly lost to all reality; she had
returned to that wonderful dreamland from which
there would be no escape.

Gradually all restraint left her body. Those novel
and powerful feelings mysteriously stripped away any
desire to pull free from him even after the fifth kiss.
His silvery tongue softly whispered stirring words
which stormed her defense, leaving her quivering
within his grasp. She could feel the entire length of
their naked bodies as they pressed closer together,
dissolving those last remnants of icy resolve. Unaware
of her peril, Alex surrendered to his command and
direction.

His embrace was possessive and his onslaught was
intoxicating. A curious mingling of lanquor and
tension surged and mounted within her. Her mind was
blissfully dazed by overwhelming lust for him. She
needed him; she wanted these rapturous sensations to
go on forever. A magical, unbreakable spell was woven
tightly and securely around her.

He moved cautiously and very gently, knowing she
might still be too sensitive. He did not want to arouse
her to the reality of what was actually taking place
between them. It appeared she had become ensnared
in that beautiful, responsive dreamland once more and
he certainly didn't want to awaken her. His voice
huskily coaxed the responses which he wanted while
his kisses and caresses drugged her. The ache within

his own loins cried out for release; yet, he fiercely controlled the urge to possess her too soon.

He quelled his guilt when she murmured his name over and over again. Well, Stephen was his first name! He hadn't exactly lied to her. Maybe it was what she said along with his name that really bothered him. "Love me, Stephen," she had whispered several times. He somehow knew she did not really refer to physical love—but he quickly discarded these thoughts.

Her hands moved up and down his back, revealing the growing intensity of her passion. Still, he cunningly continued his loving assault, determined to make her totally unable to rebuff him this time. If this was the last time he would ever make love to her, he wanted to taste her complete and willing surrender.

Spencer had delivered many women into the throes of frenzied passion, but none had ever engulfed him completely as this girl did. As his fingers gently rubbed her nipples, she arched forward to press her heated body to his. When his hand slipped below to seek out her womanhood, she moaned and writhed in his arms. He stroked her gently and masterfully, creating a greater need within her.

When he had stimulated her to the point where she cried out in urgency and clung tightly to him, he gingerly parted her thighs and eased within her receptive body. He moved slowly and provocatively, not wishing to alarm her until she was totally past the last instant of resistance and awareness. His rhythmic movements created a rapid build-up of fire. Noting the depth of her passion, he threw all caution to the wind. He plundered her body, gathering memories which would forever remain with him.

There was no turning back for either of them. Alex writhed against him. Waves of desire stormed her senses. Those instinctive, smoldering flames cried out for appeasement. Her body and her will belonged to him. Her breathing was erratic; her entire world careened wildly, then receded to leave her floating in a wondrously entrancing state. All tautness and re-sistance vanished in the flames and heat of shared passion.

Even in her innocence, she reached out to him and claimed him as no other female had ever claimed him before. He took her with an intensity and hunger which was new and exciting in slow, tantalizing tenderness which soon erupted into turbulent, wild fervor.

They scaled the heights of desire until they could no longer bear their shared need. His thrusts increased in speed and in titillation. Suddenly, wave after wave of ecstasy crashed in upon them. They clung to each other and willingly went with the raging tide which was helplessly carrying them away. The release was so powerful and stunning that Alex nearly fainted from the sheer force of it. Never had they known such feelings were possible. Never had they even dreamed love could be this consuming and potent. A blissful aftermath settled over them. Their bodies and passions had joined to forge a bond which could not be easily broken or endlessly denied . . .

Spencer pressed lingering kisses upon her lips and closed eyes, each more possessive and tender than the one before it. He gently stroked her satiny cheek and silky shoulder as a strange sense of serenity and affection washed over him. It was his resonant voice which promptly returned her to the present, "Ah, my love, didn't I promise it wouldn't hurt again? A most rewarding experience, is it not? See what magic and pleasure you would have denied us both?" he murmured fondly, perplexed by this acute craving to possess her yet again! What mystical spell had this siren cast upon him?

Her sea-green eyes opened and gazed up at him. The languid, adoring look was instantly replaced by one of intermingled shame and utter astonishment. Within moments, racking sobs were uncontrollably torn from her throat and lips. Spencer was at a complete loss. Nothing he said could calm her down until her weeping was spent. Normally, this was the time he would wisely desert a woman. Yet, this woman was not one to be nonchalantly cast aside or forced to suffer without solace. Why, he couldn't fathom.

Yet, her torment and vulnerability touched him. Spencer tried to comfort her, but she would not permit it. Her eyes blazed with unconcealed fury and shame as she accused, "You tricked me again! Do your words and honor mean nothing to you?"

Ignoring her challenge, he mischievously taunted, "Did I, love? I recall promising to let you go 'afterwards.' Can I be blamed for your misunderstanding me?"

72

Shocked by his deception, anger flooded her. "You beast! You knew what I meant! You claimed kisses and my name were all you wanted! How dare you make my own body traitor to me! Get off of me!" she defiantly stormed at him. "Surely even your vile and cunning bargain is met! You not only have my name and kisses, but you have also twice taken me against my will!" she panted, terrified by the raging fires which had consumed her mind and body.

Spencer actually laughed at her dismay. She beat against his hard chest, frantically trying to shove him away. Tears of frustration and helplessness poured from her green eyes, dancing with fury and hatred. "If it salves your guilty conscience to call what we just shared rape, then by all means do so. But I did not force you, either time," he said. "Perhaps I did seduce you the first time, but neither time did I brutally ravish you. Never have I known a woman with so much fire or stubbornness. Why can't you admit you enjoyed our encounter? Face it, Angelique, you made love to me. You have only yourself to blame for being so delectable and available," he arrogantly declared.

"You black-hearted bastard! You rutting beast! You lying, conniving rogue! Get off of me! If you value your miserable life, you'd best get as far away from here as possible!" she shouted with renewed fury and false bravery. "My family will have you arrested and flogged to death, if they do not cut out your evil heart and mutilate you first!" she boldly threatened, still trapped in the iron confines of his embrace. She used the words "family" with the hopes it would stir up intimidating images of many avenging brothers and an irate father.

His eyes grew piercing and chilling. His tone was withering as he gritted out a glacial warning of his own, "If you wish to leave here at all, my spiteful Angel, don't threaten me. Such foolhardy rantings are dangerous and annoying. Get washed off, then we'll talk," he sternly ordered the startled girl. "If there's one thing I can't tolerate, it's a two-faced, spiteful bitch! First, you blow hot; then, you wax cold. Make up your mind, woman!" he harshly rebuked her, irritated by her anger and obstinance.

While Alex was fearfully wondering if Stephen planned to silence her tongue with death, he was speculating upon how he could salvage this enticing opportunity when she was so clearly set against him. It was the haunting thought of losing her which had unknowingly inspired his volatile fury, that and the idea of her family hindering his mission. What a tempestuous and passionate wildcat to tame and to enjoy!

"Talk?" she tremulously echoed. "You wouldn't . . . kill me . . . if I promised not to . . . tell anyone, including my father . . . would you, Stephen?" she hesitantly asked, wide eyes searching his stormy face for a favorable answer.

"Kill you?" he growled incredulously. "Whyever would I do such a terrible thing to the most beautiful and satisfying woman alive?" Yet, he realized she was serious.

"But you looked so angry. I . . ." she faltered.

"Furious because you threatened me, love. But enough so to harm you? Never, Angelique. Does that ease your worries?" he asked, smiling tenderly.

Knowing it was wise to comply with his demands for the present, she controlled her impetuous temper and sharp tongue. It had been dangerously stupid to say such rash things to this treacherous rogue. She summoned her courage and forced back her tears.

How dare he make her grovel and plead with him! No man had ever forced her into being a whining weakling. He was actually making her feel the villain rather than the victim! She would punish him yet! No man degraded or abused her in this selfish manner. She was not a female to be taken lightly, then cast aside like some cheap harlot. But Spencer realized this too late.

He would pay dearly and heavily when the right time presented itself, and it would; she would make certain of it! Soon, Stephen, she vowed . . .

III

"For Fate with jealous eyes does see
Two perfect loves; nor lets them close . . .
And therefore her decrees of steel . . .
Us as the distant poles have placed."
—"Definition of Love," Andrew Marvell

Observing the smug look upon his face, Alex could not resist one last stab at him, "Can I trust you to honor your word this time, Stephen? After we talk, will you let me go home immediately?" This time, she left no room for deception.

He chuckled, then sighed in reluctant resignation. He agreed. Still skeptical, she stared at him in doubt. Noting her expression of mistrust, he dramatically placed his hand on his bare chest near his heart. He vowed, "I swear it upon my life and honor. Stay a while to talk, then I'll see you safely home."

She bit her tongue to hold back her stinging insults about that proclaimed honor and safety. He unexpectedly rolled aside, exposing her nakedness with its sheen of perspiration to the brilliant sun and to his igneous blue eyes which instantly scorched her flesh with their sweltering heat.

Mortified, she hastily flipped into the protective covering of the water. Annoyed by his chuckles of amusement, she placed her slender back to him. She then sought to remove the accusing traces of his prior lovemaking without the aid of soap and a soft cloth. By now, her mind was ensnared in a more distressing and violent maelstrom than when she had arrived in her now tarnished paradise.

Never had she been so ashamed in her entire life. A total stranger had ravished her, viewed her naked, and was presently humorously watching her bathe! Those transgressions were unforgivable; yet, there was an even greater offense leveled against him: he had persuaded her to let him seduce her! She scolded her traitorous body which had made his vile deed so easy for him. She raged at the wanton emotions which she had experienced for the first time ever. How dare this man teach her such intimate things! How dare her body actually enjoy them . . .

She recklessly turned around and glared at him. The heat and force of his still smoldering gaze unnerved her, provoked her. "Stop staring at me!" she shouted at him. "Haven't you shamed me enough already! Must you embarrass me further? Damn you, Stephen! If you cannot turn around, at least close your eyes!" she commanded, unintentionally revealing his power over her. Her arms were crossed over her chest as she vainly tried to conceal her breasts from his leering gaze.

Her cries of protest and outrage simply drew lusty laughter from him. He observed the way she attempted to shield her bosom from his intense stare with those small, ineffective hands. He enviously watched the sky-blue water as it played around her slender waist and lapped at her silky flesh. At his piercing scrutiny of her, she fused that lovely shade of crimson. "You are far too modest, my lovely Angelique. Where is that plucky, venturous streak which caused you to brazenly discard your clothes and to lie naked in the warm sunlight?" he teased cheerfully. What a stunning, fascinating combination of fire and ice, of passion and promise all wrapped up in the same beautiful package!

"I was alone then! And I told you I've never done this before. It was a stupid impulse. I was angry and upset. Just because you have no morals or conscience doesn't mean I do not!" she indignantly snapped, vexed by his noticeable indifference to her humiliation and anguish.

He grinned, thoroughly enjoying this stimulating duel of wills. So, she did have spunk and mettle after all. "Do I make you nervous and shy, Angel? Or do you merely feel threatened by my unchivalrous revelation of that fiery, passionate soul of yours? Are you afraid of my great prowess and power over you? Most women would give their right arms to experience what you just did," he arrogantly boasted.

"Oh-h-h! Well, I'm not most women! In fact, I'm not your type at all! I wouldn't give a pence for anything you have to offer! Besides, you cannot take credit for Mother Nature; you did tell me such feelings and responses were as old as time itself! But since I know nothing of such intimate situations, I cannot be blamed for falling prey to your cunning seduction!"

"So you do find me and our encounter delightful," he teased.

"You overrate yourself, sir! I found neither enjoyable!" she blurted out, her guilty expression belying her denials. What good did protests and taunts make? The conceited knave! She would like nothing better than to claw that mocking smile off his laughing face.

Cautioning herself to patience and wisdom, she timidly wheedled, "Please, Stephen, must you strip away all my pride? Surely a valiant man such as yourself understands pride? Would you meekly permit a total stranger to make you feel degraded and defeated? Would you allow a female to treat you as you are treating me? I daresay you would rebel and resist with every ounce of strength and daring which you so vividly possess. You seem to forget something very important, my swash-buckling rogue; I am not a willing strumpet whom you've paid to accept these cruelties. Is it truly necessary to treat me as a highly paid harlot or some cheap doxy? After all, I am at your mercy." Her emerald eyes welled with tears; her dainty chin quivered. She lowered her head, her silvery gold hair falling forward to conceal her expression which might unwittingly give away her crafty deceit.

Her wily scheme had the desired effect upon him. She had shrewdly selected arguments which he could readily comprehend and accept. Her vulnerability and sadness touched him deeply. As she sniffled, he was sorely tempted to go to her and to comfort her, but decided that would be unwise. She was like a fragile budding flower who was frightened and confused by the torrid rays of the sun, enticing her to unfold her delicate petals and present her beauty and freshness to him.

"You're right, Angel. I need not wither such a lovely flower with my blazing eyes. Wash off; then we'll talk, love," he crooned in that husky voice which stirred her.

He grinned at her fetching sight before his gaze. He lay down upon the grass which still boasted of her shapely impression. His body was temporarily sated, although stirrings of new desire were lapping at his mind. This place was tranquil and the sun was relaxing. A feeling of contented drowsiness and total peacefulness came over him. He shut out the azure sky and white clouds above him. The twittering of birds, the droning of bees, the singing of other busy insects relaxed his taut body and soothed his battle-weary brain. Thoughts of other matters entered his mind, that critical mission which had deserted his attention in favor of enticing plans for this alluring angel whom he had fortuitously discovered. She was beautiful and intriguing and he definitely planned to savor her. Dispatches, Spain, and Madison could wait just a wee bit longer . . .

Alex chanced a quick glance at him. Watching the steady rise and fall of his manly chest, she hoped he was not deceiving her with feigned slumber. Had he given in to her too easily to be trusted? Did he think her too mesmerized by him or too faint-hearted to attempt escape? The ruthless tyrant! The arrogant nincompoop! He had just demolished her world of beauty and innocence; and now, he was calmly taking a snooze! Fury consumed her.

She held her breath and dipped beneath the surface of the water to lift a heavy rock with her two hands, the weapon which she had been gingerly seeking out with her toes, that device to better the odds between them. Terrified, but determined, she slowly and carefully eased over to the edge of the pond to carry out her daring assault upon him. He was resting close enough to the bank for her to strike him senseless with a properly placed blow upon his handsome head. She struggled to silence her noisy respiration and to still her shaking hands. Her heart was racing wildly; shivers washed over her. As she forced her shaky legs to move forward, she held the rock beneath the surface of the water, ready to drop it if discovered. One wrong move . . .

Lulled into a delusive sense of security and power, Spencer's keen instincts were not at full alert; they failed him for the first time ever. Nearly asleep, he did not detect his angel's stealthy approach or his imminent danger until it was too late to react. He dreamily opened his eyes just as the rock was about to land upon his forehead. A last minute attempt to quickly roll aside only served to bring the stone down upon one temple. There had been no time to seize her wrists or to avoid the stunning impact. A groan of pain escaped his lips as instant blackness claimed him, carrying him to an empty void.

In her panic at discovery by those dark sapphire eyes, Alex had struck him harder than intended. The heavy thud of the rock against his skull tormented her gentle nature. The sight of his crimson blood which steadily flowed into his sable hair nearly caused her to faint. She hurriedly cast the offensive stone aside and splashed cool water upon her ashen face to clear her head and to hopefully control her churning stomach. Violence was new to her.

She stared at the motionless man, witnessing the green grass as it grew red and wet beneath his dark head. Had she killed him? Was his crime against her worthy of such a fatal punishment? Her wide eyes riveted to his chest. She exhaled loudly in relief; he was still breathing. She hastily left the water and nervously pulled on her clothes, ignoring the water which made them cling to her trembling body.

Just as she was about to flee, Alex couldn't help but glance back at him. Some mystical, overpowering force tugged at her tender heart as she eyed him. He had not moved. He was bleeding badly. What to do . . .

She timidly edged her way over to his prone body. She wondered if he would be all right. He suddenly appeared so vulnerable, eliciting her guilt. She instantly scolded herself for her inexplicable and ridiculous concern for him. Still, her heart demanded that she do something for him. Spying his white linen shirt, she picked it up and tore a long strip from its tail, piqued by the wealth and station to which his rich garments attested. She knelt by the water and dipped the makeshift bandage into the pond. She hesitantly turned to him, praying her action would not awaken him.

She sat upon the ground and struggled to bind his wound. Completing this generous task, her eyes helplessly slipped over the full length of his virile physique. She flushed in modesty; yet, she boldly scanned him from raven-black head to bare feet. His body was lean and hard; his muscles were smooth and flexible. His brute strength and leashed power permeated her senses. She was astonished to find herself admiring his manly frame rather than being repulsed by her first view of a nude male.

To be honest, he was magnificent; he was undeniably perfect in all but manners. Her hand tested the vitality of his sable hair, relishing the sleek fullness of it. From the dark mat upon his chest, she playfully curled wisps of shiny hair around her fingers. She lifted his right hand to study the fingers which had the ability to incite such pleasure and to bring such delight to her once pure body.

Despite her daring perusal, she defensively withdrew her bold gaze from the lower portion of his stalwart frame, that secret area which had stormed her womanhood and rashly rewarded it with both pleasure and pain, that provocative area which even now sent shivers of forbidden and strange yearnings over her. Her gaze lingered upon his face, visually tracing and memorizing every inch of the handsome features emblazoned there. She ran a quivering finger over his sensual lips, then, for some unknown reason, placed a fleeting kiss upon them.

Her fingers moved over his clean-shaven, strong jawline and toyed with his cleft chin. She captured his head between her trembling hands and positioned it to gain a better look at him. Why did he have to be so devastatingly attractive and so utterly irresistible? The Fates had certainly smiled generously upon this valiant creature! Her hands travelled down his neck, aware of the strength represented there. Unable to stop herself, she ventured over his broad shoulders and leisurely migrated down his brawny arms. A strange sadness plagued her.

She softly whispered, "Why must you be such a villain, Stephen? If only we had met under different circumstances, for no man has ever made my heart and body sing this dangerous melody. If father would present a man such as you, I would marry him this very day! But alas, arranged betrothals do not permit such blissful miracles . . ."

Abruptly noting her shocking actions, wanton thoughts, and absurd statements, Alex ordered herself to cease these foolish and wicked notions. But he was so splendid. His body was the pinnacle of masculinity and vitality. His face could send sparks of envy through Apollo himself! She could envision the pile of broken hearts which he had surely left behind. She speculated upon his attraction to her. Had it simply been inspired by her availability and sensuous allure? Had he merely viewed her naked body as a new conquest?

"Who are you, Stephen? Where did you come from? If you lived nearby, your reputation and name would be widely known to all women. What cruel fate brought you here today?"

She cursed him for teaching her to feel and to ponder such wishful things. She cursed fate for defensively tearing her from his side after cruelly binding her soul to his. To discover such a tempting dream and then to lose it was sheer agony. "Be gone from my sight and mind, Sir Demon, for we shall never meet again! What madness assails me that I should grieve at your loss? What vicious spell have you cast upon me that I should wantonly desire you after what you have done to me? What power and magic do you possess that tempts me to remain at your side, to crave another union with you? What strange and wicked feelings you instill within me. Damn you, Stephen! Damn you . . ."

Tears of frustration and guilt pooled in those sea-green depths. She slowly and reluctantly stood up, taking one last long look at him. She turned and hurried through the dense line of trees. She whistled for her beloved Ivory; he came galloping to her. Alex gripped his flowing mane and pulled her light weight upon his broad back. She gently kneed him and raced for home and safety, never expecting to ever see the dream lover whom she was leaving behind.

When she reached the stables, she hastily dismounted and called for Jim to give Ivory his rub-down and feeding. As if pursued by some unseen evil, Alex ran to her room. She promptly summoned her maid to prepare a hot bath for her while she angrily stripped off the clothes she was wearing, her intention to discard them immediately. Never would she ride in such a get-up again. If she had been properly attired in a velvet riding habit and had placed the uncomfortable English saddle upon Ivory's back, her meeting with Stephen might have begun and ended quite differently. Never would she venture into that lovely paradise which had changed her life and heart forever. Never could she risk meeting that intoxicating creature again. She vowed that no man would ever gain such a frightening, powerful control over her body and will. "Never again, Stephen . . ."

Even as she solemnly pledged these things to herself, she was tormented by tempting visions of that incredible man who had shown her what it was to become a woman. The knowledge that she would never see or know him again brought sudden and rending anguish, a disturbing sense of denial and loneliness. How was it possible for a complete stranger to attain such a grip upon her heart, mind, and body? It must be sheer madness, some contagious wantonness which he had injected into her! "You arrogant stud!" she swore.

As she soaked in the hot tub of fragrant bubbles, she relived every moment of the past afternoon. Envisioning Stephen's face, those new and fiery longings returned to haunt her. As tears of self-betrayal and sacrifice eased down her cheeks, Alex painfully admitted to the exquisite pleasures and fulfillment which she had discovered with him . . . feelings and sensations which she wanted to know again someday.

Recalling his lordly demeanor, she vowed softly, "If we ever meet again, Stephen, you will feel the wrath of

Lady Alexandria Hampton! Father was correct; there are men I have yet to meet. If our paths ever cross again, you will be in for the shock of your miserable life! I can hardly wait to see the look upon that smug face when you discover my identity and realize your great crime! I will let you squirm in fear of what action I will take to avenge myself!"

She began to wash her sun-kissed golden skin. She asked herself why she did not feel dirty and soiled as she had proclaimed to him she had felt. As she imagined the wrinkled hands of some lord or rough duke with whom her father might betrothe her caressing those same curves which Stephen had touched and stroked into sublime surrender, shudders swept over her entire body. After knowing Stephen and experiencing real passion, how could she settle for anything less? God help her, for she could not!

Debating a coerced marriage with him, she quickly realized how dangerous such a rash move would be. A ruthless, volatile streak ran in him, one she would be stupid to challenge. He was not a man to cross. He would make a deadly and destructive enemy. Still, he owed her . . .

Perhaps he could be tricked or enticed into marriage . . . She instantly scoffed, "You could have any woman alive, Stephen. Why should you be interested in me? Sure, a lot of men have asked for my hand, but a man like you . . . You're dreaming, Alex," she warned herself. "What could possibly set you apart from his endless list of conquests? Intimating revenge is one thing, but enforcing it is quite another," she fearfully concluded.

When her lengthy bath was over, she leisurely dressed in a satin nightgown and stretched out upon her feather bed. The hour grew late; the sun vanished. The spring air became chilly and Alex closed her window and snuggled under her covers. When the evening chimes sounded, she refused to go down to dinner, pleading a headache and fatigue. More time passed.

When her concerned father came to her room to test this excuse to avoid him and to renew their discussions, he found Alex fast asleep. Her face was pale and her cheeks were rosy. She slept so deeply and soundly that neither his knock upon her door nor his hand upon her forehead awakened her. Detecting no excessive warmth upon her brow, he assumed that she was indeed exhausted. He quietly left her to her dreams after placing an affectionate kiss upon her temple.

After dining alone, Lord Charles Hampton went to his library to complete the final preparations for his daughter's departure, one which would unknowingly be her permanent move to America. He wished he dared to reveal his plans to his willful child, but he could not for fear of an innocent slip into the wrong ear.

He pulled open a desk drawer and sought the hidden compartment which held a sheet of paper upon which a pre-arranged code for secret messages between himself and Henry Cowling was clear in bold black ink. He diligently made notes upon small scraps of cloth which would be artistically shaped into tiny balls to fit unnoticeably into the centers of several flowers upon the fashionable hats which Alex would carry to America with her, messages which Henry would then pass on to another traitorous Englishman helping the American cause.

Charles mulled over the crisis which was making this deception necessary. His shipping firm was taking devastating losses every day. With the continued conflicts between France, Great Britain, and other adversaries, he would eventually be financially ruined. His export/import company had been crippled by the King's Orders-in-Council and that arrogant Frenchman's Continental System, by greedy privateers and dangerous pirates, and by America's retaliation to each of these threats to her own survival and prosperity. He would inevitably lose everything, and to be penniless and disgraced was a reprehensible, unbearable fate.

Great Britain, particularly King George III, was to blame for his desperate and uncontrollable attempts to ward off such a distasteful situation. Lord Hampton knew his actions were treasonous and grimaced at that nasty thought.

Once Alex was safely settled in Philadelphia with his dead wife's brother, he would rapidly make plans to join them there. From past experiences and personal contacts, he fully trusted Captain Burns who craftily used his American ship the *Moon Maiden* to feign being a British privateer. Burns would deliver his daughter to Henry in complete secrecy and safety, Lord Hampton confidently concluded.

Before returning his attention to his task at hand, Charles absently wondered if Madison had acted upon his last message. If so, the treacherous and daring feat had not yet been uncovered or announced. Perhaps Madison hadn't sent anyone to steal that vital packet in Grantley's office. He was relieved that his personal identity was known only to Henry Cowling and President Madison. From Henry's letters, Madison had agreed never to entrust his name to anyone, including his unknown accomplice, that sly and dauntless agent who could slip in and out of England with ease. He was either extremely brave or very reckless.

Charles mused upon this elusive and intrepid spy. Who was he? How did he carry off such deadly, intricate missions without a trace? He shuddered in fear at the thought of being connected with such a fearless American, or perhaps another traitorous Englishman. He sighed wearily, wanting this taxing situation resolved very soon, as well as the onerous affair with Alex.

Alex . . . with any luck, some masterful and worthy American would sweep her off her feet! He really couldn't blame her for rejecting a loveless, pre-arranged marriage. She was proud and wanted to choose her own destiny. He could only pray that some virile, strong, magnetic man would vanquish that troublesome problem for him. For certain, it would require a man of steel nerves and an iron will to tame his defiant daughter! "I pray your Lancelot is real and that you find him soon, Alex," he murmured softly, totally unaware his prayers had already come true . . .

IV

"O' for a falconer's voice
To lure this tassel-gentle back again."
—*Romeo and Juliet*, William Shakespeare

Spencer Farrington gradually became aware of the throbbing pain within his wracking head. He groaned as he tried to sit up. The stabbing sensations which shot fiercely into his injured head instantly sent him back to the ground. He carefully opened his eyes, shielding the last rays of sunlight from them with his arm.

At first, he was disoriented and alarmed. Why did his head want to split wide open? Where was he? What had happened? Had his ship been attacked and overrun? Had he been wounded, captured? Why was it so quiet and cool?

Slowly and painfully, his dazed mind and fuzzy vision cleared. He cautiously remained upon his back for a while, bringing his knees upwards and planting his bare feet near his nude buttocks. Assorted facts began to filter into his spinning head.

The pond . . . Angelique . . . her vengeful attack! It all came hurling back to reveal his carelessness and her deceit.

Disregarding the excruciating agony which shot

through his head, he forced himself to sit up and to look around. Naturally she was gone. He quickly glanced down at his nude body, surprised it was not covered with hundreds of vindictive scratches from that sneaky little she-cat. His hands flew to his handsome face to check it for damage: none.

That vicious, conniving bitch would rue the day she had dared to attack him and then leave him vulnerable to danger or death! So much for thinking her dim-witted or fragile! At least she hadn't betrayed him to her family or alerted the British authorities; the late hour proved those facts. Neither had she returned with a gun to slay him. Very strange indeed . . .

He chuckled satanically as he noted the smudgings of her virgin's blood upon his limp manhood and sinewy thighs. He briefly enjoyed the fact he had also caused her pain and humiliation in return. How dare she play the wanton and willing female with him, and then try to kill him!

He frowned, wrinkling his brow, calling attention to the bandage. His hand went up to touch the binding around his head. He jerked it off, gaping at the dried blood upon one side of it. "What the devil!" he exploded in astonishment. His torn shirt lay beside him. His startled gaze went from the shirt to the bandage and back again.

Why had Angelique bothered to dress the same injury which she had spitefully inflicted? He recalled her look of sheer terror as he had opened his eyes and witnessed her impending action. Had she panicked and struck him harder than intended? Was she contrite afterwards? Had she only feared the crime and punishment which might be handed down to a common serving girl for brutally slaying some highborn lord? If she hadn't meant to kill him, surely she wouldn't have troubled herself to bind his wound.

When he found her, which he most assuredly would, he would learn the truth! He rolled into the refreshing, invigorating water which had grown chilly with the evening breeze. He rubbed his hands over his body, removing both her blood and his own. Drops of fresh blood were visible upon his fingers when he touched the tender and swollen area upon his left temple. She would pay dearly for this unforgivable act! He had grossly misjudged her courage and guileful nature. She had looked so delicate and innocent; yet, she most certainly was neither.

"Damn you, Angelique! Damn all wily females! Before I leave here, you will feel the full measure of my wrath and power. If you think today was degrading and painful, just wait until we meet again, my lovely and cunning vixen. You'll never be able to run fast or far enough to elude Joshua Steele or Spencer Farrington! Be forewarned, my little nymph; your day of payment is coming!"

He dressed, thankful she had not realized the joke in stealing his clothes. It was nearly dark. He would seek out this mystery girl later. Tonight, there were more pressing matters upon his mind, matters which had been stalled by his meeting with her. His head ached; he cursed her anew. His schedule was already tampered with by the lateness of the day. Because of his mission, he couldn't even take something for his throbbing head or grant his body a much needed sleep. He left the pond, once again relieved by her oversight in leaving his horse behind. He absently wondered if these mistakes were accidental or intentional. Perhaps she was pleading for his forgiveness and leniency.

Once home, Spencer bathed again. But unlike Alex, he did not turn in for the night. Instead, he headed toward London to pursue the crucial information which had unexpectedly spurred this sudden trip. He only halted his journey about halfway in order to rest his horse and to sleep for a few hours, hoping it would assuage his physical torment which steadily increased with each mile travelled. Each time his chestnut roan put his hooves down upon the hard ground, a new wave of agony would shoot through his skull. With each twinge of pain, he cursed and doomed the girl by the pond.

Early that next morning, he reached his destination. In London, he made his way to the Boar's Head Inn late in the afternoon. Dressed as a common seaman, little notice was given to him by the other men who were present for their nightly row of drinking, whoring, and merrymaking.

Once the King's dragoons were well into their cups, he furtively moved closer to them, listening intently for any news which might prove useful to him before he boldly attempted to steal certain maps and documents from Lord Grantley's office.

The inn was crowded and noisy. The air was filled with the odors of hot food and smelly men. Crude and simple talk was being passed around. Raucous laughter filled the room each time a burly seaman or lusty officer managed to pinch a buxom barmaid or fondle a plump bottom on a serving girl.

After his annoyed reaction, a persistent doxy got the message that Spencer wasn't interested in her charms. It also took some doing to discourage a ruddy-faced seaman who wanted to drink and chat with him. The evening seemed endless and fruitless. Following the departure of all soldiers, Spencer returned to his lonely and dark room to wait until the next night.

His time here was limited; he might be seen and recognized. Once his theft would be brought to light, he knew someone would recall that Spencer Farrington had been around that particular night. He had no choice but to make a try for that file. How much stock could he place in that secret message to Madison? Who was this nobleman who could be trusted so highly and completely by both sides? Why did Madison insist upon keeping his name a secret from everyone, including him? Very curious indeed . . .

Then again, Madison was like that. He practiced the policy that a man could not reveal what he did not know, an often vexing trait which Madison had learned from his predecessor and good friend Jefferson. Each American spy worked independently of all others, then reported to Madison who filtered through the information to sort out the facts and fallacies.

Unable to sleep or to keep his mind off of Angelique, Spencer focused his attention upon past and present troubles. He briefly speculated upon Madison's idea to involve Edmond Genet, the ex-French diplomat, in their covert schemes. Surely Madison would realize how unwise and dangerous that ploy could be. Genet was now married to Clinton's daughter. Since the New England states had seriously mulled over the idea of rejoining the British Empire, that connection was perilous.

For a moment, Spencer wished his superior was either Washington, Adams, or Jefferson. Madison was a good man, an intelligent and honest one. But he was too easy-going and far too trusting. He made an excellent second-in-command, but he lacked the skills and qualities to be in the control of this situation. Too many selfish, disloyal men were hopping upon his political carriage for their own gains.

Madison's worst mistake was in sitting patiently and confidently in his office while handing out responsibilities and passing orders along to men who either ignored them or altered them to suit their own ideas of what was best for their country—or themselves. With powerful men like Clay, Webster, and Calhoun demanding reprisals upon Great Britain, it was extremely doubtful that Madison could hold them off much longer.

Hopefully these secret papers contained facts which would help Madison make the best decision for all concerned. Those men from the Ohio Valley didn't have Madison fooled; they only wanted a legal excuse to gobble up Canada. The same was true of those Southern War-Hawks; they lusted after the Spanish-held Florida territory. Greed and lust for power! Was this the new trend? Spencer pondered.

He fumed at several American inconsistencies. That Embargo Act and those Non-Intercourse Acts had been futile and foolish if America refused to comply with them or remained unwilling to enforce them. What country would respect or fear another one who had been intimidated, humbled, and crippled?

Spencer sighed heavily. If he could personally do anything to help America recover and prosper, he definitely would give it his best effort, perilous or not. In all honesty, the President was a cunning genius. Madison's political writings had stirred the hearts of countless men, earning him much respect. He could claim great pride and intelligence in his past work with the *Constitution*, in his daring stand against Britain's offenses, and in his *Federalist Papers*. It was an honor and a privilege to be working for and with such a great man. If only he wasn't so nonchalant and trusting . . .

No matter, there were many other questions and doubts which plagued Spencer tonight. That unseen file was said to be in Lord Grantley's office for safekeeping until the King himself came to London to study it four days hence. What if that furtive message was inaccurate? What if this whole set-up was only a scheme to infiltrate the American spy system? What if it was a trap to catch him? If only he knew who had sent Madison this urgent message. With that information, he could check out his unknown source's honesty.

Spencer realized only too well that if he were

captured or exposed he would break his grandfather's heart. He would blacken the Farrington name for all time. He would be viewed as an American spy, not a loyal and intrepid American hero. Possibly due to his family ties and holdings here in England, he might be treated as a traitor, not an American patriot. In any event, he would surely face execution by hanging, following a humiliating public flogging. No doubt dear, sweet Angelique would enjoy that fate for him!

There she was again, haunting his mind and stirring his body with desire for her. Damn Angelique and damn the danger! If that mystery folder really contained the important information, it was vital to attain it at all costs.

Endlessly his brain returned to the mysterious, but lofty, Englishman who sparked his intrigue. Who could be in the position to know about this file and its contents? Why would he pass such valuable information to the American government? Did it truly contain reports from Admirals Nelson and Wellington? Suggestions from Spencer Perceval, Robert Jenkinson, and Castlereagh? Notes from General Isaac Brock in Canada about New England's defenses and unrest? Papers stolen from John Quincy Adams in Russia? George Canning's favorable ploys to settle the conflicts with American commerce?

Many of those men were powerful Tory Ministers or smug men with the King's ear. As for Adams, there was no telling what secrets his stolen papers revealed. If that file existed, it was explosive; it was absolutely essential to put it into Madison's hands!

War was a dreadful and costly affair, more costly and savage when the two warring sides claimed members from the same families. If King George's plans could be peacefully and craftily deterred, a bitter and demanding confrontation might be prevented. Friends and family members would not be compelled to take sides and to battle against each other. There was no easy choice. Spencer's mission was clear.

Shortly after midnight that next day, the tense and alert Spencer slipped into Grantley's office without a single hitch. It almost seemed too easy for him, inspiring feelings of disquiet and suspicion. His keen instincts and astute mind were watchful and alive against a possible deception. He followed the coded instructions which he had received. All went as planned.

He found the safe right where the message had indicated. He used the combination which had been smuggled to Madison; it also worked beautifully. He removed the bulging brown folder and stuffed it into his billowy black shirt. He didn't waste any precious time by even glancing over the contents. Another time and place would be wiser and safer. He stealthily made his way out of the darkened office, expecting an attack at any moment. None came. Nothing! Luck was surely riding with him tonight—or could this be some elaborate hoax to pass along phony information? But then again, his unknown contact had vowed that no one was supposed to know of the file's existence or location.

He thought it best not to return to his room at the

inn and promptly rode for Farrington Manor. It required nearly two days to reach home by the roundabout trail which would deny anyone the chance to follow him, just in case. He would not risk endangering his grandfather's life or holdings at this late date. That lovable old cuss didn't deserve the troubles and burdens Spencer could unintentionally heap upon his silver head.

Once home, he concealed the notorious file in a secret compartment in his sea trunk. Now that he had his mission completed, there were only two other matters to hinder his impending departure: a serious talk with Will and a search for a certain little viper with beautiful skin and nasty fangs.

For the past few days, Spencer had attempted to shut out all thoughts of both people and the problems which each represented to him. He contrived a truce with Grandfather Will, giving his word he would seek out a proper wife and would settle down within two years. Will was overjoyed with that piece of news. At long last, there would be a woman and children to carry on the Farrington line. His old heart bubbled with happiness.

Spencer and Will shared a tranquil dinner. Over a brandy in the morning room, they talked about days of yesterday and made plans for their future. Spencer cunningly avoided any talk about politics and the portentous war which was brewing on both sides of the Atlantic Ocean. Will brought him up to date on the current gossip and their business holdings. For the first time ever, they conversed and planned as two men, as a family. In this genial setting, the evening passed swiftly.

Spencer generously and selfishly allowed Will to believe he would eventually settle down at Farrington Manor. The time to inform the gradually weakening old man of his intention to live in America could come much later. This peaceful and relaxing atmosphere was too fragile and delightful to shatter so quickly. Besides, he had two years to fulfill his promise!

As Spencer lay in his bed in his old room, memories of a tawny-haired, golden-skinned female with emerald eyes came to lie beside him. He was aroused by simply remembering their splendid moments by the pond and by calling her enchanting face to mind. Who was this angelic witch who had made such a vivid and unforgettable impression upon him? Who was this mere slip of a budding beauty who caused all others to fade from thought and to dull in appearance? Why had she taken the time and courage to minister to his injury after causing it? The thought of never having her again bothered him more than he cared to admit. Why worry, she would be back at his side very soon, willing or not! he smugly decided in the darkness of his room.

He mused over his earlier talk with Will. He had subtly questioned his grandfather about a certain peasant girl with locks of spun gold and silver, eyes of leaf green, skin of warmest and tastiest taffy, and with the name of Angelique. Will had never seen or heard of any such female. He had grinned that knowing and mocking way of his and playfully teased Spencer about the smoldering lights which had filled his eyes and the softened inflection of his tone as he had spoken of her. Will wasn't a man easily fooled; he had quickly realized that some pretty young thing had captured his grandson's eye, had even jested about capturing his heart!

Yet even at this very moment, Will was speculating about this pleasing mystery. What else could explain Spencer's sudden agreement to marriage? Spencer had labelled her a peasant girl or a servant. Naturally Lord Spencer Farrington could never wed such a lowly creature; but this beauty had encouraged domestic desires within his grandson. If she could be located, she could make him an excellent paramour.

Will wondered if this unknown girl was as drawn to his grandson as he so obviously was to her. He laughed at his foolishness. Of course, what woman with any intelligence and clear eyes wouldn't be! If she were unique enough to catch Spencer's eye and affections, it was a shame her breeding didn't match his. Thankfully Spencer had a dutiful head upon his shoulders!

For the next three days, both men avidly searched for the identity and whereabouts of this elusive goddess who had successfully vanished into oblivion. On Spencer's last night in England, he was forced to give up his futile hunt for the evasive Angelique. Evidently she was lost to him forever. He could almost believe she had been an illusion if it hadn't been for that painful lump upon his head. But who could honestly say where reality and magic separated?

Where did one leave off and the other begin? Perhaps she really had been a mischievous naiad, he mused to ease his intense yearnings to know who and where she was. Yet, he was also infuriated and troubled by her disappearance.

Was she perhaps in danger? Why had she fled to some other haven which he could not find? Was she cunningly avoiding him? Why had he allowed that tempting sorceress to get under his hide? Why was he giving her a second thought? Second thought! he exploded mentally; it was more like ten thousand thoughts! Damn her! Where was she? Who was she? Was she simply afraid to confront him or to allow him to find her? How could she vanish without a clue? Who could say, perhaps one day she would magically and unexpectedly sail into his seafaring life again. If so, she wouldn't get away so easily!

Since Spencer would be sailing with the pre-dawn tide, he bid his cherished grandfather farewell until next year and went to sleep upon his ship; the disguised *Black Mist*, terror of the open sea when it came to British ships. Humor flooded his mind as he realized the very scourge which they feverishly and frantically sought had been docked under their aristocratic noses for nearly two weeks! But what Englishman would suspect the trusty British privateer *Wandering Siren* was in truth the American privateer *Black Mist?* He had given them no reason to suspect him. He laughed at their carelessness and stupidity.

The last words from Will's lips had been a promise to continue his own search for this mystery girl who had claimed so much of Spencer's time, energy, and interest. For some ridiculous reason, Spencer had not discouraged him. Spencer wondered if he only wished for her to learn his true identity as a punishment or was there more to it? He concluded she was gone for good.

How? Where? No one he had questioned had even heard of such a unique female! How could that be possible? A woman of her overwhelming beauty couldn't remain hidden! Was she perhaps the private property of some wealthy nobleman? Was she perhaps the bastard daughter of one? But what of her innocence? If such was the case, what would this protector do to her upon discovery of her defilement by some stranger? Would he even believe her declaration of innocence? Would he inflict some terrible punishment upon her lovely body? Such perilous contemplations worried him, annoyed him.

"You shouldn't have deserted me, Angelique," he mused to himself. "I might have taken you to America with me. How very foolish you were, my dear. May the winds cease to blow the day you can forget me."

He shook his head to clear it of such wistful speculations. It never once entered Spencer's mind to seek out a wealthy, single lady who lived within twenty miles of his family's estates! He had wisely questioned the Hampton fieldhands about a certain peasant girl. Naturally no one realized he was actually referring to their young mistress, assuming he already knew her. He covered a lengthy distance in all four directions without any success.

Not once had Spencer recalled the scrawny, blond lass who had been only ten years old when he had left home to seek his fame and fortune in America. Why should he remember the two people who had inherited his neighbor's estate? He had met the father Lord Charles Hampton only a few times on subsequent visits. He had paid little attention to the skinny tomboy who was always racing off in one direction or another in pursuit of some impish adventure. Of course he had met the young Lady Hampton many times when she had come home to visit his parents so long ago.

Nor had Sir William Farrington considered Lady Alexandria Hampton to be his grandson's dream-girl. After all, Spencer had called her a commoner. Had Spencer agreed to meet this unusual lady more recently as Will had urged and pleaded several times, the truth would have come to light. Even though Will spoke of joining the two estates, Spencer had no interest in that "spoiled brat" on the adjoining estate, not with Angelique around somewhere. Will fretted over the loss of such a refined prospect. Even if his secret talks with Lord Hampton succeeded, how could either of them postpone an arranged marriage for a year or so as Spencer had indicated he wanted? What a predicament! Will had decided Alexandria Hampton was the perfect mate for Spencer. But how could he convince the reluctant and obstinate Spencer of that fact? His only hope lay in the fact revealed to him by Lord Hampton himself; Alexandria didn't wish to marry anyone anytime soon. Who knew what difference a year could make in both of them? If he could locate this Angelique and offer her to Spencer as his mistress, could he be convinced to marry Alexandria? Since they were both so much alike and neither desired marriage, they seemed a perfect match! If only Spencer could see and meet her . . .

When the first streaks of dawn's gray light touched the English countryside, a frigate in full sails could be seen moving against the distant horizon, her mizzen-mast catching the first breeze of this new day. Spencer watched the *Moon Maiden* capture the wind with her three wings of white and dig her wooden heels into the foamy cobalt waters on her voyage to America.

He chuckled to himself. Old Burns surely had them all fooled. Spencer, too, called out his brisk orders and set his own ship upon a different course. He headed his three-masted frigate southward, while the *Moon Maiden* headed almost straight into the northeasterly winds, listing slightly to the leeward side. He absently observed the other ship until she was lost in the early morning mist, having no known reason to pursue her. His boots firmly planted upon the rolling deck of his forecastle, Captain Joshua Steele issued crisp and lucid commands to his loyal crew.

The *Moon Maiden* sailed on toward Philadelphia, carrying the very treasure which Spencer had been eagerly and vainly seeking for the past few days . . .

*   *   *

Alex strolled along the polished wooden deck upon the arm of Captain Burns. The air was becoming cooler and brisker as they headed toward their destination. Perhaps the spring weather in northern America was different from her homeland. Dread and apprehension washed over her as she glued her watery eyes to the distant skyline. America for a month or so . . .

Alex was pleasantly surprised at her early attainment of her "sea legs," as Captain Burns described it. He proudly and cheerfully labelled her a natural-born sailor in body and spirit. While her dear maid and chaperon Tessa lay deathly ill in their adjoining cabins, Alex was thrilled by the intoxicating beauty and vastness of the watery world which totally surrounded them. The sea was relatively calm and the wind was utterly invigorating.

The previous nights had revealed a breathtaking view of starry skies and silvery full moons. A sense of adventure and independence sang within her veins. This trip was just what she needed. Thankfully, Captain Burns had ordered an earlier sailing date. In the beginning, she had adopted an artificial air of great excitement about this visit to her uncle, a feigned exuberance which she now truly felt. She had clung to the house and to her room following that fateful day at the pond with Stephen, pretending to prepare for this journey. She had feared discovery by that strange demigod who had descended upon her so mysteriously and unexpectedly. Once out of her homeland, she would be safe and free, no more Stephen or wanton temptation.

That time had been well spent, for they had

departed sooner than previously planned. She had faithfully promised her father to conduct herself as a lady for the entire duration of this trip. She had also promised to consent to marriage upon her return home, but not until she had inspected his selection of suitors! He, too, had readily agreed with a sly grin.

Perhaps her father was right after all. Perhaps it was time for her to cast away silly dreams of knights and romantic love. Perhaps it was time to settle down and to begin a life of her own and a family . . .

But if such facts were true, then why did she feel so sad, so threatened, so utterly miserable? If the marriage bed—that facet she had feared and dreaded—was anything like her experience with Stephen, could it be all bad? What if she could find some vital man with similar looks and qualities, but minus his dark and forbidding nature? Did another such man exist? She feared Stephen was one of a kind!

She gradually comprehended that such an idea was too good to be true. How could any mortal man possess both looks and a valiant character? It seemed to her from past experiences that men either had hints of one or of the other. But never had she met any man with with a pleasing supply of both. That is, if she didn't count Stephen!

Stephen . . . Stephen who? Where had he come from? Where had he gone? What did it even matter now? She was half an ocean away from him. Perhaps he had only been an unhappily married man who was seeking an afternoon of carnal pleasures. No doubt he had mistaken her for some country lass, a defenseless woman with whom he could have his lecherous way. Envy and wild jealousy stormed her mind and heart. He was certainly old enough to be married, wed and to have perpetuated little Stephens! What could be worse than to be in love with a married man!

She grinned in wicked pleasure, contemplating his surprise upon awakening from her stunning blow. A prickling of fear and anxiety tugged at her. What if he had been injured badly? What if he had later died from that injury? What if he had been unable to seek help? She had been too frightened to risk going back to the pond to see if he had recovered and left. In spite of his vile treatment, she prayed for his survival. She resolved to return to the pond when she went home. She could only hope she would not find his body still there. To ease her guilt and tension, she had to learn his fate and identity . . .

She gazed up at the round yellow moon overhead and sadly murmured, "America for a month . . . Oh, Stephen, please be all right . . ."

While several hundred miles southeastward, another pair of dreamy eyes was watching that same moon and whispering softly, "Spain, then home . . . Virginia at last . . . Farewell, my enchanting siren, until we meet again . . ."

V

"O brave new world
that has such people in't."
—*The Tempest*, William Shakespeare

A voice full of confidence and pride shouted, "Strike the Union Jack! Hoist the Spanish flag! Pile all canvas! George, check the mizzenmast! She looks to tangle! Danny, bring 'er around to 40° yaw! Then, hold her steady as she goes; give 'er her leeway!" The deep tone could be heard over the snapping and popping of the white wings above them, the crashing of the mighty waves against the hull and the gusty breeze which filled those awesome sails to take them into the Spanish port. "Tim, stow those hawzers! Harley, check the mainsail knot on the bowsprit; her shape's changing!"

Spencer's proud gaze lazily eased over the stirring sight before it. His crew of one hundred seventeen men was skillful and loyal. He couldn't have located a more qualified, steady-handed wheelman than Danny if he had searched the world over. As for his good friend and first mate Andrew Pennington—Andy was his bright, brave right-hand man. After this present trouble was settled, Andy would become the new captain of the *Black Mist*, while Spencer returned to

Great Britain to honor his promise to Will. Naturally his ship would require a new coat of paint and a new name; her reputation and colors were too well known for private business. Once Spencer's personal life and family duty were realized, he could then decide whether or not to return to his ship and the carefree life of the sea. Two more measly years of freedom, excitement, and happiness!

He shuddered in repulsion. Matrimony? Horse feathers! He focused his sights and attention upon his ship. She was a beauty. She was sleek and swift; she responded to his commands with grace and promptness. Her aura was majestic and proud. She, along with her crew and captain, demanded recognition and respect. Her decks were always scrubbed and polished; her sails boasted care and attention. Her crew was cheerful and responsive, both to her and her intrepid captain. No scar from any past battle marred her sides or decks. Like a special lady, she was loved and pampered and she was a compelling and intoxicating sight to behold.

Normally painted black to conceal herself at evening tide when she did most of her work, she now displayed a swatch of blood red around her entire hull with designs of white waves as a disguise. The black coverings for the white sails had been taken down and stowed out of sight. Spencer frowned in annoyance, wishing his beloved ship was not colored up like some brazen harlot! "Soon, my love, you will be your old self again," he softly crooned to her as if she were indeed some female lover. "Once we leave Spain, you can become your mysterious, elusive lady self again."

Those lazy thoughts called another one to mind: the mythical legend of the black mist. He humorously pondered the days of yore when seamen actually took stock in such legends and tall tales; even now many still believed and feared them. To this very day, no man had ever seen Circe, sea-sirens, mermaids, sea monsters, or the black mist; yet many drunken, terrified weaklings claimed they had. Spencer chuckled at the recall of such foolish rantings. If such things existed, he would have glimpsed at least one by now in all his countless journeys.

He had played upon those irrational fears and superstitions when he had named his ship after the most frightening legend of all. He frequently went out of his way to increase his foes' fear and to further that legend to his own advantage. Whenever a dense gray mist was sighted, he would use its cover to lie in wait for an unsuspecting enemy ship who failed to observe his black ship which vanished before that stygian backdrop. When that ship was within range, he would suddenly swoop down upon her, catching her by complete surprise, appearing out of nowhere, easily conquering her, then vanishing back into the protective covering of moonless night.

He had become so skilled at this cunning ploy that most ships would instantly give quarter, knowing a fierce battle would be futile and would leave them helplessly stranded in mid-ocean. This crafty ploy and his infamous reputation prevented a great deal of bloodshed and destruction, for Spencer's main purpose was to confiscate messages and supplies between Great Britain and her accomplices on American soil. As he stood there in the moonlight with the gentle breeze caressing his bronzed face, that legend ran through his dreamy mind.

In times long past when the face of the mighty ocean was dotted with the wooden ships of good and evil, a powerful goddess watched over her watery world and gave her aid to those deserving ships and captains who found love and favor in her starry eyes and who were in grave danger of destruction by the forces of greed. It was said that when a ship and her captain proved worthy of survival and success in her eyes, she protected them with veils of misty, night-black hair. For when such a worthy ship was set upon by those who would plunder and dishonor her, this benevolent goddess removed the silvery pins from her midnight mane and trailed it over the chosen ship, concealing her from view.

To the eyes of evil, those stygian tresses appeared as some mysterious and deadly black mist. No one knew where it came from; no one knew to where it vanished. But once that magical black mist had lifted, one ship sailed on in safety while the other one lay forever lost within some shadowy realm of magical nothingness. The goddess then replaced her silvery pins and once more the sky was clear and the sea was tranqil.

If that legend were true, it could explain that odd mist which seemed to magically and mysteriously appear when he had great need of it! For once again forces of greed and evil were drifting upon the face of the sea, endangering the ships and lives of a newly born nation. Had this promising land mutely cried out for her help? Had she actually heard them and was she taking note of at least one certain, brave ship which bears the name of her legend? Strange, it did seem to be present each time he was in danger. Stranger still, no other ship seemed capable of using it safely. Was it merely his own keen instincts and talents, or was there more to it?

He laughed at such ridiculous speculations. Yet, another inexplicable mystery invaded his mind: Angelique. Like the curious black mist, she had come in secret, offering no clue as to where she came from or to where she vanished, disappearing just as mysteriously without a trace . . . It was utterly impossible that Angel had truly been the black mist goddess who had decided to finally make her face known to him! Had she, like Zeus, come to Earth to mate with a mortal of her choice? Why hadn't he been able to locate her? Why had no one ever seen or heard of her? Why was she unknown and unseen by all human eyes except his?

He instantly scolded himself, "Stow it, Spencer, old boy! You're sounding as crazy as the rest of them! The legend is pure fantasy, but Angelique is very real." Somewhere she was alive and undoubtedly laughing at him. One day, he would find her!

He threw back his head and inhaled deeply, savoring the smell of the ocean. That never-ending feeling of freedom and excitement coursed through his veins like molten lava. After two weeks on dry land, it felt exhilarating to have his feet planted upon the deck of his powerful frigate, soon to be sailing homeward.

The wind whipped through his sable hair; seaspray drifted into his smiling face, leaving a salty reminder of its presence. He absorbed the crisp fragrance which was the sea's alone. The heady song of the open water and harmonious melody of daring adventure called out to him. Braced against the rolling of the awesome sea, he refused to deliberate further upon the breathtaking girl who had entered his life one sunlit day, only to leave it that same glorious afternoon. Already they were miles and miles apart . . . perhaps even a lifetime by now. At a running speed of thirteen knots, the distance between them was steadily widening with each hour. She was somewhere in Great Britain; soon, he would be in America. Well underway to Spain, he finally left the forecastle to get some much needed rest.

About mid-morning that following day, Spencer went to his cabin to withdraw the papers for which he had risked his life, fortune, and name. He studied the pages and notes carefully and intently. His blue eyes widened in shock; his jaw dropped and tensed. Viewing the incredible facts and figures upon those sheets of paper, he hurried top-side and called out new orders to his crew. He commanded a faster pace if at all possible.

118

Distressed by the reports which were now hidden in his cabin, he debated the necessity of his voyage to Spain. Which destination was more vital, more pressing? He furiously cursed the girl who had caused him to delay; he berated and lambasted the lovely female who had taken his mind from his critical mission. While that monumental file had rested in the secret compartment of his sea trunk, he had been racing across the British countryside in search of an elusive angel. So much for being the benevolent sea goddess! If he ever got his hands upon her tawny throat, he would strangle her!

He seriously deliberated his two choices. If he had set out for Spain to confer with Joseph Bonaparte immediatley after that file was in his possession, he would be on his way to Virginia and Madison right this moment. If that folder was accurate, which he dreaded it was, America was in deep trouble. It was clear that the British were well aware of the power and hostile intent of the War-Hawks; they were now plotting to be one step ahead of the Americans at all times. What a fool he had been! Careless and selfish! For at this moment, his new country was in greater danger— because of him!

He apprehensively paced the deck in deep and brooding speculation. Spain or America? Since the French Minister Serurier should be reporting to Napoleon within a few weeks, was it truly necessary to take the time to discuss a possible American stronghold at San Augustin? The problem was that America couldn't risk the British taking possession of a port so near to them. Spencer wondered if Napoleon knew of the talk in America about going to war with both Britain and France if these conflicts continued. Americans wouldn't take much more interference in their commerce, especially not the wanton destruction of her ships and goods upon the open seas. Could he convince the French, who held Florida through their grip on Spain, to permit the Americans to protect the properties of both countries?

He sighed in frustration and uncertainty. Florida and Spain were only too conscious of the greed of certain Americans. America's determination to affix Florida to the United States was no secret. Had Joseph Bonaparte received news of Mathews's and Smith's aggressions in Florida only a few weeks past? If so, he wouldn't be in a cooperative mood. Did Spain also know that Commandant Justo Lopez had recently surrendered Fernandina to Campbell's flotilla? Had they been alerted to Smith's march on San Augustin? If so, none of these events would sit well with them.

Hopefully Madison's prompt reactions would soothe their ruffled feathers. The President had disavowed the hostile actions of those overly zealous colonials. He had immediately ordered the Americans to withdraw and to settle themselves upon nearby Amelia Island to await the results of his talks with Joseph Bonaparte in Spain, Foreign Minister Luis de Onis, and Governor Juan de Estrada.

Spencer laughed bitterly to himself. How could he possibly convince Spain of America's unselfish, generous proposals when Rhea had forcefully seized western Florida and had declared her free of Spanish rule? How could the American intention be viewed as friendly and helpful when Mathews, Smith, Campbell, and McIntosh were doing their damnedest to conquer northeastern Florida as well?

Spain should realize that Florida was too distant to be advantageous to her. She had been drained financially by her conflicts; she was being presently ruled by Napoleon's incompetent brother. Was the entire world going insane? What had happened to peace and prosperity? Too many men from so many lands were out for personal gain and glory. Why was it so impossible for Britain, France, Spain, and America to sit down together and to intelligently work out some peaceful and lasting solution to joint problems which seemed interwoven with each of them? The whole bloody situation was too complicated.

The dazzling sun reflected off the choppy waves, causing Spencer to squint his blue eyes and to furrow his brow. He absently rubbed the smoothness of his neatly shaven face as bits of information jammed the steady flow and progress of logical ideas. He shrugged, making his decision. Spain could wait; those papers could not. With a little more effort and energy, he could settle matters with Luis de Onis and de Estrada. Besides, he hadn't relished the idea of meeting with that popinjay who sat upon the Spanish throne.

"Ahoy, crew!" he called out from mid-ship. "We sail for home!" he shouted above the roaring elements of nature, bringing cheers from his men. "Bring us about, Danny! The cross winds are greedy today; strike half-sails on the mizzenmasts! We're listing too far portside! Strike the Spanish flag, Andy! Hoist the Virginia white; that should bloody well confuse any contemptuous British frigate! George, hold the Grand Union and Jolly Roger in readiness! Let's see if we can make the shores of Virginia within two weeks," he encouraged them, knowing it would more likely take three to four weeks.

Within moments, the crew was diligently performing their chores while singing a bawdy ditty. A mirthful grin flickered upon the captain's face; his eyes twinkled in elation. Feet clad in shiny Hessian boots, he swaggered agilely to the poop deck. Fawn colored breeches clung tightly to his sinewy thighs like a second skin. His white linen shirt was opened half the distance between his throat and waist, full sleeves billowing in the gusty breeze. A silver saber, always present upon his lithe body when at sea, swung from his narrow hips with each nimble movement. A black bandana was secured loosely around his neck, ever ready to be tied into place about his forehead, denying all enemies the identity of the notorious and fearless Captain Joshua Steele, the invincible and puissant pirate who paraded as a patriotic American privateer . . .

"Coffee, Capt'n Steele?" the cook called out from his side.

Spencer turned to face him, smiling amicably with the sheer delight of being alive and skimming across the expanse of blue before him. "It'd be much appreciated, Tully," he replied in a lazy drawl. The awe and affection which always shone brightly within his cook's eyes never ceased to warm him. He smiled at the barrel-chested man with his shiny, bald pate and sparkling brown eyes. If ever there was a man totally satisfied with his lot in life, it was Tully O'Shay. His impish smile and engaging charm could melt the coldest heart or brighten the dullest day. To add to his favorable traits, he was a superb cook; he had a knack for making the worst fare look, smell, and taste better. The crew adored him.

Tully nodded and grinned, then left to fetch the coffee. First mate Andrew Pennington joined his captain. He chuckled roguishly and playfully teased, "Tell me, Josh; why do you keep casting those wishful looks over your shoulder? Something special you left back there?"

Smoldering flames radiated a light from the captain's eyes which baffled and astonished Andrew. Spencer confessed before thinking, "You might say she was really something else!" Annoyed by his unwitting admission, he chuckled and smugly declared, "But not unforgettable. What female is?" he arrogantly sneered, rubbing the tender spot where that little witch had struck him. He moodily gazed off into the unseeable distance.

Andrew observed him suspiciously and perceptively. The captain could deny any real interest in that unknown female all he wanted, but Andrew knew him well enough to realize that his best friend had not dismissed some bewitching creature from his mind.

Odd, Joshua didn't normally give any female an afterthought, but especially not any pensive meditation like this girl was receiving. Unable to stifle his curiosity, he casually quizzed, "Who is she, Josh? Have you known her long?"

"Who is who, Andy?" Spencer parried, feigning indifference. For once, his blue eyes belied his words and cunning.

Andrew wasn't fooled and laughed heartily. "The female who makes your eyes light up when you think about her, the beautiful woman you reluctantly left back there," he smugly declared, pointing past the stern of the *Black Mist* toward Britain. "Somehow I don't think missing your meeting with Bonaparte, or deserting some tavern doxy, or leaving an old friend behind explains that miserable dejected expression and your somber mood. I'd venture to say that some ravishing feline gave you more to think about than your current mission. Right?" he challenged.

Spencer's penetrating gaze engulfed Andy's mocking grin and taunting amber eyes. "Since when does your duty include harassing and teasing your captain?" he genially rebuked Andy.

Andy chuckled humorously. "We've been mates too long for you to conceal such a troubled spirit. If you don't want to talk about her, fine; but don't go trying to convince me she doesn't exist," he exclaimed—yet, his gaze revealed concern and sincerity.

"Exist?" Spencer gloomily echoed. "I'm not positive myself that she does! One minute she's lying beside me; the next, she's vanished like a morning mist. I scouted the entire area. Not a soul knew anything about her; and, mind you, she wasn't a female who could go unnoticed! If she were real, someone would know something about her. A girl that beautiful and exquisite couldn't be overlooked. Maybe she was only an illusion. Maybe naiads and sea sirens do exist. Either way, as far as I could discover, she presented herself only to me and then only for two hours," he snarled in renewed frustration and disappointment.

"She must have been some beauty to intrigue and warm the black heart of Joshua Steele. Why, rumor claims your heart is as cold and hard and deadly as your name. Evidently the gossip is false. Tell me, Josh; what did this siren look like? And how'd you let her get away from you? With all that charm and prowess, I'm absolutely stunned. What female would hide from you?" he jested.

Spencer scanned Andy's boyish face and merry eyes. He grinned. "Let's just say she made a delightful pastime. Fact is, I wouldn't have minded her tagging along to Virginia. She was young enough to be trained very nicely, a shave under twenty. I'm telling you, Andy, she could spark jealousy's flames in Aprodite herself. Wouldn't surprise me any if she was the goddess of love and beauty herself!"

"That beautiful?" Andy questioned in astonishment.

"More so, my friend. Her hair was a silky mixture of

sunlight and moonlight, streaks of silver and curls of gold. Her eyes were the shade of brilliant emeralds and her skin was as creamy and succulent as golden taffy. Her face . . ." he faltered as he mentally envisioned it, ". . . was that of an angel's. I've never seen such purity and total innocence blended with such potent and vivid seductiveness and sensuality. A witch? A goddess? An illusion? Who knows, Andy?" Spencer confessed, followed by lusty laughter. "One thing for certain, I wouldn't mind running into her again."

"By total innocence and purity, do you mean you were the first man in her life?" Andy couldn't help but ask.

Spencer chuckled wickedly. "The first, but definitely not the last! A female with that much fire and beauty won't lead a celibate life. Damn her!" he stormed at that vexing thought.

"It bothers you to think of her with other men?"

"Hell no!" he furiously disclaimed. "Fact is, I have a little score to settle with Miss Angelique," he murmured in an ominous tone, eyes chilling and narrowing, jaw growing taut.

"About what, Josh? For deserting your side?" he jested.

"For cracking my skull before doing it!" he snapped.

Uncontrollable laughter filled the warm air. Andy shouted incredulously, "She did what? From what I hear, virgins normally get testy after a cunning seduction. Is that what happened? I thought girls and virgins were no-nos to you." Radiant brown eyes glimmered with amusement and intrigue.

"Never mind!" Spencer sneered irritably, unaccustomed to being the butt of a painful joke. "Suffice it to say that a certain sun-goddess owes me a hefty debt. If I ever get the chance to collect it . . ." he muttered underbreath, hope edging into his vow of revenge, remorse lacing his fury. "Don't you have something else to occupy your time and mind, Andy?"

Andrew Pennington grinned mischievously, then left Spencer poised against an azure skyline, again staring back toward the East. Finally Spencer shrugged off his wistful brown-study and headed for his cabin for some privacy.

The warm days and breezy nights coalesced into one noneventful blur which added up to three weeks. In all that time, the *Moon Maiden* did not come into close contact with any enemy ships; most unusual, was Captain Burns' opinion.

Alex had spent most of her time in her cabin, reading and making notes about this splendid adventure: a diary for her children. She was growing restless with this stuffy confinement and boring stage of her intriguing journey. She eagerly anticipated her stay in America.

Three times she had dined with Captain Burns and several other passengers of genteel breeding. She had politely listened to their meaningless banter and had made the appropriate comments in just the right places. She hated to be so selfish, but taking care of her sea-sick maid at least gave her something profitable to do with her abundant time and excessive energy.

With the sun sparkling off the blue waters during the day, she couldn't remain outside for very long. The strong reflections burned her eyes and enticed little lines to tease at her brow and to mar her most flattering feature: her forest green eyes. The heat dried her lips and devoured their softness. Besides, it wasn't proper for a young lady to have such golden skin! She was grateful that her caramel coloring was natural and complimentary. She had seen women who lived and worked in the harsh sunlight; their complexions became leathery and lined. To appear older and weathered didn't appeal to Alexandria Hampton!

At night, she was also forced to remain within her cabin, unless she strolled the deck upon the protective arm of Captain Burns, the only man her father would permit near her and the only man Captain Burns would trust around her! The brisk winds trimmed her walks to short strolls, for it savagely tore at her hair and clothes.

Perhaps it was unladylike to stand at the railing and to allow the wind to whip through her long hair, but it felt so exhilarating. The smell of the salty ocean would fill her nose and send shivers of excitement over her body. Surely the life of a sailor was stimulating and intoxicating! How she would dearly love to travel the world over, sailing with the tides, visiting foreign ports, living a carefree and suspenseful life.

The day finally arrived when the lookout shouted loudly, "Land ho! Port in two hours!"

Sitting in her cabin and intently concentrating upon Shakespeare's Love Sonnets, the news reached her ears. She flung the book aside and raced up to the wooden deck, oblivious to all eyes and ears. She put her hand above her eyes to shade them; she avidly searched the distant horizon for a strip of dark matter. She squinted and strained until a dark, narrow strip could be detected just above the ocean.

Alex jumped about in excitement and pleasure. The crew scurried about as they prepared to land in America. The ship sailed northward through the Delaware Bay, up the river, and eventually docked at the bustling and thriving seaport at Philadelphia. There was so much to take in all at once! Each of her five senses was vying for the most concentration. Sounds, sights, feelings, and odors stormed her simultaneously. She savored all of them, hoping to separate and digest each of them later.

It was May, 1812. The hills around this American city were alive with color and beauty. Alex had not believed any place other than the English countryside could be so lovely or inspiring. She stood at the railing on the port side of the massive frigate which was now flying the American flag, docking easily as if she were a slender and graceful sloop.

Alexandria's emerald gaze eagerly scanned the sea

of strange faces. It instantly halted when it seized upon the jovial face of her Uncle Henry. He was frantically waving to her in an attempt to gain her attention amidst this merry bedlam. A brilliant smile touched her lips. She waved back at him to let him know she had sighted him. She impatiently waited for the three-masted ship to be secured by other heavy ropes to the dock. At last, the sturdy gangplank was let down and tested for safety.

Moments later, her uncle was embracing her and bussing her cheek with a fatherly kiss. It was so good to see him again after all these years of separation. He held her back at arm's length to study her. He smiled in open pleasure and joyful surprise.

"You've transformed into a real beauty, Alexandria, just like your mother was, God rest her soul. I've missed ye, girl," he confessed, that slight burr noticeable in his voice even now.

"And I, you, Uncle Henry. It's been so long. The trip was so exciting. I saw so many strange and wonderful sights," she bubbled with vitality and delight. "I can hardly wait to tell you all the news from home. Papa sends his love and good wishes."

"Let's get ye home where we kin talk in private. I'm glad you decided to come. You're a sight for sore eyes, child," he murmured happily at the enchanting young woman before him.

This dislocated Englishman revealed no trace of sadness or regret. He promptly sent two of his servants to fetch her belongings and chaperon while he escorted her to his carriage. As they sat waiting for her luggage to be gathered and brought to them—along with a weakened Tessa—Alex questioned Henry about several curious and puzzling facts.

"Uncle Henry, if there is indeed an embargo against British ships, why are they permitted to sail into American ports? Is that why the *Moon Maiden* travels under different flags in different countries?" she reasoned. "What if she had been an enemy ship sneaking into port?"

Henry chuckled and then cordially explained, "We live under what Madison calls the Non-Intercourse Acts. They apply to British ships, but not privateers. Commerce and shipping would be at a standstill if it wasn't for privateers like Burns. Certain ships and captains are granted permits to dock at almost any port in America. But if you asked me, Captain Burns owes his loyalty to no one other than Captain Burns," he whispered in a low, conspiratorial tone. "He flies whatever flag is safe. As long as his services are needed and he doesn't harm anyone, why should we halt him? Frankly, I find the old gent most likable and trustworthy."

"But that seems contradictory," she remarked.

"The point of an embargo is to reveal strength and unity to the Crown. You might call it a show of defiance and disagreement, a way of making our point. There are a great many problems between here and there. To allow British ships to dock anytime and anywhere would be dangerous to our security, just as you keenly surmised, young lady. Several ships of supplies and soldiers landing at numerous points along our coast could spell disaster for us. This is our way of preventing an attack, which I wouldn't put past Old George."

"You keep saying 'us' and 'our.' Do you now consider yourself one of these crude and wild Americans?" she asked, amazed at Henry's boastful disloyalty to the Crown. "I don't understand this conflict. America is free of the British Empire now. We're too busy fighting Napoleon to attack a country clear across an ocean. Besides, probably half of the people here are of English heritage. To attack America would be like assaulting your own family and kinsmen," she naively concluded.

Henry smiled indulgently at her wide-eyed innocence. "If only King George felt as you do, Alex. Yes, lass, I am now an American and I'm mighty proud of it. As for your rustic image of us, you couldn't be more mistaken. In time, you will see for yourself," he said proudly. "America can claim men from the best families in England and from other countries," he exaggerated with an engaging grin and twinkling eyes.

Perhaps Uncle Henry was right, Alex thought. Perhaps her image of America and her people had been colored by false gossip. For certain, she would soon learn for herself. Glancing around, she admitted how wrong she had been so far. This definitely wasn't a wilderness! America for a month . . . she sighed dreamily and leaned back in Henry's comfortable carriage.

Shortly after, the luggage and a wobbly Tessa were loaded into the carriage and another wagon. The coffee-skinned driver took the reins and they headed for Henry's home. Alex's eyes darted this way and that, trying to gather every fact she could.

Within hours and two hundred-fifty miles southward of Philadelphia, another privateer was docking at the port of Norfolk, Virginia. The still disguised *Black Mist* eased into harbor flying the Grand Union just above the flag of Virginia, a place normally occupied by a banner with snow-white skull and cross-bones upon an ebony background.

The mooring was efficient and quick. Andrew Pennington was placed in charge while Spencer Farrington met with the trusted courier from President Madison's office. Instead of placing the monumental file in the messenger's capable hands, Spencer hastily accompanied him all the way to Montpelier where the President was currently staying. Spencer had previously determined to hand deliver this weighty dispatch himself.

Along the way, Spencer questioned John Lindsdale about the news in Washington and America. He was relieved to discover the business of "Henry's letters" was gradually fading in light of more pressing matters. No one knew better than Madison and Monroe what a fiasco that business had been! John told him the sloop *Hornet* had docked on the nineteenth with the news of Castlereagh's appointment to be British Foreign Minister. Weighing the notes made by Castlereagh which were presently resting in his possession, he sighed in relief.

Spencer waited patiently while he was being announced to the President of the United States of America. Within moments, the massive oak doors to his library swung open wide and in strolled his elderly superior. Spencer respectfully arose from his comfortable seat and crossed the wide expanse of polished hardwood to greet this vital man.

In his sixties, Madison was still a commanding figure of a man. His shiny, bald pate was surrounded by thin, wiry hair. His gaunt face with its beakish nose, bushy brows, and full lips suggested toughness and determination rather than his easy-going manner. The puffiness beneath his dark, hooded eyes made him appear older and wearier than when Spencer had last seen him. Was this an indication of how badly things had been going while he had been away? Madison's somber, serious mood indicated yes.

Madison smiled crookedly as he accepted Spencer's firm handshake. "Good to have you back safely, Spencer," he remarked. "The British have been causing quite a ruckus up and down the coastline. Any trouble, son?" he inquired, his smile fading.

"None, sir. Things went almost too well," Spencer replied suspiciously. "Tell me, sir; can you trust your

English informant?"

The unexpected question caused Madison's brows to lift inquisitively. "Come into the library. We'll talk there." He turned and led the way into a room which boasted of history in the making and history already made. "Sherry?" he cordially offered, pouring two glasses before Spencer could nod yes. He handed one to Spencer, then picked up his own and sipped it.

Sitting down, he motioned to Spencer to take a seat upon the short sofa nearby. "Your look tells me the news isn't good," Madison surmised aloud. He sighed in resignation and stated, "Well, let's have it, son. It couldn't be any worse than matters here."

Spencer passed the parcel over to him, saying, "I think you best look over these papers yourself, sir; then we can discuss them. Or, more accurately, what to do about them." He settled himself back against the plush cushions and sipped his sherry while Madison glanced over each document.

When Madison had sufficiently gone over the facts and figures listed upon the numerous pages, he lay them upon his desk. His gaze came up to meet Spencer's; his expression was grave. "I see why you questioned the loyalty of my informant. Rest assured, Spencer; he can be trusted as much as you and me. The problem is, do we trust these reports?" Madison candidly announced.

"If they're accurate, that file's dynamite. If those countries join Britain's offense against France, she'll finish off Napoleon within months. Then her ships and resources will be turned against us. Adams is in Russia now; what does he report?"

"His report isn't due for another few weeks. If it agrees with the one here, we've got real trouble." He ran his slender, shaky fingers through his sparse amount of hair as he mused over this devastating enlightenment. "This British ship *Guerriere*, is she a threat to us?"

"The only frigate we have who could match her is the *Constitution*," Spencer answered frankly. "At sea, we're no competition for the Royal Navy. We have capable captains, but our fleet is small and ineffectual. The only way I could help out is to lose my cover with Steele and the *Black Mist*," he suggested.

"No. We need you right where you are. We couldn't afford to lose your cover and your strength. With Virginians like you, no wonder the rest of the country is worried about so many Virginians in power! Can we be blamed for giving them Jefferson, Washington, Clay, Madison, Farrington, and Monroe? Can we help it if our statesmen are smart enough to dominate the government?" he teased.

Spencer laughed with him. He quickly explained his reasons for bypassing Spain and his meeting with Joseph Bonaparte. "I think we can accomplish just as much with Governor Juan de Estrada and Minister de Onis. Did you call off Campbell and Mathews?"

"They didn't take kindly to it," Madison replied, "but I sent them a stern message to withdraw and to cease attack upon the Spanish holdings down there. We all know Florida is a viper's nest for runaway

slaves and hostile Indians, but we can't just stroll in
and take over. We have enough animosities to handle
without creating another hornet's nest to our south.
Rhea's already taken over western Florida. If we keep
pressing them, they're going to fight us over this
matter," he concluded. "I say hold off for a while. The
Spanish might come around to selling her to us, too.
Jefferson got a good deal on the Louisiana Purchase;
maybe I can better him with the acquisition of Florida.
We've got Britain and France breathing down our
necks we surely don't need Spain too!"

"What's next for me, sir?" Spencer asked.

"Go back to Farrington Oaks for a few days' rest.
There's a delegation of hotheads here to see me. After
I confer with Clay, Webster, Calhoun, and Gallatin,
I'll send word to you. Perhaps Clinton can enlighten
me on the news from the New England area. Monroe
will be over in two days. Once I have their reports and
suggestions, I'll be better qualified to make my final
decisions. They howl and shriek for war, Spencer; but
war is a mighty nasty business. They're all too young
to recall our last one with Great Britain. They're
lawyers and orators; what do they know of blood and
fighting? They're blind dreamers, Spence; they think
we can vanquish Britain within a few months. But
once committed, there's no turning back," Madison
muttered, well aware of the grave responsibility
which was upon his shoulders.

He smiled. Changing the subject, he softly inquired,
"Did you see your grandfather?"

Spencer chuckled mischievously. "He was as ornery

as ever. After we settled some family matters, we shared a pleasant visit. The sly dog's trying to select a wife for me. Can you imagine me married and with a slew of brats?" he jested in horror.

"Why not? It happens to the best of us. You're in your prime, Spence. You've established yourself well here. What harm could a nice wife and family do? Did he suggest anyone in particular?"

"I'm afraid so. A neighbor's daughter, a real spoiled brat from the way I heard it! Lady Alexandria Hampton," he sneered disdainfully, bringing a curious light to Madison's eyes. Spencer alertly noted his odd reaction. "You've heard of her?"

"Her? Not exactly. But Lord Charles Hampton's name is no secret to anyone. A fine gentleman. Too bad he isn't an American. What has this daughter got to offer besides wealth, beauty, breeding, and a matchless bloodline?" he jested in a strange tone.

"I wouldn't know. I refused to meet her. But I promised Will I would return within two years and make some sort of decision about wedlock. With any luck, she'll be wed by then! The last thing I need at Farrington Oaks is a wild she-cat."

"Surely a man of your reputation wouldn't have any trouble taming a beautiful and audacious feline," Madison taunted merrily, eyes filled with amusement and mischief.

"Right now, the only wild-cat I want to tame is the Royal Navy. I'll leave shortly for home. I'll wait there until I receive word from you."

The two men stood up, shook hands, and departed

company. As Spencer exited, Madison grinned in secret satisfaction, suspecting the paths of Lady Hampton and Lord Farrington would cross very soon.

"As Shakespeare aptly put it, Spence, 'Lest too light winning make the prize light' . . ." Laughter filled the room.

VI

"The strongest oaths
are straw to th' fire
i' th' blood."
—*The Tempest*, William Shakespeare

An almost timid knock upon Spencer's bedroom door pulled his stormy reflections from a golden-haired siren who was claiming too much of his mental energy. Irritably dismissing mysterious Angelique from his mind, he tossed the cover aside and stood up, flexing his strong frame. He reached for a mono-grammed robe in a rich wine shade and pulled it over his naked physique which rippled with each agile movement. He cast a nonchalant glance over his shoulder at the sultry beauty who was fast asleep in his massive bed. Not since his strange encounter with that bewitching girl by the pond had he been able to totally dispel Angelique from mind. To his annoyance and dismay, he seemed to be comparing every female to her, finding them all lacking in one way or another. He cursed her for her unforgettable image and matchless passion.

Spencer quietly opened the door to speak with the ruddy-faced Thomas Canter, his loyal servant of many years. The seemingly ageless man with salt and pepper hair grinned affectionately as he handed Spencer the sealed letter from President Madison. "I didn't want to disturb you, sir, but you're abed mighty late. I didn't think you'd want me to delay this particular letter." His lively gray-blue eyes filled with merriment and deviltry as they flickered past Spencer to the woman sleeping peacefully in his master's bed. He secretly wished some enchanting and worthy creature would come along and capture the heart of this valiant man whom he respected and loved like a son. It was past time for Spencer to think seriously about a wife and children! How long would he continue his carefree and dangerous life?

"You're a good man, Tom. I couldn't do without you. I'll be down to eat shortly," Spencer replied in a mellow drawl, shrewdly noting the look on his friend's face and reading it clearly. They exchanged smiles as Spencer closed the door to head to his bath closet and read this portentous message before he bathed and dressed to leave, for surely this was some type of summons to work. About time, he fretted to himself. He had been lazing around too long to suit a restless, vital man like himself!

Weary of Marianne Flannigan, he quietly went about his grooming without awakening her. With luck, he could be packed and gone before she awoke. Women! he scoffed in unsuppressed annoyance. Once their passions had cooled, why couldn't they leave as sweetly as they had arrived? He'd never met one worthy of a serious thought or continued glance—except that little blond spitfire in England.

Having been at Farrington Oaks for over a week, Spencer was becoming anxious to have seaspray caressing his tanned face, to feel the gentle rolling of his ship upon the sea, and to experience that intoxicating feeling of total freedom and stimulating adventure. Nothing was more exciting or enlivening than to boldly confront danger and to skillfully best her.

Eager to learn what Madison had in mind for him, Spencer hurriedly bathed and dressed. He rushed down the staircase to eat as quickly as possible. "When Marianne wakes up, Tom, would you see her safely off?" he asked with a mirthful twinkle in his steel-blue eyes and a devilish grin tugging at the corners of his mouth. "Tell 'er I'll be gone for months. Maybe she'll find a new interest while I'm gone," he teased as his elderly servant smothered a laugh behind his wrinkled hand.

"I'll see to everything, Master Spencer. Not to worry. How long will you be away this time?"

"I'll send word back to you after my meeting. Probably six to eight weeks," he ventured his guess. "If not, you're in charge here until I can make it back home."

In less than an hour, Spencer was astride a huge chestnut roan galloping to his meeting. His spirits soared with each mile. Soon, the journey was over and Spencer was dismounting before the impressive home of James Madison. He handed the reins to the groom and took the steps two at a time.

He knocked upon the massive oak door and waited

for Madison's servant to answer it. The door opened and a man clad in a black jacket and pants with a white cotton shirt stood before him. "Spencer Farrington to see President Madison," Spencer announced.

"This way, sir," the servant replied in a respectful tone, leading the way into the book-lined office of the President of the United States. "Have a seat. The master will be here shortly. Brandy, sir?" he politely asked, his expression stoic and his voice even.

"Yes, that would be nice," Spencer replied, crossing his long legs and leaning back against the plush sofa.

When the servant handed him the fragile glass, he accepted it and thanked the fellow. The doors closed and he was alone. He slowly sipped his brandy and let his mind wander—and returned to delicious thoughts of Angelique. But Spencer instantly forbade his mind to dwell upon that vexing subject.

The door opened and in strode Madison. From his worried expression, things hadn't gone well during his meetings with his cabinet and advisors. A serious man, Madison paced the floor a few times as if summoning the right words to open this vital conversation. He abruptly halted and turned to look directly into Spencer's expectant gaze.

"You were right, Spencer. Things look pretty bad. It doesn't seem as if Napoleon will take England's attention from us. King George thinks he can take us both at the same time! I've no doubts he'll go to war with us. Problem is, how far is he willing to push and how soon? Those boisterous Warhawks think I should declare war while he's occupied elsewhere. They think we can set England on her heels in less than a month! Between Clay, Jackson, and Calhoun, I must admit I don't know what to do," he admitted. "They're demanding war, Spence. Even old silver-tongued Webster can't reach them."

Madison poured himself a brandy and dropped wearily into his desk chair. He levelled his somber gaze upon Spencer before going on. "The South's complaining about that hornet's nest in Florida; the Northeast is raising Cain about the new Embargo Acts. Those hot-tempered men in the Ohio and Mississippi area are screaming for something to be done about Canada and those Indian raids. And here we sit trapped between Napoleon's Continental System and England's Orders-in-Council! A country can't enter war with her eyes and ears closed!" He paused and turned to Spencer. "I've drafted a message to Congress. Clay's the Speaker of the House; he'll read it tomorrow. Then we'll see how those men truly feel about a bloody war, and not just loud, boastful talk."

"You mean a message to suggest war?" Spencer asked for clarification.

"I had no choice, Spencer. New England is practically threatening to rejoin the British Empire; the South is raving about concessions to the Northeastern shipping interests. Florida's under Spain's control, and Spain's under Napoleon's control. Now, England's furtively strengthening her forces in Canada. We've got the British prodding those Indians on to the west. If England goes ahead with her threatened blockade of the entire coastline, we'll be trapped between warring factions. It's strike now, or we'll be at a critical disadvantage later. You know England has just about convinced Russia to side with her against France. With combined forces, they could call a halt to that Corsican's assault. If so, England'll turn her full sights on us. If we've got to battle the Royal Navy, it's best to do it while she's weak," he speculated.

"What did you have in mind for me?" Spencer asked quietly, realizing the gravity of this moment.

"I want you to head up north and see if you can detect a build-up of forces there. If England's planning to dig in there and then head down this way, I want to know before she gets too strong."

"That should be simple enough," Spencer confidently agreed. "I can use Steele's cover to capture a few ships to see what I can learn," he suggested.

"Excellent. Any dispatches between here and there would be invaluable," he remarked.

"When are you supposed to address Congress?" Spencer reluctantly inquired.

"On June eighteenth," Madison answered.

"June eighteenth!" Spencer echoed in shock. "But that's less than two weeks away. I doubt I can confiscate any critical information and have it in your hands by then, sir," he mildly protested this impossible mission.

Madison shook his thinning head of hair. "I know, son, but it can't be helped. If I don't hear from you before then, I'll have no choice but to follow the wishes of the majority," he concluded in a strained voice. "Do the best you can, then report to me in Washington," he advised as calmly as he could manage under these trying circumstances.

Two lousy weeks, Spencer grumbled to himself as he rode off. What could he possibly accomplish in one and a half weeks which could change the course of this impending tragedy? Spencer headed for a secluded cove near Norfolk to meet with his crew, having previously alerted Andy to call them back to his ship. In his state of turmoil, the ride was a swift blur of dirt roads and green trees.

Once aboard the ship, he called all his men to the main deck to hear their new and pressing orders. "We set sail for the northeasterly coast, men. Hoist the Virginia White until we meet another ship. Hold the Jolly Roger, Spanish flag, and the Grand Union in readiness. Pull in the anchors and hoist sails. Let's see if we can overtake an important British frigate. We sail until we do," he informed the crew of loyal men.

The thrill of adventure filling them, the crew shouted and laughed in abandonment as the ship left her hiding place to seek out their enemy. Hands and minds were quickly involved with their beloved ship and her dauntless captain. Risqué ditties could be heard above the sensuous song of the ocean and her sweet breezes. The sails popped and cracked as the winds passed and filled them with air. As the waves crashed against the black hull of this mighty ship, seaspray dampened the rails and parts of the deck.

Days of endless blue skies and tranquil seas and

nights of scintillating stars with variations of half-moons passed without the sighting of another ship of any interest to this indiscriminate crew. With a calm and deserted sea and the skillful Danny at the wheel, there was little need for the restive captain to remain on deck. Spencer had grown weary of scouting the expanse of empty blue and the numerous papers before him. With an irrevocable war at hand, how could he concentrate upon business matters which concerned his plantation in Virginia? How could he discover England's closely guarded secrets when every ship they sighted was either a merchantman or a privateer?

Not one to sit idle for any length of time, Spencer found this solitude and lack of adventure much to his disliking. His nerves were taut with anticipation; his keen instincts were alert and tense. Just as the waiting seemed too much to tolerate, a ship was sighted to the port side.

"Ship a' port, Capt'n," came the signal he had long awaited. "She's flying the Union Jack. Looks well-armed. Three-masted frigate," the news was swiftly passed down to him from the lookout.

"Bring 'er around, Danny. Let's see where our lovely lady is heading," he ordered. His eyes sparkled with new life and intrigue. This was the moment he had been seeking.

"We gonna take her, Capt'n?" George excitedly asked.

"As surely as the sun rises, George," came his confident reply. Within minutes, the sleek ship was in

148

pursuit of the sluggish English frigate. She rode heavy
in the water, carrying some weighty load.

"Think we've got enough daylight left, sir?" Tim
asked in merry delight as he nimbly descended the
swaying ropes, knowing they could take a ship in the
pitch of night if they wished.

"I'm counting on the Lady of Darkness to help us.
Let's keep our distance until dusk, then close on her
like the wind. George, stand ready to lower the black
sails. Tim, hold the Jolly Roger in hand. Andy, get the
boarding party alerted. Tully, stow the fire; supper's
going to be a little late tonight," he quickly issued his
orders, orders which were performed readily by this
well-trained crew.

They persistently trailed the burdensome ship upon
the gradually darkening horizon. Just as the setting
sun first kissed the face of the ocean, they increased
their speed. The midnight sails were expertly lowered
before the virgin white ones. The Virginia white was
replaced by the Jolly Roger. The crew was armed and
steady. The wooden board which read *Black Mist* was
suspended from the same hooks which had so recently
carried the sign reading *Wandering Siren.* All measures
taken, the distance between the two ships quickly
vanished.

The door to the ship's interior opened and out
stepped their captain, imposingly dressed for the raid
in his pirating attire. Andy grinned in unsuppressed
amusement. His gaze eased over the tall man walking
his way. Captain Joshua Steele of the nefarious *Black
Mist* was at his best. He was dressed in knee-high

polished boots of finest leather in a shade of sooty black. His muscled legs were clad in snug-fitting black pants which clearly revealed their agility and strength with each pantherlike movement. His white linen shirt billowed with the breeze and revealed a furry chest of black hair through its opening to his narrow middle. A bright red sash was secured around his waist as was expected of any well-dressed pirate. A silver cutless swung to and fro as he swaggered toward Andy. Only a small portion of his sable hair could be seen below the mask which concealed the upper portion of his handsome face and head, a mask which reached from crown to upper lip and encircled his entire head, a mask which prevented anyone from learning the identity of the scourge of the ocean and of the English. Yet, the arrogant stance of this valiant man, the clarity of his commanding voice, the firm set of his squared jawline, and the sensual play of a noticeable contempt for danger upon his full lips vividly exposed all any enemy needed to know about this dangerous and puissant pirate.

Naturally the English frigate was aware of the smaller ship tracing her stern for hours, but foolishly assumed her to be sailing to the same port since she obviously made no attempt to overtake them. But the moment those satanic black sails were sighted, it required very little to guess the intent or identity of their elusive aggressor. The warning was sounded, but it was too late to make any difference. It was almost as if that black witch was sailing straight for them, as if she feared no power or man. She moved swiftly and gracefully upon the sea's surface, easily gaining on them. The English captain wondered if he should stand and fight or give quarter to a ship he knew from reports could sink him in less than an hour! The *Black Mist* and Steele weren't myths; their power and skills were well-known and feared. But another fact was also known: Steele didn't sink ships unless they demanded it through a futile battle. Which was best, humiliating wisdom or reckless courage and dangerous pride?

The infuriated English captain watched the *Black Mist* as she played the waves and currents with natural ability. The way she maneuvered from port to starboard with each smooth plunge, there was no way he could hit her with cannon fire. The battle had been forfeited the moment her black sails appeared! Previously alerted to the wrath of Steele if attacked, the disgruntled English crew cursed as the captain issued his orders to come about and peacefully await Steele's boarding. Intimidated and cowed, the crew obeyed. The *Wind Rover* lowered her flag to signal surrender.

"She's yielding, Capt'n. Guess she don't want to tangle with us," Danny yelled over the roar of the ocean and wind.

"That's the reward of having a fierce reputation," Spencer laughingly retorted, relieved the English ship wouldn't force a bloody and futile battle with him.

Before the moon could gain any height, the crew of the *Black Mist* was in full control of the English frigate and Spencer was searching the cabin of its captain. Finding nothing of importance, Spencer turned to face the scarlet-faced captain who was standing at rigid attention behind him and curiously watching his every move. Spencer strolled over to the irate man, halting within two feet of him.

"You seem to be travelling heavy, Captain Stovall," he noted. "Is it true you British plan to take over my territory? I don't think I'd take kindly to your intrusion," he remarked, goading the helpless man, hoping his inevitable anger would reveal some clue Spencer needed.

Stovall whitened, then flushed a guilty red. He stuttered as he replied, "Don't . . . be absurd! I'm . . . taking supplies to . . . our men up Canada way," he lied.

Deep, rumbling, mocking laughter filled the dim room. "This is June, not Christmas, Captain Stovall," he teased the vexed man before him. Stovall glued his wide eyes to the steel blue ones of glacial intensity before him as Spencer sneered contemptuously, "Don't play me for a fool. Just what does your king have in mind for my territory?" he demanded. "This is an expensive cargo to rest upon the ocean floor," he subtly warned.

With false bravado, Stovall scoffed, "You can hardly call the entire ocean your territory, Captain Steele. As to the King's plans, I am not privy to such knowledge," he huffily declared.

Spencer strolled around the stiff frame of his foe as he ventured, "You mean he doesn't intend to attack America or blockade her ports? Ports which my trade needs easy entrance to?"

A sudden inhalation of air and startled look told Spencer he had struck a nerve. He halted before the stubborn man and glared at him. "Tell me, Captain Stovall; would you care to see your ship scuttled, your spotless record demolished, and your crew executed before your eyes? I'm not asking for permission to see those hidden dispatches, I'm demanding them. Now be a good fellow and give them over," he casually handed the anxious man his ultimatum. "The papers in exchange for your honor, your ship, and your crew," he reiterated his unflinching terms.

Suspicious lights danced in Stovall's eyes. "Why would a pirate be interested in political matters?" he asked.

"Why indeed would a privateer be interested in a war which might damage his most profitable business?" Spencer sarcastically questioned. "Besides, I wouldn't want to go against the entire Royal Navy. Since I have an interest at stake here, it just might profit me and the Crown if I were to side with the inevitable winner," he calmly hinted, seating himself at the captain's desk and negligently propping his booted feet upon the cluttered piece of furniture which was securely attached to the wall. At Stovall's hesitation, Spencer snarled, "Well? What's it to be, my good man: an alliance with the Crown or my own declaration of war against it? As you know, I'm not a man who bluffs. I can give your fleet a Royal pain in the flank of its regal pants," he ominously warned with an aura of self-assurance.

"The Royal Navy doesn't need the likes of pirates

like you to help her defeat those foolish colonists!" he stormed in rising indignation and haughty pride. "Once the fleet sets sail, they'll squirm like the snakes they are! They'll regret the day they turned against the Mother Country."

"And just when does the Mother plan to take her errant fledgling back into her nest?" Steele inquired casually as he studied the neatly trimmed nails on his left hand.

"I'll not commit treason just so an arrogant pirate can line his pockets with gold! I gave quarter, but I will not forfeit my honor and loyalty!" he snapped angrily, his round face flushed with rage and humiliation.

"Pride can be a costly possession, Stovall. I'm a smart man; I fully intend to side with the obvious victor in this approaching conflict. Who's the commander of your fleet? I'll offer my services directly to him," he cunningly attempted another path to prevent being forced to settle this matter in an unpleasant way.

Stovall gave those words careful consideration. Steele wasn't a man to tangle with. Choosing to compromise, he smiled maliciously and replied, "You're no threat to his majesty's fleet, so what harm could it do to tell you? Captain Philip Broke commands the fleet," he proudly announced, then smugly anticipated Steele's cowering reaction.

Spencer grinned roguishly as he nodded his head in acceptance of that interesting fact. "That means the *Shannon* is the flagship. Well, well . . . So Broke finally made it to the top," he mysteriously commented, sounding as if he knew the man personally. "What other ships are heading this way?" he asked, undaunted.

"If you think you can out-sail the fleet, you're sadly mistaken, Steele. You're no match for the combined forces of the *Guerriere, African, Aeolus, Belvidera,* and the *Nautiler!* They'll blast your *Black Mist* back into the hell she came from!"

"Do tell," Spencer mocked his false courage and eagerness. "Why not ask Broke how many of his ships have won battles against mine? If your British courage matched your British boasting, you'd never have given quarter. Give Broke and Byron my regards when you see them. Tell 'em to keep an eagle eye to their sterns. I'll be seeing them real soon."

Spencer stood up and lazily stretched his agile frame. He withdrew his poniard from the carved leather sheath hanging next to his deadly cutlass. He leisurely strolled over to Stovall and glared into his brown gaze with eyes as cold and awesome as his steel blade. Kicking the door open, Andy and Migget rushed in, seizing Stovall's hands and securing them behind his flabby waist. With the flat side of the cold, sharp blade, Spencer tapped Stovall's bulbous nose as he spoke.

"Time's a'wasting, Captain. I know you have some papers on board which interest me greatly. Since your honor, ship, and crew are of little value to you, just how much is the safety and survival of this?" he asked in a glacial tone which caused the Englishman to tremble as Spencer lightly tapped his groin with his sword. "One skilled flick of this blade and you'll be talking like a woman for the rest of your life—if you don't bleed to death first."

"You wouldn't dare mutilate one of the King's subjects! Have you no honor?" he asked in a shaky voice.

"As you so aptly put it earlier, pirates have no honor or loyalty to any man or power but their own crews and ships. The papers. Now!" he fired the last word like a pistol shot in the midst of a deadly duel. "My patience has grown thin, Captain. I'll give you to the count of ten to make your decision."

As Spencer began to count aloud, Stovall struggled to pull free of the powerful hold by Andy and Migget and cursed Steele mightily.

Thundering laughter filled the room, mocking Stovall and his wild rantings. "Nine . . . Ten . . . Well, Captain? Your decision?" he prompted.

"You wouldn't dare!" he squeaked.

Within inches of Stovall's perspiring face, Steele vowed through white teeth, "I dare anything, Stovall, as you well know. When I leave this cabin, I'll either carry those papers in my hand or your manhood upon this knife." Before Stovall could speak or think clearly, several deft swipes of Spencer's dagger had severed his belt and had opened his dark blue pants from his flaccid waist to his quivering groin. Steele's art matchless, Stovall didn't even receive a scratch.

Stovall inhaled in stunned disbelief. Another swipe and his baggy drawers were slashed aside, divesting him of his pride and protective clothing as his limp manhood toppled out before the taunting gaze of Captain Joshua Steele. Outraged and shamed, Stovall shouted, "You black-hearted devil! You'll pay for this offense! The fleet will chase you across the face of the entire ocean!"

"Too bad you won't be around to see it," Steele retorted. "From the way I hear tell, few men survive castration. Those who do never show their faces in public again. Your time's up, Stovall. What's it to be?"

Repulsed by the idea of touching another man, but knowing this was Stovall's one weak point, Spencer gritted his teeth and reached for the stubby organ. Petrified by the seriousness of Steele's threat, Stovall shrieked, "No! You can't!"

Steele's cold laughter was his answer. Holding his blade securely and reaching for the terrified man's privates, Stovall yielded before his hand could make contact with that sensitive area.

"All right! There's a sealed dispatch hidden in the wall over my desk!"

Spencer replaced his knife and headed that way after warning, "If you're lying, Captain, you'll rue this day."

After a few moments of testing the wall for a hollow ring, Spencer smiled in satisfaction. Withdrawing his knife, he pried the board free to reveal the dispatch. Without a care to the royal seal upon it, he severed the binding and withdrew several papers of ivory parchment. He quickly scanned the contents, then smiled in pleasure. He turned to Andy and remarked, "You know what to do."

Before the *Black Mist* crew departed the frigate, the entire English crew was sleeping peacefully with the aid of the liquid secured from certain plants from a faraway island paradise. Amidst hearty chuckles, Spencer's confident gaze eased over the group of slumbrous Englishmen. "That should prevent any heroic idea of following us. Let's head home, men. You did your usual excellent job: success without any casualties. Put me off near Washington, then get the ship ready to head out again. From the looks of these papers, we'll be very busy before the new moon."

Safely aboard the *Black Mist* once more, the black sails were drawn and secured out of sight behind the virgin white ones; the Jolly Roger and name board were returned to their storage place. The crew laughed and joked as they altered the notorious *Black Mist* to the neutral privateer *Wandering Siren*. In the slight evening breeze, the white sails gently fluttered as if content to return to port from a stimulating holiday. Never one to berate the elements or his beloved ship, Spencer reluctantly accepted this sluggish pace which would slow his progress and vital mission to see Madison.

His keen eyes scanned the empty and moonlit horizon in each direction as he made his way to his cabin to study those critical papers. So, Perceval had been assassinated by a lunatic on May eleventh . . . General Issac Brock, that wily old sea-dog, was in Canada . . . How much power and influence did those Tory ministers have? How would Jenkinson, Canning,

Liverpool, and Casterlaugh vote? Too damn many variations and factions to consider! It was June fourteenth; surely he could make port by the sixteenth, two days prior to Madison's deadline of the eighteenth . . .

Spencer entered his cabin which boasted of his mercurial, strong personality. It was an artistic and intriguing mixture of American, nautical, and English decor. One thing he demanded even at sea was comfort in luxurious style. He poured himself a stiff brandy and lay down upon his large bed, propping himself up with several feather pillows. He rested his head against them and closed his eyes. Things didn't look good at all, he mused.

He placed his arm behind his head and downed the entire contents of his glass. He set the glass on the wooden table beside his bed and relaxed. It wouldn't change matters if he read those documents a third time, so he tossed them aside. He picked up the oblong wooden box near his bed and opened it. He pushed aside the velvet covering to reveal a striking painting he had foolishly purchased in Washington months ago. He could still distinctly recall that curious day.

He had been heading toward a shop where secret meetings took place when a painting in the shop window captured his eye. He had stopped immediately and backed up a few steps to take another look at it. He wondered why it had seemed to call out to him to obtain it. He absently moved his nimble fingers over the dried oils upon the surface of the exquisite painting, suddenly annoyed to find himself tracing the delicate and graceful lines of a lovely and wild sea creature who was seductively poised upon gray rocks at the edge of an ocean. As the colorful waves crashed against those rocks and sent white spray over her lithe frame, she was smiling provocatively as if utterly intoxicated by her freedom and beauty while luring some unseen lover to join her revelry. His eyes sought out her enticing, yet sensually innocent, expression.

Had this mysterious painting had any bearing upon his actions in England by that serene pond? Had Angelique's resemblance to this dreamy creature provoked him into cunningly seducing her? Was it this mythical creature he had imagined come to life? As if mesmerized by the allure of this fanciful mermaid, he had irresistibly bought the painting that very moment. As if viewing this absurd act of indulgence as some sign of foolishness and weakness, he had later refused to hang the sensuous wandering siren in his cabin.

With a muttered curse, he flung the box across his bed. If he didn't know any better, he would swear Angelique had posed for it! To buy a picture of a beautiful dream and then to meet it in the flesh was a little too eerie to suit Spencer Farrington. Damn her for taking away his peace of mind! Damn her mystery and unforgettable aura!

He rubbed his temple as if her dauntless attack still sent forth pain. If ever their paths crossed again, Miss Angelique Whatever would discover what it was to cross Captain Joshua Steele! He grinned roguishly at that delightful speculation, then frowned at its impossibility. Angelique was just as elusive as that luscious mermaid!

As her face floated before his mind's eye, his cabin suddenly felt stuffy and confining. He jumped up to seek fresh air and a change of scenery on his rolling deck.

"Be gone from my mind, Sea-Witch," he murmured angrily as he swiftly left the painting and the disturbing documents behind.

VII

"Out of her own goodness make the net,
That shall enmesh them all."
—*Othello*, William Shakespeare

Philadelphia was marvelously exhilarating in early June. Lady Alexandria Hampton was thrilled and pleased by her visit to this unexpectedly magnificent city in this surprisingly civil and thriving country. She was constantly amazed at her friendly reception by the people in America; she had fully expected them to dislike her on sight because of her loyalty to England. Yet, she was anything but scorned by those amicable people whom she had come into contact with since her arrival two weeks before. The dinners and parties had delighted and enchanted her, as had this wonderful land. Discounting the few women who treated her as a threatening rival, her stay with her uncle had been enjoyable and enlightening.

After Henry Cowling's party to introduce her to his circle of friends and acquaintances, she hadn't been allowed a moment's rest from invitations and sieges by eager young men. Feeling deliriously happy and desirable, she revelled in her femininity. What cloud could possibly darken this glorious trip and her heady adventure to what she had erroneously considered the end of the earth?

Henry glanced down the lengthy table at her and lifted a quizzical brow, wondering at her suppressed giggles. "What butterfly flutters within you, my dear?" he genially teased his lovely niece. "That smile could light the darkest corner and your laughter could lift any dismal heart. I'm so glad you decided to come visit your lonely, old uncle," he remarked.

"Henry Cowling, you sly fox," she mirthfully chided him. "You're anything but lonely or old. Isn't it wonderful to be alive and well?" she commented, her vitality and youthful zeal sparkling within her enchanting eyes. "You were absolutely correct; America is a fantastic land. I can hardly wait to tell Papa all about my experiences here," she excitedly told him. "There's so much to see and do," she stated.

"Ah, to be young and carefree again," he sighed dramatically, then chuckled. "Once you've returned home and settled down, you'll always remember these gay times," he unwittingly ventured.

"Settled down! What a dire thought to dampen this happy occasion. I could live this blissful way forever," she exclaimed. "Wouldn't it be stimulating to seek new and different adventures every day for the rest of your life?" she dreamily suggested, a note of sadness entering her eyes and sending her previously elated spirits downward.

"Why do you talk in such a miserable way? You sound as if marriage is a prison," he jested, failing to return a smile to her somber face. "You can't go gallivanting around the countryside much longer,

Alex; it wouldn't be proper."

"You're sounding more and more like Papa every day, Uncle Henry," she rebuked him for spoiling her sunny mood with reminders of her imminent fate in the bonds of legal wedlock. "Why must I be chained to a marriage I do not want? My blood sings with wanderlust, Uncle Henry. I cannot bear the thought of being housed away in some country manor. It isn't fair I was born a woman! I'd love to be a sailor and travel to distant ports. Besides, I'm still a young girl; there's no rush to see me wed!"

"You're far past being a young girl, Alex; you're very much a woman, a beautiful and desirable woman. Why do you so despise the idea of marriage?" he seriously questioned, intrigued and dismayed by the wretched irritation lining her striking features.

Horrified, she caught herself before shouting back, "Because it wouldn't be to a vital and interesting man like Stephen!" She flushed and glanced away from his probing gaze before saying, "If Papa would allow me to select my future husband, I wouldn't be so rebellious! What happiness can lie in an arranged marriage? It's humiliating and disgusting! I didn't think Papa so cruel and selfish." A mental image of Stephen flashed before her mind and annoyingly warmed her very soul.

"Now, now, Alex. You did say your father had given you some time to find a husband on your own," he mildly corrected her. "Why, you've at least fifteen young lads pursuing you here, not to mention countless swains back home," he reminded her of the

165

hot-blooded males who seized any chance to catch her eye.

"I want a man, Uncle Henry, not some foppish wastrel. You'd think at least one real man would come calling!"

"What about Daniel Grey or Seth Carter or Steven Hardy?" he argued.

At the mention of one particular name, she grimaced and wailed, "You call those men? Daniel has more appendages than an octopus! Seth sits under his father's fat thumb! And Steven . . . Steven is boring to tears," she issued her criticisms of each male suitor.

Henry laughed, then suggested, "Are you perhaps being too choosy or just plain stubborn, Alexandria Hampton? A perfect man doesn't exist, child. If I were you, I would study each one carefully and select the best man among them," he wisely hinted.

She sighed wearily and agreed, "You're right, of course. But that doesn't make marriage any more acceptable." Naturally she couldn't blurt out there was a perfect man around, near perfect anyway . . . Besides, Stephen was lost to her forever and it was best to put him completely out of mind.

In an attempt to alter this explosive and offensive subject, she asked, "How did your meeting go with Mister Clay? He certainly seemed piqued about something when he arrived this afternoon."

Immediately Henry paled and looked down at his plate. He toyed with the roasted chicken before him. Alex watched him with rising intrigue. "Uncle Henry, is there some problem with Mister Clay? You've been as nervous as a colt near a branding iron."

Henry shifted apprehensively in his chair and sipped some red wine from a stemmed glass. "Nothing to worry your head over, Alex, just a business matter," he stated, hoping to dismiss the topic.

"You have no dealings with Mister Clay, Uncle dear. What are you keeping from me?" she demanded softly, but seriously.

"That imagination is running wild, Alex. You best concentrate on choosing a husband before your time is up," he suggested, yet his tone was strained and riddled with guilt about something.

"Look at me, Uncle Henry," she gently commanded. "Your eyes and voice tell a different story from your words," she refuted his casual excuse.

"A beautiful girl can't fill her head with politics and business. We have to discuss our dinner party for next week," he made another attempt to change the subject.

"Isn't Mister Clay one of those Warhawks?" she unexpectedly asked.

Henry paled again and squirmed in his seat as he searched for an appropriate answer. His reaction told her a great deal. "Has he convinced his countrymen to go to war with us?" she inquired in a shaky voice, observing him closely.

His head jerked up; his expression betraying an affirmative reply. Yet, he teased, "Whyever would you think such a thing? War's a nasty business. It wouldn't do to charge into it blindly."

"I wouldn't call discussing and planning it for months charging blindly and impulsively. How soon?" she asked, her knees quivering and her stomach knotting.

"How soon what?" he stalled as he desperately pondered an explanation.

"You know what I mean, Uncle Henry. Has war been declared yet?"

"No, Alex," he replied honestly, but nervously.

"When?" she demanded succinctly, her eyes never leaving his ashen face.

"In a week they will meet to hear Madison's suggestions and to vote," he finally gave in to her demand to hear the truth.

Alex stared at him in disbelief. She had previously overheard talk of the dissatisfaction and dissension. It was actually coming to an open confrontation! What would happen at that June eighteenth meeting? She was in America and her father was in England. How could she get home if . . . She trembled and stammered, "I've . . . got to get . . . home before . . . they vote." Aware of how lengthy and costly English wars could be, she knew she would be stranded in America once the decision was made.

"Leave here? Now?" he reasoned aloud. "You can't, Alex. Sea travel is dangerous. There's no way I could get you safely home before . . ."

"Before what, Uncle Henry?" she asked at his abrupt hesitation.

"There's no way I could arrange passage before the eighteenth, Alex; that's only four days from now," he argued with the defiant girl.

"If you can't or won't, then I will! I refuse to remain here while your country wars against mine. It could be years before I could get home again. What about my father?" she wailed in panic.

"He knows I'll see to your safety. I cannot allow you to sail under these perilous conditions. Besides, Tessa is still unable to travel. She's been ill since your arrival," he reminded her.

"Tessa's only problem is a difficult pregnancy. She should have told me the truth before we sailed! Papa would have forced the groom to marry her. She can remain here until it's safe to travel again, but I'm going home," she willfully announced with fierce determination. "Even if I have to stow away, I'll be on the next ship which sails for England."

"Surely you jest, child!" he thundered at her, his nerves taut and his patience sorely tested.

"No, I do not jest. Before June eighteenth, I'll be on my way home. Either you arrange it or I will," she stubbornly refused to relent.

"But, Alex . . ."

She promptly cut him off. "Until you declare war, business on the high sea will continue as usual," she debated.

"As usual, yes! There are pirates and privateers! There are English ships scouting the coast, dropping off spies in every port! It wouldn't be safe or wise.

169

Please reconsider this wild idea," he pleaded with her.

"Don't you understand, Uncle Henry? It's now or never!" she dramatically presented her case. "I have to sail before Congress meets. Surely there's some acceptable ship who can take me aboard?"

"Your father will thrash both of us! Perhaps I could send word for him to join us here," he suggested.

"Papa move to America? Don't be absurd! I'm going home with or without your assistance," she concluded, rising gracefully from the dinner table to head to her room to pack. She turned to say, "I'll be packed by morning, and I'll head to town to see about a ship."

Henry shook his head in dismay. He couldn't reveal the information he knew. When she learned the truth about her father, it would have to come from his own lips! "All right, Alex," he called out as she was mounting the tall staircase. As she halted and looked down at him, he sighed and stated, "I'll see what I can do. But I refuse to let you leave on any ship that doesn't seem safe. Tessa can stay here with us."

She smiled radiantly. She rushed down the steps and hugged him tightly. "Thank you, Uncle Henry. I'm sorry, but I must go home."

He smiled faintly and said, "I know, Alex. But if anything happened to you, I'd never forgive myself. If I can't locate a proper ship and captain, I'll lock you in your room to prevent any foolish behavior," he warned.

She laughed and tweaked his plump cheek. "For once, I'll be a good girl," she teased merrily, her eyes dancing with mischief. "I promise to be very careful."

Once in her room, Alex had this same argument with Tessa. When nothing worked to change her young mistress's mind, the maid sullenly helped Alex pack her belongings. "Ye Papa's gonna be furious, Mum. He'll flog me somethin' terrible when he finds me," she fearfully stated.

"Don't be silly, Tessa. Papa knows how determined and headstrong I can be. How could a sick maid stop me?" she teased the dimpled, squat servant of seventeen who was revealing her condition more and more every day. Even after a year of service, Tessa was still guarded and strange.

"You remain here with Uncle Henry and take good care of yourself. Once you come home, Papa will see that you're legally wed to Timothy. Right after he thrashes him good and proper," she impulsively added.

"No, Mum. You mustn't get Timothy into trouble. 'Tweren't his fault. When them fires rage in ye body, they ain't no putting them out," she declared unwittingly, her face closed to Alex's scrutiny.

When Alex halted her progress to stare at her, Tessa brazenly went on, "Ye wouldn't be knowing about such things, Mum. But I tell ye the truth; when ye blood boils with passion, ain't no controlling yeself. When Timothy holds me and kisses me, the whole world is wild and wonderful. Ever'thin' spins and dances, and I only thinks about him and cooling the heat in me body. I'm a bad girl, Mum, for I kin not

171

fight the weakness of the flesh." Tessa shamelessly locked gazes with the shocked girl she was trying to embarrass and spite.

I wouldn't know about such things? Alex mentally echoed. If only I didn't know exactly what you mean . . .

She looked at Tessa and modestly argued, "No, Tessa you aren't a bad girl; just an impulsive and foolish one. I should think love would be that way. Besides, why should men have all the pleasure at such special moments? I daresay you are fortunate to have known such a unique and wonderful time. But marriage should come before such carnal pleasures. As you can see, there are punishments for wanton desires," she teased, patting Tessa's protruding stomach, refusing to expose her dismay and shock. "First the husband, then the romps in bed and babies. Agreed? No more dallying?" she demurely hinted.

"Yes, Mum," she quickly and resentfully consented. "Ye be a joy to know, Miss Alex," she deceitfully remarked, jealousy filling her heart and eyes. "How kin I ever thank ye?"

"Stay well and have a healthy baby. And no more fiery blood," she couldn't help but add with gay laughter to visibly reprimand this audacious servant who was much too brazen and defiant.

Not once during this conversation did Alex consider her own good fortune in remaining slim and unfettered by a fatherless child from her own wanton experience by the pond. Somehow, she never imagined herself as being unwed and blossoming with a bastard child. To her disadvantage, her education in that vital area was sadly lacking . . .

When the persistent Daniel Grey came calling that following afternoon, a sullen Tessa civilly sent him on his way with the lie that Alex wasn't home at present. When Tessa returned to Alex's room, she was giggling like a young girl as she came forward to relate the humorous scene below delighting in turning away a handsome and wealthy suitor.

"He surely be determined to have ye, Mum. He be planning to call again after dinner. He said to give ye this package."

Alex scowled in displeasure at the news of another appearance by that irritating rake with the wandering, groping hands. "You'd think after three pinches, two slaps, and several refusals he would get the idea I cannot tolerate him! However shall I discourage him, Tessa?" she declared her vexation. "What bribe has he sent this time?" she asked, taking the package wrapped in scented paper. "First flowers, then lace kerchiefs, now what?" she ventured as she ripped open the unwanted gift.

When she lifted the top to the box, her eyes widened in surprise. "Look at this, Tessa!" she squealed in astonishment. "Do my eyes deceive me, or is that a diamond and emerald bracelet?"

"My, oh my, Mum," Tessa murmured in wistful approval of the expensive gift. "'Tis real jewels, I do believe. He be lining his trap with treasures," Tessa enviously concluded, eying the wealth before her greedy gaze.

"You're right, Tess. A trap for sure," she readily agreed. She hastily closed the box and handed it to her servant. "Please wrap this and have it returned to Mister Grey this afternoon."

"Ye be returning it?" Tessa shrieked in disbelief. Was her haughty mistress daft!

"Certainly! I couldn't possibly accept such a costly present from a man I dislike immensely. Besides, he would surely attempt to collect some reward in exchange for it. Nothing comes free, Tessa dear, not even love," she warned, patting her tummy again to stress her point. "Everything has some price. And I'm not willing to pay Mister Daniel Grey's!" she asserted contemptuously.

"But ye be leaving soon, Mum. How can he collect if ye be gone?" she tempted her mistress to keep the exquisite bracelet which was of great value and beauty, hoping it would cause trouble.

"That wouldn't be proper, Tessa. Please return it to Mister Grey, and I don't want to hear it mentioned again." She turned and left the room, totally dismissing Daniel and the gift.

Tessa gazed down at the lovely bracelet which was worth so much money. Since Lady Alexandria was leaving in a few days, she would never know if the bracelet never found its way back home . . . Thinking of how much money could be made from its sale, she smiled and placed the bracelet in her pocket.

Humming cheerfully, she collected the wrapping paper and left the room.

That afternoon raced by in a flurry of plans and decisions. Uncle Henry informed Alex, "The *Sea Star* is the only ship leaving port within the next few days heading for England. Captain Thackery assured me you will be safe under his protection. He's agreed to let you use the first mate's quarters for a hefty purse. I've gotten you a perfect disguise and you must wear it at all times."

As he withdrew the garments from a large package, Alex placed her hand over her mouth to prevent her giggles from spilling forth. "You expect me to travel to England dressed like that?" she mocked his careful plans in unleashed merriment.

"Most assuredly, my dear. Don't you ever leave your cabin dressed any other way! Under the circumstances, it would be seemly if you remained in your cabin as much as possible. For certain, this should protect you from amorous seamen. The *Sea Star* crew didn't have any leave this port, so those men will be looking for any diversion. Please, Alex, don't tempt them to forget you're a lady and a well-paying traveller," he warned, his expression grave.

"I've given you my promise to be good and careful. I won't entice a single man. But I can't remain in a stuffy, dingy cabin for weeks on end. I'll wear this . . . disguise every time I leave it," she vowed, then laughed as she studied the clothing which he had provided for her protection.

"I know this isn't much warning, but Thackery sails with the morning tide. He wants you on board by nightfall. I just wish Tessa could travel with you," he grumbled.

"I will not be cooped up with a woman throwing up every few minutes! If I'm to be confined to my cabin, then let it be alone. I'll take several of your books along to keep my mind occupied," she stated.

Henry went to call Tessa to help Alex with her final packing. Alex looked around the room for one last time. This trip had been good for her. She had savored life and freedom for a short time. She was torn between remaining here to protect that freedom and returning home to prevent a lengthy separation by war. Would she be able to stall her father's plans for an arranged marriage? If not, she would check out every available bachelor in England and select the best one! But first, she might see if she could locate the mysterious man by the pond . . .

"Forget it, Alex! That's sheer madness," she cautioned herself.

"What's sheer madness?" her uncle questioned from the doorway.

Caught by surprise, she whirled and glanced sheepishly at him. She lied most convincingly, "To find the perfect man when I return home. You know Papa insists I be wed before this year's out. I was just preparing myself to settle for the second best man," she wretchedly stated.

"You're finally talking intelligently, my dear girl.

I'm proud of you. Charles only wants the best for his only daughter," he remarked fondly.

"I know, Uncle Henry. But is marriage to some stranger really the best for me? What about love?" she protested miserably, her nerves tensing at the idea of marriage and her trip home.

"Love comes with time, Alex, not at first or even second sight," he admonished his romantic niece.

Doesn't it? she mentally argued. If not, how could she explain these crazy feelings about Stephen? She cursed this magical spell he had cast over her heart and body. She cursed the nights she had awakened longing for him and those wild passions he had unleashed. Why was life so cruel and demanding? Why couldn't she marry a man she could love and desire?

"Alex?" her uncle called her from her dreamy state. "Is something troubling you?" he probed.

She forced a buoyant smile to her lips and shook her head of tawny curls. "I'm just fine. I'll be ready to leave shortly. I promise to come again when the war's over."

"I doubt your new husband will permit you to leave his side so soon."

"You sound as if you think America will win this conflict in a matter of months," she snapped, then promptly apologized for her curtness.

"I fully understand. You've a lot on your mind. Just remember this if you leave your cabin for any reason, any reason," he stressed, tapping the hat.

Henry called two of his servants to take her baggage

to the waiting carriage. Alex completed her disguise and turned to face him. "Well?" she inquired, twirling before him like a dancing doll.

"Excellent! You should be perfectly safe if you practice caution."

Arm-in-arm they left her bedroom and walked down the steps and out the front door. Henry helped her into the carriage and waited for her to situate herself before telling the coachman to head for the dock. They travelled in near silence, each absorbed in thought.

Within a mile of the port, Henry leaned over to whisper his final warnings to her, "Don't forget, Alex; no one must learn your real name or see those messages stitched to your petticoat. They're innocent enough, but they could be misconstrued. At the first sign of trouble, get rid of that petticoat. And tell no one your name. Understand?" he entreated gravely.

"Why, Uncle Henry? If trouble came about, wouldn't it be wiser if I told them I was the daughter of Lord Charles Hampton? Surely that would halt any problems?" she quietly reasoned, confused by his caution.

"No, you mustn't," he instantly replied. "If there's trouble on the ship, Lady Hampton would command a hefty ransom or her life could be endangered by some hot-headed loyalist. Who better to trade for information than a highborn lady? Think what foolish ideas a desperate man could get plotting ransom for you. Besides, some crude males think it sporty to ravish a lady of quality. As to those messages on your petticoat, there's no telling how some unscrupulous man might use them against me or your father. Why, they might call such messages treason," he boldly hinted.

"Treason? But what do they say?" she curiously inquired.

"Nothing of interest or concern to you or the Motherland, dear. Just some vital business facts for Charles's use. Still, other shippers wouldn't take kindly to such a trade of critical information. If you wish to protect both mine and your father's business interests and reputations, destroy that petticoat if the ship is attacked."

"Attacked? By whom?" she nervously demanded.

"I told you when you demanded this voyage home it could be dangerous. I'm referring to English scouting ships or privateers. Plus, I'm not too sure how far we can trust this Thackery. Just remain in hiding as much as possible," he reiterated his warning for what seemed the hundredth time.

"Not to worry, Uncle Henry, I'll do as you say: remain hidden; rid myself of this naughty petticoat; guard my name from all ears," she merrily repeated her lists of commands, then laughed as if this were some exciting and harmless game.

"I'm not teasing, Alexandria. The seas are perilous; many men can't be trusted. You're a beautiful woman travelling alone. This isn't a joking matter," he sternly scolded her, frowning.

Alex sobered instantly at his grave expression and apprehensive mood. It seemed pointless to revoice her promises or to offer him comfort, so she remained silent and attentive. "Tell Charles to send me word of your safe arrival as soon as possible. I'll not sleep a wink until then."

"How can Papa send word to America during a war?" she reasoned.

"He'll find some way. We both know many privateers who'll carry messages for a tidy sum of gold. Just follow my words and be careful."

Alex sighed heavily. "Please, Uncle Henry. My ears are crowded with dire warnings and advice."

"Just hope you find no need for any of it," he said under his breath, but she heard him.

Alex was briefly tempted to call off her return voyage just to calm his frayed nerves, but couldn't force herself to be that selfless. She honestly didn't know if it was the war, her father, or Stephen who was drawing her back to England . . .

When the dock was in sight, Henry quickly told her to put on her hat and to get ready to follow his every suggestion. She hurriedly complied, knowing her best interests would be served. The carriage halted and Henry jumped down to help her out. She held herself erect and silent as a man clad in dingy gray pants and shirt came forward to greet them. Alex wished for a scented kerchief when he was within smelling distance. His hair was scraggly and unkempt. His beard needed a good trim. Repulsed by his stench and filth, she almost changed her mind about this untimely trip.

"Ye be Cowling?" the rangy man asked, his age indeterminable.

"Yes, and this is my sister Maria Hathaway. As you can see, she's in mourning for her recently departed husband and only son. I pray the crew will follow my request and leave her to herself as much as possible. It was a tragic accident and she's not quite over the shock," Henry quickly offered his ruse and an explanation for her heavy black veils and mourning gown of midnight black.

As a pair of the bluest and gentlest eyes focused on the slender woman whom they could not see, Alex's heart was warmed by the sympathy which she could read through the lacy material which fell from the crown of her hat to her breasts. "I be sorry fur ye misfortunes, ma'am. We'll see kindly to'er, sir. Capt'n Thackery be a strict man, but a fair un. He'll allow no'um to bother ye sister. I'll see to her meals meself."

"Thank you; you're most kind. Take this for your extra troubles," Henry stated, handing the man a handful of gold coins.

A bony hand gripped the cold metal tightly and thanked him profusely. "Yessir. Ye sister be in good hands," he vowed once more. "Come, ma'am; I'll show ye to ye cabin. Old Pete'll let no'um trouble ye whilst ye be under my care."

Henry and Alex embraced affectionately and slowly parted. "Take care . . . sister. If you need anything, ask Pete."

181

With Pete holding her left arm, Alex was assisted up the slanted wooden walk to the ship. Pete hurried before her to open the door which descended into the heart of the ship. Careful not to trip, Alex slowly moved down the steps into the passageway. Pete led her to a door and opened it. He placed her baggage inside and came back to tell her she could enter.

In a muffled tone to disguise the youthful quality of her voice, she softly thanked him and closed the door. She was immediately distressed to discover the first mate's cabin door had no lock! Glancing around the small room, she quickly lifted the room's only chair to place it securely under the doorknob, hoping to prevent anyone from coming inside. She sighed in relief, feeling a little bit safer. Yet, she fretted over how to protect her valuables when she left this cabin.

She walked to the bunk and sat down. Panic and dejection filled her. Perhaps she should disembark and forget this wild idea. But it was too late for that; Henry had probably left by now and the streets were deserted at this time of night. If she changed her mind by morning, she could always leave at dawn before the sailing . . .

Alex removed her shoes and paced the floor for hours, keenly aware of the loud singing and laughter coming from below her cabin. Why was she being so cowardly? Hadn't she ranted about wanting adventure and suspense? Surely this voyage would provide both! With her uncle's knowledge of her presence aboard and her disguise, she would be safe. Wouldn't she?

As time snailishly passed, her thoughts went to Daniel Grey. She grinned impishly as she envisioned his reaction to the returned bracelet. No doubt that refusal added to her hasty departure would deflate his puffed-up self-esteem!

Alex walked to the solitary porthole and peered out. She thanked her lucky star this was only mid-June. Else, how could she tolerate the summer heat of this stuffy cabin for three weeks? She observed wispy clouds as they trailed their fluffy wings across the face of the full moon and watched stars twinkle and glimmer on the indigo backdrop. Her gaze followed the moon's pathway across the water's dark surface. A light breeze entered the round opening and played in her amber tresses. She inhaled the heady smell of the ocean which mingled with floral hints from the nearby shore. It was such a romantic setting. How she dreaded the loneliness of this impending voyage.

"Where are you, Stephen? Who are you? Will I ever see you again?" she softly repeated questions she had uttered countless times since that fateful day in April.

When the moon disappeared over the ship, she finally went to recline upon the bunk. She sighed in weariness, at least delighting in the clean linens.

As if drugged, Alex gradually aroused from her heavy slumber. Suddenly aware of the gentle rolling of the ship, she jumped up to peer out the porthole. Her eyes widened in disbelief. How long had she slept? They were already at sea! If she had any doubts about

183

this voyage, it was definitely too late to change her mind now!

A light knock caught her attention. Just before heading to the door, she wisely recalled her concealing hat. She hurriedly retrieved it and put it on, arranging the veil to totally obscure her face. As quietly as possible, she moved the chair aside and opened the door. Pete was standing there, grinning amiably, carrying a tray of food.

"I let ye sleep, ma'am. I figured ye be tired after that late night. I heard ye pacing most the night. Not to fear; ye'll have ye sealegs soon."

"You heard me? How?" she softly asked, remembering to keep her voice even.

"Me bunk be under here and I got sens'tive ears," he proudly boasted.

"I'll settle down today, Pete. Thank you for your kindness," she stated, saying more than she should.

Pete flashed his lopsided grin once more and brought her tray inside. "I'll come back later to fetch it. If ye need fresh air or a walk on deck, I'll take ye later. The men git kinda rowdy sometimes. Ye know what I mean?"

"I think I understand, Pete. I'll be fine. Thank you."

He left, closing the door behind him. Alex studied the tray of food, wondering if she could consume any of it, deciding she would have to in order to keep up her health and strength. Summoning her courage, she nibbled at the nearly tasteless fare. When she could stomach no more, she placed the tray outside her door and secured it with the chair. She went to her baggage and unpacked a book to read. This was going to be a very long trip, for she was already bored on the first morning at sea!

Alex halted her reading when she heard noises outside her room. She relaxed as she realized it was only Pete getting her tray. It was nearly dark when that knock came to her door again. She politely greeted the short man with his genial smile and sunny disposition.

He chided her, "Ye didn't eat much the last meal, ma'am. I know the victuals be poor, but ye must eat."

"I wasn't very hungry, Pete." This time, she kept her comments to a minimum, knowing she was pressing her luck to strike up a casual friendship with this apparently lonely man.

"Losing loved ones be hard on a woman. But ye'll find another husband and have more children," he ventured.

Alex wondered at why he assumed she was young enough to have other children, but didn't question this assumption. "Would ye like to walk on the deck, ma'am?" he asked.

"Perhaps tomorrow evening, Pete. I'm still a little weak and tired from the journey."

"Just let me know when I bring ye supper," he replied before leaving her alone.

It was the third day before Alex decided she needed the stroll on deck before she would go mad from the silence and confinement. She asked Pete to wait until most of the crew was below eating, playing cards, drinking, or sleeping. It was around ten o'clock when Pete came to get her. Dressed in all black and her face obscured from all inquisitive eyes, Alex followed Pete up the steps and onto the deck.

She glanced around her. If Thackery was as strict as Pete had claimed, why were the decks so grimy and the ship so cluttered? "Are there any other females aboard, Pete?" she inquired in a low tone.

Flustered, Pete stammered before answering. "They be two females aboard, ma'am, but no other ladies," he replied in a manner which clearly revealed her position.

"I see," she murmured demurely. "I thought you told my . . . brother that Captain Thackery was a strict man. His ship certainly doesn't prove it."

Pete actually lowered his head in shame. "I know, ma'am. But if I'd told ye brother the truth, he'd have not let ye sailed with us. The Capt'n would've flogged me if he lost that fat purse of gold fur ye passage," he anxiously confessed. "That's why I be taking good care o'ye. Ye trust old Pete; he'll let no harm come to ye."

Alarm raced through her entire body. "Are this ship and crew safe?"

"If ye stay in ye cabin unless ye be with me, ye'll be safe," he answered candidly.

"I think I'm ready to return to my cabin, Pete," she stated shakily.

Comprehending her panic, he smiled ruefully and said, "I'll take care of ye, ma'am."

In the cabin, Alex paced the floor for hours. She still had over two weeks to survive on this ship. After tonight, she would cautiously remain here even if she had to tear her hair from boredom and agitation.

Her guarded plans were thwarted that very next day. When a knock came to her door, she unthinkingly pulled it open without asking who was there, assuming it to be Pete. Through her veil, she observed the visage of a strange man who was clad in drab blue except for his time-yellowed cotton shirt. He sported a neatly trimmed beard and heavy mustache. His wiry hair teased at the collar of his faded blue jacket. His boots mutely begged for a good polishing. His washed-out pants negligently declared several careless stains. Bushy brows which were a mixture of chestnut and gray perched over hooded eyes of chocolate brown. His cheeks were plump and rosy. For an outdoorsman, he noticeably lacked a natural tan or even a healthy color.

He spoke to her in a raspy voice. "Pete tells me you've been keeping to your cabin, Mistress Hathaway. Ain't no need to be scared to go for walks on my deck. My crew's been warned to be on their best manners. Wouldn't do to go offending a proper lady or a wealthy man like Cowling. If you be needing anything, give Pete a message for me. Just wanted to make sure you ain't ailing."

"Pete's been most kind and helpful, Captain

Thackery. Under the circumstances, I wanted to be alone. But thank you for your courtesy," she said as softly as possible, feeling compelled to be polite.

She could tell the offensive man was straining to catch her words and was somewhat too curious about her. His next words proved her recent suspicions, "Sad to think such a young woman has met such tragedy."

"One can hardly call forty young, sir. But thank you for the compliment," she replied, holding a kerchief to her lips to muffle her voice.

"Would you care to take a stroll on the deck with me? Might be nice to have some good talk for a change," he boldly suggested, his eyes revealing his intense scrutiny as they struggled to pierce her heavy veil.

"Perhaps another day, sir. I'm reading a most fascinating book and I'm presently in a place which intrigues me," she offered what she knew sounded like the flimsy excuse it was.

"But you need fresh air and sunshine, mistress. You can't stay locked in here for weeks. Ain't healthy for you," he dashed her reasons.

Feeling cornered, she couldn't decide what course to take. If she was too cordial, he would be inviting her to dinner next! However, she certainly didn't want to offend him. Why had he mentioned being locked in? A figure of speech or keen insight?

"Perhaps you're right, sir. I'll join you shortly," she acquiesced.

He nodded and pulled the door shut. Alex's terrified gaze flickered around the small cabin. She cautioned herself against conversation, her agile movements, her graceful walk, exposing her unlined hands, and any other action which might betray her.

With the aid of a small mirror from her baggage, she checked her appearance. Thankfully the black gown was loose, obscuring at least part of her enticing figure. She pulled on black lace gloves and adjusted her hat and veil. She wisely refrained from applying any provocative perfume.

She opened the door to find Thackery leaning against the wall near her cabin. "I'm ready, sir."

He grinned in a strange manner, then took her elbow to lead her down the hallway to the steps. He climbed up first, then held out his hand to assist her when she was within reaching distance. Even through the thin gloves, she could detect the clamminess of his palms. She wished he would release her trembling elbow and would move away from her. He did neither.

They headed toward the stern of his ship at a leisurely stroll, gradually covering the distance until they were heading for the bow on the starboard side. The ship was moving across a relatively calm sea, the sails billowing and swaying in a slight breeze. They had walked in complete silence until this point.

"Hope we keep up this nice weather. The sea can be mighty hateful when she takes a mind to," he aimlessly began a conversation.

Alex simply nodded in agreement. "How long was

you married?" he suddenly asked, cunningly forcing her to speak.

There was no way to politely avoid answering, so she softly replied, "Twenty-three years."

"You only had the one son who was killed?" he continued his nosy line.

"Yes," she answered.

"Too bad, seventeen is too young to die," he muttered as if thinking aloud.

"Yes, it was," she responded, unaware he was entrapping her with the false information supplied by Cowling.

He lightly clutched the damp rail as his gaze focused on the distant skyline of clear blue. In pensive thought, he pursed his large lips and rocked back and forth. Innocently thinking him to be giving her time for fresh air as he politely submitted to her annoying company, she relaxed against the rail a few feet from him.

As several dolphins began to leap and frolic to her right, she slightly turned in that direction to watch them. The sun was nearly touching the deep blue water; the blue horizon was peaceful and free of dark clouds. The dolphins played in carefree abandonment before a backdrop of subtle lavender, muted gold, and fiery pinks etched upon serene azure. There was so much beauty, tranquility, and exhilaration at sea at this time of day.

In spite of her alarm and tension, Alex relaxed and enjoyed her surroundings. So enchanted was she by this setting, she failed to realize she actually laughed in soft and silvery tones. A sudden updraft from the ocean below lifted the veil just enough to present the stunned Thackery with a view of tawny curls, sparkling emerald eyes, flawless skin, and exquisite, angelic beauty. As she gasped and clutched at the veil, he instantly looked the other way as if this impish trick of nature had gone unnoticed . . .

VIII

"How poor are they that have not patience!
What wound did ever heal but by degrees?"
—*Othello*, William Shakespeare

Alex fearfully glanced toward the captain, relieved to find him half-turned the other way. She promptly resolved to secure the veil to her dress with a brooch on future outings. It wouldn't do for these crude men to see her face! With quivering hands, she held tightly to the veil to make sure it did not lift again.

As the dolphins moved further toward the stern of the ship, she followed their adventures. Facing the bow, Thackery was grinning lewdly. Absently rubbing his swollen manhood, he couldn't turn around until he had his lust under control. So many delightful ideas raced through his eager mind and inflamed body. Now he knew why she was hiding behind that veil and in her cabin! One look at her and his men would go wild! How lucky could a man be than to have a living goddess on board his ship? A ship under his control and out of the reach of any authority but his!

"Ready, sir?" she inquired for the second time, startling him out of his lecherous reflections.

"Sure, Mistress Marie," he replied, huskily using her first name with a tone she didn't like at all, but wisely let the offense pass.

She wondered if every man was so carnally minded that any female enflamed their unruly lusts, even a proclaimed widow! Annoyed, she held her shoulders erect and stiff as she hurriedly crossed the deck to the doorway. She cautiously went down the steps to avoid tripping on the long gown. She mutely went to her cabin and opened the door. After a cool offer of gratitude, she closed the door before he could speak.

Without the slightest hesitation, Alex placed the chair under the knob. Unsettled, she paced the floor for hours before turning in for the night. Plagued by doubts and tense nerves, she slept very little. For the first time, she was acutely aware of the captain's movements in the next cabin. Evidently he wasn't sleeping well either! Why?

New qualms filled Alex when Pete offered to bring in a tub and water if she wished to bathe. She instinctively knew she should refuse this strange offer, but she didn't. After three days of merely sponging off, a real bath sounded too tempting to sacrifice. While she sat patiently upon her bunk, Pete and a youthful boy hauled in a wooden tub and water. Placing a thick cloth beside the filled tub, Pete turned and smiled before walking out.

Alex went to the door and made certain the chair was firmly implanted against the knob. She dropped a bar of scented soap by the tub and quickly removed her clothes. She immersed herself in the water, surprised and delighted to find it warm. As swiftly as possible, she scrubbed her body from head to toe. Stepping out of the tub, she knelt beside it to pour the extra bucket of water over her long hair to rinse it a final time. Checking to see that no one was leaning over the rail above her cabin, she sat on her table and hung her lengthy curls out the porthole to dry them in the sun and air.

Afterwards, she sat on the bunk and brushed her silky mane until it shone with shimmering highlights. Deciding to reject the captain's company today should he offer, she donned a skin-caressing day dress in dark green. Clean hair and body and a colorful dress did wonders for her deflated spirits. She quickly put her hat and veil in place when Pete and the youth returned to remove the tub.

Pete grinned in pleasure and genially announced. "Ye be looking fresh as a spring mornin'. Ye be wanting to get some air on deck?"

"Not today, Pete, but thank you. I really should rest after all this activity. Tomorrow?" she said in her normal tone of voice.

"Me pleasure, ma'am," he replied like a lad of eighteen. He left this time whistling cheerfully.

Around eleven o'clock, another knock came to her sealed door. Alex teased herself that Pete was making another try to coax her outside. As she answered the light knocking, Pete shifted anxiously as he informed her, "Sorry to trouble ye, ma'am, but the captain wants to see you. Says it's mighty impo'tant."

"Why would he need to speak with me, Pete?" she asked, panic edging into her tone. Perhaps to share a cordial lunch?

"He said fur me to fetch ye to his cabin. Seems upset 'bout some'em," he stated in uncertainty, his tension increasing hers.

She pondered the worry lining his brow. Did Thackery simply wish to behave in a cordial manner he assumed proper for a lady on board? Was this merely a polite and harmless invitation to tea? Was there perhaps trouble brewing and he wanted to personally alert her to that possibility? Perhaps give her some orders of what to do in such an event? No matter, she couldn't adamantly refuse to comply. She was alone on his ship and it wouldn't be shrewd to displease or openly disdain him.

Closing the cabin door, she followed Pete the few steps to the captain's cabin. Pete knocked almost timidly and apprehensively waited for an answer. The door opened and the captain smiled at her. "Aw, Mistress Marie. Do come in," he suggested, as if surprised to see her standing there! "I won't be needing you anymore, Pete. Return to your duties," he ordered in an authoritative manner.

Alex remained in the hallway, suddenly aware of her green gown. She asked, "Did you wish to tell me something, Captain Thackery?" She hoped she could handle any business they might have here and now, then return to her room immediately.

Thackery gently, but firmly, took her arm and pulled her inside his cabin as he spouted, "Come in, come in, Mistress Marie. We'll have some tea or sherry while we chat."

Sherry? Chat? This meeting didn't appeal to her at all! What was this old buzzard up to this afternoon? "I really don't care for tea, sir; and I don't partake of strong spirits," she lied to hurry this talk. Fear claimed her senses as she noted the captain's heated stare as his glowing eyes eased over the perfectly fitting green gown and the black veil which his keen eyes couldn't penetrate. "I'm not good company today, sir. I'm weary from all my exertions," she tried to excuse herself again.

Thackery beamed as he stated, "Thought you might enjoy a nice bath. Sit down and join me. A glass of sherry might lighten your spirits," he encouraged, twisting his clasped hands in apparent anticipation.

Despite her protest, he poured two glasses and placed one before her. Without accepting the glass, she unthinkingly interlocked her fingers and rested those silky-skinned, graceful hands on the table before his astute vision. She remain rigid and straight in her seat.

"You're in private now, Mistress Marie. Why not give yourself some fresh air; you can take off your veil in here," he boldly offered.

She tensed. "It wouldn't be proper, sir. I am in mourning, and we are strangers."

He chuckled in a way she found disturbing. "You

seem nervous. That sherry'll calm you down," he coaxed. When he turned as if to get something from his desk, she hastily took several sips to do just that!

He came back to the table, carrying a small box of scented powder. "I thought you might like to have this," he offered, holding the fragrant box out to her.

She inhaled sharply. "I do not accept gifts from strange men, Captain Thackery. If you don't mind, I would prefer to return to my cabin to rest," she stated indignantly, resolved to end this unpleasant meeting even if she had to offend him! He was as repulsive, persistent, and obnoxious as Daniel Grey!

She felt as if her racing blood froze in her veins when he calmly announced, "But I do mind, Marie. You see, my dear lady; I don't mind your play-acting around my crew, but I dislike deceit and haughtiness where I'm concerned. If you can't trust the ship's captain with the truth, you're in deep trouble out here alone," he murmured in a tone laced with innuendo.

"I beg your pardon, sir?" she apprehensively stated, doubtful of what to do or say. Did he imply he knew who and what she was?

"Did you think I was too low to be trusted? Why didn't your brother, if he's really your brother, tell me why a beautiful lady would travel the perilous sea alone?" he abruptly stated.

"You were paid well to see me safely to England, sir. My personal affairs are none of your concern. You accepted the money and the responsibility for my safe voyage. My friendship and company were not part of that bargain," she tersely informed him.

He stood up and walked around a few minutes in deep thought. He halted near her. "Perhaps you're right," he mumbled, yanking her veil off before she realized what he was doing. He leered at the young beauty before his smoldering eyes as he sneered, "Then again, perhaps you're not."

Alex jumped to her feet, knocking over her chair. She blanched white, then flushed crimson in fury. "How dare you! Your behavior is unforgivable, sir! Be assured my uncle and father will hear of this outrage!" she boldly threatened the laughing man. Snatching her hat from his loose grip, she whirled to leave.

Thackery seized her arm in a painful grasp and yanked her around to face him. Fear and anger flooded those dark green eyes. "Release me this instant! This conduct will not go unpunished!" she stormed.

"How can you report something when you might never get ashore?" he threatened.

Alex paled in shock. "Surely you would not murder an innocent woman! Have you forgotten my uncle knows I am aboard your ship? He is awaiting word of my safe arrival in England. I assure you he will not rest until you are located and punished!" she daringly informed him.

"Who said I was going to kill such a breathtaking creature?" he asked, reaching out to caress her satiny cheek.

She slapped his hand away. He chuckled heartily. "Women get sold to them foreign slave ships all the time. Who's gonna challenge my word when I sadly relate how you took ill and died, how we was forced to bury you at sea?" he smugly challenged the panicky girl before him.

Trying to appear poised and brave, she scornfully asked, "Just what is it you want from me, Captain? More money? Jewels?"

"Two things, Marie," he easily came back, then abruptly asked, "Is Marie your real name?"

"Yes, but Henry is my uncle, not my brother," she stated.

"Why are you dressed in that silly black outfit?" he demanded.

"Uncle Henry felt it was safer since I was forced to travel quickly and alone. He wanted to send me home before a war broke out. He thinks England is getting ready to attack the Colonies. My brother and maid had taken ill with some strange fever and couldn't come with me," she fabricated a new story as she went along. She prayed he might suspect her of carrying that unknown fever and would leave her alone.

"Why does he think there's gonna be a war soon?"

"He said men were talking about it all the time now. I think he mentioned some vote in Congress this week. He felt America wouldn't be safe for me, so he's sending me home." She inwardly fumed as she watched skepticism fill his eyes. She added, "He assumed I would be safe aboard your ship, but evidently he made a bad choice in judgment."

Thackery laughed coldly. "You said you wanted two

things from me, what are they?'' she returned the conversation to his greedy demands.

"First, the whole truth about you. Second, a nice little diversion along the way," he drooled.

"You must be mad! You cannot accost a lady in your care!"

"Not mad, dear Marie, just determined to enjoy a tasty treat placed within my reach," he calmly replied.

"I would die first!" she screamed at him. Would his crew come to her aid if she yelled. No, probably not.

"Come, come, Marie. There's no need to preen those lovely feathers for me. Let's relax and have some sherry. This is gonna be a long voyage, but a pleasant one," he ominously warned.

"If you lay one finger on me, I'll slit your miserable throat!"

"Do tell?" he mocked her.

"Yes," she dauntlessly vowed, annoying him.

She attempted to pull free from his grip, but could not. She recklessly slapped and kicked at him, actions which only infuriated the lust-filled man. When she managed to rake her nails down the side of his face and produce rivulets of blood, he angrily shoved her backwards with such force she toppled and fell. His hand went to his face to check the damage she had done. He looked at the blood on his fingers, then glared at the girl on the floor.

He cursed her with words she had never heard used before and stalked forward to tower over her in a menacing fashion. Alex defiantly returned his glacial stare as if daring him to touch her again. He seized a handful of golden hair and yanked her to her feet. She screamed in pain and beat him with ineffectual blows.

"You little hell-cat! You'll pay for that!" he snarled through gritted teeth. He threw her against the wall, knocking the breath from her body. Grabbing both sides of her dress at the neckline, he yanked fiercely and ripped the material. She screamed again, but no one came to her rescue. She never knew old Pete was outside, chewing his nails and praying for the courage to come to her aid, knowing he would never find it.

Alex wrestled with the stodgy Thackery with all her might, fearing she could never resist his intentions to ravish her. Still, her battle was as necessary as it was futile. Just as she felt she had no energy left to fight with, the alarm sounded.

The ensuing fight lasted only a few more moments as Pete pounded upon the door to capture Thackery's attention. At long last, Thackery shouted, "What the hell do you want?"

"Pirate attack, Capt'n!" came the answer all captains dreaded.

"Pirates?" he echoed as if stunned by this untimely intrusion.

"Yep! The lookout says the sails are black, Capt'n," came a far worse announcement.

Alex watched the evil man before her actually pale

and shudder in noticeable fear. He quickly attempted to hide such weakness from her. "You wait here, Marie. I'll make short business of these pirates and be back to take good care of you. To make sure you stay put, I'll prevent any ideas of your escaping over the side."

He pulled her struggling body over to his bunk and secured her hands tightly above her head to the post which reached from ceiling to floor. To vex her, he kissed her soundly. Alex thought she would retch. When she spit in his leering face, he slapped her hard across her cheek, slightly stunning her with its brutal force.

"That's another night you owe me before I sell you to them desert snakes, Miss High and Mighty," he sneered, then strapped on his sword and left her alone and helpless.

Alex pulled on the ropes and twisted this way and that. She only managed to cut rope burns into her wrists until the blood ran down her arms. She clenched her teeth against the pain as she attempted to free herself once more. Tears eased down her cheeks as she realized how degrading her situation was. As the sounds of battle reached her ears, she prayed the pirate ship would sink them before Thackery could return to his cabin and complete his vile act.

Fatigued and terrified, she rested her forehead against the post as she awaited her impending fate. The ship shuddered as a cannonball made a direct hit on her starboard side. Alex laughed as she thought how lucky she was this cabin was on the port side. Shrieks of pain and loud shouts could be heard from above her. The clattering of booted feet running back and forth alerted her to the desperation of this battle. A thunderous crash suggested a severed mast and possible defeat.

What would happen once this battle was over? Would Thackery return? Would he hopefully be slain? Would the pirates kill all on board and sink them? Never in her life had she experienced such soul-shaking fear. No matter the outcome of this day, her fate was cloudy . . .

It took a few minutes for Alex to recognize the portentous silence which indicated the fierce conflict for power was over. She dreaded to guess the victor. She could hear the softened sounds of boots as they made contact with the wooden deck overhead. The voices were so low, she couldn't make out what they were saying or who was talking. There was nothing she could do but wait and pray.

When she heard the door open behind her, she tensed in dread and suspense. She held her breath in anticipation of Thackery's renewed assault. God forgive her, but she would try to kill him in any way possible! She refused to move. Her face remained between her bound arms, her tawny tresses falling forward to conceal her face as her forehead rested against the post. She could sense someone standing beside her and staring at her, but she couldn't force herself to look into that evil face.

His sapphire eyes started at her bound hands whose bloody injuries bespoke her futile attempts at freedom. He noted her erratic respiration which announced her panic. Her figure was exceptional. Her skin and hair were those of a young female, a female who had unfortunately captured the eye of this stupid captain. Should he give her a lift to the nearest port? Did he have the time and patience? She was defenseless, but could he afford the danger of having a female on board his ship who might see or hear too much? No, he decided. The consequences were too grave.

"Hand over the papers, Thackery, and I'll forget you challenged me," the never-to-be-forgotten voice commanded in a smug tone.

"Not on your life, Captain Joshua Steele," Thackery rashly declined, furious at the way Steele was eying the female tied to his bedpost.

Steele? Captain Joshua Steele? The notorious scourge of the sea? But that was Stephen's voice! Her head jerked upwards and she stared at the man beside her whose face was concealed by a black mask. When he glanced at her, she couldn't help but witness the shock which registered briefly in those entrancing blue eyes. The half-grin which claimed his sensual mouth was the same one she had viewed at the pond. Her gaze spontaneously slipped over his powerful physique from head to foot, the truth of his identity exposed there. She licked her suddenly dry lips as she stared at him.

His calm, mellow voice stated, "Take the good captain out for a few minutes. I have another matter to settle first."

Confused, Andy quickly complied. Spencer placed his hands on his narrow hips and grinned at her. "You certainly have a way of getting into trouble, Angelique." Hearty laughter filled her ears.

"You?" she whispered, all doubts cleared away. "No wonder I couldn't find you," she foolishly remarked, making it sound as if she had searched for him when she really meant she hadn't known where to locate him.

Chuckles came forth again, but he allowed her words to pass unquestioned. As if noticing the mask for the first time, she recalled that no one knew what this infamous rogue looked like. Instantly, she realized she did. What would he do with her now that he knew she could identify him? Catching the irony of her predicament, she laughed aloud.

"What's so funny?" he quickly demanded of her curious behavior.

"I take it your name isn't Stephen," she responded. "I should have guessed there was some reason your face and name weren't known. I was just wondering which fate was worse: your revenge or Thackery's."

He laughed too. Funny they should meet again this way! "Looks as if he's been giving you a difficult time," he joked, nodding at her bonds.

"I was just planning how I was going to kill him when I got free," she declared, then laughed nervously again.

"What were you doing in America? You must have left England soon after our . . . meeting," he suggested with a beguiling grin.

Her stare grew cold and angry at the recall of that portentous day. "Yes, I did. I was hoping to never see you again, but it seems I've fallen into your brutal hands once more. Captain Joshua Steele . . ." she murmured aloud, her eyes slipping over his stalwart frame a second time. "Should I say it's an honor to meet you, sir?" she scornfully questioned.

"Perhaps the first time, but not today," he answered in an inexplicable manner. "I asked what you were doing in America," he repeated.

"How do you know I was in America?" she sneered disdainfully.

"Because that's the origin of this voyage," he casually stated, yet she could sense some irritation behind his words.

"I was returning home after visiting friends there, but the good Captain Thackery didn't take kindly to my refusal of his attentions," she scoffed bitterly.

"What friends? Where?" he demanded.

"None of your business, Captain Steele," she saucily replied.

"Then I take it you would prefer I leave you to the discretion of Captain Thackery? You wouldn't be interested in a ride to the nearest port?"

Her face and eyes brightened instantly. But her smile and hope both vanished as she noted his taunting grin. "I doubt I would be any safer with you than I was with him," she panted angrily.

"Safer? Perhaps not. But surely in gentler hands," he devilishly teased.

"That's a matter of opinion!" she flared at him in rising annoyance. Should she accept his offer? Was it genuine? Should she beg him to rescue her?

He gently seized her chin and forced her frantic gaze to meet his steady one. "And what is your honest opinion, Angelique?" he murmured huskily, his gaze causing her to tremble.

Alex quickly lowered her lashes to conceal the desirous look which she knew must be revealed there, too late to prevent him from seeing it. "My opinion is that you're a black-hearted rogue who preys on innocent girls and weaker ships," she stated in a strained voice.

"You know what will happen to you if I leave you here to face Thackery again," he said, observing her closely.

Her emerald eyes came up to look at him. She suddenly looked so young, so vulnerable, so damn innocent and alluring! Besides, she could identify him. He had never confronted that danger before. If he left her here, she would have two reasons for revenge against him. That is, if she survived to reach England . . .

"Would you let me off at the nearest port?" she challenged.

"I'd grant you your freedom from Thackery in .

exchange for your silence," he cunningly offered.

For a moment, puzzlement filled her eyes. Astonishment replaced it. "Surely you must be teasing me! How could I possibly tell anyone about you without giving away how I know the truth?"

He grinned in pleasure. "You're right, Angelique. To tell what you know, you would also be forced to tell how you learned such facts."

She was watching him intently. He was still calling her Angelique. That could only mean one thing; he didn't know her real name or identity. "I was visiting my uncle Silas Grimsley in Massachusetts when he decided I should return home. He thinks a war between England and America is coming soon. I was travelling disguised as a widow, but the wind played havoc with my ploy by lifting my veil on deck," she deceitfully offered the tale. Recalling how coy females acted, Alex called upon all her feminine instincts to fool him. Tears began to ease down her cheeks as she added, "I was so afraid, Stephen. I remained in my cabin as much as possible. I kept my face hidden with that veil all the time," she demurely stated like a wronged child, nodding to the hat on the floor.

Spencer glanced down at the hat and sighed. After all, she had been an innocent virgin when they met. She was apparently here in this cabin against her will. He'd never heard of this Grimsley, but he didn't know everyone. Still, something imperceptible nagged at him. He scanned her up and down several times and he mused upon this pleasing enigma. To her bewilderment, he started laughing.

She watched his manly chest vibrate with the mocking, heady sound. "Did I say something amusing, Stephen?"

"That provocative gown and your intoxicated breath seem a wee bit suspicious, love. Is this some lover's spat or a plot to secure your safety from bloody pirates?" he merrily accused.

Practically calling her Thackery's mistress, Alex inhaled in surprise and shrieked indignantly, "You vulgar beast! How dare you speak to me in such a crude manner! No man has ever laid his hands upon me except you! And if you ever do again, I'll slit your throat!" Her eyes glittered with icy fire. "As for Thackery, I'll do the same with him!" she breathlessly added.

Spencer stepped to within inches of her, staring down into her defiant expression. "You're saying no man warms that fiery blood of yours except me?" he mercilessly teased her as his hand slid down her cheek and his fingers passed over her lips.

When she attempted to bite him, he jerked his hand away and chuckled wickedly. "Such sharp teeth for a mermaid," he added roguishly.

"You blasted demon! Just wait until my father learns of these outrageous insults! He'll see both you and Thackery hanged!"

"And what about all your brothers?" he mocked her bravery.

Before thinking, she shouted back, "I don't have

any brothers; I'm an only child!" She instantly grimaced as she recalled her tale by the pond and groaned.

"No doubt a father could handle only one child such as you." Spencer playfully carried on this delightful game to provoke her into saying more.

"How would you know? I doubt you even have a father or a mother! I venture you're the spawn of the devil himself!" she charged haughtily.

"Such a temper!" he laughingly asserted. "Perhaps you and Thackery deserve each other."

That insinuation sobered her. Tears welled in her eyes. Her chin trembled. "Please, Stephen, don't leave me here with that monster," she pleaded. "You do owe me something," she reminded him. "Please release me; my arms ache."

His mood altered drastically at that statement. "Look at me, Angelique," he commanded. "Swear you're not here of your own free will."

Her teary gaze met his as she honestly vowed, "I swear it, Stephen. I swear I was returning home dressed as a widow. Sink this miserable ship or kill me, but don't leave me here like this."

He withdrew his knife, then instantly replaced it. He paced the floor in uncertainty.

"What did I do to make you hate me so much?" she asked dejectedly. "You can't do this to me!"

He whirled to glare at her. "Are you conveniently forgetting how we parted last time, my sweet and innocent Angelique?"

211

The color drained from her face. "But you left me no choice! You tricked me! You lied to me! Isn't silly revenge beneath the dignity of the infamous Joshua Steele? I thought your reputation boasted of leniency and mercy to helpless victims," she sarcastically sneered.

"Helpless? You, Angelique? The day'll never come when a woman like you doesn't have some weapon to use on a man," he charged. "The only way you'll come along with me is to pay your way."

Alex naively misconstrued his meaning. "I have money and jewels in my cabin. You can have all of them. When we reach England, my father will also reward you for saving my life," she promised sincerely.

Spencer laughed and shook his head. "Still feigning the innocent lass, love? Don't you think that a wee bit absurd considering our previous relationship?" he cruelly hinted, vexed by the powerful pull of this girl.

"I haven't been innocent since you brutally ravished me, Captain Steele! But neither have I been wanton since that despicable day. Do not judge me by your standards!"

He pushed a straying lock of hair from her flushed face. She pulled back from his disturbing touch. "You are surely heartless, Steele. How I wish I had never known you," she declared softly, but her gaze told a much different story.

"And I, you, Angelique; for you have plagued my mind day and night since our meeting," he huskily confessed before leaning over to imprison her mouth with his.

Alex's head was spinning wildly as his mouth seared hers time and time again. Capturing her head between his hands, he explored the inviting recess of her mouth and sampled the sweet hunger within her. All thoughts and worries cast aside, she eagerly responded to this moment which had filled her dreams for weeks. As his lips moved over her cheeks to allow his teeth to nibble at her ear, she moaned softly and whispered his name. His lips possessively claimed hers once more, burning away all reality but him.

How she yearned to slip her arms around him and to nestle against that hard chest! Such raging fires and urgent needs consumed her. She could not resist the stirrings of passion which he so easily brought to life after their separation. When Spencer leaned back to gaze down at her with his igneous blue eyes, she weakly gazed back at him with eyes of sparkling green fire.

"You are surely a dangerous enchantress, Angelique, for you tempt a man to dare much to possess you," he huskily murmured.

"Then possess me, Stephen," she carelessly and wantonly entreated. "For you have haunted me each hour since that day at the pond. Be you devil or man, God, how I want you," she confessed in a fiery moment of total weakness and overpowering desire.

Reading those flames of passion which matched his own, Spencer filled with panic. This wasn't the time or place to test her honesty, but he damn well would later! To cool both their fires, he asked, "Didn't you just vow to kill me if I touched you again? Methinks your words don't match your fiery blood, Angelique. I'm not a Captain Thackery to be toyed with and then rejected. If you come with me, my reward will be your warmth in my bunk."

She gaped at him in utter disbelief. How could he speak so at a time like this? "Damn you, Stephen; I hate you! Compared to you, Thackery is an angel! Complete your business and be gone. You interrupted a most enticing adventure."

Spencer studied her for a time, keenly aware she was deceiving him. "If that is how you hate a man, love, perhaps your love would be so all-consuming as to burn a man to cinders. I shall give this matter some further thought before deciding your fate," he calmly announced, smugly telling her it was definitely in his hands.

He pulled a strip of cloth from the hem of her dress and gagged her. "Just to make sure you don't get any idea of telling lover boy who I am," he sneered, as if she could! He called his man to bring Thackery back inside.

The infuriated man's gaze went straight to Alex. He wondered at the gag upon her mouth and the stormy look in her eyes, eyes which never left that arrogant pirate!

Mortified, Alex witnessed Joshua Steele assert his will over Thackery. When the rebellious Thackery refused Steele's demands, she watched in horror as

Steele actually proceeded to castrate the terrified man before her very eyes. Just before Thackery yielded, she fainted.

Spencer glanced over at her and noted the limpness of her body. When Pete rushed over to check on her, Spencer eyed him curiously and resolved to question him later about this mysterious girl. Right now, he and Thackery had some unfinished business . . .

IX

"Alas, how love can
trifle with itself!"
—*Two Gentlemen of Verona*, William Shakespeare

A curious weightlessness surrounded Alex as she slowly returned to reality. She discovered herself lying upon a plush bed in a strange cabin, a cabin which reeked of strength and masculine charm. She sat up and glanced around. She looked at her injured wrists which were now bandaged. Her eyes widened in shock as she noted her manner of attire: one of her own nightgowns, one whose material just barely concealed her body!

Where was she? How had she come to be in this unfamiliar place? How long had she been unconscious? Who was the kind benefactor who had simultaneously rescued her from Steele and Thackery? Had the pirates been defeated while she was unconscious? Had she been taken aboard an English ship and cared for by some generous English captain?

Befuddled, she sat up and walked around, testing her strength and studying her new situation. Without a doubt, this was the cabin of a very wealthy and well-bred man. But who was he? She opened the tall chest and scanned the costly garments hanging there. Her

keen senses quickly told her he was a gentleman of
good taste and high quality. But where were her own
clothes? She glanced down at her provocative gown in
dismay. Hopefully her attire proved her baggage had
been saved; but where had it been placed? Surely these
bandages indicated a doctor had tended her . . .

Alex aimlessly strolled around the neat and
comfortable cabin, trying to envision its proud and
brave owner. She lifted a book and read the inscription
on the first page:

To my beloved son,
Forever remember your name and heritage.
Wear them with honor and pride. These things
your father and I give to you our only child with
great love and confidence.

M.S.F., December 10, 1796

Alex curiously noted the beautiful sprawling script
dedicated to "S.S.F." Alex calmly walked to the
porthole and gazed out. Without clothing, she
couldn't very well leave this cozy cabin. She must
remain here until the captain came to describe her
rescue. What greater honor could any English captain
earn than to defeat the notorious scourge of the sea?

Undesirable sadness filled her, then unreasonable
fear. What had happened to Stephen? Had he been
captured, injured, or killed? How could she brazenly
inquire about the fate or condition of an infamous

pirate without revealing a personal interest? But surely it would seem like normal curiosity to ask about the fate of an illustrious rogue who was England's bitter enemy! She chided herself for even worrying about him. He could take care of himself! Perhaps he had fled at the first sighting of an English ship. She angrily hoped that dastardly Thackery had gotten his just desserts. If not, she would see to it upon her arrival home!

Stephen was Joshua Steele? Who was this mysterious, mercurial man who slipped in and out of her life at will? Stephen . . . Steele . . . S.S.! No! It couldn't be! She rushed to the desk and pulled out the book once more to study it. Could it be possible? S.S. Stephen Steele? But what about the "F"? Had her first impressions by the pond been accurate? Was he some highborn nobleman who had turned to piracy and privateering after some family misfortune? She shook her spinning head to clear it of such foolish and intimidating ideas. Surely some silly coincidence . . .

Alex replaced the book and returned to the porthole for some much needed fresh air. The door opened behind her. She almost reluctantly turned to see who had boldly entered without knocking. She closed her eyes and stiffened in panic as he swaggered forward in vivid self-assurance.

"I see you've finally decided to rejoin us," he murmured in a vital and stirring tone, stopping before her and assuming a masterful and commanding stance. "Needless to say, you had me quite worried, Angelique. You've been unconscious for several hours," he commented in a disturbingly gentle tone.

Alexandria opened her eyes and gazed up into his arresting features. "I see you no longer have need of your disguise, Captain Steele," she acidly remarked.

"Nor you, yours," he promptly retorted. "Your little adventure doesn't seem to have tamed that wild spirit of yours in the least," he playfully teased, tugging upon a lock of spun gold.

"I had the mistaken impression you had been sent scurrying and I had been rescued by an English ship," she informed him. "This isn't exactly how I imagined a pirate's style," she caustically sneered, pointing to their slightly elegant surroundings.

"Evidently I'm the only pirate you've met so far, or perhaps the only one to enjoy your company in his cabin," he lazily remarked, grinning mischievously.

"Under the circumstances, your cruel teasing is misplaced, Captain Steele. Who are you, Stephen?" she suddenly asked.

He eyed her strangely, then asked, "What do you mean?"

"Well, you're obviously not Stephen whatever. And I seriously doubt Captain Joshua Steele is your real name either. No man would intentionally blacken his family name. Who are you, and why did you become a pirate?" she inquired in an entreating tone. She decided not to tell him about reading his book and certainly not to ask him what the "F" stood for!

"Stephen is my real name," he casually replied, to her great surprise. "But my last name must remain a secret. I'm sure you understand why. Family honor and personal safety . . . I took the name Steele when an enemy once told me I was as cold and hard as that deadly metal. It seems a befitting name, so I use it. As for Joshua, it belonged to a good friend long ago." He shuddered and glanced down at her. "Call me whatever you prefer for the short time you're here," he stated. "As for you, I still lack your last name, Angelique."

She met his probing gaze and stated bravely, "The day you give me your last name, I'll give you mine. Until then, let's leave it with Stephen and Angelique. When do we reach the first port?"

He chuckled. To demand an answer might reveal too much interest in her, so he didn't. "Content yourself to remain the coy and mysterious siren, love. Your name or identity hold little interest for me. Perhaps you've some reason to be ashamed of it," he hinted.

"You're wrong, Steele. I merely see no reason for you to know it or where to find me again," she retorted in rising annoyance at his nonchalance.

"You flatter yourself, Angelique. I seek out no woman to warm my bed or heart," he vowed with a fierce coldness which was frightening.

"You possess no heart or soul, Steele! As to any future pursuit of me, I have no illusions about you in that area. But the mere fact you selfishly seduced me long ago and then took the trouble to rescue me speaks for itself," she sweetly asserted to vex him. "For a man who doesn't seek out any female, you certainly come in and out of my life at the oddest moments . . ." She smiled provocatively, her eyes merrily taunting him.

"If memory serves me correctly, Angelique, it is you who recklessly and brazenly invades my life when I least expect it. You were the one lying naked and inviting by the pond. You were the one being held prisoner by Thackery. And, I might add, wearing a most enticing dress and with liquor on her breath. Tell me truthfully; did I interrupt a private party?"

Her eyes widened. She stammered, "I was not waiting by that pond for some roué like Joshua Steele to happen by to ravish me! As to my attire and breath in that scoundrel's cabin, he forced me from my cabin to his. I only sipped the sherry to calm my nerves when he began acting so . . . so unpredictable and frightening! I am not a harlot! You of all men should know that since you were the first to . . ." She flushed scarlet and hushed.

"Since I so wickedly claimed your purity," he triumphantly finished for her.

He tenderly caressed her rosy cheek. "Dear, sweet Angelique, you do possess a rare talent for rashly wandering into the most unusual and perilous situations. Don't worry this time; you'll be home safely before you know it," he encouraged the distraught girl who was close to tears.

"No, you don't understand, Stephen. How could you possibly know what heart-stopping fear and utter helplessness are like? I seriously doubt you've ever experienced either! I hate being a defenseless vulnerable woman," she childishly stomped her foot. "If I were a man, I would have killed Thackery!"

Spencer laughed softly this time. "If you were a

man, love, Thackery wouldn't be interested in you," he tenderly murmured, his gaze appreciative and serene.

She automatically smiled at that statement. "I suppose you're right," she admitted absently. His manly aura and compelling smile enchanted her. How many times had she dreamed of meeting him again? But never under these dangerous, stimulating, and suspenseful circumstances!

Her radiant smile and alluring eyes tugged at him. Her state of dress—or undress—didn't help matters either! She was so bewitching, so close, so . . . He cautioned himself against her magical charms. But even as he raised his guard, he played with a lock of tawny hair which wound itself around his finger. "What happened to Thackery?" she unexpectedly asked, calling him back to reality.

"I put his crew in lifeboats and sunk his ship," he casually announced.

"You what?" she blurted out. "But I thought you never sank ships!" she argued.

"Only those who challenge me. I have a reputation to uphold," he asserted. At her stunned look, he went on, "It helps to have a colorful reputation, love. They know I'm a man of my word. No fight; no trouble," he remarked smugly.

"You actually depend upon your infamous name to win battles for you?"

"It usually does. But Thackery was a fool. He was probably afraid I would find you in his cabin and steal you. Which I did," he arrogantly announced. "If he had given quarter, he could have sailed away unscathed."

"But you attacked him! Surely a man's pride would demand he protect his ship and men?" she argued in bewilderment.

"To give quarter is wiser, love. That way, he could save himself, his infernal ship, and his crew. I've worked long and hard to be known as a generous victor. Whenever possible, I never shed blood or sink a ship. But if I didn't make examples of those few defiant captains, my word wouldn't be worth a tinker's damn," he snarled.

"But why did you bring me along?" Alex asked. "Aren't you afraid I might give away your real identity?"

"Being the gentleman I am, I couldn't very well leave you in the evil clutches of Thackery, could I? As to revealing my identity, you can't because you really don't know me. Plus, it wouldn't be to your advantage to do so. Like me, you also have a reputation to protect," he humorously enlightened her. "I doubt you wish history to record you as Joshua Steele's mistress."

"You're very sure of yourself, aren't you? Still, it might be fun to sail with the infamous Joshua Steele for a few weeks. Perhaps I'll discover if your vile fame is well-deserved. Whatever will my grandchildren say when they hear about this one day?" she mused in humor.

The subtle hint of wedlock nagged him. "Have you married since I saw you last?" he asked from nowhere.

"Heavens, no!" she shrieked, insulted. "At least not yet," she worriedly added, sighing in dismay.

"I take it you're planning to be married soon," he implied, intrigued and nettled by images of her future.

"If Papa has his way when I get home, yes! But not if I can stop him," she angrily vowed, hardly aware of their curious conversation.

"Does he know about me?" he abruptly asked.

"About you?" she echoed naively, their gazes fusing.

"I should say about us and that day at the pond?" he clarified.

"You think me daft! He'd never had allowed me to leave home for one hour! As for you . . . he would have searched heaven and earth to hang you! I haven't told a single soul about that day!" she declared.

"Why not?" he calmly demanded.

"Tell them what, praytell? A stranger took advantage of me while I was . . . indisposed? Who would believe such a wild story? I would sound like a fool, a dunderhead who was guilty of some . . . whatever!" she said peevishly.

"Captain Joshua Steele and a water nymph frolicking by a tranquil pond . . . Yes, it would sound like some fairytale," he playfully agreed.

"I'm not a water nymph, Captain Steele. Besides, we were merely at the same place at the wrong time. Evidently neither of us expected anyone else at the pond that afternoon. Why did you seduce me that day? You hardly seem the heartless, bloody scoundrel your reputation paints you to be," she complimented him, hoping she could manipulate him into quickly releasing her.

He took her face between his hands and murmured tenderly, "How could I resist such beauty? Never have I looked into a face of such perfection and enchantment or eyes with such a powerful enticement. Every time I remembered you, I was amazed by my good fortune and how you had remained untouched for so long. Surely you have trampled upon countless hearts, my lovely Angeliq̄ue. How could such loveliness be so cruel and cold?"

Entranced, she replied dreamily, "I have danced upon no more hearts than you have, Stephen. I was so afraid I had hurt you badly. Every night I prayed for your survival. I'm so glad you're all right, but I was too cowardly to return to the pond to discover the truth. I have never known a man such as you. If Papa would bring home a suitor like you, I would happily have yielded to his demands that very day," she unknowingly confessed, mesmerized by him and his closeness.

"Then yield to me now, Angel. I'm here and I want you beyond all reason," he huskily coaxed the wavering girl who had lost the knowledge of where she was or why.

His mouth came down on hers, hungrily and pervasively. His arms went around her slender, shapely body and drew her tightly against him—and Alex had no choice but to return the intoxicating kiss. Her arms slipped around his waist and up his strong back. Clinging desperately to him, she helplessly surrendered her will to him and to those longings which had haunted her since their first meeting.

Her gown slid to the floor, as did his shirt and pants. She was gently and mindlessly placed upon his bed. He whispered stirring endearments into her ears and deftly explored the body and face which had plagued all his hours. For all he knew or cared, his ship could be attacked and he couldn't answer the alarm.

When he placed moist kisses upon her swollen breasts, Alex moaned in need of him and fulfillment. Every place he touched burned with a consuming wildfire. Her womanhood ached to feel him within her, to ease the anguish of long-denied cravings. Still, he teased and tantilized her until she feverishly sought their union. Love me, Stephen, she thought. Love me with fury! He entered her, savoring each tormenting moment of intense control. He moved slowly and provocatively as her body instinctively and helplessly matched his fluid movements.

"Never will another man possess what is mine alone, love," he hoarsely spoke into her ear as his teeth teased at it, his warm breath bringing tremors to her molten body.

"You're mine, Stephen, mine," she responded passionately, pulling him closer to her.

The flames of desire increased until Spencer could no longer deny himself total possession of this bewitching goddess beneath him. His rhythm increased as his mouth almost savagely took hers. The summit reached, they clung together and rode the wild and wonderful waves of sheer ecstasy into a calm sea of blissful aftermath. He gradually relaxed upon her as he awaited the return of his normal breathing. He rolled to her side, pulling her along with him. She snuggled into the protective and inviting embrace of her lover, sighing peacefully.

Some time later, Alex turned her head and looked over at him, her eyes revealing an emotion he dreaded to read. He smiled impassively. "I told you my company would be far more pleasant than Thackery's," he cruelly remarked, harassed by these unwanted feelings which pulled at him. He was determined to prove to both of them this was simply a mutual experience of passion.

"What?" she foolishly asked, not comprehending his meaning or change in mood.

He grinned. "Yep, this promises to be a most rewarding voyage. I hope the nearest port is weeks away. I think saving your life is surely worth that much of your time and efforts."

She stared at him as dread washed over her tense body. What was he saying? "I don't understand, Stephen . . ."

"What's to understand, Angel? I told you the price of your rescue before we left Thackery's ship. Surely you didn't think I was jesting. After all, you did just comply . . . most eagerly and willingly."

"You think this was only a . . ." She didn't continue as she viewed his mocking expression. Was she the most gullible, naive woman alive? Had she honestly thought this fiery union meant more than wanton lust? She should have resisted him and her own carnal emotions. "What a cunning thief you are, Captain Steele! A deceitful seduction is no less than a gentle ravishment."

"I didn't ravish you or trick you, love. You wanted me as much as I wanted you. You can lie to yourself, but not to me."

Mortified, betrayed, and angered, a stricken gaze met his. "If I were as versed and practiced in the arts of seduction as you are, Captain Steele, I would have possessed the knowledge to reject you. I'll kill you if you ever come near me again. I despise you!"

"To kill me would be most unwise, little one. For then you'd find yourself at the mercy of my entire crew. I daresay to vengefully exchange me and my safe quarters for my spiteful crew and the deck of my ship would be absurd."

"I see. A choice? Whore for you to earn my freedom or endure the wrath of your men . . ." A strange, faraway, unreadable look tinged with anguish and bitterness filled her expression and eyes.

"Admit it, love, you did find pleasure with me. Until I free you, wouldn't it be better to enjoy me rather than fight my crew? Besides, I wouldn't like having to tie you to my bedposts each night to protect my life."

She blanched so white at his empty threat that he feared she would faint. He ignored this strange reaction, but wisely noted it. "Agreed?" he pressed. "No violence or rash behavior?"

Without meeting his discerning gaze, she whispered, "Agreed."

"Where are the rest of my clothes?" she abruptly

asked in a noticeably strained voice, anguish knifing her heart.

"Stored below, but you won't be needing more than this to meet our bargain," he replied lazily, trailing his fingers over her bare skin.

Incensed, she snapped, "I don't intend to walk around naked for two or three weeks, Captain Steele!"

"I don't intend for you to walk around at all, love. I much prefer you right where you are." He chuckled in amusement as she flushed.

Her heart surely breaking at this cruel deceit, she retorted, "Even a prisoner deserves fresh air and exercise! I can't very well stroll around like this!"

"When and if you have need of other garments, rest assured I will provide them at that time. This way, you won't be tempted to escape or run around my ship enticing my men to mutiny. I personally know how irresistible you can be. A sailor can get mighty bold and reckless when he's been without a woman for a long spell, especially if a dream like you walked before his eyes."

"You filthy scum! How dare you treat me like some cheap slattern! You're a conniving, deceitful rogue, Steele! You planned to trick me all along! Oh-h-h-h . . ." she stormed at him as she beat upon his chest.

He easily captured her hands and pinned them above her silky head. "Cheap, you're not; slattern, not yet. But if you ever doublecross me, love, you'll wind up in the filthiest brothel I can locate." He gritted out his warning to frighten her into complete obedience of his commands. There would be times when her instant compliance could mean life or death for more than her! He wasn't about to confess he had actually lost his head moments ago! Never would this ravishing creature learn of her power over him! He was a man who loved and guarded the freedom this girl threatened.

Alex glared into his stormy eyes. He had tricked her once more. Who was this quicksilver man who blew hot and cold, waxed tender and cruel? She winced at the ruthless aura which he emanated. What a blind and romantic fool she was! "No matter what you think, Steele, I did not willingly go to Thackery's cabin. I will not be treated like some street harlot!"

Spencer had gotten up and was pulling on his clothes. As his shirt slipped over his head, his gaze flickered over at her. "If such were true, Angel, you wouldn't be here now. Common whores have never intrigued or pleasured me, and they never will. If the most beautiful woman alive walked in that door this minute but was a whore, I wouldn't look at her twice." As he reached the door, he turned and roguishly added, "But that would be impossible since the most exquisite creature alive is in my bed this very minute." With that statement, he left.

Not knowing what else to do, Alex lay there in deep and troubled thought. There was no way to escape the ship just now, nor was there any way to prevent Joshua Steele from taking his pleasure with her. He was a dangerous and unpredictable man. The wisest and safest course of action would be to bide her time and control her temper until these circumstances changed or she could make another assessment of this mysterious and moody man who was holding her prisoner. It would be rash to challenge a man who arrogantly accepted any dare.

She got up and bathed off with the water in the basin near his bedside. She hastily pulled on the gown which offered very little privacy from his piercing eyes or protection from his roaming hands. The mussed bed seemed to accuse her of wanton conduct, and she hurriedly straightened the covers. She nervously paced the confines of his cabin for what seemed like hours.

The longer she endured this tension and silence, the greater her apprehension and fears became. Thoughts of her father, her uncle, her predicament, and the impending war tormented her distraught mind and aching heart. How could she rebel against a man with Stephen's strength and magnetism, a man who now held her destiny in his hands? One false or foolish move and she could face a worse fate than Captain Joshua Steele.

Had he been toying with her and teasing her? Did he really think her beautiful and irresistible? He was undoubtedly a man who took what he wanted! When she was obedient or responsive, he was tender and gentle. But the instant a hint of defiance or rejection surfaced, he was cruel and hateful. Did she dare to play him the fool with sweetness and charm? Fool a man who had known countless women, women of great experience? No . . .

Feeling helpless and defeated, Alex dropped wearily into a chair at the table. Folding her arms and placing them upon the wooden surface, she rested her head upon them and wept. So entrapped in her world of despair and worry, she did not hear the door open or feel the intense stare of Spencer upon her.

Spencer studied the silvery gold head which was lowered in dejection and fear. Pangs of guilt and tenderness pulled at his wayward heart and chewed at his warring mind. Perhaps her bravery and defiance were only an act to cover her shame and anguish. In spite of her carefree behavior, she had been an innocent that first time. If she were a coy tease, she was certainly apt at it. If only she didn't appear so natural . . .

He soundlessly came forward to stand beside her. He reached out his hand to stroke her silky mane. She jumped at his contact and jerked her head upwards to look at him. Thick, dark lashes were wet with freshly shed tears which still slipped down her pale face with its rosy cheeks. At being caught in such a private moment, a scarlet flush suffused her face and neck. She hastily lowered her lids to conceal the naked emotions exposed there and silently berated her weaknesses.

"Are you all right, Angel?" he softly inquired, distressing her further with his mellow tone and mood. "Don't be sad or afraid," he encouraged her.

"I'm not!" she snapped at him, shoving his hand away. "I'm just mad. I was minding my own business that day you attacked me by the pond. You had no right to take advantage of me while I was sleeping. You're just like Thackery! He'll pay for kidnapping me and trying to rape me! You will too! You're all cruel and shameless. You should never have touched me either time. I should be home with my family planning my wedding. What will my father and husband say when they learn the truth? Damn you, Stephen; you've ruined my whole life," she miserably accused. There was no future for them; and yet, he was in her blood like some all-consuming disease which tormented her day and night. "And stop calling me Angel!" she spat.

"You have no cause to worry, Angelique. Any husband you select will be lucky to get you in any condition," he scoffed in irrational fury, desperately wanting her for himself.

"How would you feel if you suddenly discovered your new bride wasn't a virgin?" she heatedly challenged. "You'd probably choke the truth from her and then kill them both," she blurted. "It's bad enough to have your father arrange a marriage with some offensive stranger, but worse to have him despise you for something beyond your control! Because of you, I'll be miserable for the rest of my life! And how will I explain my strange and tardy arrival home? I can hear the laughter and gossip now. My God, Stephen, I'll never live this down," she wailed in a forlorn tone, more unbidden tears dropping from her emerald eyes.

He stared at her as hysterical laughter seized her. "Maybe you've done me a favor. Once the truth about us is out, who would accept my father's offer of my sullied hand? But surely there are better ways to avoid coerced wedlock! Do you plan to drop me off somewhere or turn me over to some other ship captain along the way?" she sarcastically sneered.

Astutely reading her pain and doubts, he stated, "I said I would take you home, all the way to your front door. With your run of luck, you'd probably meet disaster between my ship and your home," he teased to lighten her dismal spirits.

Terrified at that news, she shrieked, "No! You can't!"

Her curious reaction stunned him. Who was she afraid of and what? "I could help ease your father's worries by explaining how your ship was attacked by wicked pirates and how I rescued you and gallantly saw you safely home," he devilishly hinted to entice more information from her.

Green eyes wide with panic, her face drained of all color. "Are you this afraid of your father, Angelique? Or do you simply wish to keep your identity and home a secret from me?"

"Naturally I don't want you to know where I live. Can you blame me considering what happens between us every time we meet?"

He smiled. "Can you honestly swear you didn't want me as much as I wanted you, either time?"

She could feel her face grow warm. She stammered in shame and guilt, "That . . . isn't what . . . I meant. Don't you see, Stephen? This . . . thing between us is wrong, dangerous. We don't even know each other, and we'll never meet again. I mean nothing to you," she concluded painfully, her turbulent emotions revealed in her voice and eyes.

He pulled her to her feet and into his comforting embrace. "Sometimes I wish that weren't true, Angel," he hoarsely admitted as his grip tightened and he rested his cheek against her fragrant hair. "You were right about meeting at the wrong time. A few years past or a few years from now, who knows?" he murmured, briefly sharing her anguish and need for solace.

Such intense hunger filled her. Her arms slipped around his narrow waist as she clung tightly to his strong body. Her face lay against his powerful chest. "How can I refuse my father's demands, Stephen? Yet, how can I marry another man when I want you so much? I wish I had never met you," she cried out in an undeniable yearning for him.

"Then don't go home, Angel. Stay here with me," he huskily whispered.

She leaned back and looked up at him. "But what would people say? You're a pirate, Stephen; they hunt you day and night."

"No one would see you, love. I'll protect you for as long as you wish to sail with me."

"Sail with you? But don't you have a home somewhere, another identity? If you use that mask all the time, only your crew knows who you are. When the war starts, it'll be dangerous on the sea," she reminded him.

He tensed and released her. He turned away to think

clearly. "This is my home and Steele is my identity now. You can stay as long as you wish, then I'll take you wherever you wish to go," he offered, sounding selfish and unfeeling.

A flurry of thoughts raced through Alex's mind. "You mean stay with you for only a time, then return home? Become your mistress? Is that it?"

Her tone of voice alerted him to her obvious misconception. "What did you think I meant?" he asked a little too coldly.

"I . . . wasn't sure," she hesitantly answered. "What does a prisoner and hostage expect of her kidnapper? I wouldn't put it past you to hold me hostage for ransom. Become your mistress? Never!"

"Hold you for ransom? That isn't my style, love. However, the idea does sound intriguing. As to complying with my wishes, you really haven't much choice in the matter."

Alex backed away from him until her back made contact with the bedpost, preventing a further retreat. "You wouldn't dare force me to sail as your mistress! With all your previous crimes added to that one, you would hang for certain!"

Spencer's manly presence seemed to fill the entire room. "Who said I would resort to compulsion? Your will has been mine since the moment of our first meeting. There's no way you can remain at my side and resist me. Besides your attraction to me, you lacked the skills to resist me. I want you; therefore, I'll have you. So don't play the coquettish maiden with me. I've read the sweet invitation in your eyes. Admit it," he softly demanded.

"Why should I want to become any man's harlot, especially yours?" she angrily inquired. "Your carefree days are numbered, Captain Steele."

"I would never consider you that, Angelique. We could enjoy each other for a long time. You could be free of your father's demands to marry some 'offensive stranger,'" he boldly alluded.

"At what price, Captain Steele? I think you've tarnished me enough without flaunting me in every port as your mistress! A man like you shouldn't have any trouble supplying himself with a cabin full of willing females! No doubt you have one or more waiting for you in every port! But of course you must keep your identity a secret. Such are the costs of being bold and famous," she taunted him.

His chilling look giving her a warning, she smiled sadly and promised, "You needn't worry about my wagging tongue. As far as it goes, you and I have never met. You didn't say; when and where will you release me?"

"In England in two weeks," he tersely replied. "If you wish me to escort you home, fine; if not, be careful of hungry rogues," he teased arrogantly.

"I can promise you I'll be very cautious from now on." To win his trust and to disarm him, she softly added with a smile, "If you saw me home, my father would never believe your chivalrous intentions. One look at you and he would suspect the truth. He would flog me and kill you. Besides, it could be dangerous for him to come into contact with Captain Joshua Steele.

Your secret identity might not remain a secret forever. I love my father and I wouldn't want to endanger his life because of my mistakes . . . or misfortunes as you call them. This time, could we part as secret friends and forever?" she entreated, her green eyes dancing with mischief and allure.

"You constantly amaze me, Angelique," he stated with a chuckle. "As you wish, my fair-haired maiden. If we do meet again someday, I promise not to enlighten your husband to your adventurous past," he mirthfully jested.

"Nor will I betray you to the hangman, my love," she parried.

"Two weeks of blissful freedom left. If I were you, I would thoroughly enjoy them," he suggested wickedly, smoldering eyes enticing her to think wanton thoughts.

"If it's possible, Captain Steele, I would prefer separate quarters and some privacy. I wouldn't want you to become a nasty habit."

"If I'm to only have you for two weeks, then I demand every available moment of your time and attention."

"Under the right conditions, you could have me for keeps," she brazenly offered to test his strength of purpose.

Flames danced in his eyes and his body tensed in anticipation. "Is marriage that condition?" he fearlessly took her bait.

"Naturally. I would have you and a freedom of sorts. You would have my silence and anything else you desired from me. No matter what you said earlier, I know you have another name and a home somewhere. To avoid suspicion, maybe you also have an urgent need for a wife . . . Such a bargain could be profitable for both of us," she speculated aloud.

"Why would you want to marry a man like Joshua Steele?"

"I don't, but I might find marriage to Stephen most compelling and exciting," she murmured in a sexy tone. "Besides, marriage to me would offer Steele a respectable image to hide behind."

"Stephen doesn't exist anymore," he bitterly informed her.

She stepped before him and caressed his taut jawline. "He does when you allow him to come alive. You were Stephen by the pond; you were Stephen earlier when you made love to me. Why do you suppress him and punish him, Joshua?" she asked seriously.

Her touch tantilizing, he captured her hand and imprisoned it within his. He couldn't explain Steele's cover. This strange girl was too unsettling and too perceptive to suit him. He had to get rid of her before she learned too much for his own good! She was much too tempting and dangerous to keep around longer than necessary to see her safely to port! He was unnerved by the way she was looking at him and the way she was talking with him. She was wavering on the edge of falling in love with him, and he couldn't permit that. A scorned woman was even more trouble! She had altered her charge of seduction to lovemaking.

Was she actually trying to disarm and seduce him now? He would prove to her he wasn't a man to fall in love with . . .

"If you had a choice between being a poor Stephen or a living legend as Joshua Steele who could have or take anything you desired, which would you choose? Would you be willing to settle for only one woman when you could have a new diversion every day? What makes your sole ownership so valuable?"

Alex flinched as if he had physically struck her. "What makes you think Joshua Steele is worth any price to possess?" she shouted back at him.

"If my ears didn't deceive me, you just offered yourself to me for any purpose I desired," he brutally taunted her.

"You're vastly mistaken, Captain Steele. I offered you a bargain: my freedom and marriage to you in exchange for my . . . silence and services," she clarified. "I wouldn't want you or need you under any other circumstances."

"Then why did you so eagerly and willingly submit to me?" he charged.

"You simply caught me at a moment of distress and weakness. After all, you are the more skilled and experienced of the two of us. I was distraught and afraid. You do have a way of appearing when a female is vulnerable and defenseless."

"Then you don't find me irresistible?" he devilishly mocked her.

Knowing he would detect her deceit, she smiled and shook her head. "As Stephen, I find you utterly overpowering and attractive. Sadly, you're Steele most of the time. I have no wish to become entrapped by Steele, but Stephen is entirely a different matter," she craftily eluded his trap.

"Neither man is interested in marriage, love. But we can make the best of our time together."

"Considering you claim to be the world's best lover, you could spoil me for my husband. Surely you wouldn't be so cruel as to leave me pining after you?" she continued her joke, alertly noting the way he stiffened each time at the mention of her impending marriage to another man.

"We could always see each other if I'm ever around," he suggested with a beguiling grin.

She lapsed into deep thought. She suddenly laughed and replied, "If Papa weds me to some feeble man, perhaps your generous offer might have some appeal after all. Then again, he might be virile and handsome; he could put even Joshua Steele to shame—in bed and out."

A tic quivered in his jawline. His eyes chilled and narrowed as she kept referring to her future husband. "Perhaps I might find you too irresistible to release in two weeks. You just might miss that delightful chance at marriage," he growled in displeasure and anger.

Alex laughed in rising spirits. "I doubt I could become unforgettable in two short weeks, Joshua. I'll admit I'm attractive and desirable, but utterly magnetic . . ." She sighed dramatically and went on, "Don't tempt me to foolishly and futilely try to win your heart. To tell the truth, I wish I had the courage to stay with you for a time."

She walked over to the porthole and gazed out across the blue water. "I share your love for adventure and freedom. To sail the ocean with the breeze caressing your face, to visit strange lands, to face danger and excitement every day, to do whatever your heart desires, to have no cares or responsibilities, to be free and happy . . . sailing with the winds and tides . . . You're a lucky man, Joshua. You have the courage to be your own man. If I weren't a female, I'd sign on with you today."

"Why don't you?" he asked.

Tears eased down her cheeks. "Because I wouldn't be a sailor or a pirate. I would be the same thing here as I will be at home: at some man's beck and call for only one reason: his pleasures and needs."

Spencer found himself arguing, "That isn't true, Angel. You could do anything on my ship that's not too dangerous. You can learn to climb the rigs, sail the ship, handle cargo, scrub decks, repair the sails . . . You can even become my cabin boy. But I wouldn't let you board other ships," he jested mischievously.

"Don't make fun of me! You'd never allow me enough time out of your bunk to do any of those things! You'd be afraid I'd mess things up or the crew would laugh at you. The only place I would sail is in your bunk!"

Lusty laughter filled the quiet cabin. "I would train you personally if you decided to stay with me. You can dress like a sailor and get your skin all golden by the sun and hide that golden head beneath a cap. No one would recognize you. You could do all those things and see all those places if you stay," he coaxed.

"You would really let me visit in the ports?" she asked.

"Sure. But only when I say it's safe," he added cautiously.

"What about your crew?" she debated.

"My crew is loyal; they obey my orders. Do you want to stay?"

"I don't know. It sounds crazy. My father would . . ." Her eyes widened in alarm as she shrieked just before the signal was given, "A ship, Stephen! Look!" she cried out, pointing out across the expanse of blue.

He pushed her aside and gazed out the porthole. The lookout then shouted, "Ship to portside!" A loud knock came upon the door. A man's voice called out, "Captain Steele, ship sighted. No flag, sir."

"I'll be there shortly. Alert the crew." He quickly changed into his pirate's clothes and tucked the black mask into his waistband. As if suddenly recalling her presence, he turned to face Alex. She was shaking in dread and watching his every move with wide eyes.

"Will they attack?" she apprehensively questioned. "Is it English?"

"I don't know yet, Angel. Stay here until I come back," he commanded, his mind clearly on deck.

"Should you tie me up in case they defeat you?" she asked for some unknown reason, never once imagining such a deed.

He turned at the doorway to stare at her. "What?"

he stormed in disbelief and fury. "No ship will ever defeat the *Black Mist!*" With that explosion of temper, he left, slamming the door after his departure.

Alex fumed in fear and anger. Was it always like this at sea? Did peril loom on any wave? Stephen led a very precarious existence; he could be killed, injured, or captured at any moment. She couldn't remain with him any longer than she had to, regardless of her feelings.

She screamed and covered her ears as a crash split the air. Almost immediately another cannon fired upon Stephen's ship, coming close enough to send water splashing upon her highly polished decks. Boots clattered upon the decks above her; loud voices could be heard issuing or passing orders. The *Black Mist* shuddered under the stress of firing her own guns. Alex suddenly realized the ominous sounds of battle were besieging them from both sides; more than one ship was attacking them!

In terror, Alex slipped to the floor against the wall and curled into a tight ball. She closed her eyes and prayed for survival. Could this ship be defeated? Should she worry about her safety?

The door flew open and some clothes were carelessly tossed inside so quickly that she failed to see who had done this deed. She gaped at the pile of clothes on the floor, then at the closed door. She summoned her courage to retrieve them and put them on. She wondered why Stephen was allowing her this measure of generosity unless he feared . . . Had he relented because . . .

No! Her hands shook violently as she struggled into the petticoat and dress. Suddenly the door opened again and in walked a strange man. She began to retreat in panic, eyes wide and throat dry. He halted long enough to say, "Captain Steele told me to assist you and bind you."

"Why?" she fearfully inquired, noting the way he was studying her with surprise and interest.

"Just in case of trouble," he calmly informed her. "If the ship is overrun, tell them the truth about what happened on Thackery's ship. But tell them Steele kidnapped you and was going to ransom you. Understand?"

As he buttoned the back of her dress, she asked, "Are things that bad?"

"We're under attack by two frigates. But we've seen worse fights," Andy cockily stated. "Do as I said and you've no worries. They're English," he enlightened her. He pulled her over to the bunk and bound her hands tightly after removing her bandages. He grinned sheepishly as he tore her dress and mussed her hair. "Captain's orders, ma'am."

"What will they do to Captain Steele if they capture this ship?"

"I think you already know the answer," he murmured, respect and admiration glowing in his eyes for his captain. "But Josh hasn't lost a battle yet," he confidently stated. "I can see why he's been spending his time in here since we took the *Sea Star*," he playfully teased her. "You're the girl he met in England, aren't you?" he could not help but ask.

"Yes, why?" she curiously inquired, wondering why Stephen had told this man about that fateful day. "Who are you?"

"Andy. Josh is my best friend," he replied to her unspoken question. "I've got to get back on deck. Just remember what I told you." With that, he was gone.

She stared after him in mounting confusion. Stephen had actually talked about her with this man? If she truly held such little interest for him, why? The noise of the battle banished those musings from her mind. The ship lurched to and fro as the siege continued. When it seemed Alex could bear the suspense no longer, a deathly silence filled the air. All movement ceased; the crew's voices were so low she couldn't make out their words. She tensely waited . . .

X

"To unmask falsehood, and bring truth to light."
—"Rape of Lucrece," William Shakespeare

"To do a great right, do a little wrong."
—*Merchant of Venice*, William Shakespeare

The petrifying feeling of having lived through this before plagued Alex during the lengthy silence which followed the last shouts and gunfire. When the door finally opened, she dreaded to see who would enter. Relief and joy flooded her as Stephen and his best friend strolled in as calmly as if just coming from lunch! Nerves tingling, she waited for him to release her.

"Untie her, Andy," the pirate nonchalantly ordered, then glanced her way as he added, "I've agreed to ransom you to that persistent English captain in exchange for letting us sail away. I'm to put you in a small boat as soon as we're out of their range. I told him you were a highborn English lady and he bought it," he stated.

In her state of shock, Alex didn't see the look of astonished amusement which flickered over Andrew Pennington's face at his friend's cruel joke. "There you go, miss," Andy murmured as he completed his

249

task, smiling down at her.

"What if it isn't safe?" she protested, ignoring Andy.

"They're English and so are you. You wanted to go home, so here's your chance," he coldly announced.

"I doubt warships will be heading home so soon! With you at sea, I'm safer here!" she exclaimed.

"You're wrong, my fetching tart," he argued.

Before Spencer or Andy comprehended her intentions, Alex had rushed forward and slapped Spencer across the face. Assuming she was about to throw herself into his arms in relief and gratitude, he was taken by complete surprise. The blow sent a loud popping noise into the silent room just as she screamed at him, "You black-hearted demon! How dare you trade me like some war booty! I won't go!" she defiantly shrieked, stomping her foot, green eyes sparkling in obstinance.

Unable to prevent his instinctive response, he cursed aloud, "You vicious bitch!" and returned the blow with a stunning force which sent Alex staggering backwards to fall upon the bed. Andy inhaled sharply and took several steps forward to come to her aid, but quickly controlled the impulse. He was stunned by the actions of both people. Embarrassed, he hastily dismissed himself and fled the room, ignorant of what to say or do.

As she rubbed her smarting cheek, Alex gaped at Stephen in disbelief and fear. She pushed herself to a sitting position. "Thank you, Captain Steele. This should certainly convince them of my enforced imprisonment," she acidly announced, indicating the flaming cheek. "May I leave now?"

He came forward as if stalking her like some helpless prey. "On my ship, everyone obeys my orders. You will come and go as I say. Do you comprehend, Angelique?" he stormed, angered that she had caused him to strike her.

"I did ask permission, sir," she sneered. "I take it a truce of sorts is also viewed as a victory?" she sarcastically inquired, eyes blazing with fury and hatred.

"I was only teasing you. The battle was won by my cunning and skill. I sent those ships scurrying to doctor their wounds!"

Her eyes widened as his words hit her. "Then why did you send these clothes and have me bound?"

"When I saw how long the battle would take, I was afraid you might get reckless and come on deck. I did it for your protection. I would let them sink me before giving quarter! But the day hasn't come when some measly English frigate can out-maneuver or outwit my ship."

"You hateful bastard! That was mean and spiteful. You said to remain here, and I would have! I'm not an idiot!"

He charged the remaining distance between them and seized her arm, yanking her to her feet. "One more crude word from those pretty lips and I'll wash your mouth out with soap! Be satisfied I spared your life and reputation. But if you ever strike me again, woman . . ." He glared at her, the need to complete his

251

ominous warning unnecessary from the look on her face and the quivering in her body. "If anyone besides Andy had witnessed that rash conduct, I would flog you with the cat-of-nine-tails to make an example of you," he gritted out another warning.

"Just take me home as quickly as possible and our problems will be solved. And save your lousy jokes for someone else!" she retorted.

"One more outburst like that, and you won't ever be going home," he added to wipe the sneer from her rebellious face.

Cautioning herself to patience and a milder manner with this dangerous man, Alex replied, "I couldn't help myself, Stephen. You frightened me. All that time I didn't know what was going on, then you waltzed in here and said you've traded me for your ship and freedom. What did you expect?"

"I expected you to be overjoyed at that news! Not attack me as if I had betrayed you! Damnit, woman, you're the one who said you didn't want to stay with me!" he snarled.

"I can't stay with you! Besides being dangerous, it isn't good for either of us," she argued wretchedly. "How long could I have withstood their badgering questions and demands for your identity?" She abruptly asked, "What day is this?"

He eyed her strangely. "Why?"

"What day is it?" she demanded again.

"June twentieth. Why?" he repeated, witnessing the distressed look on her face.

"How soon before we reach the first English port?"

she questioned, ignoring his demands and curiosity.

"Why is the date so important?" he snarled in rising annoyance. "Afraid you'll miss your joyous wedding?"

"The Americans were going to declare war on June eighteenth. I must get home as promptly as possible. My father doesn't know yet."

"How would you know when Congress was voting for war?" he inquired suspiciously. "Why would your father be interested in that news?"

"I heard some men talking about it. That's why I left America in such a hurry. My father's business will be affected by a new war, so I need to tell him soon," she explained only briefly, serving to further intrigue him.

"What kind of business?" he demanded.

"I can't tell you. How soon can you get me home?" she pressed.

"Right after you answer my questions," he calmly replied.

"I can't. You promised to see me safely home," she reminded him. "You said you were a man of your word."

"The answers first," he refused to budge.

"That wasn't in our original deal, Captain. Why are you so interested in the war? You're a pirate, not an American."

"A war will naturally affect me and my business," he lied smoothly. "Besides, I have friends and family in America, as well as valuable property. So, you might say I'm an American," he stated.

253

"I thought you English. I fail to understand how a man who was born English could side with America. I believed you Americans a unique breed of man who hungered and fought for freedom, but you constantly tempt my country to destroy you."

"England will not devastate America, love. She's well established and strengthened now. I propose to side with the imminent victor when the time comes to take a stand."

"You feel their cause is just?" she questioned sincerely.

Was this radiant creature trying to trap him? Did she suspect the truth about him? He had better be careful!

He craftily lightened the subject, "What would a beautiful, carefree lass know about the hunger for freedom?"

"I know the loss of it can be like a disease eating away inside of you until you'll risk or do anything to regain it. Not wishing to sound treasonous, but no country—including mine—has the right to imprison or oppress others."

The bitterness and anguish in her tone confused him. She spoke like she knew from experience what she was saying, not just reasoning aloud. "I hate to agree with you, Captain Steele, but I think you've selected the winning side. After what I saw and felt in America, I believe she will win her struggle against my country. Considering my country's history, I hope she does; I only pray it is over quickly," she wistfully stated.

"What vital business could a peasant girl's father have?" he asked again, intrigued.

"Peasant girl?" she echoed, then smiled at something which had amused her. "Farmers supply food for soldiers and lumber for ships," she craftily speculated aloud. "Two of the suitors Papa was studying are ship captains. When we go to war, they'll be out of the running for a long time. If fate shines on me, I could turn out to be a wealthy widow. Who knows, one of them could be the victor over Joshua Steele and return home a hero. It wouldn't be too bad to be married to a national hero," she taunted him.

"If you wed an English captain, you'll certainly wind up a widow, love," he smugly and tersely concluded.

"Then make haste, Captain, before I lose this valuable opportunity," she entreated with feigned eagerness.

"Why do I get the feeling that isn't the real reason for your rush? I doubt a war will be of any surprise to your papa. England's been begging for it for years."

She drew herself up indignantly. "The Americans started it first! They rebelled against the Crown. They declared war, not us."

He laughed at her. "You need a few lessons in history, love. Your country's the aggressor and always has been. Didn't you learn anything in America?" he teased, watching her closely.

"Yes! They do have just charges, but I'm still English. You sound more like an American than a pirate!" she rationalized.

"Would that be so terrible?" he mocked her distress.

"It is surely better than a bloody pirate! Will you tell . . ."

Before she could complete her next question, the signal was given once more. "Another attack?" she fearfully inquired, tensing in new dread.

"Your English navy is spoiling for fights today," he scornfully growled. "You know the routine; stay here and remain quiet. Agreed?"

She saluted him to break her tension as she murmured, "Yes, Captain Steele."

Irritation flickered over his handsome features. "I'm serious, Angel."

"I know, Stephen," she replied softly, wanting to embrace him and warn him to be careful. But she did neither.

He left her standing there in pensive silence. This time, there was no cannon fire. The waiting seemed endless. An unfamiliar man brought her some food and lit the lanterns in the cabin to dispel the gathering shadows of late evening.

"What's happening? I haven't heard anything," Alex anxiously pressed the roughly dressed, middle-aged man.

He pointed to his mouth and shook his head, indicating he was mute. She tried another approach, "Is there going to be another attack?"

He shook his head. "The ship was friendly or sailed on by?" she probed for more information. He nodded to her first question. "They're talking?" Again, he nodded yes. She sighed in relief and sat down to eat, suddenly ravenous.

As time slipped by, she could hear singing and talking. It was evident the men were having a carefree time. She sighed in loneliness and despair. Home was beginning to look good to her. The tension of these past few days was working upon her nerves. Alex longed to walk across open meadows and smell the fragrance of the wildflowers, she wanted to hear the singing of the birds. She hungered to ride her horse over dales and hills with the wind stealing her breath. And, she wanted to see her father. She needed to relax and feel safe once more, no matter the price.

She took Spencer's book to the bed and propped upon the pillows to read. She was too keyed up to sleep. What was taking so long? Was he celebrating his recent victory with the other ship captain? Were they plotting some joint attack upon other unsuspecting ships from her country? Her eyes becoming fatigued, she lay the book upon her stomach and rested for a few moments. Then, she absently flipped to the front page to study the inscription once more.

Thinking her asleep by this time, Spencer eased the door open and came inside. Already near a stormy rage following his meeting with Captain Morris about Madison needing to see him immediately, his eyes darkened in anger as he noted the book and page which had her attention. Irrationally venting his pent-up fury on the innocent Alex, he came forward and snatched it from her grasp. "Don't ever touch this book again! Why aren't you asleep? It's late!"

Witnessing the height of his irritation and anger, her voice trembled as she said, "I'm sorry, but I didn't mean any harm. What does the 'F' stand for?" she boldly asked, knowing he knew she had seen it.

"None of your business!" he fiercely exploded. "It belonged to a close friend of mine; he's dead now," he scathingly dismissed her curiosity, glaring at her to instill fear and silence, but failing to do so.

She dared to ask, "What ship was that?"

"A fellow privateer," he responded, but she felt he was lying. "I see you couldn't get to sleep with me gone," he murmured, his tone softening at the look of anxiety upon her ashen face.

"If you had bothered to send word we weren't in danger of attack, I could have! Don't you ever think of anyone besides yourself?"

"A captain is only concerned with his ship, his crew, and his friends," he indifferently answered, waving his hand in mid-air, dismissing the subject.

"For the present, I am one of your crew," she asserted. "I would appreciate a little consideration."

He gave her a mocking bow and murmured, "Yes ma'am. And what consideration would you like first?"

Her eyes glittered with fury at his taunting manner, and for once, she was at a loss for words.

Spencer began to slip out of his clothes.

"What are you doing?" she shrieked in dismay as she watched his knee boots hit the floor, then his pants and shirt follow them.

"Getting ready for bed," he replied lazily.

"Here?" she questioned in rising alarm.

"Where else? This is my cabin." He picked up his clothes and lay them across a wooden chair, then placed his boots next to it.

"But what about me? Where will I sleep?"

He halted briefly to stare at her. She was serious. "Here with me."

"Surely you jest!" she squealed in panic. They had made love several times, but sleep together like . . . She swallowed with difficulty at that idea.

"Not this time, love. For the next few weeks, this is the arrangement. When I make a bargain, it's full time." He slowly came forward.

"Never! I can't sleep with a man!" she panicked, backing against the wall and holding the pillow before her chest as if it could protect her.

He chuckled in amusement as he stood nearly naked beside the large bunk. "The only available bunk is with my men below, and I certainly couldn't permit you to sleep there."

"You could sleep there!" she debated.

"Not on your life. This is my cabin, and you'll share it for a while. You're not a child and I'm not your lenient father. So stop behaving like a spoiled, rebellious brat with me. In light of our past relationship, don't you think playing the coy virgin a bit ridiculous?" he teased.

"You ravished me before! But sleep together? We can't; it isn't proper," she reasoned to no avail.

"I seduced you the first time, but not this afternoon. You were just as willing as I was. Get ready for bed and stop all this chatter. I'm exhausted."

Alex couldn't very well argue his point about their last union, but this was asking too much! "No!" she defiantly stated.

"Shall I do it for you, love? If you make it necessary, your dress will be ruined," he threatened in a low tone.

She gaped at him. "You mean undress right here?"

"I've seen you nude several times, love," he mirthfully reminded her. "But if you value that dress, it better come off quickly."

She shrank against the wall and stared at him. "I'll sleep in it," she relented.

"No, you will not. I'll give you to five to get it off," he warned.

Alex paled. "You gave Thackery to ten," she sneered angrily at this degrading event.

"Thackery's choice was a little more critical than removing a dress, love."

"I won't be treated like some cheap harlot! I'm not your mistress; I'm your guest!" she frantically argued, knowing the battle was lost.

Ignoring her, Spencer began to count slowly, "One . . . two . . . three . . . four . . ."

"All right!" she quickly responded, fearing he would tear the dress off the moment "five" was out. "Turn your back," she ordered.

He laughed once more, a vexing, but somehow pleasing sound. "No."

"You're a . . ."

He lifted his hand in warning as he snarled, "One more foul word and I'll take you over my knee and teach you better!"

She pouted and mumbled, "I wasn't going to use vulgar talk."

When she didn't move, he asked, "Do I start counting again, Angel?"

"I think you're the meanest man alive!" she shouted in frustration, sliding across the bed and standing up. She remained with her back to him for a few moments.

"You're slower than a snail. I'm tired, woman!"

She glanced over her shoulder and snapped, "It buttons down the back!"

"Then why didn't you ask me to unfasten you? I'm not a mind-reader!"

"Would you please unfasten me, sir?" she sarcastically requested. "Or do I have to struggle by myself?"

Tempted to grasp both sides of the dress and rip it off, he curbed that impulse. He fumbled with the row of tiny buttons, muttering curses at the difficult task. She clucked her tongue and saucily warned, "Shall I wash your dirty mouth out with soap, Captain Steele?"

"If you dare," he parried her jibe, completing the chore.

Alex eased the dress over her shoulders and down her hips. She wiggled most provocatively as she stepped out of it. She walked to the table and lay the dress over a second chair there. Then she sat down and removed her shoes. As she came toward the bed, he chuckled and remarked, "The rest of the garments, love. When a female's next to me all night, I want to feel warm flesh."

She flushed a bright scarlet and inhaled sharply. "You mean remove all my clothes?" she asked in horror.

"All of them. I want nothing between us. We have a lot of time to make up for in only a few short weeks. You only whet my appetite by the pond and this afternoon. Now, you can appease this hunger you created."

"But we've already made love today!" she declared, wondering at his insatiable appetite.

Rumbling laughter filled the room. "What an innocent you are, Angel. Who says a man and woman can't make love more than once a day?"

"I just thought . . . I mean I heard . . . I . . ." she stammered, confused as to how to explain her obvious misconception. "Do all men . . . Gossip says wives hate . . . Do husbands and wives . . ." Distressed by her ignorance and his beguiling grin, she halted in frustration.

"Wives dislike sex because their husbands are selfish and in too much of a hurry to sate their own desires," he began in reply to her unfinished questions. "Wives dislike sex because they've never been truly satisfied or romanced with leisure and skill. To them, it's like another chore. But with you, I doubt your husband will leave bed for more than a few moments at a time. With your fiery nature, you'll do just fine. But if he fails to give you the same pleasures I do, I'll be around off and on. That is, if you ever tell me where you live and your name.''

Stunned by his casual attitude about sex and marriage, she stared at him. "I would never carry on like that!" she informed him when she found her voice. "What an evil rogue you are, Steele. Besides, where would I find time to fit you in if he keeps me occupied all the time?" she challenged.

"I would find some way to distract him if you gave the word," he calmly informed her. "I could be enticed to make you a wealthy widow for the right price," he devilishly hinted.

"Pay you to murder my husband?" she asked incredulously.

"With the same terms as this present bargain, why not? To have you waiting for me is a mighty big temptation."

"If you find me so appealing, why not have me waiting for you all the time?" she seductively entreated him, then couldn't believe she had actually said that.

"I'm not the marrying kind, Angel. I like my freedom too much. A wife and home demand too many strings." He negligently leaned against the bedpost, relishing this unusual conversation and the intoxicating view of her lush body.

"I wouldn't. I would demand only your real name and freedom from my father's wishes," she tartly offered.

"No female alive is worth my freedom, love."

"What price does your freedom carry, Joshua?"

"Can you afford to even ask?" he teased.

"Can I afford not to?" she fenced. "You're certainly better than any man my father's brought home so far. It could be a marriage in name only. You could loan me the use of your name for whatever price you set. After a while when my father's temper has cooled and his urgent need to see me wed is sated, I could quietly divorce you and we would both be free and happy. You wouldn't have to ever see me again," she suggested with a bewitching smile. "Name your price," she encouraged him, thinking this only some amusing game.

"With my name in your possession, you could recover any expense by profitably betraying me to your countrymen."

"I swear I would never reveal who you are, with or without any bargain. I don't need or want a husband, only a name upon a paper to satisfy my father. Besides, how could I explain marrying Joshua Steele?" she debated cheerfully.

"You could always say you learned the truth after the marriage, giving you an undebatable reason to divorce me."

"Surely the use of your name for a few months and my eternal silence has some price, Joshua?" she scoffed.

He studied her for a time, smoldering eyes travelling up and down her body several times. "Ten thousand English pounds," he declared to her surprise.

Observing him for the same length of time, she smiled provocatively. He actually looked serious. Such an amount would require less than two pieces of her jewelry! She called his bluff, "In gold, jewels, or money?"

Astonished, Spencer asked, "Are you serious? Where would a peasant girl get that much money?"

At calling her a country lass once more, Alex smiled and shrugged. "If you're serious, then I positively am. Since you're a man of your word, give it to me in exchange for the money. We can be married in the first port we make, then you can take me home . . . all the way to my front door. We'll break the news to my father, show him the license, then you can leave. Naturally when you never return, I'll pine for a spell, then divorce you," she delivered her ploy with great ease and confidence.

"Come here and sit down. This sounds most intriguing. I've never been so enchantingly propositioned before."

She hurried over to sit down beside him, disregarding her state of undress. This sport was fun, but it could become more than a joke with a little effort and cunning! "Well? Do you honestly want to earn an easy ten thousand pounds?" she challenged.

"Ten for the marriage, ten for the divorce," he slyly altered his demand. "Payment before the marriage and definitely not in name only. It wouldn't be legal if we didn't consummate it. You remain my wife until I divorce you."

She pondered his added stipulations. The money was no problem, neither was making love to this virile man who made her pulse race. But why would he want the divorce option in his control? "Are you serious,

Joshua? You aren't just playing games with me?"

"I'm deadly serious, Angel. Meet my terms and you have a bargain."

"Your word of honor?" she insisted.

"My word of honor," he promised, knowing she couldn't meet those terms.

"I accept your terms," she promptly agreed before he could add more conditions. "Where is my baggage?"

"Your baggage?" he echoed, baffled by her change of topic.

"You said pay now and marry at first port, so I will. The money is hidden in my baggage. Your name in exchange for twenty thousand pounds. The date of our divorce is up to you."

"You have twenty thousand pounds in your baggage?" he stormed in disbelief.

"I have jewels which will more than cover that amount," she calmly announced. "You can select whichever pieces you want."

"I don't believe you," he argued, dismayed by the serious look in her eyes. If she could meet his terms, how would he extract himself from this absurd trap? He laughed at his foolishness. There was no way this country lass had that much money!

"Have someone bring the baggage here and I'll show you," she challenged. "You did give your word of honor, Josh. Are you backing out so soon?"

"This is only a trick to get your clothes, isn't it?" he charged.

"Since I'll be your wife soon, I won't have need of

any. You did say my husband would keep me occupied," she saucily retorted. "Since we won't have time for a honeymoon afterwards, why not share one before?"

He ran his fingers through his sable mane as he studied her. There was only one way to halt this game now. "Stay right here," he ordered, pulling on his pants and leaving.

Congratulating herself for solving her problem with her father, Alex envisioned his face as she plotted her impending tale of love and marriage to an overpowering American. She could say he swept her off her feet. He would be impressed by Stephen Whatever before he was supposedly forced to leave on business, never to return. Free . . . Later, she could feign a broken heart as a reason to stall another marriage until she found a man who suited her. If Stephen never returned and she discovered another man like him, she could always divorce him on grounds of desertion or presumed death . . . the plan was perfect!

Spencer stuck his dark head in the door and commanded her to cover up. When she had done so, her baggage was brought into the room by two husky men and deposited in the middle of the floor. Once the men had departed, he turned and challenged, "Hand over the money, love. If you can't, these trunks go over the side and you will pay dearly."

She smiled as she rushed forward to open one of the trunks. "Thanks for bringing them along. I would hate to think of them at the bottom of the ocean."

She withdrew all her clothes and piled them neatly

upon the floor. Spencer noted the elegance and expense of the fine wardrobe within the trunk. Was this innocent in fact a thief? Whose possessions were these? Had she stolen them from some wealthy mistress?

Alex glanced up at him, her smug expression fading to one of confusion. "Why are you looking at me like that?"

"I was just wondering how you came in possession of such clothes."

"They're mine! If you doubt me, check the sizes." She took a small bejeweled dagger and pried open a secret compartment on the lower left side of the trunk. "Thackery didn't have time to rob me. He was too busy trying to rape me. No doubt he would have gotten around to it later!"

She held up a box and taunted, "See, I can hold up my end of the bargain." She stood up and opened the box to reveal a collection of very expensive jewelry. "Any piece is valued at half your asking price. Which ones do you want?"

He took the box and walked to the table to remove them and to inspect the costly collection. Without a doubt, they were real. "Where did you get these?" he demanded harshly.

"From my father, mother, and my grandparents," she answered, puzzled by his anger.

He glared at her, his skepticism vivid. "We have a deal, Joshua. I've kept my part. What about you?"

"What if I demand the entire collection?" he tested her.

Dismayed by his apparent greed, she still relented, "It isn't fair, but I agree. I'll tell my father they were stolen and he'll buy me more."

"What's your name, Angel? How does your father earn this kind of money?"

"I'll answer any question you have . . . after we're married," she stubbornly declared, feeling he might trick her after all.

"How do you expect to marry me without a name?"

"You can find out at the ceremony," she rebuffed his ploy.

"You want me this badly?" he asked.

"Your name and my freedom, yes. Consider those a wedding gift, my dowry."

Desperately seeking a way to end this farce, he stood up and paced in deep concentration. He couldn't marry anyone, especially not a mere country lass. No doubt her family was involved in some profitable and illegal activities. Had this been her intention all along, to snag a wealthy and prestigious husband to better her station in life? But why him? Why was she travelling alone? Why had she been by the pond? Too many suspicious questions without logical answers . . .

"Why would you want to marry a stranger? Particularly me?"

"I told you I don't want to marry anyone at all, but my father will arrange a marriage if I come home single," she stated in exasperation. "Since you can't make any demands upon me and you'll be gone soon, you're the perfect solution to my problem. You promised, Joshua."

"That was before I knew you could meet my terms!" he blurted.

"Then you were teasing me!" she hotly charged. "Well, that doesn't matter. You gave me your word!" she defiantly reminded him.

Spencer went back to the table and sat down. Once she discovered they were heading back to America on top of his refusal to comply with their silly deal, she would be furious.

As she impatiently awaited his next words, her eyes found the petticoat upon the floor: the one with the messages from her uncle to her father. She tensed in panic. If Joshua saw it, there was no telling what he might do with that information. He was most assuredly not beyond blackmail! He could ruin both her uncle and father with the coded messages there. He could take her jewels and her body and refuse to meet his part of their bargain. How to get rid of it?

She recalled Henry's caution about disposing of it. She glanced at the porthole, then at the man whose attention was upon her jewelry. She leaned over and picked it up, pretending to toy with it. She nervously rolled it into a tight bundle and began to aimlessly, but purposefully, head toward the porthole. Standing before it, she pretended to gaze out at the moon's reflection upon the indigo water. She dared to glance at him again, but he seemed preoccupied by the fortune in his hands.

She tightly clutched the treacherous material and began to ease her hands upwards to stuff it through the porthole. Just as it was halfway out, a hand snaked out and seized it. She began to struggle with him over its possession. It was imperative to throw it out.

"Let it go!" she yelled at him. "It's mine; I can throw it away if I wish!"

Spencer shoved her backwards to the bed and pinned her down with the weight of his powerful body. He snatched the garment from her tight grip and glared at her through stormy eyes. "You seem mighty anxious to toss this outside, love. Why?"

He got up and started to unroll the petticoat. She jumped up and grabbed for it. Another fight ensued. Within minutes, he was sitting on top of her, her arms imprisoned beneath his knees. "Now, let's have a closer look at this," he breathlessly stated.

"No!" she shrieked in dismay, fearful of the unknown stitches there. Why had she forgotten about this dangerous evidence? Why hadn't she gotten rid of it before? She trembled in alarm as she watched him.

To a man with Spencer's experience, the irregular stitches stood out as clearly as a black storm cloud. He studied them for a time, then more closely as he held the fabric up to the light. Amazed to find an obvious code sewn there, he glanced down at the helpless girl beneath him. "What does it say, Angel?" he asked in a deceptively calm tone.

She belligerently returned his stare. "I don't know what you mean," she lied noticeably.

Who was this bewitching girl with expensive clothes and jewels who had mysteriously entered his life on two critical occasions? "The code's as clear as the nose on my face, love. What does it say?" he harshly demanded.

"What code?" she sweetly inquired, failing to disarm him.

"Come now, Angel, I'm no fool. What does it say?"

"What would I know about such things? And better yet, what would you know about such things? You're a pirate, or so you claim," she sneered with bravado.

"Who's sending this message and to whom? How are you involved, my beautiful English spy."

"Spy?" she incredulously echoed. "Me? If there's some message there, I know nothing about it."

"Then why were you trying to discard it?" he demanded, his eyes narrowing at his apparent misjudgment of this girl.

She turned her face from his piercing eyes and sighed as if unconcerned. "I don't know anything about it. Someone must have put it there. Perhaps that was what Thackery really wanted. How should I know?"

Spencer got up and stared down at the rebellious girl. "You won't leave this ship until you decipher this code," he suddenly warned.

She jerked upwards. "But we have a deal! You promised!"

"Is that what you're after, love? My name for your superiors? That's where the gowns and jewels came from, isn't it? How long did you and Thackery hang around hoping I would attack and 'rescue' you? You almost had me fooled, Angel," he angrily admitted aloud.

"What are you talking about?" she cried in dismay. "You sound as if you honestly think I'm some scheming spy!"

"Aren't you? Wasn't this some trick to worm your way into my confidence? Trouble was, you didn't expect the man by the pond, did you? It looks as if the joke's on you this time, Angelique."

"You're crazy! I've told you the truth, Stephen. I'm English, but not a spy!"

"Then tell me what message is on this petticoat!" he growled.

"I don't know! My uncle is sending it to my father. It's nothing to concern you; I swear it!" she vowed, her apprehension rising.

"Who are your father and uncle?" he instantly inquired.

"I can't tell you. I won't allow you to blackmail them! Why are you so eager to know what's written there? You sound more like a spy than I do!" she screamed at him.

To make light of her charge, he laughed heartily. "If the message wasn't critical, love, it wouldn't be in code. I find this most intriguing. You'll remain here until I know its contents."

"Damn you, Stephen! I don't know what it says!"

"Maybe that's true and maybe it isn't. But for certain you know who's involved. Tell me if you desire freedom and home again. Your little ruse about marriage doesn't fool me an instant."

"I was serious! There might be something there that

could endanger my father's life. I honestly don't know what it says, but it isn't important to you! Keep the jewels, just take me home."

"We're heading for an American port at first light. You can either trust me with the information, or I'll turn you over to some American officers to extract it. I owe several of them favors. Handing them a beautiful and devious spy should repay them," he coldly threatened.

"You can't do that. I'm not a spy. You must take me home. Please, Stephen. My father will pay you any ransom you name."

"Your father or your employers? I doubt a cunning witch like you even has a father. During war, there are ways of dealing with crafty spies," he threatened. "The price of freedom is high this time, love. You can either give me their names or the contents of this message. You have my word I'll release you."

"Your word is as fake as your name, Steele!" This man could not be trusted, she decided. If he did take her back to America and leave her, she could claim innocence. Her uncle was one of them; he would come to her aid. She would tell Joshua Steele nothing!

Reading her look of defiance, he came forward and halted before her. "Do you have any idea what prison is like, love? Do you realize what they'll do to get the truth from you?"

"I'm innocent. They'll believe me," she bravely declared.

"When I hand them this petticoat, they won't."

"It's your word against mine. Who would accept the word of Joshua Steele over . . . mine? If you take me there, I'll tell them who you really are," she issued a threat of her own. She was alert to catch the concern in his eyes before he shielded them against her probing gaze.

"I would strangle you first," he sneered arrogantly.

"How can they extract information from a dead woman?" she scoffed. "You turn me in, and I'll blow your cover so fast you won't be able to leave the port before they blast you from the water!"

Spencer couldn't afford for anyone to learn his secret just yet. But the information on this petticoat could be vital. That would explain her actions: the panic to discard it, her sudden flight home, her presence here and in England, and her possession of such wealth. Had he simply blundered into her current mission? Had Thackery been a part of it or not? Was she reckless enough to want to add his capture to her list of daring and successful exploits?

"I think it's past time we have a serious talk, love. There are things I must know and now," he icily informed her.

Confused, frightened, and angered, she sneered, "Talk about what, Captain Steele? Your kidnapping? Your seductions? Your lies and tricks?"

"About you and your furtive activities in America," he snapped.

"You have no right to know anything about me! I am your prisoner, nothing more," she retorted.

"I am captain here; everything and everyone are my concern."

"Not me!" she hotly protested.

"It could prove most dangerous and embarrassing for me if a British spy is found upon my ship."

Mocking laughter vexed him further. "Spy? You really think that?"

"Aren't you?"

Stubborn and vengeful, she haughtily sneered, "You may think anything you wish, sir."

"I demand the truth, woman!" he thundered in rising impatience.

"I will only say this much; I have never been a spy in my country or yours. You have committed far more offenses than I ever could. Will you turn yourself over to your American friends to be punished?"

Deciding upon another ploy to disarm her, he yawned and suggested, "I say we sleep on this problem and discuss it again with fresh minds. I don't know about you, but I'm exhausted. This has been a most enlightening and baffling day," he turned on his charm. If force wouldn't work, perhaps another course of action would . . .

Needing this reprieve to regain her wits, Alex instantly agreed. Lying side by side in the darkness, she murmured softly, "I'm not a spy, Stephen, no matter what you believe." She turned to her side to try to relax. His nearness and manly scent assailed her senses. Was it possible to love and hate the same man at the same time?

He propped himself up on his elbow, gently and enticingly trailing his other hand down her arm. "Think it over, love. I wouldn't want to see you harmed," he murmured.

She turned and gazed up into the moonlit shadows. "Why are you doing this to me, Stephen? What difference does the war make to you? You can't honestly believe I'm a dangerous spy. What if they imprison me or execute me? If you take me home, I'll do whatever you say."

"Tell me what the code says or give me the names involved, and I'll set you free. War will most definitely affect me and my business. What am I supposed to think when a beautiful girl is caught with secret messages stitched to her petticoats? In my place, what would you think?"

"In your place, I wouldn't see why it would make a damn! I can't comprehend why the messages are more important to an infamous pirate than jewels and money. What am I supposed to think?" she returned his query. "If there's a suspicious spy in this room, Captain Steele, it's you."

"I need the information now, love. We can't make England for weeks."

That slip enlightened her to his prior deception about their schedule and destination. "I'll never tell you anything!"

"There are terrible ways to extract information from a woman . . ."

"Such as lash me to the mast and flog me ten times?

Do so if you dare," she dauntlessly challenged, her chin trembling to belie her courage.

Alex began to weep. She was so frightened and confused. Why was this pirate so intrigued by her petticoat?

Spencer strained to see her in the dimness. Was this some new ruse to win his mercy? What if she was telling the truth? What if she was an innocent player in this deadly drama? The fact remained, this situation was suspicious during these perilous times. Morris told him three English spies had already been captured, one a lovely and ice-hearted female. Did he dare trust this curious girl? This time, as always, his head had to rule over his loins . . . and heart.

If only he knew more about her. It would be dangerous, perhaps fatal, for him and her if he callously handed her over to the American government. The only path opened to him was to find some way to win her trust and cooperation . . .

Spencer stroked her hair and pretended to soothe her fears. "Don't worry, love. I won't make any drastic moves. We both need time to think over this matter. But I can't release you until I have some answers."

"I can't tell you anything, Stephen. I'm sorry," she sadly murmured, wishing the traitorous garment didn't exist.

"I understand," he softly replied, mentally planning his strategy. He leaned over and kissed her lightly upon the lips. "You're very unique and beautiful,

Angelique. I wish things hadn't worked out this way."

"We can't help who or what we are, Stephen. You could change that if you wanted to. We've reached an impasse; the next move is yours."

He smiled. "How about this one?" he huskily whispered, kissing her soundly this time. She struggled briefly before relenting to his magnetic charms.

"Let's make the best of it until we talk again," he coaxed as he nibbled upon her ear.

"You're a fiend, Steele," she mumbled, easing her arms around him.

He chuckled. "I've been called much worse, Angel."

"I'm sure you have, and justly so," she teased, returning his kiss with heated passion.

Soon, nothing mattered except dousing the fires of passion which consumed them. Spencer used every skill and charm he possessed to tantilize her beyond reality. As his mouth tenderly ravaged hers, his deft hands gently and enticingly explored her pliant body. As he trailed kisses over her face and throat, she moaned in unleashed desire.

He teased her taut breasts and eased his hand lower to remove any thoughts but him. Such wild and wonderful feelings washed over her as she delighted in this fiery union. No matter who or what he was, Alex wanted him desperately. She clung to him, moving her hands up and down the rippling muscles of his firm, smooth back. There was such strength and tenderness combined in this complex man, such power and passion. His contempt of danger was like a heady drug which numbed her wits and tormented her body.

Each time his manhood plunged into her receptive body, his kisses would deepen. They challenged her to match them. She trembled as the fires of passion raged within her, crying out for appeasement. Shouldn't it be a crime for a man to possess such magic and appeal?

Each stroke of his manhood served to increase her blissful agony. Her fingers played in his hair, then she pressed his mouth more tightly against her. It seemed as if she couldn't taste him enough or get close enough to him. The intensity built to a point she felt she could no longer endure. She cried out in need of the pleasure only he could give her. Her mind reeled and her body shook with the force of her release, and over and over she murmured his name.

Caught up in this savage storm of volatile emotions, Spencer held her tightly and possessively. Wave after wave of blissful ecstasy washed over them, carrying them along in its powerful force. Gradually the tremors and sensations ebbed away, leaving them in a peaceful ocean of serenity.

Still, Spencer did not roll to her side or withdraw from her moist body. His mouth continued to demand kiss after kiss. Later, his respiration returned to normal, as did his thudding heart. He leaned back and stared down at her, an inexplicable expression in his unreadable eyes.

"You are the most tormenting creature alive, Angel. You're a mystery which I plan to understand.

You can give everything one minute and nothing the next. What spell have you cast over me, my lovely sea witch?"

Her hand went up to wipe the glistening beads of moisture from his upper lip. "You, Sir Demon, are the one who has cast the spell over me. I am but a woman, but you are far more than a mere man. I can't understand you at all. One moment you're kind and tender, the next you're cold and cruel. For a man who can have any woman he desires, what do you want with me? Why must you so cruelly dance in and out of my life? Who are you, Stephen?"

He captured her hand and placed a kiss in its palm. "Your missions are over, love. You'll never deliver that petticoat or me to your countrymen. You're an artful teaser, Angel; but I won't fall for your pretense of innocence or your magical charms. Be satisfied I'll grant you the time to confess, but don't play the coy maiden with me."

"Are we back to your absurd charges and suspicions again? Have it your way, Captain Steele, but I've nothing to confess. The messages are about business, Stephen; I swear it. My uncle and father would never ask me to become involved in any dangerous or traitorous activities. If you wish to pretend you believe such charges for some ulterior motive, then do so. But don't expect me to play along with this ridiculous game. All I want is to get home and forget all about you."

"What ulterior motive could I possibly have?"

"My jewels . . . using me . . . a choice between who will pay the most for me and that petticoat: the Americans or my family . . . How should I know what you have in mind? Perhaps you hope to intimidate me with these wild ideas while taking advantage of me, then play the gallant hero by releasing me. You know I would never reveal any of this to anyone, including my family."

He chuckled playfully. "You are more cunning than I realized. You play your role with perfection. How long have you been helping them? If they're forcing you to do this, I can help you, love. You can keep the jewels and I'll grant your freedom in any port you choose if you cooperate. I'll even offer you my protection if you're afraid of them."

Exasperated, she protested, "There is no one to fear or obey, Stephen! The only ones forcing me to do anything are you and my father. You're holding me captive and he's forcing me to marry some fool!"

"I have to admit, you're damn good at this for one so young. You have a heart of stone and a cunning mind I envy. Of course, your many other assets aid in your disguise," he teased. "You strike me as a natural heroine and courageous patriot. With your charms and beauty, you could ingratiate yourself into the hearts and lives of the most important men in the American government. You could easily worm out every secret they have, and no one would ever suspect such an innocent, enchanting woman of spying."

"I'm afraid you overestimate my patriotism and

skills. I can be brave when the moment demands it, but I'd never make a successful spy. I lack the talent for deception and dishonesty that job demands. I despise deceit and deceivers," she vowed, accusing him of such actions. "Besides, the requirements needed to worm one's way into the hearts of influential men would be impossible for me. Such a price for patriotism is too great to pay."

"Are you still interested in marrying me?" he abruptly asked.

Startled, she watched him closely. This was only some trick to disarm her. "No," she wistfully replied. "You aren't the man I thought you to be. You fooled me."

"You sound disappointed," he mocked her sad tone of voice.

"Strange as it seems, I am. I'm just too gullible and naive for my own good. Thanks for the lessons, sir."

"There's one more you'll soon learn: I always get what I want. And you know what that is," he hinted.

To nettle him, she smiled coyly and sighed, "Me, of course."

"That was true before I discovered what a cunning and dangerous witch you are. Now, I only want information. And I'll have it before you leave this ship."

"Then you had better relax, Captain; it's going to be a mighty long voyage. I'll never tell you anything," she bravely asserted.

"We'll soon see. I think you'll tire of me and this

seclusion before I tire of having you along," he teased merrily, eying her appreciatively.

"I don't think I could ever tire of you, Stephen," she admitted.

"What about Steele?" he instantly came back at her.

"Him? He's a different story all together. Who knows, maybe I'll eventually come to like and understand him too," she parried softly.

"Name your price," he entreated.

"Price?" she repeated in confusion.

"Anything in exchange for that information," he clarified.

"Anything?" she provocatively inquired.

"Anything," he stressed.

"Including you?" she fenced.

"Which one of us?" he played along.

"Both of you as one husband," she casually replied.

"Back to that crafty marriage again?" he teased.

"I need a husband, and you're the ideal choice. Why not?"

"Why not indeed?" he echoed, lying down to gaze into the darkness.

"Well?" she challenged.

He spoke clearly and evenly, "I'll give it some thought. Go to sleep, Angel."

She lay down and closed her eyes. This was the most perplexing conversation she had ever had. If she was to be his prisoner for several weeks, why not make the best of it? She had craved adventure and suspense. She had hungered for this man for weeks. Why not take advantage of this unusual situation until she was free?

"Good-night, Stephen . . . Josh . . ."

He chuckled. "'Night, Angel," he murmured.

They were both asleep within minutes.

XI

"She speaks, yet she says nothing."
"So loving-jealous of his liberty."
—*Romeo and Juliet*, William Shakespeare

Those next two days passed sluggishly for both Spencer and Alex. Spencer spent much of his time on deck to avoid any contact with the beautiful and suspicious girl in his cabin. Andy teased him unmercifully about his restlessness and stormy moods. He had never seen any female treat his good friend this way or affect him in this curious manner. Josh wasn't one to take something like this from a woman. Why was this girl different? If she was truly a spy like Josh suggested, why didn't he turn her in? What strange hold did she have over his captain? Did he care about her more than he dared to admit, even to himself?

Alex roamed the confines of Joshua's quarters with rising dismay and apprehension. It had been two and a half days of verbal battles and challenging bouts in his bunk. They had quarreled, talked, loved, and pleaded. Nothing changed either one's mind.

Most of the time Alex spent alone, too much time alone. She and the captain shared chilly dinners and stubborn arguments. But at night, all things faded but fiery passion. Who were these two men sharing the same body? Alex thought. Why did he keep pretending he was trying to force some information from her? Did he honestly believe those messages were critical? Even so, why did they matter to him? Was *he* really an English spy?

She longed for fresh air and exercise, anything to break this nerve-racking monotony of silence and seclusion. Dressed in a nightgown, she couldn't leave his cabin. True to his ruthless nature, he had sent her baggage back below. She could only await his . . . his what?

Bored, Alex went to the porthole to look out. Land! They were actually in sight of land! Where were they?

The door opened and in swaggered Stephen. He glared at her, then walked to his clothes chest. He withdrew a pair of fawn-colored knee breeches, a white linen shirt, and a dark brown coat and matching vest. Without even speaking to her, he began to dress.

"Where are we? Are you going to release me tonight?"

"I'm going ashore. You'll remain here under guard. I won't be back until morning," he snarled his responses.

"But what about me? I've been locked in this room for days. I need some air and a stroll. You said I could leave at the first port," she petulantly protested.

"I doubt you would find an American port safe, love. I have some business. Don't leave this cabin. Understand?" he growled.

"You can't hold me prisoner forever, Captain

Steele! I want to go home!" she shrieked at him.

He faced her. "You know the terms for your release." As with his crew, he was also starting to ponder his motives and actions where this girl was concerned. She was a deceitful, cunning, and defiant spy who resisted his charms and powers. Why should he feel guilty about holding a spy captive? Why should his harsh treatment of such a devious woman bother him? Yet, it did. Why did her continual refusals deal him such an infuriating blow? What did her fate matter to him? If he had any brains and courage at all, he would simply beat the information out of her! What scheme could terrify her into compliance? Nothing seemed to work on this stubborn female!

"Damn you!" she screamed at him, rushing forward to beat upon his chest.

He captured her hands and imprisoned them in his tight grasp. She fought against his brute strength, finally yielding to it. "Please, Stephen. Let me go now," she pleaded, tears sparkling in her eyes.

He seized her and kissed her savagely. He released her so suddenly she almost fell. He steadied her and smiled mischievously. "I think I'll see an old friend while I'm here. She'll certainly be better company than you are," he stated to annoy her.

She paled. "You're going to see another woman?" She seethed with anger and jealousy. "What about me?" she stormed.

"Tell me what I want to know, and you can have my full attention for as long as you wish," he unexpectedly declared.

"You're an animal! I despise you! Go to your little harlot! I could care less!" She should have realized his sudden gentleness had only been a trick to win her confidence. What cruel fate had forced her to fall in love with a demon lover? Would she ever be free of him?

He threw back his head and laughed. "Methinks you're jealous, love."

"Methinks you can think anything you damn well please!" she snapped.

"You could come with me," he nonchalantly remarked.

Her head jerked upwards and her face brightened. "I could?"

"If I could trust you?" he cunningly added.

"But you can."

"How can I trust a female who won't trust me?" he reasoned.

She realized he was only teasing her. "How long do you plan to continue this cruelty? Don't answer!" she said angrily, knowing what it would be. "You'll be sorry for this one day, Stephen."

"I already am, love. I wish I had never laid eyes on you. From our first meeting, you've been nothing but trouble and pain. If we could re-live that day by the pond, I would reject your charms like the plague. Seducing you was the worst mistake I've made; the second one is allowing you time to confess. I doubt you'll relent even to save your own deceitful neck! Why I even care about your fate is beyond me!" With those stinging insults, he left.

Alex cried for hours. She envisioned Stephen in the arms of another woman. She cursed him and swore vengeance upon his head. If she only knew what that code said, she might tell him in hopes he would release her.

As she lay there, a daring plan came to mind. She hurried to his clothes chest and withdrew a pair of tight black knee breeches and a white shirt. She quickly put them on. Since they were close to shore, she could jump off the ship and swim to safety and freedom. She would go to the authorities and give them some tale about escaping from ruthless pirates. She would tell them about her uncle and surely they would send her to him.

Dressed in Stephen's baggy garments, she knocked on the door until a man came to answer it. "What'cha need, ma'am?"

"I fell. I think my arm is broken. Is there a doctor on the ship?" Just as she hoped, he opened the door and came to check on her. Before he caught her deception, she landed a heavy blow to his head with a paperweight.

Alex struggled to pull his body inside to prevent anyone from seeing it. She stuffed the money from Stephen's desk into a pocket and concealed her flowing mane of gold beneath a black bandanna. She eased the door open and looked out. All was quiet. Terror filled her as the steps creaked beneath her footsteps. Still, she bravely continued her plans.

The door to the deck was open. With only a quarter moon, it was very dark. She strained to see if anyone was about. She tensed. There was a man on guard near the bow. He was leaning against the rail, staring in the other direction. She glanced at the rail nearest her and calculated the distance to it. She was agile and light. She could doubtlessly make it before he could reach her. Her only drawback was the distance to the water. How soon could he sound the alarm if she was sighted? How quickly could they pursue her?

She soundlessly made her way across the wooden deck to the rail and looked down. The water was a long way off. White waves could be sighted lapping against the hull of the ship. It was now or never. She had already gone too far to turn back now. She summoned her courage and placed her leg over the side. Throwing the other one over, she momentarily hesitated as she sat upon the wooden barrier to her freedom. Should she dive or just drop in?

The ship lurched suddenly and her decision was made for her. Feet first, Alex struck the water with force. Alarmed, she struggled to regain the surface. Finally, she rose to the top and struck out for the shore.

She didn't realize she had cried out as she was tossed from the rail into the deep water. The man came running over to see what had happened. Her scarf gone, shimmers of golden hair reflected the moon's light as she swam toward shore. He called out to her, but she ignored him. Alarmed at discovery, Alex increased her speed. He shouted again, but the shore was near.

Nearly breathless, her feet touched bottom. She

fought the pull of the water against her slender body and saturated clothes and staggered toward the shadowy beach. At last, she was standing upon dry ground. She sank to it to catch her wind. She had made it this far. Yet, she needed to conceal herself before they could pursue her.

She forced herself to her feet and raced toward the woods. As she passed the first large tree, a hand snaked out and grabbed her. She screamed and fought with this unseen villain who was hindering her progress.

"What do we have here?" the stirring voice of Joshua Steele taunted. "A mermaid escaped from the sea and her master?" he teased.

"You! You said you would be gone all night," she shrieked, trapped in the iron confines of his arms.

"I changed my mind," he lazily stated. "I discovered you're far more satisfying than most females."

"Let me go. I'm getting your clothes all wet," she foolishly ranted.

Tugging at his stolen shirt, he roguishly concluded, "Both sets from the looks of it. Just where did you think you were going?"

"I don't know, just out of your reach!"

"You could have been injured jumping off my ship. Not to mention eaten by sharks."

"Sharks?" she fearfully stammered. "You mean there're sharks here?"

"Plenty of them," he lied most convincingly. "I'm surprised they missed a delectable piece of meat like you."

Alex nervously glanced out across the darkened waters. She hadn't even considered that danger when she planned her daring flight.

"What should I do about you, Angel?" he devilishly teased her.

"Let me go," she instantly answered. "Please, Stephen . . ."

He looked up to see a small boat heading their way from his ship. "It seems you saved me the trouble of signalling my ship. My men are hot on your trail now." He motioned to the boat about to beach. Noticing the way his white shirt clung to her wet body, he removed his jacket and ordered her to put it on. "You leave little to the imagination, love. I wouldn't want you to tempt my crew. It's been a long time between shore leaves." Roguish deviltry sparkled in his sapphire eyes.

Her eyes flew to the revealing condition of the shirt. She gasped and picked at the material to conceal her breasts from his laughing eyes. She quickly slipped into his proffered jacket and held the sides tightly together. "It'll be ruined," she stated apologetically. "Thank you, Stephen," she added softly.

"Your manners never cease to amaze me, Angelique. You were well trained, love," he complimented her in an insulting tone.

Two men came forward, their expressions sheepish. "Sorry, Capt'n. But I didn't see her in time to stop her. We came as quickly as we could."

"Doesn't matter, Tom. Angel's a sly and daring vixen. Let's get back to the ship. We sail at dawn."

"We can't!" she wailed. "Please, Josh, let me stay here."

"I'm almost tempted to let you. But it isn't safe. You'll come with me until I say you can go home."

What little moonlight there was seemed to play in her wet locks, and Spencer gently reached out to wipe the beads of moisture from her nose and chin. She pondered the tenderness in his expression and touch. If he was furious with her, he certainly didn't act like it. Yet, his keen mind seemed to be on some disturbing topic.

She smiled as she realized he had not spent the night with that female he had mentioned earlier. "Do I detect some amusement about something?"

"I was just thinking you came home mighty early," she flippantly hinted.

"I did, didn't I?" he murmured, alertly catching her insinuation. "Were you looking for me?" he jested, an arresting grin upon his sensual lips.

"Naturally. I can't afford to allow some other woman to take my place."

"You're a brazen flirt, Angelique. Come along, my slimy siren." He grasped her hand to lead her to the waiting boat.

"Ouch!" she cried out, leaning over as if she had something in her foot. She rubbed it, eying him from beneath her trailing hair. While he waited patiently for her to solve her problem, he turned away to scan the horizon. Too much was happening too fast to suit him.

She rashly grabbed his ankles and tripped him, then

ran for the cover of the trees. The sand slowed her progress, as did her wet and baggy garments. Spencer was upon her in an instant, throwing them both to the ground. A struggle followed. With little exertion, he had her pinned to the gritty surface beneath her.

"That was a foolish thing to do!" he snarled at her, glaring down into her defiant features.

"I won't let you take me back to your ship! I'll scream until someone comes to help me," she threatened.

With a few swift moves, she was gagged and bound, his belt surrounding and immobilizing her arms. Alex squirmed in the sand, but Spencer only laughed. He lifted her and tossed her over his powerful shoulders and calmly walked to the boat. His two men couldn't suppress their grins at this humorous sight. Spencer captured her feet and pinned them against his chest to prevent her from kicking him in the groin, which is what she appeared to be trying to do. What a little she-cat to tame!

He settled himself in the forward section and placed her in his lap. The craft was shoved into the water and they headed for the ship. With Alex dangling over his shoulder, he agilely climbed the rope ladder to the deck. He placed her bare feet upon the wooden surface and chuckled in amusement. Alex angrily twisted her shoulder to slam into his rumbling chest. The stalwart captain imprisoned her against him, taunting, "What a little she-cat you are."

He lifted her in his arms and strolled off, whistling merrily. He called over his shoulder, "Back to your duties, men; the fun's over for now."

They encountered Tully, the ship's cook, along their way. Spencer ordered, "Tully, send a tub and some water to my cabin. I have a slimy fish to bathe."

Tully laughed heartily and went to comply. Once inside his cabin, Spencer sat Alex down in a chair. "You're a lot of trouble for such a little package. Sit still before my temper gets out of hand." Following a knock on his door, Spencer went to let Tully inside with the tub. "It'll take a while to warm some water, Capt'n."

"No need, Tully. Bring it on now," he indifferently commanded.

Alex sat there wide-eyed as cool water was hauled in and the tub filled. What was this fiend up to now? When the men left and Spencer cautiously locked his cabin door, he came toward her and pulled her to her feet. Her curses were muffled by the gag which she still wore.

He undid the belt and let it drop to the floor. He forcefully pulled the shirt over her head as she wiggled to get free. The thin camisole quickly followed it. She clutched her small hands over her breasts in embarrassment. Outraged, she had no choice but to move one to yank the gag off. As she did so, Spencer practically ripped the pants from her slender body. Her hands struck out at him to prevent the removal of her last garment.

His greater size and strength were no match for hers. One hand over her bosom and one before her most private region, she stood trembling naked before his leering gaze. "You'll pay dearly for this insult!"

"You'll pay, love, for trying to make a complete fool of me! When I give orders, I expect them to be obeyed," he revealed his tightly leashed anger for the first time.

He picked her up and promptly deposited her in the tub. "I don't want sand and salt in my bed. You're prickly enough."

He took the washcloth and soap and began to scrub her, none too gently. "Ouch! You're hurting me! Stop it!" she protested as he laughed and worked on.

When her head and body were to his liking, Spencer seized Alex from the tub and began to dry her off. "I'm not a child, Steele! I can do it myself!"

"But I prefer to do it, love. I've never washed a mermaid before—and a man should do everything once!"

"Stephen! You'll regret this unforgivable insult! My father will see you flogged and hanged!"

"Who is this all-powerful father?" he snapped, hoping to trick her.

"He's . . . none of your business!" she halted just in time.

Her hair settled around her shoulders, making her a wild and alluring creature. Her flesh was pink from his intense scrubbing. "Get into bed," he commanded harshly.

"No!" she rebelliously declared.

In no mood to argue, Spencer seized her and threw her onto the bunk.

To hide her nudity and humiliation, Alex quickly

scrambled beneath the covers. What else could she do? He stripped naked and joined her. To her surprise, he turned his back to her as if to go to sleep!

Irritated with the perilous turn in events, Spencer punched his pillow several times to vent some anger. His keen mind flickered back to his previous meeting with Madison and other officials. He had fully intended to tell them about Angelique but hadn't, for some strange reason. Maybe it had to do with the fates of those other spies captured. After hearing about their tortures and executions, he couldn't bring himself to turn this lovely girl over to those headstrong men. The mere fact she knew his identity made her a deadly risk to all of them, or so he used that logical excuse to keep silent.

He had been tempted to send her to his plantation, but thought more wisely of that idea too. He couldn't trust this mysterious piece of fluff! His mind was in a turmoil; it was dangerous to keep her aboard, but just as perilous to release her. If only she would confide in him, his decision would be easier.

The war was a fact now. The American fleet had put to sea this very day. He went over the list given to him by Madison: Rodgers on the *President,* Smith on the *Congress,* Decatur on the *United States,* St. Clair on the *Argus,* and Hull on the *Constitution.* What a measly force to send out against the mighty Royal Navy! But for these captains and a few trusted officials, no one knew the *Black Mist* was in the employ of the United States government.

Considering the British fleet already in this area,

the open seas were dangerous. That last dispatch
Spencer had taken from Thackery was a real gem.
Madison was pleased to have a partial list of the British
ships dogging the coast. There wasn't too much
concern with the *African, Aeolus, Nautiles*, and
Shannon; but the *Belvidera* and the *Guerriere* were
definitely ships to be reckoned with. The build-up
around the northern border and Great Lakes didn't sit
well with any American.

Spencer wondered why Madison was ignoring Andy
Jackson's offer of assistance in the southern areas. A
man of his courage and skill should be used to their
advantage. Perhaps political rivalry was at the bottom
of it. If Mathews and his group were forced to leave the
Florida territory, someone needed to guard the
southern borders. It was too bad Mathews, Campbell,
and the others had arrogantly and aggressively
overstepped their orders and infuriated the Spanish
government.

In light of the letters from Russia from Adams,
things didn't look good over there either. Napoleon
was pushing too hard. With the Russians and other
countries joining England to battle him, they could
make a quick finish of the infamous pirate. In that
case, England would have more men and supplies to
attack America. No matter, Spencer still couldn't pray
for Napoleon to keep the English busy in Europe.

Spencer recalled his argument with Madison. Was
the President so certain the *Black Mist* would be of
more help than the *Wandering Siren?* If Madison
wanted him to continue as before, he had no choice. In

this role, he did secure an awful lot of vital information. So he would do as requested; he would sail up and down the American coast acting the part of a greedy and daring privateer . . .

But what about Angelique? Madison had found the petticoat of great intrigue, but no one could imagine what the curious code meant. He planned to turn it over to his best agent to decipher. Spencer was unsettled at having to lie to Madison about where he had obtained it. From the look on Madison's face, he had suspected Spencer was deceiving him. Why he had allowed this odd situation to go unquestioned, Spencer couldn't venture a guess.

"You awake, Angel?" he asked, turning toward her.

She tensed, but did not reply. "What will it take to win your trust and help?" he went on, knowing she was listening. "I gave the Americans the petticoat, but they couldn't make heads, or tails out of it. They wanted to know where I got it."

"What did you tell them?" she asked in a tremulous tone.

"I didn't turn you in, if that's what you mean. The last two spies were tortured and executed. I thought I'd give you another chance to comply before . . ." He didn't complete his threat.

She remained silent, relieved they couldn't read the messages.

"The war's getting nasty, love. I can't hold you here forever, but I can't free you either. What should I do about you?"

"You have the petticoat, my jewels, and my vow of silence. What more can I offer?" she sadly inquired.

"I need information," came the demand she knew by heart.

She sat up, holding the covers before her. "I can't, Stephen."

"Damnit, Angel! I don't want to be responsible for your hanging!"

"Then take me home and forget you ever met me," she pleaded.

"I own property in America and I plan to settle there one day. I can't permit England to win this war. If those codes mean what I think, they outline our defenses. If it comes to a choice between you and my country . . ."

"I see," she murmured, her voice shaky. "I can't read the code, Stephen, but I can swear it is about business. My uncle is American and my father English. Neither would betray his homeland. With all my heart, I know that to be true," she fervently vowed.

"One or the other is a spy, love. Don't be so naive, Angel. They're using you and you're too blind to see it," he harshly retorted.

"You're wrong! They love me and only want what's best for me. If the messages were dangerous, they wouldn't have asked me to carry them," she heatedly argued.

"In light of your present circumstances, you don't consider them dangerous? You don't find it suspicious you were told to dispose of them in case of trouble? If your father's in England, I can't touch him. Why risk your life to cover for him?"

"You came there once before! Are you forgetting how we met?"

"For as long as I live, I'll never forget that day," he murmured softly.

"Nor will I," she snapped.

He smiled in secret pleasure. To disarm her, he tenderly asked, "We're caught in the middle, aren't we? I didn't expect to ever see you again, but surely not under these conditions. I wish it weren't so, love."

"Does it have to be this way, Stephen? Do I mean nothing but profit to you?" she wretchedly challenged.

"If that were true, you wouldn't be here now. I want to protect you, love, but you make it impossible."

"Would you really turn me over to the colonial authorities? If you don't believe me, they never will. Nothing has gone right since I met you."

"Good. At least you're as miserable as I am. It's bad to want something and can't have it. If matters were different, I'd take you home with me right now."

Stunned, she asked, "Would you really?"

"In a minute! You're a breath of fresh and invigorating air, Angel. I've never met a woman like you. Frankly, you irritate the hell out of me."

"I do? Why?"

"You're the first woman who's fit into my life so nicely. But I can't take the time or energy to keep you right now."

"What if I agree to wait for you?" she boldly offered.

"What about your father and his demands?" he countered.

"I could refuse to go back. I could wait at your home."

"Until I left? You'd be gone the moment my back was turned, just like tonight," he challenged her honesty and feelings.

"You know why I tried to leave! You've been mean and cruel."

"Were you heading for your uncle's?" he inquired.

"Yes. He's probably frantic by now."

"Where?"

"Why do you always do this? You're only trying to trick me!"

"How else can I protect both you and me?"

"You don't care about me, only yourself and your greedy pockets. By the way, I took some money from your desk. It's in your clothes I borrowed."

He burst into laughter. "Too bad you aren't this honest all the time."

He reached and pulled her down to him. Before she could pull free, his mouth was covering hers. He pressed her into the softness of his bed, his hands taking command of her body. It was useless to resist him—and Alex realized she didn't want to resist him. It was sheer madness, but she couldn't help herself.

Once their passions were sated, she snuggled into his protective arms and went to sleep. He gazed down at her. Why did she have to look and act like such an innocent? In and out of bed, she was an intoxicating delight. Too many secrets were between them. First the truth, then . . . He shook his head as if to clear it of these unwanted intrusions. Even if Angelique were innocent of all wrongs, he couldn't seriously consider a future with a peasant girl. When his sons were born, their bloodline would be matchless. Of all men alive, he knew how important a spotless heritage was!

In spite of his vanity and arrogance, he couldn't keep her dangling for years, and he couldn't make any commitments to any female at present. Still, she was too rare a treasure to lose. He fumed at the fate which had borne them of different classes. If a woman this unique had to enter his life, why couldn't she be a lady? For the time being, she was his. He determined to take all she had to give until the day came when he would be forced to send her away . . . and that day would come.

To dismantle her guard, Spencer began a new and compelling tactic that next day. He resolved to have her so enamored of him that she could confess the very depths of her soul. He spent every moment possible with her, assailing her mind and body with his multiple and irresistible charms. He was mellow and loving; he was tender and passionate. He entertained her with tall tales about his adventures. He waited upon her like a devoted slave. He was overpowering and charming, everything a dreamy hero should be.

Spencer would take her walking on the decks twice a day: during the early morning when the mist was just rising from the sea and the sun was dancing over the water, and just at evening tide when the moon was scanning her face in the serene ocean. The colors, odors, and sights set a very romantic and tranquil mood . . . and Alex found herself loving every minute of her captivity.

They would share marvelous dinners by candle-light, and would dance in the privacy of his cabin to the haunting strains of music coming from the deck. They would converse on many subjects; yet, Spencer never questioned how she knew so much or why she was so polished and educated. Amidst the display of her refined qualities and best behavior, he refused to comprehend what fineness was before him. He denied all his perceptions and reactions but his delight in vividly charming her.

Two weeks passed as they savored each other without pressures. The more Alex relaxed and warmed up to him, the more he suspected her eventual defeat. Spencer dreaded the thought of her final submission; for once she capitulated, he would have no reasonable excuse to keep her. For that reason alone, he ceased to make any demands for the truth. With her and the ominous petticoat in his possession, she was no threat to America.

Skirting the southern coast to watch for a fleet coming from that direction, the days were long and lazy and the nights heady and short. Once while anchored in a cove, they went for a moonlight swim and made love on the beach. Alex wondered at this gay abandonment she was experiencing. Was she becoming as wanton as some street slattern? No matter what her head told her, her heart always overruled its logic. There was no denying the fact she was in love with this magnificent man who was so strong and so tender. In view of his present conduct, she assumed he was feeling the same way she was. With all her heart, she honestly felt he loved her and wanted to keep her. She concluded she had won his trust and his affection. Even his crew had come to treat her with respect and fondness as the captain's woman.

During the third week with her love, a terrible event took place: the American Captain Rodgers sank the English warship *Belvidera*. From the talk she overheard, Rodgers's ship had become separated from the rest of the American squadron and was laying waste to many British merchant ships up and down the coast. Following the *Black Mist*'s capture of an English frigate, they learned the English fleet was pursuing Rodgers for revenge.

As the men rambled on without awareness to her nearby presence, Alex was horrified to learn the greatest ship in the American line, the *Constitution*, had outwitted the British who were lying in wait for Rodgers. She held her breath as she listened to their versions of the fierce and bloody battles going on near the Canadian border. Somehow she couldn't find joy in the British victories at the cost of so many lives. Why were her countrymen employing savages to slaughter friends and kin? She feared to hear the names of Englishmen or Americans whom she knew.

Not wishing to refresh Stephen's suspicions about her, Alex stubbornly refused to question him about the war and depended upon eavesdropping for her news. Thinking of her beloved uncle, she fretted over this ghastly war which didn't sound promising for the Americans. The Royal Navy had never been defeated; how could America defend herself against such a force when she could only boast of a few meager ships? Their only hope lay in the mighty *Constitution,* and she could only do so much. In a way, Alex was slightly perturbed with Stephen for not lending his ship, men, and himself to this obviously just cause!

Before leaving home, her father had been distressed and angered by America's embargo, Napoleon's Continental System, and England's Orders-in-Council. Did those messages between her uncle and her father contain treasonous information? Had they decided to use privateers to save their shipping business? If only she knew what those baffling stitches said! Until Stephen proved his love and faith, she dared not trust him with their identities. But, oh, how she wished she could!

New fears and doubts tormented her. They had outsailed several ships and attacked others. How long could their luck hold out? What future did this life offer either of them? How she wished he would become a loyal American, for then she would accept him.

Each time they docked or anchored near the

American coast, Stephen would go ashore for hours. She would pace the confines of his cabin until he returned safely. After each separation, no matter how brief, she would fall into his arms and make almost savage and desperate love to him. When he returned after an overly long visit, she would rant angrily in relief before he would scoop her up in his arms and toss her on the bed to make leisurely and tormentingly tantilizing love to her.

Time seemed endless; and yet, it was passing swiftly. August was half over when the final straw to their bittersweet stalemate came. The *Black Mist* had boldly taken many British merchant ships and daringly sunk several English frigates. They had delivered confiscated booty to different ports and had restocked simultaneously. Not once had Stephen given in to her pleas to go ashore. He steadily warned of her dangerous predicament if anyone learned of her presence. Believing he was sincerely concerned about her health and safety, she obeyed his every command.

Alex was perplexed by the brown packets which Stephen would bring to his cabin and conceal after battles with English ships. She was even more confused when he took them with him when he went ashore. Yet, the significance of these actions never registered in her innocent mind.

Her heart sank the night he returned to his ship in a stormy rage. On August nineteenth, the *Constitution* had confronted and disabled the noted *Guerriere!* Alex couldn't believe that shocking news. Instead of being elated, Stephen was furious. During an explosive outburst, she learned why. The British army and naval fleet were making steady and deadly progress against the American forces on land and sea. Her country was even threatening to blockade the entire coast! Thousands of men had died, some brutally at the hands of Indians. Wounded soldiers lying near death had been slaughtered and scalped on British instruction! It was an awesome thing to discover about her own people.

She had been with Stephen for nearly two months now. He had not mentioned the notorious petticoat until tonight. As he paced his cabin in pensive thought, she watched him closely and curiously. She wondered what had him so upset.

Alex would never have suspected what was troubling the pirate so deeply. Matters were getting worse on land and at sea. Madison had ordered him to proceed to Florida to meet with the new Spanish governor to convince him to allow an American stronghold in his territory and to prevent the English from digging in there as a supply stop and for attacking America from her southern border. With the dangers increasing daily and his missions becoming more critical and secret, he couldn't keep Angelique any longer. Should he release her or turn her in?

Spencer wished Castlereagh's letter of capitulation to the Americans' terms had come sooner. He raged at his timing, for never had it been more costly. He had been rescuing Angelique and wasting time with Thackery while that ominous letter was slowly, too slowly, making its way across the Atlantic ocean to arrive after the American declaration of war. If only he had intercepted the *Hornet* instead! The plan set into motion, there was no turning back now. Only victory would appease the Americans.

In light of the intensity of the war, he needed his full concentration on the war at hand. Time for leniency and personal pleasures had run out. He needed to get down to serious fighting now. Whatever Angelique's connections were, he was determined to uncover them.

He halted his aimless roamings to stare at her. Confusion clouded her eyes. "Is something wrong, Stephen?" she softly asked.

"It damn well is, love. You," he added mysteriously.

"Me? I don't understand. Did I do something to upset you?"

"If you can't relate the code on your petticoat, give me the names of the men involved. I have to know now, Angel. It's vital."

She looked at him. "That isn't important, Stephen," she protested, alarmed by the way he was acting.

"Let me decide if you don't mind," he snarled.

"I do mind. I can't tell you," she refused as in the past.

"You can and you will!" he thundered, astonishing

her with his vehemence. His eyes narrowed and darkened in reckless determination.

"No," she replied, her tone carrying a pleading note.

"I've spent nearly two months playing the love-struck idiot to you. The game is over! Tell me what I want to know, woman!"

"Game?" she echoed. Only a game?

"That's right, love. I tried to win your trust and affection, but I failed. I'm weary of coddling you and coaxing you. I see no reason for your continued silence. If you don't relent soon, I'll be forced to take drastic measures," he threatened.

Drastic measures? After all they had shared, would he really turn her over to her enemies? His expression and tone said yes. She grimaced at the pain of his calloused betrayal. It would have only required three short words to extract anything from her. But in his arrogant resolve, he had stubbornly and haughtily refused them.

Alex was beyond caring now. If the choice was between her freedom and her father's life and reputation, there was none. "I suggest you set sail for the nearest port of American authority, for I'll never tell you," she blatantly resisted his fury and power.

"You'll be sorry, love," he muttered through clenched teeth.

"I already am, Captain Steele," she uttered in despair. She had lost everything she loved and desired. What little pride and loyalty remained within her strengthened her resilience.

He seized a handful of silvery gold hair and yanked her head backwards, compelling her to lock gazes with his. "Once the course is set, love, there's no turning back. If I'm to help you, it must be now. Please, Angel, trust me," he unexpectedly and tenderly entreated her.

Tears blurring her vision, Alex vowed, "I can't. There's more at stake than my life and freedom. My fate lies within your hands, sir. There is nothing I can do or say to affect it."

"You're blind and stupid, love. It would take but a few words to end this private war between us. Yield to me, Angel, else your life is worth little. Don't place this monstrous decision upon my head."

A solitary tear slipped down her cheek. "It is already within your realm of power, sir. I have yielded all that is mine alone to give, far more than I should have. There is nothing more to grant that is mine alone. I have given my word the code is of no threat to you or the Americans. After all we have known together, if you do not trust me now, you never will. I cannot understand this fierce doubt within you, nor how you could calmly hand me over to those who have declared themselves my foes. You know what will probably happen to me. Yet, you do not care. You have no mercy or kindness, Steele. I am innocent. If I die, my blood will forever be upon your hands."

Thinking her trying to play upon his warring emotions, he sought to halt the ruse, "It will not be the

313

first blood I have shed out of necessity, nor the last. You hold the deliverance of your fate within your obstinate, cunning head. If you choose to remain silent, you have only yourself to blame. You can play the patriotic martyr, but I'm no executioner. You have six days to make up your mind before we dock in Florida. When I set sail again, you will sail with me only if you earn that right."

"Plan to sail without me, Captain Steele," Alex announced, her lips and chin quivering.

"As you wish, Angel. I only pray you realize this is no game before it's too late. If I leave you in Florida, our paths will never cross again."

She wondered if there was a trace of disappointment or sadness in his tone. His expression was harsh and impassive, telling her nothing. Six days to set the pattern for the remainder of her life . . . or death. What should she do? If he had tricked her for two months with his golden dreams and promises, he could easily delude her again.

Bereft and alone, she turned and walked to the bed. As if minus all modesty and shame now, she quietly stripped and went to bed . . . as usual. Her back to him as tears of bitterness and anguish dampened her pillow, Alex could feel the force of his cold stare. She wished things were different, but they were not and never would be.

She jumped as the cabin door slammed after his departure. Unable to prevent it, Alex burst into tears, knowing whatever they had shared for such a short time had been brutally shattered by the vicious demands of war, demands which she could not alter or prevent.

Spencer's pretense of resignation and acceptance of her and her silence had proven costly for each of them. It had only served to increase their love and desire for each other. Each carefree day and blissful night spent together had forged a stronger bond between them; each day, especially now, they blindly and foolishly resisted it.

XII

"My only love . . . Too early seen
unknown, and known too late!"
—*Romeo and Juliet,* William Shakespeare

Avoiding each other as much as possible, the next
few days passed in a tormenting existence for the ill-
fated lovers. Spencer totally ignored Alex, in bed and
out. Desperately in love, but too proud to submit, Alex
avoided the moody captain.

Two days from their destination, black clouds began
to build ominously upon the far horizon, rapidly
closing in on the tall-masted ship now boasting white
sails and the name *Wandering Siren.* For an hour the
storm trailed them like a persistent hound after a
wounded deer. The winds were gradually picking up,
warning of what was to come. The waves answered her
gusty cries, crashing white tips against the sturdy hull
of the ship. The sails crackled and popped like corn in a
hot pan. Eventually all traces of white and blue
disappeared from the heavens. Only leaden gray and
portentous black could be sighted. The mare's-tails
upon the horizon forecast the bleak story of what was
in store.

"Batten down the hatches and gear, men," came
their captain's command as he stood proud, calm, and

317

self-assured upon the rolling deck on his first love. "When she hits, she'll take her toll."

"Should I warn Angelique we'll be hitting a violent squall soon?" Andy asked in deep concern for the lovely creature his friend was mentally and emotionally torturing. After being around her for so many weeks, he wasn't at all convinced Josh was accurate in his stubborn assumptions.

"She'll know soon enough," he growled impatiently, growing weary and annoyed at the way his crew was rebelling against his decisions.

The tempest hit at sunset, attacking as viciously as a starving wolf on a helpless lamb. The winds and waves seemed to join forces to test the strength and prowess of this ship and her captain. The massive craft heaved violently under this assault of nature. The ship heeled sharply to the leeward side as several crew members struggled with the heavy sails. Water surged over the sides to flood the deck.

The persistent waves tugged at gear and men, begging to take them along with their watery fingers. White-knuckled hands clung frantically to ropes and denied Mother Nature her sacrifices. From behind the thunderous clouds shot jagged streaks of lightning, dancing like eerie skeletons upon a somber backdrop. Rain beat down upon the men with a stinging, punishing force. It was impossible to assess which element rendered the most power or the loudest noise: the crashing waves, the howling winds, the roaring thunder, the defenseless sails and groaning masts, or the crew screaming over them to be heard.

The scene had been enacted many times before, but it never ceased to inspire dread and respect. Faces were lined with worry and strain; hands were taut and bleeding as they gripped ropes to steady the sails or to play them against the winds. Booted feet scuffed over wet decks as they attempted to brace their owners against the pull and tug of the mighty ocean. As the mischievous fingers of the water and wind yanked at ropes, many were pulled free to send gear or cargo rolling into the roaring waves to disappear instantly.

But even amidst their awe and apprehension, an aura of suspense and elation filled each man, especially the captain. Each storm was like a personal battle where he proved his greater cunning and courage. He revelled in his dauntless contempt of danger and fear. It was a challenge he savored, one in which he always won. He was experienced and skilled, as was his loyal crew. He knew exactly what to do and the precise moment to do it and he commanded his beloved ship to withstand it all.

As suddenly as it had come, the fierce squall headed away to blow itself out to sea. Soaking wet, but filled with excitement and satisfaction, Captain Joshua Steele gave the first shout of victory when the last sign of danger was past. He studied each mast and the riggings. A slight rip here and there but no real damage, he joyously concluded. He ran his fingers threw his dark head of wet hair. He licked his lips, tasting the salt. The peril a thing of the past, he shouted to Andy he was going below to bathe and change into dry clothes.

"We can handle the clean-up, Josh. Why not turn in?" he suggested, hoping his friend would spend some time with his ravishing captive, hoping Josh would change his mind and free her.

Their gazes met and locked in mutual understanding. "No need, Andy. We'll make port in two days."

Without caring if Josh saw him, Andy sadly shook his head and walked off. Even if Angelique was a spy, didn't she deserve some mercy? Just who was Josh trying to punish and why? Did he even know himself? He sincerely hoped Josh would change his mind, but he wouldn't interfere.

When Spencer entered his cabin, it was totally engulfed in darkness. At least Alex had the sense to douse the lantern to prevent a fire! He called her name, but she didn't answer him. He grinned roguishly at her willful streak. As he headed for the lantern, he nearly tripped and fell over her. "What the . . ." he exploded, catching his balance before tumbling to the floor. "Angel?" he called out through the obscure shadows. No reply. He shook her shoulder. No movement.

He hurriedly found the lantern and lit it. He turned to see what mischief she was up to now. Stunned, he instantly saw the bloody injury upon her forehead. He knelt beside her and lifted her head, resting it upon his quivering knee. She was out cold. He gently picked her up and placed her upon the bed. He touched the sensitive wound and she winced in pain and moaned. He took a cloth and wet it to mop the blood away to study the wound.

It was a small cut, but was bleeding steadily. He held the wet cloth to it. Dipping his fingers in the water basin, he flicked moisture into her pale face. Her thick lashes fluttered and opened. Emerald green eyes looked up at him in confusion.

"What happened?" she hazily inquired, her temple aching.

"There was a storm. Evidently you took a fall," he speculated. "It appears my wooden lady sought her own revenge for your past attack. Your injury matched the one you gave me by the pond."

She pondered his explanation, then flippantly agreed. "I was sitting at the table, but the ship was rolling so badly I moved. I was going to lie down, but I didn't make it. I think I hit the table. Is it bad? Will there be a scar?" she asked, like any vain female. "Perhaps your ship packs a heavier wallop than I do."

He chuckled, inwardly relieved she wasn't hurt any worse. "I think not. Were you ill?" he teased.

"No. I'm a good sailor. Captain Burns said so," she pertly snapped.

"Burns? Of the *Moon Maiden?*" he pressed.

"Yes. I sailed to America with him," she carelessly continued.

"The *Moon Maiden* sailed the same day I did. You escaped right under my nose?" he sneered in anger, recalling how he had searched for her everywhere.

Astounded by this fact, she blurted out, "You were on the ship heading southward that morning?" She could still envision that stimulating sight, but hadn't realized this was that same sleek and graceful ship.

He began to laugh. "All that time we were only a few feet apart," he murmured thoughtfully. It might do to check with Burns to learn who had purchased her fare, perhaps even discover her identity!

"Why are you looking at me like that?" she curiously asked.

He grinned slyly. "Inquisitive little tart, aren't you? How do you feel? Head injuries can be dangerous." Perhaps he could find out the truth without her aid . . .

"More so than your American authorities?" she sneered sarcastically at his concern, phony no doubt! This was his first smile in days.

"My American authorities?" he probed.

"If not, you wouldn't be so eager to assist them!" she hotly accused.

"I have my reasons, love," he coldly replied.

"So do I, Captain Steele," she stated acidly.

"Angel, Angel . . . Why do you make this so difficult for us?" he sighed in exasperation.

"It isn't difficult at all, Captain Steele, merely impossible." She turned her face away from his piercing gaze to conceal her tears.

He gently grasped her chin and pulled it back around, placing a heady kiss upon her mouth. As he dragged his mouth from hers, she informed him, "You're getting me all wet."

"As I recall, you did the same to me one night," he jested mirthfully, standing up to remove his clothes. Knowing the futility of resisting him, she submitted to his hands as they undressed her and eased her beneath the covers.

He joined her, but once again kept his broad back to her. He was too near and inviting to be ignored, no matter how fiercely she tried. There was so little time left. Her ravaged heart rebelled against his loss and the loss of all she loved dearly.

Just above a whisper, she solemnly confessed, "You're right, I'm not brave. I was terrified during the storm. I want to go home, Stephen. Please . . ." She began to tremble and weep.

Why did she appeal to Stephen to weaken him? At sea, he was Joshua Steele. Why did she have the power to make him forget that fact? He listened to her sobbing as long as he could stand it. He turned over and murmured tenderly, "Come here, love."

He didn't have to ask twice. Alex was instantly in his comforting, strong embrace. He nuzzled his chin against her fragrant mane of silky gold. She was too small and fragile to endure such a dire fate. Nothing worked with her, neither force nor gentleness. What was he going to do now? Soon, she would be out of his life forever. Why did that thought plague him? For countless reasons, they were an impossible match.

At her touch and smell, his passions flamed to possess her. She was warm, willing, and alluring. Her mesmerizing siren's song was too magical to resist. His mouth sought hers in an exploratory, devastating kiss. Within moments, they were entrapped in a world of fiery passion.

Spencer trailed his tongue seductively over her parted lips before tasting the sweetness of her mouth.

As he pulled his feverish lips from hers to tease at her ear, he whispered tenderly in a voice laced with heavy emotion. Ensnared by her own wild and wonderful needs, her mind absorbed only the passion which his husky voice declared so boldly. Her body throbbed with fierce cravings which only Stephen could incite and soothe.

Alex eagerly stroked the virile body which her senses had come to know as well as her own. Its strength and beauty tantalized and pleased her. She absently wondered why his masculine hands which caressed her body to such heights of frenzied pleasure were not weathered or callused from their rugged way of life. Each part of his valiant frame represented vitality, from his sable head to his warm feet. The mere sight or smell of him filled her with greedy desire. He was like a powerful and deadly drug which she could not resist sampling, to which she had become addicted.

With deliberate and agonizingly sweet movements, his hands seemed to memorize each inch of her trembling body. How was it possible for a brief touch here or there to be so stimulating? Without cupping her breast, his hand wandered over it, teasing the protruding nipple with his palm. A liquid fire which raced from her spinning head to her dainty feet burned like potent acid, dissolving and enflaming her with a greater need. She groaned as he slowly continued his intoxicating foreplay, as if to have her mindless with passion before entering her and appeasing the yearnings he was inspiring.

Spencer's mouth returned to hers and hungrily

sought delight where he couldn't find truth. His teeth
gently pulled upon her lower lip before easing down to
the hollow of her throat to place several kisses there,
then slowly moving to nibble at her ivory shoulder. As
his tongue made tiny circles around her other breast,
his hand found another place to blissfully torment.
Just as he was certain she was moist enough to allow
his easy penetration, she moaned in a strained voice,
"Please, Stephen . . . I need you now."

He moved atop her and drove his manhood into that
warm, dark haven to seek his own ecstasy. With
tightly leashed control, his rhythm was calculated and
stirring. Higher and higher they climbed the spiral of
mutual desire, their bodies joining and working as one.
Each time he thrust into her receptive body, she
arched upwards to take all of him. Each time he
slightly withdrew, she groaned with lingering hunger.

Reality had deserted them long ago. Only thoughts
of fulfillment lingered in the shadowy cabin. Soon, the
masterful strokes increased in purpose and speed,
driving almost desperately into her. Yet Alex was
beyond feeling anything but Spencer and his savagely
sweet onslaught. Her mouth and body instinctively
responded to his touch; her stomach tightened
momentarily as the overwhelming spasms swept
through her fiery womanhood; his lips seared hers,
binding her to him for all time. Simultaneously,
Spencer abandoned his guard and allowed his molten
juices to intermingle with hers. Time and time again
he plundered her mouth and womanhood until every
ounce of torturous need was filled. He had made love

to many women, but never had ever delighted him as this slip of a girl did.

Swept away, he relaxed briefly upon her before rolling aside, pulling her along in his possessive embrace. Spencer's hand trailed over her smooth stomach, then over her breasts to rediscover their soft flesh. She was calm and limp in his arms, her passions sated. He smiled into the darkness of his quarters. He had given as much pleasure as he had received.

His fingers wandered into her silky mane and pulled her head to rest in the hollow of his throat. One of her long legs was gently trapped between his as her body molded itself perfectly against him. He grinned as her hand began to move up and down his side, hesitating at his narrow waist, while her other hand toyed absently in the curly mat upon his chest. Alex sighed in contentment and snuggled closer to him.

He grasped her chin and lifted it, gazing down at the exquisite features which he could barely detect in the dim glow offered by the shafts of moonlight entering the porthole. He gazed at her for a lengthy time, bringing a look of inquisitiveness to her brilliant eyes. His finger traced over her cheekbone and across her passion-swollen lips. His manhood began to stir to new life. Alex pressed forward to boldly kiss him, so enraptured that she was unaware of her unbridled actions.

"Am I so unskilled that I can appease you for only a moment, my sensuous siren?" he teased, his voice and expression playful and mellow. "Do you hint at another union this quickly?"

Alex smiled seductively and brazenly closed her hand around his erect manhood as she provocatively parried, "It appears I am the one who cannot sate you, my lusty pirate. Surely this hint is more insistent than my meager kiss?"

"Then perhaps your suggestive kiss should try to match my bold invitation," he devilishly challenged, covering her mouth with his.

When his lips left hers and sought her breast, she rolled her head upon the pillow as new fires swept through her tingling body. Every nerve in her body was alive and afire. Vainly attempting to conceal the eagerness in her voice and quivering frame, she laughed and stated, "I fear I am too unpracticed to compete with your skills, Sir Pirate."

"Then I shall teach you all you do not already know, my luscious sea witch," he warned roguishly, chuckling wickedly.

"Somehow I don't think such lessons are proper. Wherever shall I practice such skills when you release me?" she saucily asked, his loving assault tearing away her logic.

"Once you leave this ship, you best forget them, love."

"But why teach me such things if only to forget them so quickly?"

"I'm selfish and demanding," he lazily replied.

"I see. I'm to pleasure you, Sir Pirate, but no one else?"

"Exactly. I can't allow you to go traipsing around the country enslaving every male you encounter," he jested mirthfully, suppressing his laughter.

She giggled. "What if I only want to conquer one male heart?"

"One or one at a time?" he genially fenced with her.

"Only one. Surely one perfect man is enough for any woman?"

"If a perfect man existed, perhaps it would be."

"You're saying even the formidable Captain Joshua Steele isn't perfect? What a disappointment," she wailed, sighing dramatically.

"I never claimed to be, love, and I'm far from it. You of all women should know that by now. Surely it isn't my black, steely heart you're after," he huskily teased, gently yanking upon a tawny curl.

"I was under the impression you didn't possess a heart of any kind, Captain Steele," she quickly came back at him.

"What, praytell, do you think keeps this aging body alive?"

"The power of your evil forces, naturally," she pertly quipped.

"Is my evil power so great that I could enslave your soul?"

"Perhaps if you desired it enough, but you don't. Your love of freedom and adventure are more appealing than any mortal female could ever be," she boldly hinted, hoping he would deny her statements.

"You're absolutely correct," Spencer admitted. "I doubt there's a woman alive who could tempt me to sacrifice them to possess her and to accept her bonds." Trying to recapture their playful mood, Spencer said,

"No way, love; Captain Steele is a confirmed bachelor."

"I never doubted that for a moment, Sir Pirate," Alex whispered, hoping her lowered voice would hide the loud rending of her tender heart. Yet, even as she told herself this situation was impossible, she bravely and foolishly determined to tempt him beyond his control. He fiercely desired and enjoyed her; of that, she was certain! Determined to savor her love while she could, Alex pulled Spencer's head to hers, seeking shelter in the circle of his arms. Together they boldly rode the waves of passion once more; then, exhausted, they slept in each other's arms, their troubles neither forgotten nor settled.

It was late afternoon when Spencer finally returned to his cabin that next day. Their night of lovemaking tugged unmercifully at his conscience. Alex was dressed and sitting at the table, poised like a polished lady awaiting her tea and scones. He went to his desk and sat down to work, not even speaking to her or even glancing in her direction after his entry.

The legs of his chair scraped loudly as he turned to speak to her. He couldn't avoid conversation with her any longer. "I'm going to ask you one last time, Angel; will you tell me the truth? The storm earned you another day's reprieve; she blew us off course. Well?"

He noticed her back stiffen. Alex swallowed loudly enough for him to hear it. Without speaking, she shook her head. "May I go on deck for some fresh air and a change of scenery now? You've kept me locked in here for days now. Surely a condemned prisoner has some rights?"

"Have it your way, love. But I'll grant you to the last minute to change your mind. If you don't, I promise you I'll walk away and never glance back," he stated in a wintry tone.

She squeezed her eyes tightly shut in dread and despair. She instinctively knew neither of them would change their minds. "May I take a walk, sir?" she forced the only reply she could from her dry lips.

Torn between wanting to spank her and make passionate love to her, he did neither. "Why not?"

As he stood up, the dreaded warning was given, "Ship to starboard!"

Alex paled and swayed. Another perilous battle? Would she survive to see Florida and American captivity? She barely noticed as Spencer swiftly responded to the alert by yanking on his infamous disguise and racing out, only pausing to shout at her, "Stay here, Angel!" He was gone.

Alex hurried to the porthole to peer out. Panic clutched at her heart as she sighted the massive frigate heading straight for them! She strained to make out her flag: English! The striking colors of the Union Jack waved in the breeze. Should she be overjoyed or terrified? What would they do when they discovered her aboard?

Her wide eyes were glued to the stalking ship. What was Steele waiting for? The guns on both ships remained silent. Were they each sizing up their foe, deciding whether or not to attack?

Spencer took his place on the bow, keenly observing the strategy of his swiftly approaching enemy. The intentions of the English captain were apparent to him. His crew and guns were ready and alert. He was well-manned and armed for any battle with her forty-four carronades. The guns were an assortment of thirty-two and forty-two pounders. There was also a long gun on the bow and one on the stern.

The distance between them disappeared rapidly, sealing the fate of one or the other.

"Watch the wind, Danny; hold her steady. Stay alert, men. We'll take her at a right angle and make splinters of her from stem to stern," he confidently stated.

Spencer yelled up to the man in the crow's nest, "Keep a sharp eye, Tim!" To his gunners, he called out, "Broadside her, then come about to reload. George, hoist the Jolly Roger and give 'em something to think about. Andy, stand by to order the long guns. We need to clip those masts and their steering."

"She's piling on the canvas, Capt'n! She's heading straight for us! What fool would try to ram us right off!" Tim called down incredulously as he observed the curious maneuvers of the enemy ship.

The very instant the *Black Mist* was in firing range, the other ship swayed to the leeward side and turned to broadside them, her guns booming. With luck and cunning, the *Black Mist* turned just in time to watch the shot pass between the forward mast and mizzenmast. Their guns quickly answered the awesome challenge, sending a direct hit across the deck on the English frigate. Another broadside shot was fired instantly, smashing into the aft mast, sending it toppling into the water on the other side.

The *Black Mist* swiftly maneuvered to the other side to fire those guns while the others were being reloaded. Danny was quick to respond to Spencer's commands. Several rounds were exchanged between the two ships with little damage to them. Knowing the results of this battle, the crew worked quickly and efficiently to be the victors. The *Black Mist* fired again, striking and weakening the forward mast. A roar of joy and confidence engulfed the pirate ship, the anticipation of victory entering each man.

Spencer's ship took a hit on her forward mast, the top shearing off and hanging precariously, only the rigging preventing its deadly plunge to the deck below. Tim's mangled body was tossed into the sea as lifeless as a tattered ragdoll. Spencer cursed and grimaced as if feeling the injuries himself. Enraged, he cautioned himself to self-control. "Fire all guns!" he shouted above the roar of the battle.

The English frigate seemed to stagger under the rain of blows. Her hull reluctantly accepted two hits. Smoke betrayed the fire within her wooden belly. She was a mass of splintered and smoldering defeat. Yet, her guns fired once more, tearing a hole in the starboard side near the rail of Spencer's ship.

"Sink her, George! She's asking for it!" Spencer barked.

The carronades blasted another round into the

disabled vessel, damaging her beyond hope. A deadly silence followed as they tensely waited to see if the English frigate would finally give quarter. Gallant and fiercely proud to the end, she refused to strike her flag. Flames were now licking greedily at her. She wouldn't live to fight another day.

Hastily surveying the damage to his own ship, Spencer swore in anger. They would be forced to spend a lengthy time in the San Augustin port to repair their damages. He fumed at the impending delay, but professional repairs were mandatory to survival. He didn't like this feeling of weakness and vulnerability. But far worse, he didn't like the death of any crew member.

"We going to board her, Captain?" Andy asked, pulling him from his pensive mood.

Spencer's eyes were chilled and troubled as they glanced across the choppy waters to the dying ship. "Let's not waste our time and energy. Let's make port before we meet another brave Englishman," he sneered contemptuously. "Misty took some damage. She needs some doctoring fast."

Andy caught his meaning. In this condition, they were almost defenseless. "Strike the flag and set sail. You know the destination."

Spencer turned to find Alex poised in the hatchway, watching him curiously. He stalked over to her. "What the hell are you doing up here!" he thundered at the silent, ashen girl.

"What about survivors, Captain Steele? That ship's sinking," she bravely voiced her concerns for her fellow countrymen.

"She took that risk when she attacked us! They have boats. Let 'em save themselves. If we had been disabled, they would still be blasting away until we were resting on bottom. They should thank their lucky stars I don't finish the job for them! This way, if they're smart and tough, they have a chance for survival."

Alex glanced at the ship which was weighing heavy in the water, flames engulfing her. They were close enough to hear the shouts of panic and cries of pain from the wounded. "You're just going to calmly sail away and leave them like that? What about the wounded? Those men were only following orders, just like your crew."

"We're at war, Angel. You don't aid your enemy to return and attack you another day," he shouted impatiently, drawing stares from several nearby men.

"May I take a boat over there?" she incredulously asked.

"Are you insane, woman? In less than an hour, there won't be a ship there," he exploded in rage.

"I know, but I might could help some of the wounded. They're my people," she reminded him, bringing a scowl to his face.

"Get below, Angel, before I forget you're a woman!" he warned. "My ship's damaged and Tim's dead!" he thundered angrily.

"From your accent, Captain Steele, you were once English. Why do you hate us so much now?" Without waiting for an answer, she turned and fled to his cabin, sobbing.

"Don't you think you're being a little hard on her? She's very young and delicate, Josh," Andy remarked from behind him.

Spencer whirled and snarled, "Stay out of this, Andy! She's my concern and my problem."

"Problem, yes; but I don't think you're the least concerned about her! Do you have any idea what those men will do to her?"

"All she has to do is tell me the truth!" he growled, angered at being questioned and pressed by even his closest friend.

Andy lowered his voice to a near whisper, "Listen to me, Spence; maybe she can't. My God, man, she's terrified of you. She's had a hard time. Are you conveniently forgetting how you two met? She has plenty of cause to despise you and refuse to trust you. Funny thing, I don't think she does hate you. Why, I can't imagine after the way you've treated her."

"What do you mean?" Spencer demanded in confusion.

"Are you blind? The girl's in love with you. She was standing there for most of the battle. Doing what? Watching you like a hawk! Everytime a gun fired, she would almost race to your side. The only thing she was afraid of was something happening to you."

"She has a strange way of showing her affection and concern!" Spencer retorted skeptically.

"So do you, Spence. That's the real problem, isn't it? You're too damn proud and stubborn to admit you want her! For certain, you're afraid to keep her.

You've finally discovered something you truly crave and you refuse to admit it."

"You're crazy, Andy! Sure, she's desirable and beautiful. But that's as far as it goes! Can't you imagine my Grandfather Will's face if I waltzed in with a girl like that on my arm? He'd disown and disinherit me in one swift blow!"

"Since when did you allow your grandfather or anyone to plot your course? You don't need his money; you have more than he does right now! She's the best thing that's come along, Spence. Think twice before you lose her for keeps this time. Can't you recall how unforgettable she was before you found her again? After all this time together, it'll be worse if you lose her again. If you have any feelings at all for her, set her free," he urged, utterly baffled by the inbred forces which compelled his friend to marry a woman of genteel birth.

"Never. She'll confess or go to prison."

"Is that it? If you can't have her, no man will?" he boldly challenged.

"Don't be absurd, Andy! We have our orders."

"They don't know about her yet. You know what prison's like for a female. You can't do it. It really sticks in your craw she can defy you, doesn't it? Are you still after revenge for her little attack on you? If you're expecting the Americans to hold her safely in prison until you can reclaim her after the war, it won't work. She'll never be the same . . . if she even survives such an experience."

"You know as well as I do that code has some

special meaning."

"Even so, what different could it make now? What if she was forced to carry it? It's mighty strange we haven't come across it before—nor has anyone else. Maybe she's telling the truth. Maybe it's just a family message," he reasoned in mounting frustration.

"But what if it isn't, Andy?"

"What if it is?" Andy quickly came back to nettle him.

Without an answer, Spencer turned his back on his friend . . . unable to forget his words.

The winds and currents in their favor, they sailed into the port at San Augustin that next afternoon. Alex was shocked when Spencer took her ashore this time, her and her baggage! Yet, the moment they were settled into a comfortable suite of rooms in a massive stucco structure, he left for some secret meeting with "friends."

A guard had been left outside her door to prevent any rash moves. She had been quick to pick up certain facts: the Spanish ruled Florida and the French ruled the Spanish through Napoleon's brother on the Spanish throne. For all she knew, they had simply put into port here for rest and repairs.

Before leaving, Stephen had ordered a bath for her. She reclined in the large oval tub for hours. It was deliriously invigorating. After she dressed in one of her finest and prettiest gowns, Alex relaxed in the warm sunlight on a side balcony to dry her tawny hair.

She brushed and braided it, securing it around her head like a golden coronet. She splashed on a delightful fragrance and nibbled at the food sent in by the guard.

If Stephen was determined to discard her, he would view her at her best this last time! She would make such an impression upon him, he would never forget her! She knew she was desirable; men had made that plain to her in the past. She would use every charm and feminine wile she possessed. Tears, rebellion, and submission hadn't worked any wonders for her. What would happen if she made herself irresistible and provocative? Could she persuade Stephen to change his mind? She would give it her damnedest!

She withdrew a book from her trunk and sat down to patiently wait for him. She instantly jumped up and knocked on the door. When the guard answered her signal, she boldly and confidently ordered a sumptuous dinner and a heady red wine to be served in their room. Confused, the guard complied.

In less than half an hour, a table with a lacy cloth was brought inside. A silver candleholder with creamy tapers was placed upon it. A dish of colorful and fragrant flowers joined it. A light red wine followed and the table was set in elegant style. No doubt they realized this pirate captain could afford anything his lady ordered and responded with enthusiasm.

Just as darkness closed in, the delectable meal was brought to their room, covered with silver tops to keep everything warm. Glowing with anticipation, Alex lit the candles and waited. She nervously dabbed on more perfume. A heady odor from the mixture of flowers wafted through the open windows and balcony doors.

An hour passed—no Stephen. Another hour snailishly followed it—no Stephen. She called to the guard to ask when he would return. A new man was there and replied he didn't know the captain's plans. She paced the floor until her nerves were taut. Was it possible he wasn't coming back tonight? Perhaps he had another room? Perhaps he was working out the details to hand her over to the authorities here? Perhaps he was even seeing another woman?

She wearily and anxiously leaned back against the sofa. She sipped several glasses of wine, an unfamiliar habit. Taking its toll, she was eventually sound asleep. It was past two in the morning when Spencer finally came in, reeking of cheap cologne and brandy.

He stared at the strange sight which greeted his tired eyes. Neither his attempt to forget this vexing female in another woman's arms nor to drown his guilt in strong spirits had worked. All evening, all he could think about was her waiting here alone, vulnerable. His smarting gaze went from the sleeping girl attired in an exquisite gown to the table with burned-down candles, cold food, colorful flowers, and a half-empty bottle of wine.

He staggered over to her. In her lap were two objects: a wilted flower and an empty wine glass. From the salty streaks upon her cheeks, she had been crying before falling asleep. He was transfixed by the vision of beauty and softness before him. Angel was an appropriate name for this slumbering child who radiated innocence and purity. He mentally cursed her for the effect she effortlessly worked upon him.

Effortlessly? he protested to himself. From the looks of things, she was definitely attempting to catch his attention. He was sorry he had messed up her scheme to entrap him. He was tempted to leave her there all night to punish her for her blatant and seductive game!

As with a small child, he helped her up and led her into the adjoining room to the bed. Unable to fully arouse herself, Alex was undressed by him and tucked in. He stripped and followed her, kissing her lightly upon the head.

Her lids fluttered slightly and she dreamily looked up into his handsome face. "Go to sleep, love; it's late," he tenderly murmured.

"Good night, Stephen. I love you," she mumbled in her hazy state, then closed those alluring green eyes to sink into instant slumber.

That slip sobered him. Did she really say what he thought? Did she realize what she was saying? Surely not, she was too far gone! Stunned, it was some time before he could get to sleep.

Once during the wee hours, Alex stirred and glanced over at him. Too fatigued to come alert, she detected the odor of brandy and cologne. Her mind spinning, anger and jealousy consumed her. "You vile bastard, you'll pay for this insult," she sleepily threatened before giving over to mindless sleep.

A light sleeper whose instincts were always sharp, he heard and ignored her empty threat. Maybe jealousy was good for her. When all else failed, work on a female's vanity. He grinned and sighed peacefully.

When Spencer awoke the next morning, he yawned and stretched to loosen taut muscles. His mouth felt like cotton and tasted worse. His temples ached, but he thought the pain was a result of a lack of sleep and tension rather than a hangover from too much brandy. He glanced over at the girl beside him. She looked almost regal with her exquisite features and her coronet of golden hair. Her soft lips were slightly parted and were most inviting. Thick, dark lashes lay against her flawless skin. Damn, if she wasn't the most fetching female alive!

He was sorely pressed to awaken her and make savage love to her as she lay there, an alluring mixture of innocence and provocation, carefree child and seductive woman. He wondered if Andy was right. Was he trying to punish her for being so enchanting and irresistible, so unreachable, so forbidden? Was he only trying to make certain no other man could possess those charms which he craved, yet resisted?

Spencer carefully left the bed so as to not disturb her. From the darkened smudges beneath her eyes, she needed more sleep—and he wasn't in any mood for a bitter confrontation this morning. He had other pressing matters to take care of before tonight. He went into the bath closet to wash, wishing he could purge his mind as easily. He dressed in tan breeches which fit his lower torso like a glove, leaving little to the imagination. Desiring comfort today, he pulled on a loose white shirt and left it opened halfway to his narrow waist, exposing a tawny chest with an enticing mat of furry black hair. He pulled on shiny black knee boots and strolled out, closing the door quietly behind him.

If he had been more alert this morning, Spencer would have been aware of the green eyes watching his every move. Alex had awakened long before him, but had feigned sleep to avoid an argument. She threw the covers aside, bathed, then dressed in a tea gown of muted greens.

Eying his discarded clothes from the night before, Alex absently picked them up to lay them across a chair. Catching the lingering fragrance of another woman's perfume, she angrily flung them back to the floor. She scolded herself for this ridiculous envy of another female. She had no rights where he was concerned. She had been a fool to fall in love with a man like Joshua Steele!

When she hadn't ordered any breakfast by midday, the guard knocked and inquired if she was ready to eat. Lacking any appetite, she refused without opening the door. Noting the remains of her spoiled evening staring her in the face, she finally called the guard to have the foolish evidence removed. She wondered what Stephen thought when he saw how she had planned to spend last evening. A cynical laugh passed through her taut lips. What did she care what he thought or felt? He had unmasked his true colors and intentions. All games had ended. If only she could claim one victory . . .

To pass the time away, she unpacked and neatly re-packed her trunks. She was baffled to discover her jewels still present. Why did they mean nothing to a greedy pirate? After all, they were worth a small fortune! She smiled in pleasure. With them, she might find some way to escape and buy her passage home. For the first time, those expensive baubles gave her delight and satisfaction. She carefully returned them to their concealed compartment.

Around two o'clock, the guard made another attempt to persuade her to eat something.

"I'm not hungry! How can I work up any appetite cooped up like some animal?" she vented her anger and tension upon the man.

"I'm sorry, miss: Capt'n's orders," he stated almost apologetically.

"I know, George; I'm sorry. I don't need to take my irritation out on you." She thanked him and closed the door to pace some more.

Alex went to the balcony and gazed out over the gardens below it. The rainbow-colored flowers with their sweet smells brought a smile to her lips and eyes. She reached out to pluck several from nearby trees. She held them to her nose and inhaled their stimulating odors. She leaned against the bumpy surface of the stucco wall and closed her eyes dreamily. Such a wide variety of thoughts and images flashed through her troubled mind. What if this was the last time she could enjoy nature at her peak, or feel the breeze playing through her amber hair and over her skin, or inhale the freshness of each new day, or . . .

Tears eased down her cheeks as she rebelled at the hopelessness of this trying situation and fully comprehended the price of her reckless love for a daring and heartless pirate. "Oh, Papa," she miserably cried, "I should have heeded your words. Surely no marriage could compare with this hellish existence. If I ever get home again, I'll never disobey you again."

Spencer shifted uneasily at intruding upon such a private and tormenting moment for her. He patiently, and yet anxiously, waited for her to compose herself. He dearly hoped she would not begin sobbing again; he didn't like the effect of her tears and anguish upon him! Angel, Angel, why do you make me hurt you this way? he inwardly raged.

Without opening her eyes, she wiped away the moisture teasing at her cheeks and quivering chin. "I'll never let you hurt me again, Stephen," she swore softly as if replying to his thoughts. She sighed wearily and inhaled the heady aroma of the flowers in her tight grasp. Time passed.

For some inexplicable reason, Spencer couldn't find the right words to open their talk. His normal poise and confidence were stormed by the sight before him. He couldn't allow his weakness for her to continue. He toughened his heart against his emotions. He only had a few more days before his ship would be ready to put to sea again and that last moment to decide her future would be upon him. His talks with Governor Sebastian Kindelan hadn't gone well so far. He could hardly blame the man for not trusting him and the American government. America had seized the western portion of the territory and attacked others. He hoped he wouldn't be forced to insist upon a base here to prevent the English from using it.

Alex opened her eyes, ready to order some hot tea to calm her frayed nerves. She jumped as her gaze touched upon the solemn man standing near her. Startled, she gasped, "How long have you been standing there gaping at me?"

"Only a few moments," he lied. "You looked so serene and lovely standing there, I couldn't break your magical spell," he teased, although serious.

Chips of ice flashed angrily in her green eyes. "Did you want something, or is it time to go?" she scornfully asked. She lifted her chin and shoulders to reveal her courage and pride.

His smoldering eyes eased over her body from head to foot, noting how nicely her clothes fit and enhanced her delicate air. "George says you haven't eaten all day. From the looks of it, you also skipped dinner last night. No appetite when I'm away?" he jested.

"My lack of hunger has nothing whatsoever to do with you, Captain Steele. Without exercise, the body doesn't require much food to nourish it." She noticeably failed to mention last night's fiasco. There was something different about her this morning. He dreaded to comprehend it. She was quiet, withdrawn, and tense.

"I've come to make amends for ignoring you so long, love, but I had business which came first. How would you like to attend a dinner and dance at a friend's house?" he asked, his own aura self-assured and mellow.

"No thank you, Captain Steele. I don't make a practice of socializing with my enemies," she rejected him.

"You mean you aren't bored enough yet to share my company outside my bed?" he teased.

"I would prefer not to share any time with you at all, sir," she sassily declared, looking as if she honestly meant it.

"You could dress in one of those lovely gowns and dazzle all the men and make the women green with envy," he added mischievously. "It would make a most enjoyable evening for both of us."

"I have no desire to do either, Captain Steele. As for being enjoyable, that I seriously doubt. Farewell parties have never been to my liking, especially not my own. I'm certain you can find another willing female to keep you company. Until you make the arrangements for my incarceration, I prefer to remain here . . . alone, if you don't mind."

He could sense the withdrawal and tension within her. She wasn't going to make this any easier for him. "The only female company I desire at present is you, Angel. I want you to come with me tonight."

She glared at him. "You have a strange way of revealing your interest in me, Captain Steele. The answer is still no. I find your company most disagreeable."

"Since when?" he snarled, his temper rising at her blatant rebuffs.

She laughed, a cool and taunting sound. "I am not one of your strumpets, Captain Steele. I will not be flaunted or treated as such. I'm sure you'll discover any other female more pliant and inviting than I am."

She placed her rigid back to him, waves of tawny hair flowing down her slender back. Was she still hurt and jealous? Was this some feminine ploy to punish him or to entreat him to plead for her attentions?

"You're coming with me whether you want to or not," he ordered. No woman had ever refused him anything. Who did this arrogant girl think she was!

"Are you still pouting because I didn't get home in time for dinner last night? If I had known you were planning such a special evening, I would have left my meeting posthaste," he murmured.

"Meeting, my foot!" she blurted out before thinking.

He chuckled, baiting her. "By jove, you're jealous!" he accused. "No need, love. That perfume was a silly joke; one I didn't take kindly to either. That cheap floozy should be glad I didn't beat her after rubbing all over me like that. I don't pick up cheap tarts, Angel, in case you've forgotten," he sought to disarm her with the truth for a change. "I'm sorry I missed a pleasant dinner with you."

"I'm not," she crisply replied, doubting his every word now. To nettle him, she said, "Besides, it was only meant to relax you so I could convince you to free me. With your vast knowledge and experiences with so many women, you would have seen right through my ruse. So, it really was for the best you didn't come back last night. I hate making a fool of myself, which I would have." She somehow knew the sarcastic truth would be more disturbing than a false pretense.

"Frankly, I'm not sure who's the bigger fool, you or me," he snarled.

She laughed again. "I doubt you have ever been a fool about anything or anyone, Captain Steele."

"Where you're concerned, I have, and it galls me beyond my limits of patience and endurance," he admitted reluctantly. "Now get dressed; we're going to that party."

"No," she calmly protested, keeping her back to him.

"You're coming along if I have to dress you myself!"

"I doubt you would want to tarnish your image by carrying me to a party all tied up, love," she scoffed. "That's the only way I'll leave this room. I should think you would find that most embarrassing. I'll make certain everyone there knows how much I detest you."

"I could care less how you feel about me."

"What about how they might feel if I shout your identity to them?" she retorted spitefully.

Suddenly realizing the guests at this affair would know him as Captain Stephen Farrington of the *Wandering Siren*, he chided himself for his careless oversight. He couldn't take her along. With any intelligence at all, she would figure out his identity. "If you don't want to come along, fine. Call George when you're ready for dinner, if you decide to ever eat again."

He was giving up awfully easy! Alex realized. He wasn't going to throw his weight around? A strange look had briefly crossed his aristocratic features. Why? Was he afraid to subject himself to a pleasurable evening with her? Now she had rashly condemned herself to another boring night alone, denied herself a chance to get even with him or to change his stubborn mind!

She hurried after him. He was leisurely changing clothes. Her eyes widened at his choice of garments. He had put on a pair of rich gold knee breeches which fit his fine form handsomely. They buttoned just below the knee over silk stockings which were concealed by shiny boots in the finest of leathers. Tailored to fit him perfectly, there wasn't a single crease or wrinkle to mar the seductive picture of his slender hips and muscular thighs.

A man who obviously recognized a flair for fashion and spared no expense with his clothes, she was speechless in her bold study of him. A definite sign of wealth and polish, he donned a white linen shirt which clung tightly to his chest and shoulders. A deep wine vest was added next. As if he had all evening, he gradually fastened the four buttons down its front. He slipped his arms into a matching coat which was elegant and appealing with its plain lines, snug sleeves, small cuffs at the wrists, and dangling coattails. Instead of a snowy cravat, he knotted a jabot of ivory lawn at his neck to complete his attire.

As he playfully brushed and fluffed his sable mane

which fell loosely to his collar, she suddenly realized his hair was freshly trimmed and shaped. His clean-shaven face flaunted the proud and arrogant lines of his features. He was certainly taking great pains with his appearance tonight! How she longed to be the woman on his arm tonight—on any night! He exuded such animal magnetism and undeniable charm that she scolded herself for her rash and regrettable refusal to go with him.

He turned around before her gaping eyes several times. "Well? Will I pass for a gentleman of fine breeding tonight, love?"

Unnerved and entranced, she murmured, "I didn't think it possible for you to look any better than you already did, but I can see I was vastly mistaken, Captain Steele. Like this, you could charm the Queen herself into deserting the King," she admitted.

"The Queen would be more susceptible to me than you are?" he wickedly teased, meeting her appreciative gaze in the reflective glass.

"I must confess, Captain Steele, you are most attractive, too much, so I fear. Is it too late to change my mind about going with you tonight?" she asked, causing him to tense up.

"I'm afraid so, love. I'm late as it is," he stated stoically.

"I can dress quickly when I must," she hinted boldly.

"After your little display of temper earlier, I don't think I could trust you. Tonight, I'm in the mood to relax and have a good time. I don't relish remaining on guard against your wily tricks."

"Not even if I promise to be on my very best behavior?" she pleaded.

He eyed her intently. How he wished he could take her along—but it was much too dangerous. "Don't wait up for me. I expect to be late, if I come back tonight." With that he headed for the door, opened it and told George to bring her dinner when she was ready for it. He glanced at her, winked and left.

Hearing him take the back stairs, Alex hurried to the balcony to watch his retreat. She berated herself for being so stubborn. She leaned back to hopefully catch another view of him while denying him one of her. He halted just beneath the balcony to talk with Andy, his first mate and good friend. As the words drifted to her alert ears, she couldn't believe what she was hearing.

Winking at Andy who was reluctantly a part of his devious scheme, Spencer played his role to the hilt . . .

XIII

"Delays have dangerous ends."
—*Henry VI*, William Shakespeare

"I'm tired of all her wily games and taunts, Andy," Spencer confided. "One minute she's all over me, and the next she's fighting me tooth and nail! I've given her ample time to tell me what I want to know. I can't take her back to sea with us; it's getting too dangerous out there. Besides, I'm exhausted with trying to figure out a woman who's so temperamental."

"What do you think they'll do with her?" Andy questioned, not daring to look up at the balcony.

"I wish I knew. Maybe she'll convince them she's innocent. Maybe they'll turn her loose to return to this so-called uncle of hers. Who knows?"

"What if they don't accept her claim of ignorance? Look how close you two have been, and you don't believe her for a minute."

"I could if she would tell me everything, Andy. My stars, man, doesn't she realize how suspicious her story and actions are? Once we sail, she won't be my problem anymore," he stated.

"Come on, Josh; you know you care about her," Andy injected, bringing a scowl to his friend's face at his audacity.

"Of course I care about her! She's different; she's refreshing and entertaining. But there are lots of sexy mermaids around."

"Have you mentioned her to the authorities yet?"

"I dropped a few hints about a possible spy," he nonchalantly answered.

"Is she really an English spy?" Andy skeptically inquired.

"If she isn't, she knows who is."

"Have you given any serious thought to her fate? It could even be death."

"I know, Andy, but it can't be helped. If she confesses all, I'll let her go. If not," he halted and burst into hearty laughter.

"What's so funny?" Andy quizzed.

A new idea came to mind. If Angelique didn't fear the authorities, there was another fate she would surely wish to avoid. "I have a better solution for our silent Angel. Since I don't want to endanger her life, I know a place where she'll be kept out of any further activities. She can spread a little joy while being out of the Americans' hair."

Assuming he was referring to his Virginia plantation, Andy jumped on this hint, "Where?"

His elation was short-lived when Spencer murmured in sardonic pleasure, "In Maria's brothel. She guards her girls like an eagle. Angel would never get out of there to transport any more codes."

"You can't mean that!" Andy debated, noting he was indeed serious.

"Why not? She would be alive and out of the way. It

would serve the little tease right! By now, she's experienced enough to survive there nicely. If she's cunning, she just might earn her freedom one day."

Alex winced at the coldness in Spencer's withering tone. She burned at being discussed so intimately and spitefully and fury filled her. She strained to catch his every word and inflection.

"That's exactly what I plan to do. If Angel doesn't come across by midday tomorrow, she'll be sleeping at Maria's from now on."

Alex nearly fainted. She didn't doubt his ruthless threat at all. Taking her chances with the American government was one thing, but risking enslavement to a filthy brothel? She had heard tales of this horrible fate of young girls who unfortunately fell into the hands of evil men like Joshua Steele. She could never endure such degradation. It was a far worse fate than death. How far did her loyalty to her family go when it endangered her survival and honor? Could she allow Captain Steele to confine her in such a deplorable place?

Could this man who had artfully seduced her body and claimed her heart and soul subject her to such an existence? They had shared blissful moments of unbridled passion—was he capable of such cruelty? Had she so misjudged him and their fiery relationship? Why, Joshua? she wretchedly cried. He was no human god after all; he was a sadistic demon who was devouring her heart, soul, and body.

"I have a meeting with Minister D'Onis and Governor Sebastian Kindelan tomorrow afternoon, then one with Commandant Lopez and some American named Campbell afterwards. I'll know all by lunch, or Angel will be keeping company with Maria before either meeting."

"I can't change your mind, Josh?" he worriedly pressed.

"No!" he objected arrogantly. "Let's go or we'll miss dinner."

The two men, so different in looks and character, strolled off. Alex slowly entered the room, suddenly stuffy in her highly emotional state. Yet, she did not dissolve into tremors and tears. A pleased smirk claimed her lovely lips and revenge danced brightly in her eyes. Her careless captor had just become her unknowing liberator.

She ran to her trunks and opened them. She quickly selected a special outfit for this final act to a desperate drama. She pulled two black dresses from her trunk, ones chosen by her uncle for a smiliar deception. She rolled them into a neat bundle and bound them inside a dark blue shawl. She put on a bright red gown with a daring neckline and billowy shirt. She placed her collection of jewels on the bed beside the other bundle to select a few pieces to aid her plans. Let him keep the rest; it would look too suspicious if she managed to escape with the entire collection. She headed to the door to set her desperate plan into motion, clutching a heavy object within her grasp. As a better plan came to mind, she sat it upon the table in the middle of the room.

She called George's name. The door clicked as he

unlocked it and stuck his head inside. "I need some help, George. Captain Steele is coming back for me later, but I'm having trouble with this dress. Some empty-headed seamstress placed hundreds of tiny buttons down the back. Could you do it up for me?" she sweetly entreated, smiling demurely.

Unaccustomed to helping a lady dress, he shifted nervously and hesitated. She innocently coaxed, "It's all right, George. Josh won't mind. I must hurry before he returns for me. Please. We won't tell him," she wheedled conspiratorially.

He laughed amiably and shuffled forward to comply. Just before he could fasten it halfway, Alex gasped in surprise and shrieked, "Who's that?"

George naively turned around to glance at the door. The statue thudded down upon his head, instantly rendering him unconscious. Alex hurriedly checked to make sure he was still breathing. She sighed in relief, hating to injure this genial man. To show him her apology, she placed a flower in his right hand and a diamond bracelet in the left. She stripped off the red gown and rolled it into a tight ball, then swiftly dressed in a dark blue gown and covered her head with the lacy Spanish scarf which she had bought just before leaving Philadelphia. What a wise purchase it had been!

Alex stuffed two necklaces of expensive gems into her dress near the waist and seized the red gown and her other bundle. She left without looking back, locking the door behind her. She rushed down the stairs as quickly as she could without making any excessive noise. She cautiously skirted the rear of the next building before stepping out to the main street. As if she were merely taking an afternoon stroll, she headed toward the tall white structure which was sure to be the governor's home. If she were mistaken, a large slice of her precious getaway time would be consumed.

The mantilla of midnight lace clutched tightly before her face, no one caught sight of the beauty revealed there. As she passed a heap of trash, she tossed the red bundle upon it. She had never liked the tawdry gown anyway and shouldn't have allowed that seamstress to convince her to buy it. She walked to the side gate and called out through the iron barrier. It was but moments before a Spanish soldier came to answer. She eyed his uniform in bright red and midnight black. Perplexed, he asked what she wanted.

She held her disguise in place as she calmly stated, "Please tell Governor Kindelan that Lady Alexandria Hampton is here to see him."

The guard gaped at her in disbelief and suspicion. She haughtily snapped, "We are close friends, sir. He will be most displeased that you kept me standing here like some commoner!"

Witnessing her polished manner and genteel speech, he hurriedly unlocked the gate and asked her to follow him. Once inside, he told her to wait while he told the governor she was here and wished to see him. She nodded and sat down, discarding the feigned haughty role she had seen so many spoiled females use on those of lesser stations.

Sebastian Kindelan swept into the room with his usual flair for pomp. She arose to greet him, extending her quivering hand. He gaped at her in astonishment as he took it and affectionately squeezed it. "Do my old eyes deceive me, Lady Hampton?" he ventured.

She smiled and stated clearly, "I fear not, sir. I am in dire need of your help and your secrecy." A look of sadness and fear entered those lovely green eyes. Pretense was necessary though she despised wearing its guise.

"I do not understand," he murmured in befuddlement. "Is your father with you?"

"No, sir. In fact, he has no idea where I am," she began.

"Surely you have not run away from home, my wild dove," he teased, recalling her willful nature.

"I was kidnapped by wicked pirates while returning home from visiting Uncle Henry in America," she announced in a shaky voice. "I have recently managed to clobber my guard and escape them this very day."

"What injustice is this!" he shouted in distress and fury. "I will set my guards upon them and slay them all!"

"I wish you could, sir, but they set sail earlier. Once I escaped them, I hid until their sails faded from sight. I didn't know what to do. There are American ships and men everywhere. Since we are at war, I feared to ask their assistance. I would be held for a hefty ransom should they learn of my father's name. So many of the privateers are connected with the American forces. I dared trust no one until I heard your name. It was the

359

sweetest sound I've ever heard, sir," she declared honestly, tears springing forth.

He patted her shoulder and comforted her, "No harm shall befall you now, my dear. I owe your father many favors. You have given me the chance to repay my dear friend of many years."

"You must tell no one of my presence here, sir. One careless word dropped, and friends of those ruffians might seize me again. They threatened me with dire fates. One wanted to sell me to slavers; others said to ransom me to my father. But I refused to speak his name or mine. I dare trust no one except you. Is there some way I could travel back to my uncle's without anyone, including your own men, finding out about me? I mean no disrespect, sir, but men often leak secrets when into their cups. I can hardly go unnoticed unless you keep me hidden."

"In troubled times like these, I will tell no one but my most trusted servants," Kindelan promised. "There are several privateers whom I trust implicitly. I am sure I can persuade one of them to take you safely to Henry's. With your King's men playing havoc upon the seas, it will be far easier to get you to Pennsylvania than England."

"I thought as much myself, sir," she concurred. She quickly related the protective ruse her uncle had planned for her and how it had failed. The elderly man was rankled by her vile treatment. "As you can see, if such facts came to light, my name would be soiled beyond repair. I shall be in your debt forever if you can assist me without others learning of this degrading experience. I fear I should die of shame."

"Perhaps we can solve this problem quickly, Lady Hampton. I would enjoy a short visit, but I know you wish to relieve the frantic minds of your family as promptly as possible. There are two ships anchored nearby who might be of help to us," he began. He halted briefly to pour her a sherry to calm her tension.

"You shall dress as before, the tragic widow. I will place you under my personal protection as my grieving sister. I shall even hire a trusted man to guard your life and privacy. Let's see . . ." he murmured thoughtfully. "There's the *Agatha* and the *Wandering Siren* in port now."

Wandering Siren! Joshua's ship in her elusive disguise! Alex hastily interrupted his line of thought, "The crew on the ship where I was held captive mentioned the crew of the *Wandering Siren*, sir. I think perhaps some of them might be acquainted."

"I recently met their captain, a charming and serious fellow. He looked a man who could protect any treasure from harm. But you are right; his crew is a different matter. I shan't give him any consideration at all. These privateers and pirates are a fiercely loyal bunch. Besides, he is much too handsome to be trusted with my beloved sister," he merrily jested, playfully tweaking her cheek.

"I fear it will be a long time before any man is appealing to me, sir. I did not realize such evil and cruelty existed in their hearts. I pleaded for help from many of them, but they laughed in my face and tried to steal disgusting kisses," she lied out of necessity. Never would she reveal the name of her true captor. First, she must get back to her uncle's, then home whenever possible. After all, her father assumed she was still in America. With her uncle's and Sebastian's help, he would never learn the truth.

"I will seek out the captain of the *Agatha* this very day. I believe he is set to sail within the next two tides."

"I must ask one more favor, sir. If you would be so kind, please do not ever relate this humiliating episode to my father. He does not know of it and I pray he never does. It would hurt and distress him deeply; he would feel he is to blame."

"As you say, Lady Hampton. This tale will go no further than this room," he chivalrously vowed.

She smiled in gratitude and embraced him fondly. "Whatever would I do without you, sir?"

Kindelan called one of his servants and ordered her taken to a room. He cautioned the woman that no one was to know of her presence, for she was a dear friend whose life was precious to him. The woman quickly obeyed. Sebastian called in another servant and ordered him to fetch the captain of the *Agatha*.

When the stocky man appeared to discuss some profitable business with the governor, he was surprised to learn the powerful man only wanted to pay a hefty price to have his sister taken to Philadelphia. There was no easier or quicker way to earn such a nice pouch of gold coins since that was to be his second port of call anyway.

The deal concluded, Sebastian hurried to tell Alex of the expediency of their plan. She was overjoyed to hear the ship would sail at dawn. Gone so quickly and secretly, Josh wouldn't stand a chance of pursing her! Learning she had to be aboard at first light, Alex ate a light supper, bathed, and went to bed. Understanding her fatigue and anguish, Sebastian didn't press for her company. At long last, he could repay his friend for saving his life, but Charles Hampton wouldn't even know of it. No matter, he did.

Not far away, a frantic conversation was going on between a furious Spencer, a tense Andy, and an embarrassed George. Deciding to make certain Angelique was well aware of her impending fate if she refused to obey him, Spencer had returned later to test her. If she had relented, she could even join him at the party.

"I'm sorry, Capt'n. She caught me by surprise," George meekly stated, crushing the flower in his hand as he gazed at the wealth in the other.

"She's a cunning vixen, George. I don't blame you," he vowed, rubbing the very spot where Angelique had smacked him long ago. Gone? Where? In a place like this, she was probably in trouble by now. "Bring some of the men ashore, Andy. We best find our wandering siren before she lands in someone's eager lap."

"She was wearing a bright red dress, Capt'n, one of

them fancy gowns like them rich ladies wear. We'll spot her in a minute. I'll go looking now since I'm partly to blame. What should I do with this necklace?"

"You stay here and rest, George. With luck she'll come to her senses and return before dark. If she does, tie her to a chair!" he harshly ordered. "As for the necklace, keep it; she meant it as a gift to soften her blow," he murmured, wondering at her strange action.

Outside the tall structure, he paused to curse under his breath. Andy couldn't help but say, "I told you it was a bad idea to let her hear us talking. You can't blame her for panicking and running. She's quite a surprise, isn't she? The first woman all that charm didn't work on," he jovially teased his moody friend.

"That's the trouble, Andy; she's just as stubborn and willful as I am. It's no joke, friend. She could be in real danger. Look around us: pirates, criminals, cutthroats, scum. For all we know, some villain might have truly sold her to Maria's by now! Worse, she's a treasure any captain would steal. Damn! I was too rough on her, wasn't I?"

"Don't tell me you're seeing the light this late? I hope we find her, Josh. This time, take her home," he entreated gravely.

Spencer grinned. "That's exactly what I plan to do."

Andy stared at him. "Do you mean what I think?"

"Why not? If anyone can keep her safe and under wraps, it's Thomas Canter. You're right; maybe I need to take another look at her. If she is the perfect woman you seem to think, I'd be a fool to lose her."

Andy laughed and slapped him on the back. "Now you're thinking clearly, Captain. After all, a beauty dressed like that can't traipse about unnoticed."

"Before bedtime, Angel will be lying next to me," he confidently stated. They headed off down the street to question anyone in sight.

Hours passed and total darkness claimed the seaport. Not a soul admitted to seeing a woman in a red dress. Not even the enormous reward announced for her safe return brought any results. Exhausted and alarmed, the men met in Spencer's room to discuss this trying problem. It was clear by now their search wasn't going to be easy or swift. Either someone was hiding her, had kidnapped her, or . . . or what? Spencer apprehensively pondered.

It just wasn't possible for her to escape unseen. He checked out a theory of his, bewildered and distressed to discover she hadn't taken all of her jewels, just a couple of pieces. If she was lucky enough to find some honest man, she had only enough to pay for passage and food. Trouble was, even honest men became greedy and evil at the sight of such riches and vulnerable beauty. He dreaded to imagine his beloved Angel in the brutal hands of some real pirate or slaver.

That night was long and tense for both Alex and Spencer. She feared he would find her, and he feared he wouldn't. Within a mile of each other, they both paced their shadowy rooms in pensive speculation. Had they found each other again only to lose each other once more, this time permanently? Who and where was this ravishing girl whom the earth had seemed to disappear without a trace?

Dawn finally showed her face of pinks and grays. Under the guard of Governor Kindelan and hidden behind the heavy drapes of his personal carriage, Alex passed within two feet of Spencer and his anxious men as they desperately began another futile search for her as she made her way to the dock. While Spencer's group was posting a reward for her return, Alex was being taken aboard the *Agatha* to head for her uncle's, hidden behind those similar veils of mourning.

As the hull of the Spanish privateer caught the morning tide and eased from her berth, Spencer and his crew frantically entered every establishment and house to ask about her. Days passed as Alex clung to her room, the boredom acceptable this time. The governor's guard was never far from her door. Running with the winds and tides, this voyage was brief. As Alex thanked the guard for his assistance, he helped her into a carriage which would take her back to the home of Henry Cowling just outside the city of Philadelphia.

In San Augustín, Spencer was forced to give up his fruitless hunt for his Angel after three days of checking every clue or hope to find them empty. The burden of his guilt and loss weighed heavily upon his warring mind and heart. There was nothing more he could do. His ship repaired, he set sail to return in three weeks for Kindelan's answers to his proposals.

Kindelan was mystified by the abrupt change in this intriguing man, but never questioned his sudden distraction and apparent sadness. His mind filled with other matters, he was totally unaware this same man had offered a steep reward for the return of a missing girl who fit Alexandria's description. Before he agreed to an American stronghold in his territory, he would confer with Minister D'Onis first. After all, those aggressive Americans were still camped on nearby Amelia Island and had perviously conquered the western portion of this territory!

Alex knocked timidly upon the front door of her uncle's stately home. When the servant answered it, he looked stunned to find her standing there alone and looking lost. He was even more confused when she burst into tears and begged to see her uncle immediately.

Upon hearing she was back and in a state of emotional upheaval, Henry hurried to check out this unimaginable event. Between sobs and tremors, Alex related the same tale she had given to the Spanish governor of Florida. This time, she added how she had escaped those fierce pirates and how Kindelan had aided her return here.

Henry's mouth was agape as he listened to this horrifying tale of danger and daring. "I knew it was wrong to send you away alone," he berated himself.

"It isn't your fault, Uncle Henry. I was stupid and

defiant. Even with Tessa along, the results could have been the same. You were right all along; it's too dangerous to go home now. I've learned a terrible lesson; I'll never do anything like that again."

"Your father will be furious with both of us. You could have been killed," he murmured fearfully.

"We can't ever tell him, Uncle Henry. He would blame himself. It won' ᵗ ᵖpen again. I swear it. It's over now. Let's forget ι ᵥver happened," she urged.

"But . . ." he began to protest, but she quickly cut him off.

"No, let it pass. Please. I'm so tired. I couldn't rest on the ship, not after what happened last time. Could I rest before we talk anymore?"

"Of course, child. You've been through a terrible ordeal. I'm proud of you, Alex. You showed great courage and wisdom," he complimented her.

Feeling guilty about her time with Stephen, she lowered her lashes to conceal those warring emotions from his keen eyes. She withdrew the tight bundle within her dress. "I managed to steal a few of my jewels before I escaped, but I couldn't bring the rest or any clothes along. Whatever shall I do?" she wailed dejectedly at the thought of her missing clothes.

"You are a true gem yourself, Alex. Leave it to a female to rescue her jewels at any risk," he teased her. "We'll have all new clothes made."

"Thank you, Uncle Henry," she murmured, easing up to kiss his plump cheek.

She went to her old room and threw herself upon her bed without even asking about Tessa. She desperately needed rest and solitude to sort out some plaguing thoughts and feelings. Surely she had seen Joshua Steele for the last time. But why did that reality torment her? She wept silently until fatigue claimed her. It was the first of September of 1812, and here she was stranded in a land at war with her own country. What now?

XIV

"O! Call back yesterday, bid time return."
—*Richard II*, William Shakespeare

Those first two weeks back in Philadelphia passed in a painful blur for Alex. Unable to tell anyone the truth about her recent adventures, she suffered and struggled in lonely silence. Before meeting Captain Joshua Steele, her main concern had been to outwit her father's determination to arrange a proper marriage for her. Now, her whole world seemed physically and emotionally topsy-turvy.

Many nights she had awakened in body-shaking sobs, hugging her pillow in urgent need of a fulfillment only Stephen could grant. Would this pain and hunger never cease to torment her? Would his memory always be so agonizingly alive? Her lack of appetite and sleep created a tense, moody girl in the place of the once carefree girl who had first arrived here the end of May.

Henry fretted over these new changes in his lovely niece. Yet, feeling he knew the reason behind her lingering fears and emotional turmoil, he did all within his power to draw her out of this melancholy and

reserved state. He grimaced at the sadness and lack of
sparkle in her. It was unlike Alex to be so quiet and to
spend so much time alone in her room. He couldn't
even entice her to go riding, to visit his friends, to
attend special dinners, or to entertain guests. She
seemed content to suffer in lonely silence.

Whenever he would find her playing the pianoforte
in his morning room, they were always somber songs
which matched this new and vexing mood of hers.
Even the seamstress was forced to come to his home to
fit, size, and deliver her new wardrobe. Although
knowing very little about women's clothing or
fashions, Henry had made himself present on each
occasion to prevent her selection of drab colors and
plain gowns. What was wrong with the girl? She had
never been excessively vain about her beauty and good
taste, but now it seemed to matter little what she wore
or how she looked. If she had been aware of her beauty
and appeal before this tragic episode, she was totally
ignorant of them now. These things worried Henry. It
just wasn't like a female to be so disinterested in life.

One night after dinner, with Alex picking over her
plate as usual, Henry suggested a stroll in his colorful
garden. Sighing as if utterly exhausted, the spiritless
girl declined, saying she was going to bed early:
another trait which nettled her exasperated uncle.

"Tarnation, Alexandria! You cannot go on inde-
finitely like this! You aren't the first person to face a
personal tragedy!" he suddenly exploded. "I've just
about endured the limits of my patience and temper!
I've done everything I can imagine to draw you from

this deathly state. You're too young and beautiful to wither away! How can you tolerate this morbid mood all the time? You're acting like a spoiled brat who's had some bully steal her candy! Where's all that sparkle and spirit?"

"They were lost at sea," she replied, half in anger and half in sadness.

"Then find some way to get them back! Those pirates couldn't have done more damage to you if they had killed you! You're letting them destroy your whole life, child. Is that what you want, to let them win? My lord, Alex, did you give them your soul to survive?"

Stunned by the vehemence and anguish in his face and voice, Alex began to ponder his words and her behavior.

"I know it was a terrible experience for anyone to endure, but let it die. Don't let it consume you like this," he urged her. "You aren't even trying to help yourself get over this vile act against you. You refuse every offer of help I give. You're giving in to your troubles. Don't! Fight them, Alex, and I'll help you. Put on some pretty clothes and get out of this house! Have some fun for a change. It'll do wonders for you, I promise."

"But what if I run into one of those awful men again?" she wailed, exposing one of her deep concerns.

"Pirates don't sail into guarded ports like ours," he argued. "You'd hardly meet a man like that at dinner or out riding," he continued.

Yet, Alex knew how easily Captain Joshua Steele could fit into any situation. Without his suave disguise, he was accepted anywhere he chose to go. He had been in England; he had been at the mansion of the governor in Florida. He had frequently anchored near many American ports to visit and stroll among these people. He could just as easily and safely sail into this port.

"Pirates lead dangerous lives, Alex. They spend most of their time at sea or holed up in some slimy place with their confederates. The chances of ever seeing any one of them again is practically nil," he reasoned. "Between the American and English fleets, that ship of scoundrels could be at the bottom of the ocean right now."

Instead of giving her comfort, that statement alarmed her. Stephen, Andy, George, Tim, Tully and the others gone forever? Dead or captured? She fiercely rejected that possibility with all her being. But her uncle was right; she was merely existing. Stephen had brutally and unforgivably betrayed and used her, but she couldn't allow him or any man to devastate her.

Alex glanced over at her worried uncle and smiled at him, really smiled at him for the first time since June. She sighed heavily, this time in rising determination. "You're right, Uncle Henry; I'm hurting myself as much as he did. Shall we make a new attempt to revive the old Alex?" She laughed mirthfully. "Perhaps not the old Alex, but a wiser and better one," she joked lightly. She paused, then continued. "I really was a terrible nuisance, wasn't I? I honestly didn't mean to distress you so. Papa was too lenient and indulgent with me. I was a spoiled, hateful brat. I really had some growing up to do. Change is difficult and painful, Uncle Henry. Papa knew what he was doing; he knew a marriage would settle me down. Yet even now, the thought of some empty, pre-arranged deal sounds disgusting." As she chatted aimlessly, she only half-believed what she was saying. But marriage would offer her some protection from harsh life and these feelings of guilt over Joshua. Love and passion like that surely came only once in a person's life. Her heart was ravaged by the thought of never experiencing such exquisite emotions again. Damn him, he would pay dearly for this anguish and shame . . . if they ever met again!

With eyes glimmering with renewed life, she cautioned, "Just don't push me too fast, Uncle Henry. Let me take this rebirth a pain at a time."

He chuckled and smiled, his eyes crinkling at the edges. A thought came from nowhere and she questioned, "Did you ever learn where Tessa went and why?"

"I'll never understand that girl, Alex. She's as headstrong and willful as you were," he stated, bringing laughter at his last word.

"She just packed up and left without anyone seeing her? What about the baby and money?" she asked, concerned about this flighty and brazen girl who was a mystery to her. Tessa had been her personal maid for over a year before this fateful trip. But in all their time together, Tessa had revealed little about herself or her feelings. In her pregnant unwed state and without money, why would she simply take off like that? How would she survive?

Suddenly Alex beamed with a new idea. "What about a man, Uncle Henry? Perhaps she ran off with some new love. She couldn't have gone far without money or assistance."

"That could be right. Frankly, I was glad she left. She surely liked men and let them know it," he said disappointingly of Tessa's lack of morals. "I wonder if her new fellow realized she was carrying another man's child. She was sick for a long time, even took to her bed for nearly a week after you left. The maid said she was having lots of pain and was weak for days. She could have fooled this new lad. With her plump figure, she didn't even look pregnant after her worse bout of illness. Fact is, she looked and acted like nothing was wrong when she finally got up and around."

"Perhaps she miscarried and didn't tell anyone, Uncle Henry. That would certainly explain everything. If she was ready to carry on like before, she knew she couldn't do it here. She's probably working in some tavern or roadhouse miles away. It really doesn't matter; Tessa was always strange and flighty. She never made a good servant, but I hated to tell Papa to let her go. I should be ashamed of myself, but I was partially happy about her illness on the voyage over here; it kept her out of my hair—which she never could fix right anyway," she added, giggling cheerfully.

"I hate to confess, Alex, but I had the entire house searched after her disappearance. I feared she had stolen something to pay the way for her departure. She just wasn't trustworthy or dependable."

"Was anything missing?" she asked.

"Not that I could discover, but I wouldn't be surprised to find some unnoticeable and valuable object missing. That's all in the past. Let's discuss getting you out of this confining house," he suggested, a twinkle in his eyes.

"What did you have in mind?" she suspiciously inquired.

"Shopping? Dinner with the Gillises? A small party here?" he offered her some choices, recalling her words about pressure.

"I really don't need to buy anything else, Uncle Henry. You've given me so much as it is," she protested his generosity with vivid appreciation.

"Since when was the day when a female didn't want to go shopping for some frivolous items?" he merrily ventured, delighting in this new mood.

She smiled radiantly. "Idle shopping has never been one of my pastimes, and you know it," she chided him gently. "As for a party here, I'm not sure I'm ready to be all smiles and entertain guests for an entire evening. Who'll be at the Gillises?" she asked, feeling obligated to accept one of his suggestions.

"The Hardys, the Wellses, the Howards, the Carters, and the Greys," he added the last name with vivid amusement.

"I see what you're up to, you sly fox. Three out of

those families have eligible sons."

"Sons who've previously shown a great deal of interest in my becoming niece. Plus, the Wellses have twin sons named Joe and John, twenty-three. Look alike, but oh so different in character. Joe is quiet and serious, reputed to be a fine and respectable lad. But that John, he's a rakehell who haunts the wrong side of town. About the only vice he doesn't have is heavy drinking. If you asked me, I think he likes to keep a clear head at the gaming tables and around eager, marriage-minded females! The Gillises have two daughters, one a beauty and one hopelessly plain. I think that's the reason they give so many parties for people with grown sons," he mused aloud between chuckles before going on with his perceptions.

"Of course, the Howards have three daughters to rival them. Well-bred girls, but vain as pea hens. Nice looking enough, but no comparison to you or Helen. Poor Alice, it must be heartbreaking to stand in Helen's shadow. You'd think that conceited girl was Helen of Troy the way she acts and dresses. She's the prettiest young woman around when you're not here. I doubt she'll take kindly to your intrusion of her territory."

They joined in gay laughter. "I'm not a competitor in that field, Uncle Henry. She is welcome to all of those eager swains. I'm looking for someone very special. And when I find him, I'll battle any woman who stands in my path," she mischievously vowed. "If the Gillises are trying to shove their daughters off on these lads, why would they invite a family with three rivals?"

"It wouldn't look proper to have all those males and only their daughters present. Besides, Robert and Tom are good friends. But if you come with me, Helen won't be the center of attention as always. I'd love to see you pluck a few of her fine feathers. Might be good for her and the other girls."

"Henry Cowling! You're a spiteful rogue," she stated amidst her giggles. Yet, what better way to take her mind off her troubles? Girls like this Helen seemed had always annoyed her. They were like Joshua Steele who thought he could take, use, and discard anyone he pleased.

In an uncommon state of needing to punish another person, she irrationally viewed Helen as Joshua's stand-in. People like them deserved to be taken down a notch or two! Intrigued and feeling deliciously wicked, she agreed to the party. Slightly surprised, Henry glowed with happiness and excitement. "It's tomorrow night. Can you be ready that soon?"

"Without a doubt, since you purchased that provocative emerald gown for me. I daresay this is what you had in mind for its debut. I shall be the perfect lady while I teach sweet Helen she isn't the only woman alive."

Elated with both ideas, Henry burst into hearty laughter and confessed his eagerness to see this feat. To his further astonishment, Alex relented to his prior suggestion to walk in the moonlight through his aromatic garden.

Leisurely sipping a glass of white wine, they

lingered in the light of the full moon while inhaling the intermingling of fresh air and heady flowers and enjoying a real conversation. It was like Alex had mysteriously received a heavy infusion of new life and zeal.

That night, Alex slept without awakening or dreaming. When slender fingers of sunlight played upon her face the next morning, she yawned and stretched, feeling calm and fresh for the first time in ages. Had she reached that inevitable and wonderful moment when the past was finally being laid to rest? To test herself, she envisioned Joshua. She was definitely making real progress. The pain and desire were still present, but they had lessened to a dull ache. Perhaps those twinges would always be there to remind her of her reckless adventure and to caution her against giving her heart and body so freely to any man who magically entered her life. At last, she could accept and deal with her past life with him. How deliriously wonderful this new-found peace was. A heady and dangerous sense of power filled her.

Henry couldn't believe the complete about-face in her, but relished it. He cancelled his morning meeting when she invited him to go riding with her. They rode for hours, savoring the beauty of nature. As if displeased with her face, Mother Nature was boldly altering it. Leaves were threatening to burst into flashy oranges, reds, golds, and scarlets at any day now. When October came soon, Henry promised to take her on a tour of the nearby countryside when autumn was in its peak.

They lingered over a light lunch at a quaint inn. They laughed and talked until her sides ached, a marvelous feeling she had missed. Pushing all painful memories aside, she sank her pearly teeth into this new and intoxicating bite of life. Pleasantly fatigued, their return ride passed in tranquil silence.

To look her absolute best for tonight's event, Alex rested for an hour with a cold wet cloth upon her eyes. She took a lengthy and enlivening bath in a warm tub of fragrant bubbles. Taking two hours with her hair and clothes, when she finally descended the steps, Henry couldn't take his eyes from the entrancing sight which gracefully floated down the steps and walked toward him.

She playfully quizzed, "Will Lady Alexandria Hampton be at her finest tonight, dear uncle?"

"Utterly matchless and enchanting, my child," he complimented her. "To recall how you resisted that gown is beyond me. It is perfect and bewitching."

She slowly twirled before him to allow his scrutiny. Never one to adhere to stuffy fashion, her tawny hair was artfully drawn up near the top of her head to allow a cascade of heavy ringlets to fall to her creamy shoulders. Wispy curls like golden feathers rested upon her forehead and fell beside her ears. Not a pin, comb, or ornament distracted from the lovely style which enhanced and revealed her flawless face.

Like two precious emeralds, her green eyes glittered with pride and enticement. A carry-over from her days at sea, her skin was still a soft caramel shade. A subtle hint of color played upon her cheeks and lips. His eyes lowered in vivid appreciation and affection. Emerald earrings and a solitary matching stone at the swell of her breasts were her only embellishments. A fragile gold chain held the heart-shaped stone in place.

But her dress and hair inspired the reasons for her transformation from carefree child to seductive woman. Again her lack of concern for normal fashion was revealed by her gown. Henry never knew it was the vivacious French seamstress who had designed and insisted upon this particular dress, raving about how perfect it was for her figure and coloring. Lacking the strength or will to argue back then, she had let the charming creature to do as she pleased. At this moment, she was glad.

The neckline dipped to a V which halted only in time to prevent exposing her bosom in a most immodest manner. So recently from France where fashion was at its peak and originality, the seamstress was talented beyond her age. The puffed, elbow-length sleeves were secured at the shoulders with flat bows. The bodice was plain and sized perfectly to flatter without boldness. The waist was snug and the skirt was full, highlighting Alex's diminutive waist. At the middle of her waist in the front, the outer skirt was slashed to the hem and sloped to either side to reveal an underskirt of expensive lace over satin in a color which matched the lush green of the satin gown. Except for the delicate lace and cut-away overskirt, there was nothing to detract from the elegant simplicity of the becoming gown. Gizelle had used no contrasting color to spoil its effect. Satin slippers in matching emerald green completed her attire.

As Henry caught her hand and kissed it fondly, he noted she wore only a single emerald ring upon her graceful right hand. Just before asking about the emerald and diamond bracelet Daniel Grey had mentioned giving to her, he changed his mind and offered to let her wear one which had belonged to his deceased wife.

"Thank you, Uncle Henry; you're so kind and thoughtful. But I don't want to overwhelm our hosts with a king's fortune in jewels. Besides, counting the dress, my hair, and these other stones, no one will even notice the girl at all," she impishly alleged.

"There won't be a soul present who won't know you're there, child. Ready to leave; the carriage is waiting." He took her elbow and led her outside and into his carriage.

"Drive slowly, Zachary. I don't want to muss my hair," she entreated, eagerly anticipating the impending charade.

Timed just right, they were the last guests to arrive at the Gillises. After the butler answered the door, every eye was trained upon them as they entered the drawing room. Standing poised like an earth-bound goddess on her uncle's arm, every conversation and movement ceased abruptly as they were announced, "Henry Cowling and his niece Lady Alexandria Hampton."

Alex was amused when even their host and hostess had difficulty regaining their composures before coming forward and greeting them. Robert Gillis's

admiration and astonishment was as evident as Mrs.
Gillis's annoyance and chilling manner. All smiles and
refinement, Alex politely spoke with each one and
waited patiently as her uncle did the same. It was
Robert who saved the moment by cordially intro-
ducing each guest present.

Alluring green eyes gradually followed his direction
as the names were given to her. Amidst another brief
conversation between her uncle and Robert, she made
her hasty assessments of each person. Alice was
indeed plain, but her timid smile was friendly. Alex
spontaneously returned it. The Howards' daughters
were a curious variety: one flaming redhead, one drab
blonde, and one raven-haired girl who looked the
youngest and brightest of the group.

Helen was in a class to herself. A sultry brunette
with sky-blue eyes and a ripe figure was shooting
visual daggers at this unwanted opponent. Her
carriage was haughty and sullen; her mood, childishly
envious. Decked out in bright sunny yellow, it was
clear she vividly resented Alex's presence. She turned
up her nose and chatted with the two males on either
side of her.

From her uncle's previous descriptions, it was easy
to pick which ruggedly handsome male was John or
Joe. Minus their noticeable difference in behavior,
both were identical: dark blond hair, sapphire eyes,
proud and well-defined features, and a heavy dose of
masculine appeal. Alex quickly noted one striking
difference: John's golden tan was much darker than
Joe's tawny one.

She had forced herself to smile pleasantly and nod at Seth, Steven, and Daniel. From Daniel's smoldering and displeased gaze, Alex knew he was sorry for having brought a companion along, no doubt to harass Helen. Yet, a sparkle of fury was noted in his eyes. Could it be he was still piqued with her for refusing to see him since her return? Could it be he doubted her uncle's claims of illness? Why did he keep staring at her wrists, then glaring coldly at her? No matter, she flippantly decided. She had no intention of using Daniel in her sport tonight. Thankfully, he was out of competition anyway. He turned to respond to something his companion had said. She was pretty, but no competition for either her or Helen.

Knowing it was time for dinner, both Alex and her uncle politely declined a glass of sherry. The bell rang and they strolled arm in arm to the massive dining room. Alex was impressed by what she witnessed there and during dinner. In spite of her first impression, they lived elegantly and certainly knew how to entertain with a flair, sparing no expense.

Before she caught what was taking place, she found herself seated between John and Joe Wells and across from Daniel. Her uncle was four places away, too far to converse with or retreat for reprieve. Robert sat at the head of the lengthy table with Joe to his right and Helen to his left, then came John next to herself and Daniel next to Helen. The placement of the guests seemed odd to her. Helen between her father and a man who had brought his own date? Enlightenment gradually filled her: Helen had obviously resolved to be near her and the Wells twins!

In spite of Helen's brazen digs at her and the combined attentions of Robert, Joe, and John, the dinner was swift and delicious. During brief moments between casual banter, Alex irritably noticed how Helen feigned a romantic interest in Daniel right before his companion's sad eyes. Soon, Alex felt sorry for the young woman. She was clearly embarrassed and unsettled. To aid the girl and to nettle Helen, Alex made it a point to continually draw her into the conversation. Aware of what the English girl was doing, Joanna smiled warmly and compelled herself to battle for Daniel's attention.

Frivolous topics carried the conversations until Helen, fuming with jealousy and spite, sweetly declared, "Isn't the war going well, Father? We're certainly giving those nasty, uncivilized English a fight to long remember. Such dreadful people! They're never at peace for very long. No doubt they still carry the blood of their barbarian conquerors."

Everyone at that end of the table halted to stare at the malicious girl in astonishment. Before she could prevent it, Alex flushed a deep crimson. Robert hissed in unsuppressed anger, "Cease such foolish prattle, daughter. Have you forgotten we have an English guest this evening?"

Practically cooing in a mock southern drawl, Helen pretended to apologize, "I'm so sorry, Lady Hampton. I do declare I forgot my manners and your loyalty to your homeland. Whatever possessed me to be so rude and thoughtless?"

Swiftly regaining her poise, Alex smiled and replied, "Please don't fret, Helen; everyone is rude and thoughtless on occasion. But I should remind you, England did not declare this present war or the previous one with your delightful country, nor the one against that tyrant Napoleon. Perhaps I should loan you one of my history books. It is most distressing and embarrassing to find oneself in such gross error in public. As to my English heritage, I am very proud of it."

Turning to Joe, she ended her snide attempt to humiliate her by asking, "Weren't you telling me about a carnival here soon?"

Never having enjoyed any moment so much, Joe smiled in warmth and satisfaction. No one had ever so cunningly and politely silenced that little snit across the table. "I'd be delighted to take you to see it," he offered, smiling tenderly.

"Hold on, brother," John protested. "I was going to invite Alexandria to go with me."

Alex could feel the force of Helen's venomous glares as the two males argued over who was to escort her to the fair next week. Not wishing to create any hard feelings at this early date, she smiled and thanked John, but accepted Joe's invitation. She was relieved he had asked first, giving her a logical reason to accept him. John's arrogant, self-assured, suave manner reminded her too much of another man, one she wanted to forget.

Besides, Joe emanated a gentleness and charm which evidenced peace of mind. If she was any judge of men, he would behave the perfect gentleman and be good company for her. Determined to make her presence known, Helen vied for John's attention, freeing Alex to focus hers upon Joe. Perhaps this man was someone to learn more about . . .

Yet, Helen wasn't the only one near her who radiated a strong feeling of resentment. Strange as it seemed, Daniel practically ignored Alex. Still, she was disquieted and perplexed by his coolness and reserve. Some masculine ploy to intrigue or punish her? She smiled to herself, dismissing him.

Alex hoped to seek out her uncle to converse with after dinner, but she was denied this much-needed break. Robert arose and said, "Let's retire to the drawing room. I'm sure you young people would rather talk and get acquainted outside in the fresh air. Helen, lead the way."

As Alex passed her uncle, she cast him a look of appeal to rescue her as soon as possible. He smiled and nodded in understanding. This was her first outing since her dreadful time with those bloody pirates. He would visit just long enough to be courteous, then use the excuse of her alleged recovery to depart. He was beaming with pride; she had fared well tonight.

Her second glance of appeal was sent to Joe, who quickly read and followed it. He took her arm and led the way outside before Helen could do so. At present, Helen was cooing and melting pretentiously over

Daniel and John. Alex ignored the fact Joe knew his way around this particular home.

The terrace to the side of the house was enclosed by a waist-high wall. Alex and Joe walked over to it and halted there. Placing her hands upon it, she leaned her head back and closed her eyes, inhaling the invigorating air.

"I'm sorry, Alexandria; Helen doesn't make it easy or pleasant for any female and certainly not one as beautiful as you. I've seen her at work before, but never with the intensity and spitefulness she displayed tonight. I hope that little scene won't color your opinion of all Americans."

She turned her head and smiled at him. "In all honesty, Joe, she's the only disagreeable one I've met so far. I pride myself in my manners, but I was sorely tempted to forget them several times during dinner." She sighed in relief. It was good to have a few moments to relax. "Thanks for chivalrously coming to my rescue more than once. I much prefer to avoid tense moments like that. Tell me about yourself," she encouraged, needing to begin another topic.

He grinned. "There isn't much to tell. John's the outgoing one."

She sensed a slight envy and resentment in his tone. "What do you do?" she inquired, acting as if John didn't exist.

"I finished school last spring. I'm a lawyer, or trying to become one. As soon as this war's over, I'll be working with Mr. Webster."

"Daniel Webster?" she inquired.

"One and the same," he replied without a trace of detectable arrogance.

Impressed, she smiled and remarked, "You must have fine potential for a man of his esteem to be interested in you. Even a foreigner like myself has heard of him. Do you have your own office yet?"

As if surprised she hadn't asked what his brother did, he lifted his brow and glanced at her. "I have a small one in town. I'd be honored if you visited me and shared some lunch."

Alex brightened and accepted so hastily that his astonishment amused her. "You look surprised I would accept. You were serious, weren't you?"

"Yes, but I never imagined you would agree," he admitted.

"I've never seen a barrister's office before. It would be fun to do so. Who knows, I might have need of a lawyer one day," she sweetly informed him, using the American term this time.

He laughed. "I can't imagine you ever in trouble or need of my services."

"One never knows," she declared softly. She was pleased to discover him relaxing and opening up with her. In this private setting and with her disarming manner, his restraint and sensitive aura relented to her mellow and vivacious air.

Refusing to be so bold as to inquire for a date for her visit, she used a different means to get to know him better. If she was right about him, he was the perfect choice to spend time with and to use to discourage other men. "Would you like to join my uncle and me for dinner Sunday? Do you ride?" she abruptly asked before he could eagerly accept.

"Yes, why?" he inquired.

"If you come early in the afternoon, you could show me the countryside. Uncle Henry is very caught up in business, and riding isn't much fun with a sullen groom. The leaves are changing colors and the air is crisp and fresh. I've missed riding since being here."

Her natural aura of vitality and innocence took over and shone brightly before the enchanted Joe. "I can think of nothing I would enjoy more than riding and dining with you on Sunday, Alexandria."

"My close friends and family call me Alex. Please feel free to do so," she coaxed, actually looking forward to Sunday.

Hearing the laughter of the others coming to join them and to compete for her attention, he quickly asked, "Would you like to see a play with me on Saturday evening?"

At the almost desperate edge to his hasty question, she glanced up at him. He literally blushed at his uncontrollable manner. Evidently he wanted to claim her before his brother could. "I'm sorry, Alexandria. I shouldn't impose upon all your time."

She plucked a small rose from a nearby bush and smelled its sweet odor. She handed it to him as she responded, "I find both you and your company most enjoyable, Joe. I'll be ready whenever you call

Saturday night. And it's Alex, remember?" she teased.

John headed straight toward them. A roguish smile claimed his lips as he huskily chided his twin brother, "You're being too possessive with our lovely visitor, Joe. I've never seen you so taken with a female before."

To dismiss the sudden tension in the air, Alex smiled and protested, "Joe and I seem to have a great deal in common. Your brother is a most fascinating man. He's going to teach me something about the law next week."

"You invited Alexandria to your office?" he asked, thoroughly shocked.

"Why not?" Joe indifferently stated, realizing Alex had just come to his rescue. "She's the most intelligent and refreshing woman I've met to date," he declared with unusual confidence and boldness. "Alex and I are also taking in that new play next Saturday," he smugly announced.

"Alex?" he echoed, eying both of them curiously.

"That's what my friends call me," she informed him, delighting in the way their friendliness was clearly effecting John.

"You really work fast, brother," he noted, reluctant respect in his tone. He instantly resorted to playful deviltry. "Or is our Alex kindly working upon that excessive shyness of yours?"

Joe stiffened as he caught his brother's attempt to unsettle and mock him. Incensed by this rude behavior, Alex quickly asserted, "I haven't found Joe

392

the least shy. We were having a delightful conversation," she said, stressing the past tense in her statement.

John astutely read the irritation and protectiveness in her gaze. What a provocative mixture of lava and snow! She was as finely polished and honed as a rare gem or a deadly weapon. Yet, he detected an enticing quality of gentleness. She was definitely well-bred and well-educated. But, oh, so feminine and sensitive! A seductive body, a delicate nature, an exquisite face, wit and poise, charm and breeding . . . Did she lack nothing?

"Perhaps I should explain, Alex," he began, cautioning himself to his most charming and polite manner. "Joe and I tease each other like this all the time. We're really very close," he lied outright.

His scrutiny and conclusions didn't go unnoticed by either Joe or Alex. "Perhaps it's time to call a halt to such boyish mischief. Sometimes playful jesting gets out of hand and inspires trouble," Alex wisely hinted.

"Old habits are hard to break," he fenced in a mellow tone.

"I'm sure they are, but we all grow up sometime," she lighted parried.

"Perhaps I can make amends by taking you to dinner Sunday?"

She smiled at Joe and genially declined, "I've invited Joe to come riding and dining with us Sunday."

This added bit of news rankled John. "Sunday

dinner and riding, a play on Saturday, a visit to your office, and a trip to the carnival all in less than an hour? Perhaps I should take lessons from you, brother."

John couldn't believe his ears when Joe flippantly agreed. Before this conversation could further deteriorate, Daniel came over to join them. He handed Alex a glass of sherry and boldly insinuated, "Perhaps some refreshment would be in order. We could hear this battle for Alex's attention clear across the way."

Alex pinkened at his subtle insult. Joe hastily said, "Rudeness is most unbecoming on you, Dan. You can hardly blame John and I for our brazen conduct."

"You look most enchanting tonight, Alex, but your appearance lacks one extra item." At her quizzical look, he added in a curt tone, "A matching bracelet, perhaps with diamonds, would do it."

Puzzled, she simply stared at him. "I'm sorry to disappoint you, Daniel, but I don't own one."

Missing his point entirely and in the dark as to his following reaction, she couldn't explain his irrational anger and terse response. "You don't own one?" he stormed at her so loudly the others turned to look at them.

At a complete loss as to his meaning, she innocently replied, "No."

Beyond control in his unjust outrage, he snarled bitterly, "It was quite expensive, Alex. Did you give it away or sell it?"

"What are you talking about?" she inquired,

distressed by his clear intent to embarrass her.

John caught his arm and shook him. "I don't know what your problem is, Dan, but I can't permit you to treat Alex like this. Drop it," he warned.

"Certainly not, John. A woman doesn't accept such an expensive gift then turn her nose up to you!" he finally succeeded in blurting out the motive behind his actions.

"But I didn't accept it!" Alex protested. "I never accept gifts from any man! After you delivered it, I told my maid to rewrap it and return it that same day! I gave you no reason to believe you could bribe me with expensive trinkets! In fact, I dislike you immensely, Daniel Grey. You have more hands than an oc . . ." Suddenly aware of what she was saying, she flushed and hesitated.

At the unwitting drop of that personal information, John was grinning ear to ear. "The bracelet was never returned to me, love," he sneered as if calling her a liar.

"It must have! I gave it to Tessa and told her . . ." She halted once more as suspicion filled her. Of course! That was where she got the money to leave! All this time Daniel assumed she had kept it!

Dismayed by this conclusion, she lifted her chin proudly and forced an apology, "Evidently my maid stole the bracelet. Since she ran away months ago, I can hardly demand the bracelet from her. At least I can now understand your hatefulness." She stunned the entire group by removing her emerald heart pendant of comparative value and handing it to Daniel. "If I'm any judge of such things, this should amply cover your loss. Accept it with my apology." She pressed the necklace into his palm and turned to Joe. "If you don't mind, Joe, will you please escort me inside to say good night? I'm still weak from my recent illness and this evening has been most exhausting."

As they strolled into the house, Alex heard John sneer at Daniel, "You stupid ass! Don't you recognize quality when you see it? If you keep that necklace, you're a bigger idiot than you look now!"

"What was I supposed to think?" Daniel snapped.

"Before you go accusing people of things, get your facts straight! Your conduct is unforgivable . . ." Inside, the rest of his verbal chastisement was lost to a befuddled Alex. Like his brother, there was more to John than she had realized.

Henry was upset by the paleness of his niece's face and the tremors in her body. Her poise sorely strained, she could hardly voice her gratitude and farewells. Joe walked them to the carriage. "I'm deeply sorry, Alex."

His heart raced wildly as she lifted misty eyes to his. She tenderly caressed his cheek and murmured, "My gallant and indispensable knight, I thank you for everything."

Henry couldn't imagine what was going on or what had preceded this strange behavior. Wide-eyed, he witnessed another baffling scene. Joe leaned over and placed a kiss upon her forehead and murmured, "I'll see you Sunday."

She smiled, close to tears, and nodded, unable to

speak aloud. He assisted her into the carriage and it drove off. Henry stared at her. "What was that all about?"

"Give me a few moments to calm down, Uncle Henry. You'll never believe what happened tonight," she ventured, dabbing at her tears.

XV

"... something in the wind."
—*A Comedy of Errors*, William Shakespeare

The distance between Henry's and the Gillises' was covered in strained silence and soft weeping. Once inside his study, Henry pressed a glass of brandy into Alex's shaking hand and ordered her to drink it. When she halted after the first fiery sip, he insisted she quickly down the entire contents of the glass. She did, coughing after its searing trail, watering her eyes even more.

"Now, sit down and tell me who and what distressed you so," Henry tenderly pressed.

"You recall how mystified we were by Tessa's flight without protection or money?" When he nodded, she went on, "That mystery was rudely solved tonight. When I was here last, Daniel Grey sent me a very expensive bracelet of diamonds and emeralds to hopefully halt my resistance to those seeking hands he was always putting all over me. He's such a lecherous fiend, Uncle Henry. Naturally I refused the gift for many reasons. I told Tessa to have your head servant return it to Daniel the same day he sent it here, the day before I sailed. I assumed she had done so, but evidently she kept it."

"What?" he shouted in shock.

"I couldn't understand why Daniel was so hateful to me all evening. I thought he was only upset because of my rebuffs. He was furious because he actually thought I had kept the bracelet without giving him any special favors in return. He even suggested I had either sold it or given it away to spite him. We had a violent and humiliating argument right there in front of everyone before I comprehended what Tessa had done. Since I was innocently to blame, I apologized and explained; I gave him my necklace as repayment."

"He took your necklace even after you explained about the theft?"

"Yes, sir. After all, Tessa was my servant and the bracelet was quite expensive," she tried to justify her settlement to the nasty incident.

"No matter, child; a real gentleman would never have behaved in such a disgusting manner. He should never have mentioned the gift in the first place. Gifts belong to the receiver! If you couldn't do with it as you pleased, he should never have offered it to you! What did the others say?"

"The girls, nothing. I couldn't believe any man would make such a scene over another female in front of his date. I felt so ashamed for Joanna. Seth and Madison remained with the girls and didn't interfere. John and Joe took my side. But it was John who acted as my defender, strange as that sounds. He was just as furious as Daniel. When he couldn't stop the whole matter, he gave Daniel a terrible tongue-lashing. I thought it best to leave quickly, which I did."

"I'm terribly sorry, Alex. I never wanted your first evening to end like this. But Helen was the one I was concerned about, not one of the men. Jealousy and revenge take heavy tolls on a person. Rest assured, I shall have a word or two with that offensive young man!"

"Please don't, Uncle Henry. Let it pass. I would prefer he didn't have a chance to apologize. Perhaps the lesson was worth the necklace. From now on, I'll see to my own private affairs and I won't pretend a friendship just for social amenities. I was too nice to him just to avoid any unpleasant scenes. I didn't expect to see him again. Now I see why so many women are viewed as haughty and cold; it takes such acts to prevent misunderstandings and repulsive scenes like I endured tonight. From now on, if I despise a man, he'll be sure to know it! Helen must have savored every minute of it."

"I doubt it, child. After all, Daniel behaved like an insanely jealous suitor who was being rejected after plying you with expensive gifts. Your poise and unselfish act of repayment surely stunned them and won you some respect. The men were naturally on the side of a ravishing, unjustly assailed lady. It's hard to believe John actually defended you; he's never done anything so gallant for a female before. It's usually the other way around. Why he's the most envied, sought-after bachelor around I'll never understand; he beats countless women off every single day. Could it be our roguish charmer has met his match? I think he's taken with you, Alex."

"Uncle Henry! Besides, men like John Wells are never true to any one female, including their wives. He's arrogant and selfish. He's a taker and a user. I don't like such men. Anyway, you should be delighted to know that I'm seeing Joe Wells several times in the next two weeks." She went on to relate their plans.

"How in the world did you manage not one invitation, but four? Joe's so reserved that women fail to notice him at all."

"I know. We had some time alone to chat. He's really very warm and gentle. He's very intelligent and charming, too. I just about had him relaxed enough to talk openly and freely until John swaggered up and tried to steal his thunder."

"That's the John I know," Henry humorously concurred. "Joe's a pleasant man, Alex. He's hard-working, dependable, and serious. But I should warn you to step lightly and careful where he's concerned."

Alex studied him a moment. Why was he so concerned and tense? She asked for an explanation.

"Like you realize," Henry said, "he is smart. He doesn't have his brother's colorful flair, but Joe Wells gets what he goes after. In contrast to John, he does it with cunning and persistence rather than looks and charm. Don't underestimate his power and reserved air. Be careful, Alex. In fact, I trust John more than Joe. John doesn't pretend. It wouldn't surprise me in the least to learn Joe is working secretly for the British. Whatever you do, keep a guard on your tongue around him. He knows I'm friends with some of the most powerful, influential men in America."

"What can I do now? I've already accepted his invitations. I thought it would please you if I got out some. Joe seemed so quiet and safe," she confessed.

"I thought as much. Just be on guard around him," he warned gravely. To her dismay and shock, he added, "With two visits so close together, he might suspect you of being a spy for the same side. He could be feeling you out, or he may have some far-fetched idea of enlisting your help. As incredible as it sounds, several of the English spies captured have been lovely and innocent-looking females."

Alex instantly recalled Joshua's suspicions and claims. Was it possible he had been serious and justifiably concerned? To think of herself innocently caught in another similar situation here alarmed her. She abruptly questioned him about the curiously ignored petticoat, "Uncle Henry? What was written on that petticoat you asked me to take to Papa?"

Henry paled and trembled at its recall. "What happened to it, Alex?" he choked in panic.

Witnessing his reaction, she deceived him, "I stuffed it out the porthole like you asked." She dared not tell him it was seized before success. "What was on it?" she persisted.

"Nothing important, child, just business," he stated noncommittally.

"I have a right to know what I risked my life and honor for, Uncle Henry. I insist you tell me. Was there anything traitorous upon it?"

Paling and shaking once more, he stammered, "I . . . told you . . . it was only . . . business."

"Forgive my impertinence, Uncle, but you aren't telling the truth," Alex charged.

Trapped, he deceptively explained, "Your father and I are using privateers to carry on our trade. If we don't, we'll both be financially ruined by the time this war's over. Only certain ships can be trusted and certain goods are most valuable in times like these: food, weapons, and medical supplies. Naturally such trade between us might be viewed as conspiring with the enemy. We Americans need such things and your father helps me get them."

Alex suddenly realized he was being partially honest.

"The petticoat listed names and dates for shipments and what items we needed the most," Henry continued. "Surely you can see how incriminating such information would be in the wrong hands?"

"What if I had been caught with that information?" she blurted out, angered and hurt at being used by her family.

"I knew you would handle the matter quickly and efficiently. There was no danger to you," he reasoned, unaware of how wrong he was.

To argue his point would reveal matters she wished to remain secret. She almost laughed at the painful absurdity of the entire adventure. How would Joshua feel if he learned she had actually been helping his chosen side? She had suffered for nothing! Her hat! "Did my hat contain similar messages from Papa?"

"Yes, Alex," he confirmed her suspicion.

To clarify all of her confusion, she asked, "If you

and Papa are working together, why is Joe a threat to you . . . if you're right about him?"

"I fear Joe is working for the British to help win the war for them. In his position and with his innocent air, he has access to some vital facts the British would pay hefty sums to attain. Just think what would happen to your father if Joe or anyone learned of his assistance to me."

"Why would Papa do such a thing?" she wailed.

"This time, Alex, the King is wrong, England is wrong, and this bloody war is wrong. Is he supposed to idly stand by and simply observe such a travesty in the name of patriotism? There comes a time when a man must decide his own views. Which is more important: mindless loyalty for your country or your own honor and conscience?"

"I honestly don't know how to reply," she candidly answered.

"You once asked me not to mention your misadventure at sea to your father, now I'm asking you to keep your knowledge of this matter a secret from Charles. It would distress him just as much to discover you had learned of his actions. He loves you and wants to protect you. Don't let any of this pass beyond this room ever. Agreed?" he requested.

"I promise," Alex acquiesced. "I won't mention it again, unless it's to relate something curious about Joe."

"Don't play the heroic spy and gain his suspicion, Alex. He's smart. I know how willful and eager for excitement you can be. This time, it could endanger

several lives, including your own. If Joe is what I think
he is, he wouldn't be above sacrificing you to the
authorities to protect himself."

"I'll be careful, Uncle Henry. I'll not ask a single
question. Thank goodness you told me about him. I
could have innocently done all of us great harm."

Between that night and Sunday afternoon, all Alex
could think of was this strange turn in events and her
time with Joshua. Every time she thought she had one
episode puzzled out and solved, new doubts entangled
it. Joshua was a privateer, a pirate. From what she had
seen and heard, his notoriety was justly earned. So
many pretenses surrounded her. Which side did he
truly work for? How deeply was her family involved?
How could she became enmeshed in this dangerous
and bizzare puzzle? How she longed to return home
and have her life settle down!

During her ride with Joe, Alex was just as quiet and
guarded as he was. Joe could sense her restraint and
anxiety. He chalked it up to modesty and breeding.
After all, she was a refined lady and they were newly
acquainted. She was polite, charming, and friendly;
but he was the one attempting to pull her from her
shell today! He moodily speculated that perhaps after
meeting John she was sorry she had accepted his
company so hastily. For certain, he sensed she was
slightly uneasy around aggressive men. He wondered
if her constraint and apprehension were the results of
some painful affair in the past. Frankly, he couldn't
imagine any man refusing her. Odd for a girl like her to
avoid masculine attention and adoration. Perhaps it

was only the combination of so much attention which frightened her. No matter, she would suit all of his intentions very nicely.

Alex's strain was more noticeable at dinner. It was clear she was forcing herself to be genial and poised. Where had all her spontaneity gone? Did she perhaps fear he would also resort to pressure upon her as Daniel had and treat her badly when she resisted? Of course! She was probably still suffering from embarrassment at his witnessing of that event.

When dinner was finally over and Joe had departed, Alex sighed in relief. Weary from the strain, she went to bed immediately, but not before Henry complimented her excellent conduct.

On Thursday, the carnival passed swiftly in a blur of sights, sounds, and merriment. With so much to see and do, Alex had little difficulty with her carefree pretense in the noisy crowd. She managed to relax enough to share a delightful day with him. Pleading fatigue, she sweetly refused his invitation to dinner. At the door, Joe pressed a light kiss to her lips and thanked her for a wonderful day. He said he would call for her about six on Saturday. He suggested they eat after the play at a romantic spot. When he playfully debated her reluctance to such a late evening alone, she felt compelled to agree.

"I've never pressured any female with unwanted attentions, Alex, and I promise not to start with you. You're a very special woman who deserves special treatment. I promise to control my deep affection for you."

She laughed merrily. "With such a promise from a man like you, I accept. See you at six."

That next day, Alex cast all modesty aside to boldly ride in a man's style in a full skirt which revealed a knicker cut with certain movements. Gizelle had been appalled at her suggestion of this daring and improper riding outfit, but had complied. Accustomed to riding bareback and spread-legged at home, she despised the discomfort of the English side-saddle which she was compelled to endure in public.

She gave her mount his lead and galloped headlong across the meadow at a breakneck speed. The wind snatched at her laughter and hair, spreading it out behind her like a flowing mane of amber. Seized by a heady sense of danger and elation, she encouraged the horse to an even faster pace. She was totally unaware of the frantic man swiftly overtaking her with his magnificent white stallion. She screamed in surprise as she was suddenly snatched from her saddle.

Bouncing precariously in his tight grip around her slender waist until he could slow and halt his horse, she fumed at this outrageous act of daring. She was carefully deposited upon the ground and hurriedly joined by her panicky rescuer.

He seized her shoulders and asked, "Are you all right, Alex? I was scared stiff when I saw that horse running away with you. You should never go riding alone. You could have an accident or confront some dangerous villain," he scolded her. "It isn't beyond our enemies to send scouts down here. We are at war, girl!"

She gaped at him as enlightenment settled in, caution promptly filling her. "What are you doing here, Joe? I wasn't expecting you today. I hate to disappoint you, but I didn't require any help. I had him under control; we were racing the wind. I ride all the time and I'm good at it," she petulantly stated in pride and annoyance.

He grinned. "I see. But my panic was reasonable and my rescue well intended."

"In the future, make sure I need help first," she snipped at his smug look. "Were you looking for me or taking a ride?" she asked as she calmed down.

"Both," he casually informed her. "The ride first, then I was coming to see you later." He reached out to push some hair from her face, then smiled.

She flushed at his smoldering gaze which engulfed her. His appreciation was bold and strangely disturbing. What was he doing? His manner had altered drastically since Sunday!

"How can a female be so devastatingly beautiful? You're enchanting, Alex, utterly and irresistibly bewitching," he murmured in a husky tone. "Have dinner with me tonight?" he entreated, grinning roguishly.

Unnerved by his forwardness and the effect of his mood and appeal, she stammered, "But we . . . just had dinner together. And we'll . . . be going out again in a few days."

"I doubt it's possible for a man to see enough of you, but never too much. Please," he coaxed in a tone which lacked any real hint of weakness.

"I have other plans tonight," she only half lied. Had she become so wanton since her sojourn with Joshua that a handsome and virile stranger could entice her to the point of temptation and desire?

"Are you afraid of me, Alex?" he unexpectedly asked, utterly serious.

"Why should I be? You've been a perfect gentleman and you're from a fine family," she replied unconvincingly.

"Any man makes you uneasy, doesn't he? Why?" he demanded.

Alex's face whitened beneath her tawny skin. A tremor swept over her; she moistened her suddenly dry lips. Feeling she had to give some explanation, she said, "Perhaps in some way I am. I resent overly eager men who forget their place and mine. I don't like being stormed for attention or pressured for responses which I don't feel. Now, I better get back before Uncle Henry starts to worry. I said I was taking a short ride."

Joe gently caught her arm and denied her skittish retreat. "In my case, Alex, you have nothing to fear or resist. I can assure you my intentions are most honorable. Will you marry me?"

"Marry you?" she echoed in astonishment. "But we just met. I like you and enjoy your company, Joe, but I don't love you or wish to marry you. I'm sorry to be so blunt. I hope I haven't given you any reason to misunderstand my friendship. If so, I'm sorry," she repeated in rising disquiet.

A pleased grin captured his sensual mouth and softened his eyes. She stared at him in utter bewilderment. He drew her into his arms and kissed her soundly—a masterful, heady kiss which revealed his experience and skill. Caught unprepared for this pervasive assault upon her starving senses, Alex swayed against him and accepted the passionate kiss without returning it.

When he pulled his mouth from hers, she stared at him. His igneous sapphire eyes devoured her features and exposed his desire. "Marry me, Alex," he coaxed. "We're perfectly matched and I'll make you forget every man you've ever known."

"What wicked sport are you playing, John?" she angrily accused.

"How did you know it was me? I had hoped to sweep you off your feet and have you legally bound to me before you guessed the truth," he candidly declared, grinning at her.

"You might look like Joe, but you're nothing like him," she responded in a shaky voice.

"We're more alike than people realize, Alex," he indifferently dropped a hint which agreed with her uncle's perceptions. "I'm glad you aren't falling for Joe; he could never make you feel the way I can."

"You overestimate your charms and powers, John. Needless to say, I am aware of your reputation," Alex declared, angered by his game and her response to him.

He laughed cheerfully and challenged, "If there's one thing I recognize, Alex, it's a woman's interest. You might think you feel nothing for me, but you do. I know that look and sense a warring air in you. As to my reputation, men always get a colorful one when they take and enjoy what pleases them. I don't care what others think or say. You should know envy causes more gossip and exaggeration than the truth. My proposal was deadly serious. If you agree, I'll make the best husband possible," he stated confidently.

To lead this conversation to safety, Alex asked, "Why were you looking for me?"

Guessing her ploy, he chuckled. "To return this," he replied, handing her the heart-shaped necklace which she had given to Daniel.

"Why would he return it? No matter, I can't take it back. I want no obligations to that offensive creature," she protested.

"I purchased it from him. It's yours . . . without any obligations. Its color matches your eyes and its shape proclaims your nature. Please accept it," he urged tenderly.

"I can't take it, John. You shouldn't have bought it. Still, it was a generous and thoughtful act, but too extravagant. Thank you," she whispered softly, touched by his genuine sincerity.

"What can I do with a gem like this?" he teased her.

"I'm sure you'll find some lucky female who'll cherish it," she replied, smiling.

"No one could do it the justice you do. Besides, after snuggling so close to you, how could I bear to see it upon another female?"

"Then hold it for your future wife," she playfully suggested.

"Which won't be you, right?"

"I must decline, John. I hate to admit it, but I don't trust you," she ruefully, but honestly, replied.

"Only because you don't know me, and you're afraid to trust yourself with me. Can I at least hope you'll consider my proposal?" he pressed.

"Please don't. In light of the trouble with Daniel, I wouldn't want to inspire any false hopes or impressions. But I am extremely fond of you already. You are much too disarming, you dashing rogue."

"As are you, my lovely angel," he murmured.

"Don't call me that!" she screamed at him, pale and rigid.

Startled by her outburst, John was taken aback— until he saw the tears in her eyes. A connoisseur of women, it took little imagination to comprehend the source of Alex's distress. Careful not to frighten her, he pulled her into his arms and comforted her. He fiercely controlled his raging desire for her. He could spoil any hope of winning her over if he took advantage of her now. When she regained her composure, he smiled and offered to see her home.

She returned the smile and thanked him, knowing how tightly he was restraining himself. He grinned and bid her a hasty farewell at the door. Halfway down the front steps, he halted and turned to say, "If you need or want to see me, will you send a message?"

Alex readily agreed, then watched him mount up and ride off while waving to her. Despite everything, she wished she dared to encourage him. But now it was better for both of them if they stayed apart. For the first time in her present state of turmoil, Alex realized she was holding something. She glanced down at her hand; John had pressed the necklace into it while saying goodbye.

That next morning an urgent message came for Henry from President Madison who was requesting his prompt visit to Washington. Alex witnessed his curious reaction to this prestigious summons. He was furious about something in the letter. He was mumbling about the heavy fighting going on to the northern border, Rogers's defensive movement to New York, and Madison's pre-occupation with the upcoming presidential election. Two other facts elated him: Perry had defeated the British fleet on Lake Erie and Elliott had captured two other British ships.

Henry halted his nervous pacing to ask her if she wished to tag along. "The fighting's getting rougher, Alex, and nearer. I couldn't rest easy worrying about your safety. Might be a pleasing outing," he needlessly coaxed.

Overjoyed at some excuse to avoid the men around Philadelphia, and excited about such an adventure, Alex instantly agreed. "I'll send Joe a message to let him know I've left, but only after it's a fact. When do we leave?"

"In the morning. I'd best get there quickly and see what the old bird wants. Probably needs help getting re-elected. With so many people growing weary of this war, he could inspire them to elect another man."

"I don't see why; they forced him to declare war," she astutely surmised. "Washington . . ." she dreamily murmured.

The ride took three and a half days of arduous and bumpy travel in the otherwise comfortable and roomy coach. Sensing her uncle's haste and vexation, Alex kept her discomfort to herself. How she wished this queasiness would stop assailing her during the early morning hours. At least her excessive sleepiness could be abated with occasional naps while her uncle read his papers. Even though her monthly was very late, she hoped it would be delayed a while longer until after their arrival.

Once ensconced in the hotel, Alex rested that first day. Caught up in business and political meetings, Henry was gone most of the time. Placed under the eagle eye of one of Madison's trusted employees on that next day, Alex was given several tours to intriguing locations around the large city. Later, she was invited to dinner at Madison's home.

She was overwhelmed by the illustrious guests present. She found herself smiling and enjoying the amiable, balding man who ruled this promising land. His features hawkish and harsh, his mellow mood and lively blue eyes still relaxed her. Even at sixty-one, he radiated an intelligence and warmth she found appealing and delightful.

Then, there was the famous orator and outspoken Warhawk John Calhoun. He flaunted a curious beard underneath his chin but sported no hair upon his stubborn chin or strong jawline. Bushy brows perched over dark and piercing eyes. He had a rapidly receding hairline which generously allowed his thinning hair to flow back to his nape. She couldn't decide if she liked this powerful and repellent man.

Henry Clay was a different matter. A self-educated lawyer who was known for his boldness, ardor, and frankness had no trouble winning friends and supporters with his magnetic charm and invigorating zeal. Although ̄a Southerner, he fiercely opposed slavery, as she did. Also an ardent Warhawk, he had done much to inspire this war. But for his cleft chin and shapeless mouth, his features bore an aristocratic quality.

The most impressive man present was Daniel Webster, a dashing man in his early thirties. A staunch Federalist, he was also a lawyer. From the Northeast, his resentment of the predominance of Virginians and Southerners in government could be detected in his brazen statements. Unlike the others present, he had vigorously opposed this war. Known to be an eloquent speaker, that time his arguments had fallen upon deaf ears and hardened hearts. His features were large and most prominent. His sharply pointed brows gave him a satanic look. Added to that disadvantage, a bulbous nose, thin upper lip, and large lower one presented a false impression of sullenness.

While the few ladies were present, there was no mention of business or politics during dinner or the brief piano recital by a talented, blond woman who was married to Madison's assistant John Lindsdale. Clearly vexed by Alex's beauty and unintentional rivalry for masculine attention, she reminded Alex of Helen Gillis. As if unmindful of her husband and noted guests, her outrageous flirtations with other men took

Alex by surprise. Why did Lindsdale permit such wantonness?

Entrapped in the drawing room with the ladies after dinner, Alex was compelled to listen to their frivolous conversations while waiting for this now dull evening to end. To sneak a breath of fresh air, she pretended to excuse herself, then hurried outside.

Leaning against the wooden facade of the President's mansion to the dark side of the lengthy U-shaped porch, Alex overheard a curious conversation between Cassandra Lindsdale and another young woman who was still unattached.

"I can't believe it, Lucy; he's finally back. He's been gone too long," she stated petulantly. "There's no other man alive to compare with him. He's a god and a devil."

"But what about John; you're married now," Lucy argued. "It's my turn to woo him."

"You know Spence always preferred me over all other women," she vainly announced.

"But you're married now. Spence never fools with married women and you know it, Cass! Besides, he said he never wanted to see you again!"

"That was a silly misunderstanding. I'll straighten it out," she smugly vowed.

"Misunderstanding?" Lucy shrieked in amusement. "Catching his lady friend in bed with another man to make him jealous is more than a silly disagreement. Have you forgotten you pulled a knife on him and tried to castrate him?" she reminded the molten-blooded, hot-tempered woman with tawny hair and flashing green eyes.

"He knows I was only upset by his rude dismissal. He'll forgive me; you'll see."

"Spence doesn't care what any woman feels or thinks. I hate him!"

"Liar," Cassandra cooed. "You'll accept any amount of attention from him like every other female does."

"Only because he's so handsome, virile, and wealthy," she sneered.

"I would give my soul to have him," Cassandra truthfully vowed. "What female wouldn't after meeting him?"

"Spencer Farrington can have any woman he chooses for as long as he wishes and he'd accept none of them afterwards. When he marries, it'll be to a wealthy, beautiful, and highborn lady. You mark my words, Cass; he'll never settle for less."

"Let's sneak into the kitchen and get some wine; my throat is drier than cotton." When Lucy agreed, they left.

Spencer Farrington? Could it be Sir William's grandson, their future neighbor, the catty women had been discussing? Alex had heard wild tales about him, but had yet to meet him. Could he be as irresistible and aloof as they alleged? Alex laughed as she recalled her father's last words to her about discussing an arranged marriage between herself and that rogue. Strange, Sir William had been the first to mention it. If this Spencer Farrington was such a catch, why didn't he select his own wife from his endless list of conquests?

Could he be as reluctant and discriminating as she was? Could he be forced to marry a woman of Will's choosing, possibly even her? Comparing their personalities and reputations, it could be a perfect match and solution!

Alex hurried inside to return to the drawing room before Cassandra and Lucy could arrive first. The remainder of that evening she secretly studied each woman with renewed intrigue.

The next morning revealed a glorious fall day. After her stroll and lunch, she bid her stuffy and necessary escort farewell at the hotel entrance. As soon as he was out of sight, she grinned mischievously and leisurely began another stroll down the street, stopping here and there to gaze into shop windows.

At a quaint shop where paintings were sold, she paused to go inside. She aimlessly wandered around until a particular canvas captured her attention. It was an irresistible oil painting of an infamous ship at sea, one she recalled too well. Waves were crashing against her black hull and imaginary winds were filling her midnight sails. Unable to resist this striking reminder of her bittersweet past with Joshua, she checked the price . . . but she didn't have that much money with her.

She went to the shopkeeper and asked if he would hold it for her until she could fetch the money from her uncle later that evening. He smiled amicably and agreed. For some absurd reason, she gave the name Angelique DuBois. Maybe it had to do with the effect of the painting which had refreshed her memories of life at sea with Joshua. She waved to him and headed down the street, knowing her uncle would be out until after dinner.

In less than five minutes, a beady-eyed man about sixty hurried up to her. "Miss, miss," he breathlessly called out. When she paused, he related a message for her. "Your uncle's had an accident, miss. Don't know how bad he's hurt. They took him to room seven at the hotel. He said to find you and send you there."

Without stopping to further question this man, Alex turned and rushed toward the hotel. She was oblivious to the sparkling blue eyes watching her hasty progress, the same ones which had watched her entrance and exit from the shop where he held secret meetings with his contacts and where he had once purchased a painting of a siren who looked like her . . . He couldn't decide why she wanted a painting of the *Black Mist* caught in a violent storm.

Alex hurried toward the entrance in near panic. What would she do if her uncle had met with a fatal accident? She would be all alone in this foreign and hostile land. How badly was he hurt? Her frantic thoughts fluctuated between Henry's present ill fortune and her own future distress. She rushed up the stairs without bothering to speak with the busy clerk at the long wooden desk. After all, she and her uncle were staying on the second floor of this same hotel. Why hadn't they taken him to their suite of rooms? She almost ran down the lengthy hallway until she came to room seven. She knocked upon the heavy door, impatiently waiting to be let inside to check her uncle's state of health.

The door swung open and she rushed inside. It instantly shut and locked behind her. She whirled in confusion and alarm, fully expecting to find Daniel Grey or a comparative scoundrel poised there. She nearly fainted when her gaze locked with the beguiling and taunting one of Joshua Steele. Eyes wide and lips parted, she simply stared at him in total disbelief.

He grinned in devilish pleasure. "Been a long time, Angel, but it appears you've fared well since your daring escape from me," he stated in a deceptively calm voice. He leaned negligently against the only exit to this suddenly stuffy room. From his smug expression and roguish mood, he was mentally congratulating himself on his unforeseen good luck.

"What are you doing here?" she finally managed to get out in a whisper. "How did you find me?"

"I didn't," he replied smoothly. "When I saw you strolling down the street, I couldn't believe my eyes. How did you get here? I searched half of Florida and the coast looking for you, woman! You gave me quite a scare. I was afraid you'd met with foul play," he asserted, and Alex almost believed he was serious.

"I gave you a scare?" she repeated his implausible words. "What about me? Surely you didn't think I would hang around to be stuck into a slimy brothel!"

"You mean that little conversation with Andy beneath your balcony which I foolishly allowed you to overhear just to frighten you?" he admitted playfully.

421

"You allowed?" she shrieked.

"Naturally. You were a most stubborn, young lady. I only wanted to scare you into confessing, not endanger your life with a rash escape. How did you get here?" he repeated his inquiry.

She grinned. "I'm not as stupid as you seem to think, Captain Steele. All it took was some courage, cunning, and planning. Is George all right?"

Amused by her concern, he chuckled. "A bit embarrassed, but fine. You certainly wasted a lot of my valuable time looking for you," he irritably snapped at her smug manner.

"And you didn't waste any of mine?" she scoffed.

"I see you've returned to the scene of your previous mischief. Looking for more information, my lovely spy, or only trying to replace what I took?"

"I never was a spy and I'm not now! So don't start that foolishness again! Now move and I'll leave."

"Not so fast, love. We have some unfinished business."

"We have nothing to say, Josh. If you don't move, I'll scream so loud your ears will ache for months . . . in prison, Captain Steele."

"I think it would be a wee bit difficult for you to explain your presence in Captain Steele's room, don't you, love?"

"I'll say you lured me here under false pretenses. Who would take your word against mine? I'll explain everything."

"Afterwards, you can explain how I can identify

every mark upon your lovely and traitorous body," he boldly threatened.

"You wouldn't dare!" she shrieked in dismay.

"Wouldn't I? What's the fate for the mistress of a notorious pirate?" His sapphire eyes raked over her ashen face and shaky body.

"I wasn't your mistress; I was your prisoner!" she angrily protested, trying to summon her wits and courage.

"Did you report me when you miraculously returned from your little misadventure? I doubt it. Who would accept this belated tale?"

"What do you want this time? You already have my silence, among other things," she sneered, alarmed by his effect upon her.

"If you'd like your clothes and jewels returned, come and take them from my ship. I see you were crafty enough to take a few of them with you. As for the petticoat, nothing doing, You'll leave this room after you tell me everything I want to know. If not, you're coming with me," he smugly issued his terrifying ultimatum.

"You can't kidnap me again!" she frantically argued. Even so, she feared he might do just that! She couldn't endure another bittersweet sojourn on his ship. He would make certain she never escaped again. Yet, she couldn't very well call out for help. What to do . . . the truth? No, for she couldn't discern his loyalties. Now that she partially knew what was on the nefarious petticoat, she was more determined to resist his demands.

"I want your full name and the information on that petticoat. No more stalling, Angelique. My patience with you has worn dangerously thin."

Angelique? she mentally echoed. My full name? Did that mean he was still in the dark about her? She recalled his earlier words about sighting her on the street. Whatever it took, she had to get free of him quickly before he discovered the truth. What possible reason could she use to discourage him? Did she dare?

"You can't take me back to sea, Stephen. Please," she cautiously began her daring ploy, using every feminine wile she possessed.

He stared at her. "There you go again, woman! Why do you call me Stephen in times like these and Joshua at other times?" he abruptly asked.

"Because you are Stephen sometimes and Joshua others. Be Stephen today, please," she entreated.

"I can't, Angel. You have something I want and need. Give it to me and I'll leave you alone."

"For the hundredth time, I can't decipher that code! And I can't give you my father's name. Is that so hard for you to understand and accept?"

"Impossible," he coldly stated. "What's it to be, love?"

"I can't answer and I can't go with you. Even if you don't care anything about me, there's someone you should. Damn you, I'm pregnant! I'm getting married in two weeks," she blurted out.

"Married? Pregnant?" he repeated in shock. "You

work mighty fast, don't you?" Was that jealousy in his eyes?

"Not me, you bloody fool! You do. It's your child I'm carrying! My uncle thinks I was besieged by pirates and ravished by their captain. He's somehow managed to convince a wealthy friend of his to marry me. Please, just get out of my life and stay out! You've done enough damage! Unless you want to wed me and claim your child, don't prevent this marriage with your stupid charges and selfishness! Damn you, Joshua! I'm not a spy; I swear it. Let me go; please . . ."

Spencer stared at her for a long time. "I don't believe you. How could you be carrying my child?"

"My God, Stephen! We slept together day and night for months. It isn't uncommon for a baby to follow such abundant acts of passion. You sound as naive as I was! Can't you imagine what I felt and thought when the doctor told me that news?" she challenged. "I hoped and prayed I had seen the last of you, but it appears you left a little reminder with me of our stormy interlude."

"If you're lying to me, I'll beat you to within an inch of your miserable life!" he snarled, unprepared for this news or for seeing her again. Not a day had passed without thinking about her, wanting her!

"Stick around for a month, and you'll see the evidence for yourself! Maybe sooner. What do I know about such things? Once I foolishly enticed you to assist my freedom, but all you've done was give me more chains. It isn't fair, Stephen. I'm practically a child myself," she miserably stated, weeping in fear of her ruse not working. If she could pull it off, surely he wouldn't take her along. He was ruthless and cruel, but was he totally heartless?

"You expect me to walk away and leave my child to another man?" he asked in surprise, coming forward to stand before her.

Stunned by the fury in his tone and expression, she was speechless. They stared at each other. "Are you saying you'll marry me?" she finally asked, her look of disbelief too real to discount.

"I can't. Not now. But I'll make sure you're both taken care of, Angel," he vowed, looking ill at ease for the first time ever.

"You might not care if your son is born a bastard, but I do! He'll have a name and a father when he enters this world! I don't need your help or your pity. Just leave me alone to work out this problem," she angrily spouted at him. "He doesn't need the additional stain your reputation would brand upon him. He'll already arrive too suspiciously early to avoid gossip."

"He's my son and my responsibility," he argued with the only female to ever break through his rigid guard and fill his life and heart.

"No, Captain Steele; he's my son. You ruined my life, but I won't allow you to harm his. I'll see you hanged first!" she fiercely declared.

"Why didn't you tell me you were pregnant?" he growled, his own anger rising. Damn, he wanted her!

What rotten timing he had!

"I didn't know! Everything's arranged and I won't permit you to mess things up for me again." Even while engaged in this frantic ruse, Alexandria didn't guess she might be telling the truth.

"What's the man's name?" he harshly demanded.

"And let you come strolling into our lives again someday? No way, Steele. Haven't you any decency at all? Are you so unfeeling and selfish? What about me and our child? It's all your fault!"

"I never meant for this to happen, Angel," he defended himself, wondering what to do about her and the baby.

"You're an experienced man, Steele. You should have known better," she taunted him. Seeing the infuriating effect of her stinging words, she cautioned herself to a milder approach. "Please, Stephen, there's nothing you can do to solve this problem. Don't make it any worse for me."

She turned away from him, praying he wouldn't read the deception in her eyes. His nearness sparked too many feelings of desire for him, feelings she couldn't destroy or yield to. Tears of self-betrayal flowed down her cheeks. Was she a fool? Even now, she wanted him desperately. Her shoulders trembled as she wept silently.

"Angel?" he murmured tenderly, but didn't continue.

She slowly turned to look up into his eyes, sensing she had won and he would leave soon. Misreading the anguish in her dewy eyes, he reached out and pulled her into his arms. Unable to help herself, she did not resist this much needed contact for the last time.

"I'm sorry, love. I wouldn't hurt you for anything," he whispered into her ear.

"You already have, Stephen," she sadly told him. "I've never wanted anything in my life as much as I wanted you. Why did it have to be this way?"

His embrace tightened. "Our timing was all wrong, love. Believe it or not, I wish it wasn't."

She looked up at him and inquired, "Do you really mean that, Stephen? If things had been different, could you have loved me, too?"

Too? he caught her slip. "Are you in love with me, Angel?" he couldn't help but ask, needing to hear those words from her.

She lowered her head and laughed sadly, "How could I possibly love a pirate like you? A man who blundered into my world and devastated it?"

"As much as you wish it weren't true, it is," he answered for her.

She stiffened; her lips and chin quivered. She didn't respond. He lifted her chin and forced their gazes to meet. "I'm right, aren't I?"

She didn't have to answer aloud, her eyes screamed her stifled response. "Of all men to choose from, why you, Stephen? My God, why you?" she cried out in utter despair, her composure stripped away.

Spencer's mouth came down upon hers, at first gentle and then almost savage. She clung to him in a painful last parting. It had been so long since her blood had flamed with hunger and her heart had felt alive and free. He lifted her light body and carried her to his bed. Between kisses and caresses, he undressed each of them. Their bodies and hearts yearned for this union so long desired. It would be their final farewell, but it would be remembered forever, she vowed.

XVI

"Love looks not with the eyes, . . .
And therefore is winged Cupid painted blind."
—*A Midsummer Night's Dream*, William Shakespeare

Their first joining had been with a savage and urgent intensity. But their second one was leisurely sensual and tenderly passionate. For a time, only Alex and Spencer lay upon the bed making love, no longer past enemies or future combatants. His tasty mouth explored hers as his hands expertly and gently fondled the body which had haunted him day and night since her mind-staggering disappearance. Beneath him lay the one woman who could stir his mind and heart to rebel against all he had thought or known. How could he ever give her up or lose her again? He couldn't; yet, he stubbornly refused to allow her the knowledge of her power over him.

Spencer teased her sensitive breasts and devoured her lips. To think of another man possessing her was too much to accept and he wouldn't. As he lay there beside her, he stroked her tawny hair and caressed her passion-flushed cheek. Unable to touch her enough or to halt these feelings of tenderness and love from besieging him, he declined to speak or to move.

It was Alex who broke the spell between them. She

propped up on her elbow and gazed down at him. Her fingers traced the angles of his face, stroked his hair, and played in the furry mat upon his chest. As she ran her finger over his sensual lips, he seized it gently with his teeth and held it captive. She laughed.

"What a vicious bite you have, my lusty dragon," she teased, leaning over to kiss him.

He released the finger to allow her lips to replace it. "I've missed you, Angel," he confessed.

"And I, you," she admitted, laying her tawny head upon his chest.

He caught himself before demanding why she had fled him, knowing why and not wishing to spoil this moment he had yearned for and had feared to never experience again. His hand came up to hold her head close to him. He wished the war was over and he could either go to England or to his Virginia plantation. He loved and needed this slip of a common girl!

Recalling his meeting with Cassandra the night before, he wondered why he had ever taken any time with her. He smothered his laughter at the remembrance of their argument and his stinging rejection of her offer to become his mistress. With Angelique safely returned to his side, he needed and wanted no other woman. A child . . . somehow that thought didn't distress him at all. Once Will got over the initial shock of his marriage to a commoner, his grandfather would come to love Angelique and their child as much as he himself did now.

Only a few details remained to be settled. He would keep her here with him. Naturally she couldn't be allowed to marry another man. He must retrieve his legal seal from a close and trusted friend and marry Angelique before he put to sea again. He would take her home to Virginia and place her under Thomas's watchful eye. She would be safe and happy there.

"I must leave, Stephen," she whispered softly in a reluctant tone. "I can't afford idle gossip about me right before my marriage."

"You can't marry another man, Angel; you belong to me. I have some important business which will take about an hour, love. Stay here until I return, then I'll decide how to handle everything. I don't want to ever lose you again. My cabin's too quiet and empty."

"I can't stay here, Stephen. I've already been gone too long now," she weakly protested, making no attempt to get up and dress, feeling she must use patience and love to earn his trust if she were to escape him soon. Did he still think her so gullible and naive as to recklessly fall for his disarming tricks again? Yes, he did.

He smiled. "I promise I won't be long. Please do as I ask just once," he wheedled. "I promise to bring you a surprise if you're a good girl."

She laughed cheerfully. "The only surprise I want is you."

"You can have that, too. From now on, love, I'll never let you out of my sight. Have you any objections to sharing my life and future?" he asked, flashing her a beguiling grin.

Stunned speechless, she gaped at him. Believing this was either a trick or a cruel lie, pain knifed her heart. Mistress and prisoner perhaps, but nothing more. How much longer could she endure this torturous game before this sea-devil eviscerated her heart and soul? She forced a smile. "I can think of nothing better," she vowed truthfully. To fully disarm him and to win his trust, she snuggled into his arms and whispered, "I love you, Stephen. My life is nothing without you. Please hurry back"

Tears, which he assumed to be those of happiness, burned his naked chest. The arrogant rogue was convinced she, like any female, loved and wanted him at any price. She had no choice but to use that male pride against him now. But his emotions weren't the only ones being subjected to this game.

"Within the hour, I promise. Never have I wanted a woman as much as you, Angelique," he stated clearly, denying her the full truth.

"Oh, Stephen, it's so wonderful to have you again." She hugged him tightly, offering her lips to his, dreading the final score of this brutal game between them. Neither would be a winner . . .

"You, too, Miss DuBois," he announced, kissing her soundly.

She laughed. "Since you have managed to learn my identity, do I get to know yours now?" she hinted, placing kisses over his face and eyes.

"When I return in an hour, I promise to tell you," he teased playfully. "In fact, love, we have a lot of talking and planning to do." He got up and slowly dressed, his gaze rarely leaving her.

When fully clothed, he leaned over and kissed her.

"I'll be back soon."

"Shall I wait here or get dressed?" she wantonly jested, bringing a heated look to his eyes as she curiously awaited his response.

"You'd better dress just in case I'm not alone," he lazily replied, unaware of her conclusions.

"I'd much prefer to remain right here, but if you insist, my love." She threw the covers aside and stood up. What more could she do to tempt or sway him? Was he utterly unreachable? Had this romantic cause been lost to her even that first day by the pond? She was granting him every chance possible to prove he loved her and wanted her in this same way. Please, Stephen, love me as I love you, she fervently prayed.

His eyes raked appreciatively over her provocative body. "You wouldn't be trying to change my mind, you wanton temptress, would you? I have to leave for a while; there's something mighty important to both of us which I must do. After tonight, everything will be all right, Angel."

"Me try to change your mind?" she innocently inquired. Once she was gone, she would make certain he would long remember her and this treacherous night!

He came over and pulled her to him. His mouth came down over hers. She clung to him, savoring these fleeting moments before his loss. Becoming aroused again, he pulled away and sighed. "Later, love. If I don't leave now, I never will."

"Would that be so terrible?" she mischievously taunted. "For weeks I've endured a painful separation from you. I never thought to ever see you again. I shall never have enough of you, Stephen."

"I hope you mean that, woman; forever is a mighty long time."

Bubbly laughter came forth. What a stimulating and exciting life they could share if he would allow it. Bitterly recalling those first few weeks aboard his ship when he had so easily and cruelly deceived her with the same way he was behaving now, she steeled her heart against his tender words and enticing caresses. No words of love or promises of marriage . . .

"Get dressed and wait for me, you sultry siren. I plan to keep you busy after tonight," he huskily warned.

"Yes, Captain Steele," she cooed, saluting him and grinning.

He kissed her and left, believing she would wait for him. It was clear she loved him and desired him. And, he was the father of the child she was carrying. Add those facts to his show of trust in her, she would be there . . .

The moment the door closed, Alex was up and frantically dressing. She went to the writing desk and sat down to compose a note. She could envision his fury when he came back and found her missing. No doubt he would either bring the American authorities with him or a trunk to lock her in until he could take her to his ship! "Never will I succumb to you or be your slave again, my dashing rogue."

She walked slowly to the bed and stood beside it. Tormented and accused by its rumpled condition, she hastily straightened the covers. She placed the note on the front pillow where he would be sure to see it. She leaned over and read it one last time:

J.S.,

When you return with your confederates to betray me one last time or with your trunk to steal me in, I will be long gone from your sight and reach forever. Never will I yield to the carnal weaknesses you inspire, nor become your slave again. If you thought for one moment your cunning ruse worked as it did before, you were mistaken, my treacherous love. You need not fret over the loss of your child, for one never existed. As you can see by my successful escape once more, I learned much about deception and revenge from you. May you rot in prison for what you have done to me. For as long as I think of you and recall your many betrayals, I shall curse you and hate you. Surely if you show your face again, my husband will slay you where you stand. Farewell, my dashing rogue.

A.H.

She smiled sadly as she envisioned his face and reaction to learning she wasn't carrying his child and had cunningly fooled him completely. Maybe he would be infuriated by the idea of her marrying another man. She glanced at the initials on the note.

She reached for it to change them, but changed her mind instead. Let him stew and puzzle over the implication there! Besides, they were leaving in the morning. She would be careful until then. He would never look for her right under his nose! She hurriedly departed, taking one last glance backwards before closing the door. "Goodbye, my love, this time forever," she murmured wretchedly.

Not daring to tempt fate and Joshua's persistence, Alex ordered a light meal sent to her room. It was late when her uncle returned and went to bed. The course was plotted and she was ready to sail toward some obscure future. She hoped their plans had not been changed.

One floor below her, Spencer was sitting in a chair in the dark. He had been a fool to leave her alone! Didn't he realize she would never trust him enough to wait for his return? He made no attempt to search for her this time. No doubt she was long gone as stated. Between cursing her and himself and longing for her return, he sat there numb as if grieving for a love who was now eternally lost to death. Anguish, fury, and sadness stormed him.

Spencer hadn't known what it was to love someone so much or to feel such torment at a careless loss. Three times she had mysteriously entered his life and three times she had agonizingly left it. Surely his luck had run out. Three chances to win her without success. Who was this elusive siren who plagued his life and heart? No child? Could he believe her denial?

No, there was a child and she was only trying to punish him. Did she think him totally naive? Her rounding tummy revealed the truth! He should have confessed his love and taken her straight to some minister and wed her!

A.H.? Another ruse, or was this finally the truth? If only she had waited! To find that one unique woman, to love her, to need her, and to needlessly lose her was torture. Why, Angel?

What use was there in looking for her? She had made her plans and would carry them out. Who would become the father of his child and the owner of his woman? Fury and jealousy gnawed at him.

"You best hope our paths never cross again, Angel, for you'll never escape me again!" he swore between clenched teeth.

Going over the orders received from Madison that night, Spencer threw himself upon the bed to face a restless night before returning to his ship in the morning to set sail for Jamaica. Once matters were settled, he needed to go home to see his aging grandfather once more.

Upon arising, Alex was violently ill. Concerned, her uncle sent for a doctor. When the results were delivered to her after his examination, Alex fainted in shock. Surely the fates were punishing her for her sins and deceits!

After the doctor left, Henry came in to speak with

her. Seeing his look of anguish and shock, she wretchedly inquired, "He told you?"

"Yes, child, and I'm sorry." He dejectedly dropped into the chair by the window. Surely this was all his fault. How could he have been so careless and weak-spined with her safety?

"What can I do, Uncle Henry? He's probably gone by now," she wailed.

"Who's gone, Alex?" he asked in confusion, thinking her suffering from shock, wondering why she wasn't accusing him of allowing this terrible thing to happen to her.

Almost hysterical, she shrieked, "Joshua Steele, that rogue who ravished me! He was here at the hotel yesterday. He tried to kidnap me again, but I tricked him and eluded him a second time. My God, I'm carrying Joshua Steele's child!"

Stunned by the accusation against his good friend, Henry asked, "Are you saying Joshua Steele is the pirate who kidnapped you and held you prisoner?"

"Yes, on that infamous ship of his, the *Black Mist!*"

Still not convinced of this incredible tale, he pressed, "Are you certain it was Steele? That doesn't sound like him."

"Of course, I'm sure! But he uses the name Stephen sometimes. He always wears that black mask over his handsome face so no one can identify him. But I can! I'm sorry, Uncle Henry, but he found the petticoat when I was trying to discard it. He claimed I was a spy! He threatened to turn me over to the authorities because I wouldn't decode it or give him yours and Papa's names. He tried every trick to force the information from me; he was even sweet and charming sometimes. But I didn't tell him anything! He thinks my name is Angelique DuBois, that's what I told him."

In Henry's stunned silence and her outpouring of anguish and pain, the whole story came forth: she began with the day at the pond and continued until just the day before. "I must be the wickedest girl alive, Uncle Henry, but I actually fell in love with him. I've never met any man like him. Even now, I love him and want him," she exclaimed, ending her long and painful confession. "I'm as bad as he is," she concluded.

"There, there, Alex. Don't worry, child. I have the perfect solution," he comforted the girl who was unknowingly in love with Spencer Farrington. "You rest while I make a call on someone. I'll be back shortly." Spence was in for the shock of his life!

As he closed the door, he could hear Alex weeping as if her tender and ravaged heart was broken. When he discovered Spencer had already left the hotel, he immediately headed for the dock, only to discover Spencer had sailed at dawn. Furious and desperate, he called on their mutual and influential friend Madison for his assistance. After a private discussion, they came up with a daring plan.

Madison stood before his window watching Henry Cowling's solemn departure. Reflecting upon a conversation between himself and Spencer months ago, he grimaced in sympathy for both Spencer and Alex.

The winning had neither been painless nor light. Yet, he could only presume Spencer had deep feelings for this English girl; else, he would never have kept her as his captive mistress for weeks on end. Astute, he knew that portentous petticoat and this English girl were somehow connected.

Why had Spencer deceived him, and what innocent role had this girl played in his moody silence? He shook his head sadly. So much anguish for a harmless mistake! What would Spencer feel and think when he eventually discovered that coded message was actually being passed between two of his cohorts, patriotic men whose loyalties rested with the Americans, one still unknown to him? Would Lady Alexandria ever forgive him for an error which cost her so much? Was it right to wed them by proxy? Yes, an innocent child made it so! Knowing Spencer Farrington so well, Madison felt he would accept their hasty actions. Spencer was an honorable man who would accept his responsibilities to Alex and his child.

Suddenly, irrepressible chuckles claimed the powerful man. Surely this was a union designed by the fates. Before this day was passed, Spencer would be legally bound to the very girl he had avoided like the plague, the very girl he had chosen himself! How would that proud and valiant man feel when he learned his wife and his dream-girl were the same woman?

Henry returned to the hotel and told Alex to get bathed and dressed. Without asking questions, she did so reluctantly, then joined him in the other room. She sat down, her head hung in shame and dejection.

"Everything's settled, Alex. You'll be married within the hour to a good friend of mine," he cheerfully informed the distraught girl.

"Married? To whom? How?" she stammered, dreading to believe the fates had entrapped her in a desperate snare of her own making, helplessly caught in a web of her own lies to Joshua . . .

"You probably don't know this, but your father and Sir William Farrington were arranging a marriage between you and Spencer, his grandson. But like you, Spencer doesn't wish to marry or settle down. Yet, he must to please his grandfather and avoid disinheritance. I spoke with him before he left on business and he's agreed to marry you by proxy. He left his seal with me. It's all arranged. I have a trusted man waiting to stand in for him. Then, there's a ship heading for England later today. I'll put you on it. The English are waging a bitter war to the North. They're also heading this way from the South, and they're about to blockade the entire coastline. I need to get you out of here while I can. Three ships will be travelling together for safety."

Astounded, she debated, "Spencer Farrington agreed to marry me? Does he know about the baby?"

"Yes," he continued his desperate lies, knowing he would explain everything to Spencer when he next saw him. In light of these circumstances, what could he say or do? Nothing, the irresponsible rogue! He would leave it up to Spencer to reveal the entire truth to Alex; damnit, he owed her that much and more! "He'll claim the baby as his. We'll date the license for two months past."

"But I've never met Spencer. How will I explain my lack of knowledge about my own husband?" she reasoned.

"You aren't the only one who's seen or met that dauntless pirate, Alex. In my secret dealings with privateers, I have also met him. But I dared tell no one about him for fear of implicating myself. If only you'd told me about Steele upon your return. Zounds, girl! I saw him just yesterday. If I had known the truth then . . ." He halted, knowing it was too late to recall it.

"Strange as it sounds, Steele and Spencer are enough alike in appearance and character to be brothers. Just describe Steele to anyone who questions you and they'll never guess the truth. Plus, I'll fill you in on his life and work here. I know his comings and goings, so you'll have accurate facts to relate to Will and your father. So you see, if the baby favors his father, it won't matter at all. Spencer's troubles are solved and so are yours. If either of you desires a divorce later, the other must agree."

"From what I've heard about Spencer Farrington, this generosity is hard to believe. Will it be legal?"

"Of course, child; it's done all the time when the groom can't make the wedding for one reason or another. All that is required is his signature and his seal. I have both. Time is short, so let's be off."

Her head was spinning with this curious whirl of events. Before it cleared, she was on a ship heading home: Lady Alexandria Hampton Farrington! Travelling under a letter of protection signed by President Madison himself and another by Lord Spencer Farrington, Alex was secure from danger from either side! Still, she pondered Spencer's motives. She suddenly recalled the conversation between Lucy and Cassandra. She smiled in ironic amusement as she stared at the gold band upon her finger; Lucy had been correct. He had married a highborn, wealthy, and attractive lady!

Alex's problems were solved and perhaps his were too. If only she had met him just once, this ruse wouldn't be so difficult. Her father was in for the shock of his life when she returned home not only wed and pregnant, but by the man with whom he was so craftily arranging such feats! Well, it was done. Joshua was out of her life for good. A marriage in name only and for convenience was the answer for her since Joshua would be there between them.

During the three week voyage, Alex's morning sickness vanished and her figure gradually expanded. She would need to order new dresses the moment after her arrival. If the American doctor was correct, the baby was due sometime in April, nine months after the alleged date upon her marriage license, a year after their first meeting.

Upon her arrival, Alex ordered a carriage to take her

home. When Daxley opened the door to find her standing there, he shouted in surprise and pleasure. At the mention of her name, her father came rushing from his library. He couldn't believe his eyes, which were watering with joy.

"Alex!" he joined in the merriment. "How did you get here? We're at war with America. Did Henry come with you?" his questions tumbled one over the other.

Elated to be home, she wept in joy and relief. At last, her wonderful and tormenting experiences were over. She hugged her father tightly, who instantly noticed her protruding stomach. He leaned back and stared at her, at a loss. "What's this?" he asked, patting her tummy.

She grinned and calmly stated, "Your first grand-child, naturally. Uncle Henry thought we would be safer here, so he sent us home. The President himself sent along an official letter of protection. We had a small fleet of three ships for safety. Oh, Papa, so much has happened," she rushed on excitedly, forgetting to mention any husband to her alarmed father.

"I can see that for myself, Alex. Is there some logical explanation for this condition?" he demanded, his tone stern and shaky.

She burst into laughter. "Perhaps this will explain everything," she hinted, handing him the rolled parchment secured by a blue ribbon.

He accepted it, then read it after removing the confining ribbon. His eyes widened in astonishment. "You and Spencer Farrington were married in July?"

he asked incredulously.

"July fifteenth, to be exact, Papa. You did say I could marry some worthy American if I found one," she impishly reminded him, playing this necessary role with skill and relief. "He's absolutely magnificent, Papa. Eyes as blue as rich sapphires . . . hair of shiny sable . . . so proud and strong and handsome . . . I've never met any man like Spence," she murmured dreamily as she assumed a bride of nearly four months would do.

While she had his undivided attention, she went on romantically, "Have you ever met him, Papa? He could charm candy from a baby. He's tall and has the broadest shoulders. He . . ."

He cut her off, "Where is this matchless son-in-law, pray tell?"

"Oh! I forgot to tell you," she shrieked, then laughed. "Spence was away on business when the opportunity came to leave. He left orders for Uncle Henry to put me on the first safe ship. He's to join us as soon as possible. Spence and Uncle Henry were afraid for me and the baby; things are terrible in some places. I hope it doesn't take long for him to join me; I miss him already," she pouted convincingly.

"Was it safe for you to travel in this condition?" he asked like a worried father.

She smiled. "The baby isn't due until mid-April, Papa. I'm perfectly fine. Spence wouldn't have permitted me to travel if it weren't safe."

He abruptly began to laugh, the side-splitting kind.

She gaped at him. "Papa? Are you all right?" she teased.

"Surely this match was meant to be, Alex. Will and I just signed the agreement for an alliance between you and Spencer," he mirthfully confessed.

"Papa!" she scolded him. "What if I had married someone else? You shouldn't have done that without speaking with me first."

"What difference does it make now? You two are already married. Very married," he added, patting her tummy again.

"Charles Hampton," she chided, "you are a lecherous old man!"

"But an ecstatically happy one. Let's hope and pray Spence makes it home by Christmas," he ventured, hugging her affectionately.

Christmas came, with no Spencer. St. Valentine's Day passed and still there was no Spencer. The rebirth of spring came with her lush greens, colorful wildflowers, heavy rains, and gusty winds: still no Spencer arrived nor was there any word from him. Naturally Alex understood these things, but neither Charles nor Will did. They worried over his safety during the continual war. Countless British ships of varying sizes and types had been sunk. Violent conflicts had occurred in several locations.

Afraid of an accident during the snows and rains, Will called on Alex at the Hampton Manor rather than risking her visits to Farrington Estates. They had become close friends, sharing many happy and serene afternoons and dinners. They had taken walks together and conversed for hours. She had played the piano for him and entertained him with the stories supplied by her thoughtful and cautious uncle.

Will came to love and respect Alex as his own daughter. He marveled at the growth of his great-grandchild as it vividly proclaimed its presence. He prayed Spencer would arrive before its birth. It saddened him to think of his beloved grandson separated from his lovely and devoted wife for such a long time. He was beaming with pride and love, delighted with Spencer's choice of a bride. He couldn't wait to congratulate him.

In her condition, Alex was given an excuse to decline most social invitations. She spent hours exercising like the doctor suggested to assist an easier birth and to retain her health and looks. Yet, each day which drew the baby's birth closer, fear increased within her. Her fear was enmeshed with sadness and strain. Not for one day had she forgotten Joshua. Each time his child moved, she would caress her stomach and think of him.

During that second week of April, Alex was plagued by a dull backache and irregular pains. Suddenly she comprehended what was happening. Panicked, she alerted her father to her first signs of labor. To everyone's relief, only six hours later, a small son was born to Lady Alexandria Hampton Farrington. The doctor attributed her excellent condition and the baby's tiny size to the uncomplicated and hasty birthing of the child. Still dazed after the ordeal and her exertions, when asked what his name would be, she smiled happily and stated, "Joshua Stephen," before she fell into deep slumber.

She was awakened to the crying of her son as he demanded his dinner. She gently and anxiously accepted him from the genial and competent nurse hired by her father. Almost reluctantly afraid to handle the tiny and squirming bundle of squalling life, Martha had to gently coax the apprehensive new mother. Alex flushed as she listened to the older woman's instructions on how to feed the baby. Her embarrassment faded swiftly as she gazed into the small pink face with a head of dark hair. He sucked greedily at his mother's milk-laden breasts and she laughed at the tickling sensation.

"My son," she whispered in amazement. "Oh, Joshua," she sadly murmured, referring to his father instead of to her baby as the elderly nurse presumed. Alex clutched him tightly to her and sang softly to him as he nursed. When he was done, Martha placed him in the cradle near her.

Her heart full of love and pride, she watched him for a time. Would it be over now? Had her forbidden and mysterious love come full circle? It had been a year ago this very month when she had first met her dashing pirate. They had shared a union as serene as a tranquil ocean and as violent as a storm at sea. She had lost him; yet, she would always have a part of him in their son. The love and the ache would be there for a long time, perhaps forever. Yet, his son would bring her the love and joy which his father had cruelly denied her. In a tragic way, Joshua was the real loser; he would never see or know his own son. Time, that was what she needed . . .

She snuggled into her pillow and slept peacefully, knowing April would always be special and difficult for her.

XVII

"Every tongue brings in a several tale,
Every tale condemns me for a villain."
—Richard II, William Shakespeare

"Don't be silly, Will," Alex teased the elderly gentleman. "He isn't going to break. He's six weeks old. Here, hold your great-grandson for a moment while I get his bath ready," she encouraged, giggling at his look of fear, recalling how she had felt the same way that first time Martha had offered him to her.

"Such a tiny bundle. Spence'll be sorry he missed his birth. Have you heard from him yet, Alex?" he asked sadly.

"Not yet, Will, but I'm sure he's fine. Nothing and no one could harm him or keep him away too much longer," she comforted the man who was growing weaker every day. She sincerely hoped Spencer would make it home to visit before it was too late. She also prayed her uncle had related all the necessary details of the wedding to match their stories. Besides, she was looking forward to meeting this elusive and mysterious man who had stolen and abused so many hearts.

The groom finally came to assist the old gentleman home. Alex walked to his carriage to say goodbye. "If you're feeling up to it, Will, join us for dinner tomorrow night. We'll put our heads together and see if we can come up with some way to reach my errant husband," she playfully stated to bring a smile to his face.

"How could I refuse an invitation like that? Did Spence tell you what to name the baby?" he asked from the blue.

She smiled and shook her head. "We really never discussed it; time was short," she answered truthfully, winking at him.

"Then he's in for a pleasant surprise," he remarked, not commenting further. If he had, the truth might have come to light, much to Alex's shock and pleasure. Will waved as he was driven away.

Guilt flooded Alex at her blatant ruse. How would Spencer behave when he finally came home? How should she behave? Everyone would expect them to act like starstruck lovers reunited after a terrible separation of months; could they carry it off? Would such a romantic ruse have any effect upon him, upon her? She couldn't guess until she met him.

Alex returned to her room. The baby was sleeping soundly. She watched him for a time. He would doubtlessly favor his father. She hoped her uncle was right when he said Spencer had sable hair and blue eyes, for Joshua's son certainly did. If Spencer would come home just once and meet her, she could decide what course of action to take. She couldn't keep making excuses for his absence forever. He had agreed to this mock marriage; the least he could do was make an appearance! If he wanted a divorce, she would gladly grant it. He had helped her out of a terrible situation. Perhaps he wouldn't wish one until after his grandfather's death. At least she had earned Spencer a greater measure of love, happiness, and respect in the old man's heart. Still, this ruse couldn't continue much longer without some help from him.

Seeing the wondrous product of her love for Joshua, Alex felt drawn to the spot of their first meeting. She hadn't gone there since that fated day. She yanked off her clothes and pulled on a riding habit. She told the horrified nurse she was going for a ride. She calmed the woman by promising only to allow the horse to walk.

True to her word, Alex assumed a leisure and safe pace. Since the baby was six weeks old, surely her body was healed. She revelled in the warm May air, suddenly realizing tomorrow would be June first!

How swiftly and eventfully time had passed since her meeting by the pond with Stephen. This time last year, she had just arrived in America. Now, she was safely home and had a six-week-old son by a man who would no doubt haunt her forever. She weaved her way through the overgrown path into a world set apart from reality. She looked around; it was like truly coming home at last.

She walked to the pond and sat down upon the grassy bank. Too cool to take a swim and risk a cold, she dangled her feet in the sensuous water. Her palms pressed to the ground behind her, she leaned back and closed her eyes. The sun was warm and relaxing; sweet fragrances filled her nostrils; the birds sang as if for her enjoyment alone. She withdrew her feet and stretched out by the pond, trailing her fingers in the water. She dreamily closed her eyes once more to allow her senses to extract the intangible beauty and uniqueness of nature. In this dreamy setting, her mind began to drift . . .

"I don't believe it," came the mellow sound of that never-to-be-forgotten voice.

Her eyes flew open; she stared up at the vital man towering over her. It couldn't be! As if frozen, she could neither speak nor move. He knelt down beside Alex, her gaze never leaving his arresting face and mesmerizing aura. Was there no place she could ever hide from him? Did she even want him out of her life forever? Her heart and body became instant traitors to her. Her pulse raced and her body enflamed.

"I'm sure we're thinking the same question, so I'll answer first. I just arrived." His eyes noticeably slipped to her flat stomach. A scowl lined his impressive features. "Did you lose the baby, or am I a proud father by now?" he asked coldly.

She paled and trembled. She was sorely tempted to lie, but felt she couldn't carry it off under his piercing stare. "I have a son," she whispered, stressing the first word.

"I beg to disagree, love, but we have a son. Where is he?" he demanded, furiously noting the gold circle upon her left hand. "Who's the lucky man?" he contemptuously snarled.

She suddenly moved as if to jump up and dash for safety. He grabbed her by the waist and sent her none too gently to the ground, flat on her back with her wrists pinned above her head. Lying upon her to prevent any further struggle, his grasp tightened upon her wrists. She cried out in pain.

"You're hurting me, Josh!"

"No more than you hurt me, woman! Where's my son? How dare you prevent me from having him!" he shouted at the defenseless girl.

"Did you think I would just lie there waiting for you to return with your American friends or some trunk to stuff me in until you could imprison me upon your ship again? My God, Stephen, what about our child?"

He looked at her in a strange manner. "You stupid fool! I went to get a man to marry us. I was going to leave you at my home until I could return!" he stormed at her.

Her look of shock couldn't be fake. "You were going to marry me?"

"Absolutely! You were carrying my first child. And . . . damnit, Angel! I love you and need you. A day hasn't passed I didn't think about you."

"You love me? I don't believe you! You've never even hinted at any strong feelings for me, except for carnal desire!" she resisted him.

"It's clear your fiery passions have been sated more than mine! How could you marry another man? How could you let him touch you?" he thundered his jealousy and rage.

"But he hasn't touched me. And he never will! No man has but you, Josh," she instantly argued.

"You expect me to believe a man could live with you without touching you? Don't take me for a fool, Angel!" he snarled harshly at her deception.

"I swear it, Josh! The man I wed needed a wife for business reasons, and you know why I needed a husband! We made a bargain: marriage in name only until one or the other wanted freedom. I've never been in his room or he in mine. Nothing has happened between us. How could it when I was carrying your child? I love you, Josh. I have since that first day here."

They stared at each other, weighing and absorbing these facts. "I should have told you my plans before I left the hotel. I was coming back to marry you, love."

Tears brimmed in her green eyes and flowed into her tawny hair. "I didn't know, Josh. I never even suspected such an incredible thing. I didn't have any reason to trust you. I had to think about the baby. It's like the fates are battling over our destinies. One is frantically and cruelly trying to keep us apart; another is struggling to throw us together. It isn't fair, Stephen," she cried out in anguish, weeping and trembling.

He pulled her into his arms and held her tightly. "Don't worry, love; we'll figure something out," he offered her solace with words and caresses.

"You mean you still want us?" she fearfully asked.

He smiled tenderly. "Both of you and as soon as possible."

She hugged him fiercely. "I was afraid I'd never see you again. What will we do if my husband changes his mind and refuses me a divorce?"

"I'll kill him first!"

"You can't! You're in enough danger as Joshua Steele without adding murder to your list of infamy. I'll talk with him. If he refuses to comply with our bargain, I'll take the baby and leave. You should see him, Josh. He's beautiful. He has your eyes and hair. When he gets older, he'll look just like you. He coos and holds your finger tightly. He's the most wonderful gift in the whole world. I didn't know it was possible to feel so much love and pride. Sometimes I think my heart will burst with them."

He watched the softened lights which glowed in her eyes. "Motherhood becomes you, love. I didn't think it possible for you to grow more radiant and beautiful, but you have." He kissed her deeply and Alex hungrily responded.

"Let's go see him now. You can come with me this minute," he eagerly stated.

"I can't. The minute anyone lays eyes on you, the truth will be as clear as this pond. I told you; he looks just like you. Are you forgetting the power of a man's pride? To see you standing there with me would only inspire him to fight us. Please let me handle it my way," she pleaded. She would discuss Spencer's obvious disinterest and desertion with her father. She would make him help her get a divorce, then she would leave with her true love.

"I want to see our son," he stubbornly insisted.

She pondered these intertwined problems. She brightened. "I'll bring Josh here to see you at midday tomorrow."

"Josh?" he echoed.

She laughed in blissful elation. "I'm a wicked woman, Stephen. I named our son Joshua Stephen. Of course you can change his name after we're married if you prefer another one," she jested.

He smiled broadly. "How did you plan to forget me after naming our son after me?" he merrily hinted.

"How could I possibly forget you when your son is steadily becoming your spitten image? Anyway, I was half asleep when they asked me, and I gave the first and most appropriate answer," she happily retorted.

"No need to change his name. I like your choices very much. Joshua was special to me long ago and Stephen is my name."

"Stephen what?" she boldly inquired.

"I'll tell you the moment I gaze into the face of my son," he teased. "Deal?"

"Anything you say, my love," she dreamily agreed. A worried look chased her smile and glow away.

"What's wrong, love?" he asked.

"When we go to America, would you give up the sea and stay home with us? I couldn't bear the thought of losing you again. It's so dangerous, Stephen. You could be killed, or captured, or wounded. Please give up Steele. We could live in a grass shack for all I care. I only want you safe and near."

He caressed her cheek. "Those are precisely my plans, love. I have a family to think about now. I promise to be around to watch him grow up and you grow out with our next child."

"Another child?" she echoed in wonder.

"'It isn't uncommon for a baby to follow such abundant acts of passion,'" he quoted her words from the day at the hotel in Washington. "I don't plan a celibate life like your present husband has followed."

She giggled. "I know I'm still rather green in such matters, Captain Steele, but I think he has some problem which prevents anything between us. I would kill him if he tried to touch me," she vowed seriously.

"You're right, love; I think I have some lucky lodestar guiding me. We always seem to find each other again. Maybe it's the goddess of the black mist. She certainly seems to favor me at sea."

"You will be here tomorrow, won't you?" he asked anxiously. "If you're not, I'll search heaven, earth, and hell until I find you," he playfully threatened.

"Nothing and no one can ever keep us apart again, Stephen. I'll be here. If he refuses an agreeable divorce, I'll bring the baby and never look back."

"Who is this 'he' you keep referring to?" he questioned.

"I'll tell you everything tomorrow, my love. I don't want you tempted to come and sneak a look at our son. It could spoil everything, and we're too close to our life together. Please, do as I ask this time."

"For once, I trust you implicitly."

"I love you so much, Stephen."

His mouth closed upon hers and his hand sought her breast. His mouth seared hers. God, how she wanted and needed him. As his hand slipped under her skirt and sought another place of agonizing need, she writhed in urgent desire to possess him instantly and desperately.

In frustration and anguish, she cried out and thrashed upon the grass. She opened her eyes, her body damp and taut with the emotions tormenting it. She looked around in confusion. Where was Stephen? She turned over and wept bitterly, the beautiful and all-too-real dream vanished. She cried for a long time.

"Why do you torture me this way, Stephen? That's how it should be! That's how it should be," she wretchedly moaned.

Her breasts ached with the fullness of milk. It was past Josh's feeding time. She slowly pushed herself up to a sitting position. She struggled to pull herself together before returning home. Somehow and some way, she had to dispel his magical touch . . .

Alex rode home at that same slow pace, the stepping of her beloved horse bringing discomfort to her breasts each time he put his hooves down. She dismounted with the assistance of a groom and hurried inside. The nurse was beside herself with worry and annoyance.

"I was about to send someone to search for you,

Lady Farrington. The baby has been crying for nearly half an hour. I feared some harm had befallen you," she ranted on and on.

Tempted to demand she shut up, Alex fiercely resisted that needed release. She had the right to worry and scold her. "I'm sorry, Martha. When I halted to rest, I fell asleep. I dared not rush back, so I came as quickly as I could. It won't happen again," she promised like an errant child, the realistic dream still tormenting her.

She went to the nursery adjoining her room and picked up her wailing son. She shed just as many tears as she entreated him to stop his, "Don't cry, little love; Mama's here now."

She went to the rocking chair, sat down, and unbuttoned her dress. She placed him near the left breast. Instantly he began to suckle upon it, his distress gone. She sang softly as she rocked him, her gaze tracing his every feature.

More tears eased down her rosy cheeks as she murmured sadly, "Oh, Josh . . . I love you so much."

Martha wondered at the despondency in her mistress's voice and the sadness in her eyes as she spoke softly to her son Josh. Deciding she was merely lonely and worried for her husband whom she hadn't seen since leaving America, she shook her gray head sadly and left Alex to herself.

Once sated, she placed the sleeping infant in his cradle, gazing down at him for a long time. Her dream had one point of reality: she could never forget the man who confronted her each day through his son. No matter what had happened, she didn't resent her child at all. She loved him with all her heart, as she did his father.

She ordered a tub of hot and soapy water. She needed to relax this tension in her mind and body. After soaking until the water was chilled, she got out and dried off. She dressed in a tea gown of soft yellow, enhancing her beauty and coloring. She pulled the confining ribbon from her amber tresses and brushed her hair until it shone with silky gold highlights. She dabbed on a cologne with a hint of wildflowers.

As she left her room, she told Martha she would be in the garden getting some fresh air and sun. She told the woman to bring a pallet and her son to do the same when he awakened.

Martha patted her shoulder in fondness. She softly encouraged, "He'll be home soon, Lady Farrington. Don't be so sad."

Just before asking who she meant, Alex smiled and replied, "I know, Martha. I miss him so much." Naturally the elderly nurse didn't realize she meant Joshua Steele and not her husband. But until Spencer Farrington showed up and they talked, her life would never settle down.

Angry with him for this humiliating ignorance of her for so long, Alex resolved to give him a piece of her mind if and when he finally and graciously appeared! How dare that arrogant, selfish creature treat her this way! After all, he had needed this alliance as much as she had! Besides, if his reputation and that talk overheard in Washington were accurate, he sounded to be the only man who could help her forget Joshua Steele. If fact, they sounded like the same man! Did she dare use him as a substitute for Joshua? Could she ever fall in love with another man?

So many questions! No answers could be forthcoming until she met this wayward husband of hers.

XVIII

"Twice or thrice had I loved thee,
Before I knew thy face or name."
—"Air and Angels," John Donne

"What in the devil are you talking about, Jefferson? Me married to Lady Hampton? She claims we have a son?" Spencer shouted in disbelief and fury. What could that vain girl be thinking of to pull a ruse like this? There was only one female he would ever marry!

Bewildered by the wild rantings of Spencer Farrington upon his arrival home, Jefferson couldn't make heads or tails of his behavior. "Where's Will? If that old cuss has bound me to that witch, I'll strangle him! How dare the old buzzard do this to me! For damn sure it isn't legal! Just wait until I get my hands on that conniving vixen and my brazen grandfather!" Months of agony and denial tormented him.

"You can't disturb him right now, Master Spence," the elderly servant declared, grasping the infuriated man's arm to prevent him from storming up the steps and verbally assailing the enfeebled lord of this estate. "He's bad off, Master Spence. He's growing weaker every day. I don't think he'll live to see next month."

"He's that low, Jefferson?" Spencer asked, leashing his temper. What had happened to his carefree life and control? Angelique!

"I'm afraid so," the aging servant sadly replied. "Lady Alex and the baby are the lights of his heart. They're the only things which keep him going. He loves her like a daughter. They spend lots of time together. He's sleeping now, but he's having dinner tonight at Hampton Manor with your wife and son."

"Darnit, Jefferson! I don't have a wife and son! That's what I've been trying to get across! I've never married any woman. But when I do, it won't be that spoiled brat!" he thundered near exasperation. The strain and sacrifice of the past months savagely attacked him. He hadn't been the same since Washington. How much longer would this bitterness, loneliness, and hunger plague him? He was still in love with a dream which couldn't come true.

"But, Master Spence," Jefferson protested, "it's true."

"Did Will and Charles dream up this proxy marriage?" he demanded suspiciously.

Baffled, he shook his head. "Lady Farrington came back from America already married to you. She's been living with her father until you came home. You have a fine baby, named Michael," the forgetful old man stated, using Spencer's father's name instead of the baby's.

"She claims I married her in America?"

"She said you sent her home because of the war. She talks about you all the time. That girl surely loves and misses you."

"I just bet she does," he sarcastically sneered. So,

the haughty Lady Hampton got into trouble in America and was using him to save her name and honor! Well, the little tramp wouldn't get away with this treacherous act! How dare she try to foist another man's child off on him! Did she believe herself so beautiful and irresistible as to think she could cunningly enchant him upon his arrival and entice him to go along with this bold farce? Since she arrived claiming to be wed to him, her father and Will weren't in on her little scheme. Just wait until he burst her bubble in her face!

"Don't tell Will I'm home yet, Jefferson. I'm going to Hampton Manor and find out what that little tart is up to. She'd better have one good story to tell," he scoffed angrily.

He changed into buckskin riding breeches, a blue linen shirt, and a fawn colored riding coat. He headed for the stables and saddled a horse. He rode like an obsessed man until he reined in before the stately manor belonging to his neighbor.

He knocked loudly and persistently upon the door. The head servant opened it and looked inquisitively at him. "Lord Spencer Farrington to see Charles Hampton," he stated icily.

The man beamed with pleasure and stepped aside. "Come in, come in," he repeated cheerfully. "Mistress Alex will be so happy you're finally here. She's been so worried about how long you been away, sir."

He grimaced. "I'd like to speak with Charles first. I would prefer you didn't tell Alex I was here just yet," he mysteriously stated, his eyes and voice carrying a vivid hint of annoyance and coldness.

The befuddled man led him toward the library where Charles was engrossed in paper work, wondering why this man was acting so odd. He tapped upon the door and waited for Charles to ask, "Yes, what is it?"

He opened the door and informed him, "Lord Farrington's here to see you, sir."

He jumped up and hurried forward to grip Spencer's hand and shake it. As the servant closed the door, Charles raved excitedly, "It's good to finally have you home, Spencer. I can't tell you how pleased and surprised Will and I were to hear about you and Alex. Have you seen her yet? I've never seen any girl so much in love. The way she carries on, I expected you to be ten feet tall by now," he jested as Spencer remained silent and sullen.

"Alex doesn't know I'm here. I thought it best you and I talk first," he declared in a voice of deadly and chilling steel. His blue eyes carried those same metallic qualities.

"But she's been worried sick about you, son. Let me fetch her, then we can talk later," he offered, curiously alarmed by Spencer's strange and chilly manner.

"First, I'd like a little information. Would you mind telling me how I came to be married to your daughter?"

Charles looked at him oddly. "Is this some joke, son?"

"I can assure you I'm deadly serious, sir. This is the

first I've heard of such an incredible tale. Not only am I not married to your deceitful daughter, but I've never even met Lady Hampton. As for the child, the bastard isn't mine," he sneered contemptuously.

Appalled, Charles inhaled sharply and paled. "How dare you speak of your wife and son in this offensive manner! Do you forget, sir, they are also my daughter and grandson! What is the meaning of this outrage!" he shouted, his face flushed with fury and shock.

"That's what I'd like to know! I just arrived home to be greeted with congratulations for a marriage and son I know nothing about. Whatever your sly daughter is up to, sir, I am no part of it. I have never laid eyes or a hand upon your daughter. Since she arrived home claiming to be my wife, I can assume this daring charade is all her idea. You can rest assured the law will deal severely with her devious lies!" he threatened icily.

"I don't understand. What's going on between you two?" he demanded, utterly bewildered by this alarming scene.

"Nothing, and nothing ever has," Spencer added arrogantly.

"I don't know what you're trying to pull, Farrington, but it won't work," Charles snapped, heading for his desk. He withdrew the marriage parchment and shook it in Spencer's defiant face. "Can you deny that's your seal and signature?" he harshly challenged his irrational son-in-law.

Spencer yanked the blue ribbon off and unrolled the crisp ivory page. He stared at it in utter disbelief.

When Alexandria Hampton went after something, she certainly took pains to make it credible! How had she managed this?

"Well?" Charles demanded a reply.

Puzzled and vexed, Spencer snarled, "It's my signature and seal all right. But how the hell she got them on this paper, I'll never know until I ask her! I tell you in all honesty, sir; I did not marry your daughter or father her child. It will be easy to prove I was at sea on July fifteenth, as well as for weeks before and after!"

Her uncontrollable curiosity getting the better of her, Martha listened to this preposterous debate going on inside the library. She hurried to alert her beloved mistress to the storm brewing and heading her way. She raced to the garden, pale and nervous.

Alex was sitting upon the pallet beneath a shade tree, playing with her son. Martha rushed over to her side. "Trouble, milady. Lord Farrington's here and he's arguing violently with your father in the library. It's terrible! He's shouting and ranting about not being married to you. He claims he's never even met you! Your papa's furious. They're quarreling something fierce. He's calling you awful names and vowing he knows nothing of this marriage. Forgive me for repeating such crude words, but he called Josh a bastard. Perhaps I should take him upstairs until you settle this matter," she suggested.

Alex paled. She shuddered. My God, she thought, what is he doing? If he wants the marriage dissolved, he should have come to her. How could she possibly explain his actions and words? As her thoughts flickered here and there in search of some logical meaning to the situation, her father's voice spoke from behind her, "Martha, leave us alone for a while."

The distraught woman instantly obeyed. "Alex, Spencer Farrington here claims you two aren't legally married. Would you care to argue the point? He also denies he's Joshua's father."

Spencer's eyes had briefly touched upon the baby named Joshua with dark hair lying upon the pallet before his amber-haired mother. His stormy gaze shifted to Alex as she looked up while speaking.

"Spencer, I can explain ev . . ." She halted in alarm and disbelief, gaping at the man towering above her. Joshua Steele! Here? Claiming to be Spencer? "What are you doing here?" she demanded fearfully. For revenge? For the baby? He knew her name and home . . .

He stared at her as the letters upon her note flashed before his mind's eye: "A.H." . . . Alexandria Hampton? Before he could utter a single word, she swooned. Spencer instinctively dropped to his knees and caught her limp body before it could fall upon their child. Their child! His startled gaze flew to the baby wriggling upon the ground. Joshua? His softened gaze returned to Alex's colorless face. Angelique was Alex? His lost love was claiming to be his wife? Why had she chosen Spencer Farrington to entrap? If she had accidentally discovered his identity, she certainly seemed shocked to see him.

"Would you mind telling me what's going on!"

Charles shouted, more confused than ever, as was Spencer.

"Only a terrible misunderstanding, sir," he muttered, wondering how to explain this incredible, but pleasing, situation.

Charles squatted and pressed, "Are you two married or not?"

Spencer's eyes touched upon the pin on Charles's lapel: a small lion's head with ruby eyes. Stunned, he glanced up at the distressed man and stated clearly, "A lion's eyes grow red in winter."

A look of caution filled the older man's blue eyes. Observing Spencer closely, he replied, "Only when taken from the jungle."

"Could be the English fog which irritates them," Spencer parried. Hampton, his contact? Alex, his wife? If she hadn't put the facts together, why had she lied about a marriage to him? Then again, the license looked valid. A crafty proxy? By whom? How?

"Or the heat of a new battle," Charles completed the code. Disregarding the implications in their brief discourse, he asked sharply, "Did you or did you not meet Alex while she was visiting Henry Cowling in America and marry her? Henry claims he was at the wedding himself, as does President Madison. He even gave her a safe escort and letter of protection when you sent her home. If she's never met you, how could she describe you and your affairs so accurately?"

With the mention of those facts, Spencer suspected what must have taken place and how it was carried off. "It's a long story, sir, but Alex and I are obviously married and that is my son."

"Then why the unforgivable act upon your arrival?"

"I need to talk with her first and settle some matters. Briefly, Alex met and fell in love with Captain Joshua Steele. She was travelling under the disguise of Angelique DuBois when I met her. We fell in love and sort of lost our heads for a time. Evidently Henry took matters into his own hands when he discovered her condition and married us by proxy. Rest assured we are very much in love, sir. As you can tell from her reaction, she learned my true identity at the same moment I learned hers. I had no idea my Angelique was Lady Hampton, nor did she have any inkling Steele was Spencer Farrington. In view of how we met, you can see why we never exchanged accurate names," he related the facts to the astounded man beside him. "If I had known sooner, I would have married her without Henry's assistance. Evidently Henry didn't tell her Steele and Farrington were the same man."

It was clear to him now that the message on the petticoat which had created their misunderstanding was being passed between Henry and Charles. Spence dreaded to recall his treatment of her during their encounters. "I haven't been ashore in months. The fighting at sea has been heavy. I was coming to see Will once more before I attempted to barrel through the British blockade. I had no idea what went on there after I left. Alex must have told Henry who the father was. Since he knew me so well, he took matters into his own hands. Thank goodness he did. If you don't mind, sir, I'd like to explain everything to Alex in private. She's also in for a big shock or two." Would she despise and fear him? Would she demand a divorce?

"After which, you and I have some more talking to do."

"In light of my conduct, I hope you don't mind having me for a son-in-law," he hinted to test the slightly calmed Charles's feelings.

"Not if you truly love Alex and the baby," he fenced.

"More than I thought possible, sir. Naturally with these new responsibilities, Steele will have to retire."

Charles smiled. "I fully agree. Too bad. Henry says your services have been invaluable." He patted Spencer's shoulder and left.

Spencer tenderly caressed Alex's cheek and lovingly ran his fingers through her silky hair. At last, his agony and search were over; she legally belonged to him, and he would never free her. He chuckled as he realized he had been the wealthy man whom she had planned to marry. How would she feel about him once the truth was out? "Alex," he called her name, shaking her gently, wondering at Henry's silence at their last meeting, that same fateful day. Clearly she was no spy! Would she ever forgive him for their troubled past?

She moaned and moved. Her lids fluttered and opened. In panic, she stared at him. "What are you doing here, Stephen? You'll ruin everything! What must Papa be thinking now? Whyever did you tell him you're Spencer Farrington and claim we aren't married? I told you I was getting married! I did; I married Spencer that next day by proxy. Papa's met Spencer several times, so you didn't fool him! Why are you doing this to me?" she wailed sadly. "Why use that name?"

He grinned roguishly and murmured, "Because it's mine. I take it our son's name is Michael Farrington after my father?" he speculated aloud, but she failed to grasp the meaning of his words in her distress. He should have realized she was a real lady!

"No, I named him Joshua Stephen Farrington for some inexplicable reason," she absently responded, wondering how to solve this crisis and retain her father's love and respect. Abruptly his previous words hit home. She looked up into his smoldering sapphire eyes and asked, "What did you say? What mad revenge is this?"

He chuckled as he emphasized his next words, "My real name is Stephen . . . Spencer . . . Farrington. But you, my devious and lovely wife, may call me Spence. Now that you know the truth, surely you won't betray your own husband to the hangman?"

Flabbergasted, she stammered, "You . . . mean . . . you really are . . . Spencer Farrington? The Spencer Farrington? Will's grandson?" That book in Joshua's cabin . . . "S.S.F."!

Lusty laughter reached her ears as his virile body shook with amusement. "That certainly explains our first meeting, Alexandria Hampton Farrington. The property line between our estates goes right down the middle of our secret paradise. I was home visiting Will for a few days when I met an enchanting nymph at my secluded pond. I'm sorry I caused such a scene upon my return home, but surely you can imagine my shock and anger at finding myself married to Lady Hampton when the only woman I wanted to marry was an elusive siren named Angelique, if I ever managed to locate her again," he teased.

Baffled, she debated, "Then why did you agree to our mock marriage? Why didn't you tell me your name at the hotel? Was it done by proxy so I wouldn't guess the truth? I would have married you anyway. I had no idea you were the same man."

It was his turn to show confusion. "If you explain how we came to be married, then we can both comprehend this strange occurrence. I didn't learn your name until today."

Alex gradually related the facts as she knew them. She couldn't believe her uncle's audacity when he told her his side. "No wonder you were so upset! Why would he do such a deceitful and daring thing?"

"Because he is close friends with both Spencer and Steele. He put two and two together and solved the problem himself by marrying you to the father of your child. No doubt he intended to tell me everything, but I've been at sea since our last encounter. I'm sorry for all I put you through, love. If you had stayed around as promised, his trickery wouldn't have been necessary," he alluded.

"What do you mean?" she questioned.

"I left you to prepare a hasty marriage for us. I

478

planned to reveal myself that night and marry you. I had decided to take you to my Virginia plantation to wait for me. It's been hell without you."

"What a stupid fool I was!" she berated herself.

"I really can't blame you, love. I should have told you how much I loved you and needed you before I rushed out to get the minister. I suppose I was a little too proud and stubborn to admit how much you meant to me. I'm still a bit confused by this proxy marriage between us. I thought you told me your marriage was all arranged. When I saw Henry that same day, he didn't mention it and he surely didn't act angry with me. Why didn't he tell me about you and the wedding?"

Ashamed, she lowered her head as she revealed her desperate ruse. He grinned and jested, "Found yourself ensnared in your own trap, love? I could have strangled you for deserting me again."

"I'm sorry, Josh. I didn't know you or trust you. I honestly didn't know I was pregnant that day. I was afraid and . . ."

He placed his finger to her lips. "It's all right now, love. Everything worked out perfectly in the end. You best work on calling me Spence now. God, how I feared I had lost you forever. All I've thought about is you and the baby. You're mine, woman; accept it."

"Should we change our son's name?" she suddenly questioned.

He smiled and shook his head. "Joshua was my brother. He was killed in an accident when he was twelve. One of the King's favorite archers shot him while hunting. Since my name's really Stephen, it would seem natural to name our son after the two of us."

"I'm sorry, Spence. I didn't know. Do you realize that's the first personal thing you've ever told me about yourself?" she stated in wonder. "I still can't believe this; Spencer and Steele the same man?"

"We'll have years to discover each other's secrets," he hinted playfully, allowing the months of anguish and anger to slip away.

A frightened look replaced her joyful one. "What's wrong, love?" he asked, dreading to hear her reservations about him.

"I was just thinking about Captain Steele. I would die if I lost you now, Spence. Please don't sail the *Black Mist* anymore."

He smiled. "In view of my new and delightful situation, I think Steele has mysteriously retired. I missed the birth of our first child, but I don't plan to miss the next one. I want to spend every minute with you and our son. This match is perfect and permanent."

Her eyes softened and watered. "I love you, Spencer Farrington. I have sorely missed you. We'll never be torn apart again, my love." Was her dream by the pond coming true?

"If you had told me the truth after our first reunion, I'd had fought heaven and hell to keep you. After all, Henry, your father, and Captain Steele do work for the same side. I wish I had known then the message was from Henry Cowling, or at least known your name. We certainly ripped at each other, didn't we, and all for nothing. To think I actually refused to meet you on two separate occasions!"

"You work for the same side? I don't follow . . ."

"Contrary to gossip and what you thought, Captain Steele was a secret agent for President Madison himself, love. I only used the cover of a privateer and a pirate to carry out my assignments. That's why I never sank any ship or killed anyone without it being unavoidable. All I was after were the coded messages being passed between English spies and soldiers, of which I erroneously assumed you were one because of that infamous slip. Can you forgive me, love?"

"My father knows who you are?" she exclaimed in panic.

"He does now. I told him while you were sleeping peacefully a while ago."

"Can you trust him to keep silent?" she fretted anxiously.

"Without a doubt. Once the war's over, he's moving to America. But all that can be discussed later. Right now, I only want to kiss my wife to make certain she's real and mine."

"Wife!" she shrieked as if this was the first time she comprehended that fact. "We are married!"

"That does make things easier for us. Now, you won't have to divorce your husband to marry me. We've wasted a whole year, Alex."

His mouth came down upon hers. Her arms slipped around his waist. Shutting out the whole world, they clung together and savored this heady moment. He pressed her cheek to his drumming heart and held her close. "Sweet Angel, how I've missed you."

"Is it safe to come out now?" her father teased.

As if caught in some wanton predicament, she jerked away from Spence and flushed. Spence chuckled. "Aren't you forgetting something, Mrs. Farrington?"

When she looked up into his sparkling eyes, he teased, "We are married, love. It is all right to show your husband some affection after such a long and lonely separation."

She laughed and hugged him tightly. The baby began to cry for his next meal. Alex turned and lifted him into her arms. "Would you care to inspect your first son, my love?"

Spencer trailed his fingers over the soft flesh of his arms and face, then touched the dark hair upon his head. "He favors you, Spence. How lucky can I be? Two handsome and irresistible men to love."

As Spencer took his hand and gazed at it in awe and pride, the baby grasped his forefinger and held it. "Does that mean he likes me or knows who I am?" he inquired, laughing.

"Neither, my love, it's instinctive. But he will soon," she promised. "I better go and feed him. Your son can thunder as loud as you when denied his wishes," she impishly taunted.

He stood up and helped her to her feet. "I'll return as soon as he's fed and put down for his nap."

"I'm coming to watch. I've missed too much as it is," he declared.

Before she could argue, he took her elbow and headed for the steps. "We'll talk later, Charles. We all have some things to work out," he stated meaningfully.

Knowing they needed time alone, Charles returned to his work, whistling merrily after telling the staff to prepare a fabulous feast for dinner tonight. Taking the initiative, he sent word of Spencer's arrival and the family celebration planned for that night to William Farrington—who would respond and head that way the moment the letter reached him.

In the nursery, Alex dismissed Martha who kept staring belligerently at Spencer as she made her exit. "I take it she doesn't like my replacing her?"

"I'm afraid you made a terrible first impression on her; she overheard most of your violent argument with Papa after your arrival. Plus, she's annoyed with me for going riding earlier today. I visited the pond for the first time since . . ." She blushed at her confession.

He laughed and kissed her forehead. "I see you found me as haunting as I found you, love. We've really resisted this perfect match, haven't we?"

"Yes, we did. But never again," she vowed, her gaze leaving her task a moment to look at him. Once the baby was diapered and dressed for bed, she went to the rocker and sat down. "You'll have to wait until later to spend some time with your son, Spence. If we want any peace and privacy, we best not interfere with his rigid schedule."

He sat down on the edge of the bed, his gaze glued on

the two people he loved above his own life. As she unbuttoned her dress, she suddenly halted and flushed like a timid bride on her wedding night. "Why are you staring at me like that?" she nervously asked.

"I do believe you've returned to your excessive modesty, my love. This is all new to me and I want to share each moment. Do you mind?"

"It's still fairly new to me, Spence, but you can stay." She placed the baby near her right breast this time. Relishing this nourishment and contact, his small mouth attached itself to his mother's body.

"Your son is just as greedy as his father. The way he eats, he'll be your size in no time," she commented, then giggled.

"What's so funny?" he inquired, touched by the scene before him.

"It tickles sometimes. I dread to think of him sprouting teeth and using them on me."

He laughed heartily. "Maybe I could give him some lessons in how to use them gently. After all, we do seem to have the same parts."

"Spencer Farrington! How dare you speak so crudely before our innocent son," she playfully chided him. "While you're giving him lessons, please teach him to use his 'parts' wisely and selectively."

"Just like his old man," he cheerfully concluded, coming to kneel down beside the rocker and fluff the baby's hair.

His gaze fused with hers. He traced his finger over her breast and up her throat to pass over her lips. He pulled her over and kissed her pervasively. Alex tingled and warmed; her whole being flamed with desire for him. He had always had this same effect upon her.

She pulled back, resting her spinning head against the rocker. "If you distract me like that again, I might drop our son," she hinted in a strained voice, laced with hunger.

His own body enflamed with the urgent need to be joined with hers, he leaned over and allowed his warm tongue to make moist circles around her left breast. "Perhaps I should discover why my son enjoys this so much," he huskily murmured, closing his mouth over the protruding nipple.

She shuddered and moaned. Her breath caught in her throat; she tensed and burned. "Please, Spencer, don't torture me like this. It's been so long and I need you so much," she whispered raggedly.

Their gazes met and fused once more. "Too long, Alex. Much too long . . ." Was he truly in the same room with his love?

He stood up and walked to her door. He locked it and leaned against it, torturously waiting for her to finish. She tore her gaze from his with great effort. The baby was asleep. She entered the nursery and placed him in the bed instead of the cradle in her bedroom, opening the hall door so Martha could tend him if he awakened.

She returned to her room and locked the door behind her. As if some unspoken signal was given, they slowly walked toward each other, this moment long overdue and eagerly anticipated. Stopping only inches apart, neither spoke nor moved. They simply stared into each other's eyes. The first to finally move, his hands came out to capture her face between them.

Before his head came down to fuse their lips, he said tenderly, "I love you, Alex, so much it frightens me."

Savoring this moment, he kissed her time and time again. When he pulled back briefly to look at her, she smiled and seductively stated, "I need you too much to be modest, Spence."

She eased his riding coat off his powerful shoulders and let it drop to the floor behind him. Her trembling fingers struggled with the buttons upon his shirt; it, too, floated soundlessly to the floor. She pressed her exposed bosom against his hard and hairy chest. Her arms went around him; her hands explored the rippling, smooth muscles upon his broad back. Tremors washed over her.

"Oh, God, that feels so wonderful," she sighed in unleashed passion. "A day or a night hasn't passed that I haven't dreamed of this moment. I want you so much it hurts, Spencer. Please make love to me before I die of need," she pleaded hoarsely, her mouth sought his and claimed it.

He spread intoxicating kisses over her face and throat. When his lips teased at her breasts once more, Alex could not suppress the cry of intense anguish which ravaged her smoldering body. He pushed her away to practically tear her clothes and the rest of his from their bodies.

He picked her up and carried her to the bed. The covers already turned aside for the nap she had missed during all the excitement, he placed her there and lay beside her. She instantly turned to him and pulled him tightly against her.

Aquiver with a fierce yearning, she could hardly bear his continued assault upon her senses. Tantilizing every inch of her body, she begged for their union. When he nibbled at her ears and breasts as his hand sought to drive her mindless with blissful ecstasy, she followed his lead and gently seized his erect and throbbing manhood. He moaned against her mouth as she intensified his passion with her exploratory journey there. Never before, no matter how impassioned, had she dared to touch him in this most intimate and tempting manner.

Shuddering with need, Spencer pushed her hand aside to thrust into her receptive and moist body. As he drove into her over and over, each time as if to withdraw briefly, Alex cried out at the pleasurable sensations which were so powerful she feared to faint from their effect. Her legs instinctively curled around him to trap him there.

He gently rotated his slim hips and enticingly ground his molten member into her fiery furnace. They had shared great tenderness, passion, and urgency before; but never like this. Each knew this time was different and this would become the new pattern of their joinings. Just as the summit was reached, he leaned back and looked into her passion-glazed eyes and vowed, "I love you with all my heart and soul, Alex. I couldn't survive without you now."

"As I love you, Spence," she replied, pulling his mouth to hers.

All control gone, they were caught upon the wild and wonderful sea of love. Wave after wave of overwhelming love and pleasure crashed against them, sweeping them along with its power. Love's sweet lava flowed from each and joined to create a calm sea of sated passion.

As the tranquil aftermath of their stormy union surrounded them, still he didn't move away. He held her possessively as if fearing she might magically elude him again, knowing he could never endure that loss. Spencer was a long time in rolling aside to remove his weight from her body. She snuggled into his embrace, whispering her love over and over.

His body temporarily sated, his heart brimming with love, and his mind at peace, Spencer's thoughts focused upon his previous life and the mythical legend for which his ship had been named. He had used black sails as that goddess was alleged to use her stygian hair. He had never seen a real black mist as the legend foretold. The fable claimed the benevolent goddess of the black mist used her powers to suddenly and mysteriously cover the sea and conceal whatever lay within its obscuring path. Alleged to be her magical hair which had been lowered to hide a ship whose captain and cause she found deserving of help and survival, the myth had frequently inspired some enemies to fear Captain Joshua Steele had found her favor and power.

His beloved Alex could have been that goddess. Many times she had come in secret, appearing suddenly and inexplicably, offering no clues as to where she had come from or why, disappearing just as mysteriously and quickly without a trace . . . but never again. His lovely golden mist had materialized in his grasp, never to slip through his fingers again.

Following their second and blissfully leisurely union, Alex sighed heavily and suggested they bathe and dress for dinner. He cocked his head and scowled, "In case you haven't realized it, Alexandria Farrington, this is our honeymoon. I haven't seen you since September. Surely we won't be missed this one night?"

She laughed at the wounded expression he forced upon his face. "The marriage is very legal and binding now, Lord Farrington; it was just consummated most delightfully. Will is coming for dinner. By now I'm certain a festive celebration is awaiting us downstairs. Besides, we do have a son who will be demanding his mother's attention soon."

"I see," he mischievously taunted. "Now that you have been captivated, I must yield to my son's wishes before my own."

"I fear he has even less control over his desires than you, my love."

"When it comes to you, my alluring siren, I am just as weak and helpless as he is. And just as eager and demanding for your attention."

"From your colorful reputation, Spencer Farrington, make sure I am the only female whose attention you crave from now on," she saucily quipped.

"Have I perhaps married a possessive and selfish wife?"

"Without a doubt, my dashing pirate. I will expect you in my bed every single night . . . and most days," she seductively tempted him.

"Wherever will I get such stamina, you bewitching girl?"

"I shall take excellent care of you to make certain you lose none of that vitality and virility I've heard so much about," she remarked, smiling provocatively at him.

"With you around, that's all I need."

As he moved to reluctantly get up, Alex flung herself upon him and purred, "Where are you going, my sated groom?"

He chuckled and fluffed her hair. "I have a voracious appetite, love; I shall never be sated for more than an hour. You did say we were obligated to make an appearance at dinner," he reminded her.

"Whatever possessed me to say a ridiculous thing like that? You think they would notice our absence?"

"You wanton hussy. Since the celebration is for us, we would be sorely missed. They might understand if we leave early," he slyly hinted. "Also, there's that little product of our prior relationship in the next room."

"Then I suggest we get this evening started quickly so we can get to bed early. I'm exhausted; how about you?"

"I certainly hope you don't plan on any sleep tonight," he threatened.

"Only cat-naps when we get weary," she boldly answered.

"A woman after my own heart," he concluded.

"I thought I already had it," she pouted in mock petulance.

"Now and forever, Alexandria Hampton Farrington."

After several kisses, she arose to order a bath for each of them. He was shown to another room while hers was brought into her bedroom. Finishing first, he came back to watch her.

"Are you always this slow, Mrs. Farrington?"

"Only when it's something I enjoy," she cheerfully responded.

"Does that mean you don't enjoy me?" he playfully quizzed, alluding to their past unions of swift urgency.

"Where you are concerned, my love, I have no control or will. Hand me that towel," she entreated.

"My personal services will cost you."

"Name your price. No need," she quickly injected. "I shall pay any amount you wish."

She stepped out and reached for the towel. He held it beyond her reach. She eyed his playful grin. She laughed as she made a lunge for him. He agilely avoided her and raced around the tub with her in pursuit. "Have you no modesty, my brazen nymph, to go traipsing around like so?"

As he scampered across the bed, boots and all, they were like carefree children. Just before reaching the other side, she jumped upon the bed from the foot and grabbed his coat. "I might rip it. Give quarter, Captain Steele; you've been defeated."

"Never, my cunning siren," he taunted, seizing her

by the waist and pinning her damp body beneath his upon the rumpled bed. He began to tickle her.

"Spencer! Stop it! I can't take anymore!" she squealed amidst laughter and wild thrashings.

"Alex! Are you all right?" came her father's booming voice through the locked door.

She giggled and called out, "Yes, Papa, never better!"

"Will you two be coming down soon? Will is here and we're holding dinner for you. Martha has the baby downstairs."

"Give us about fifteen minutes," she replied, tugging upon Spencer's hair to pull his mouth from her breast. She whispered softly, "If you don't stop that, dear husband, I'll soon be unable to leave this room for another hour."

"Then put some clothes on that luscious body and stop tempting me," he murmured, kissing her lightly. "You are wetting both me and the bed, my slippery mermaid." She laced her fingers around his neck and pulled his mouth to hers. "Don't start something you can't finish, woman," Spencer scolded.

"Just one last kiss until later," she sweetly entreated, but the heady kiss led to other things which hindered their arrival for another half hour. She looked up into his tranquil eyes which revealed a love she had never dreamed to view. Perhaps it had been destined for them to meet as Joshua and Angelique. Perhaps it wouldn't have been the same between the arrogant Spencer and the spoiled Alexandria.

Spencer helped Alex dress quickly after splashing

off in the cool water. As he unlocked the door, she purred' softly, "At last, my love, your timing is perfect."

As they descended the stairs arm in arm, Will and Charles were impatiently waiting for them. Martha was standing nearby holding Joshua Stephen. They simultaneously halted and glanced at each other. Known only to them, it wasn't Lord Spencer Farrington smiling tenderly at Lady Alexandria Hampton Farrington; it was the roguish Captain Joshua Steele visually claiming his wandering siren Angelique. It was like walking away from the misty past and into a bright future. They smiled at each other, their great love glowing. He placed his arm around her waist and she snuggled against his side, both excitedly anticipating their life together. Serene and eager, they happily covered the next few steps . . .